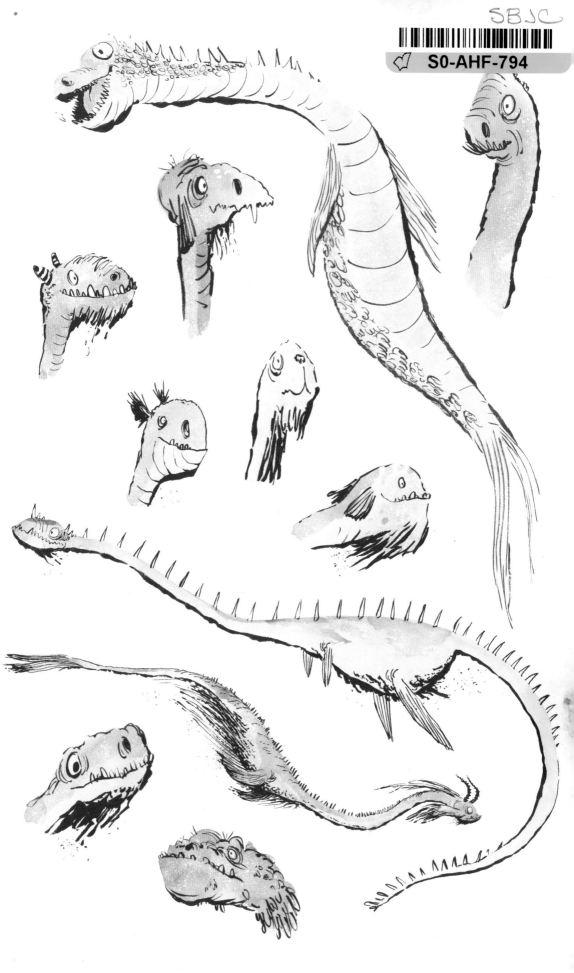

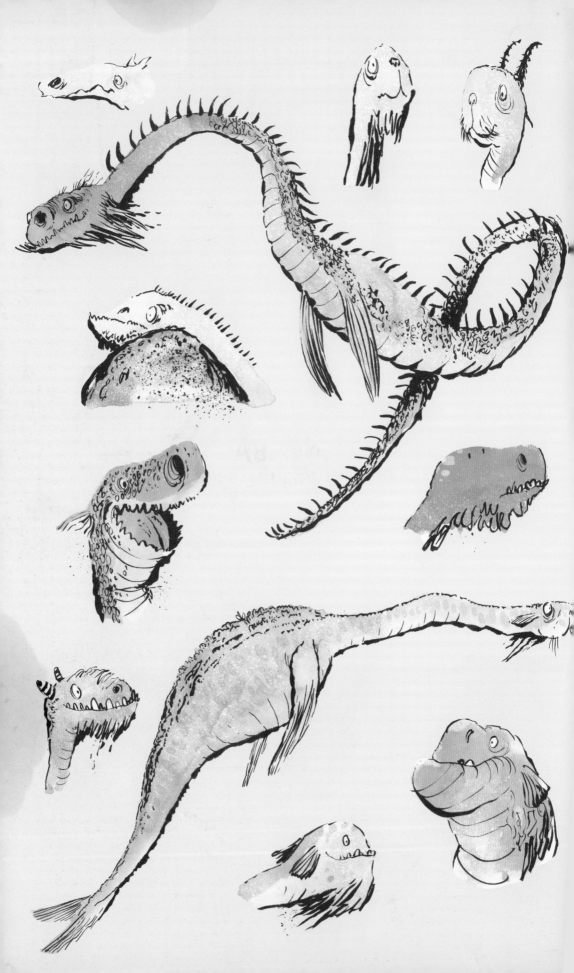

Otter Lagoon

SUEÑO BAY
ADVENTURES ❷

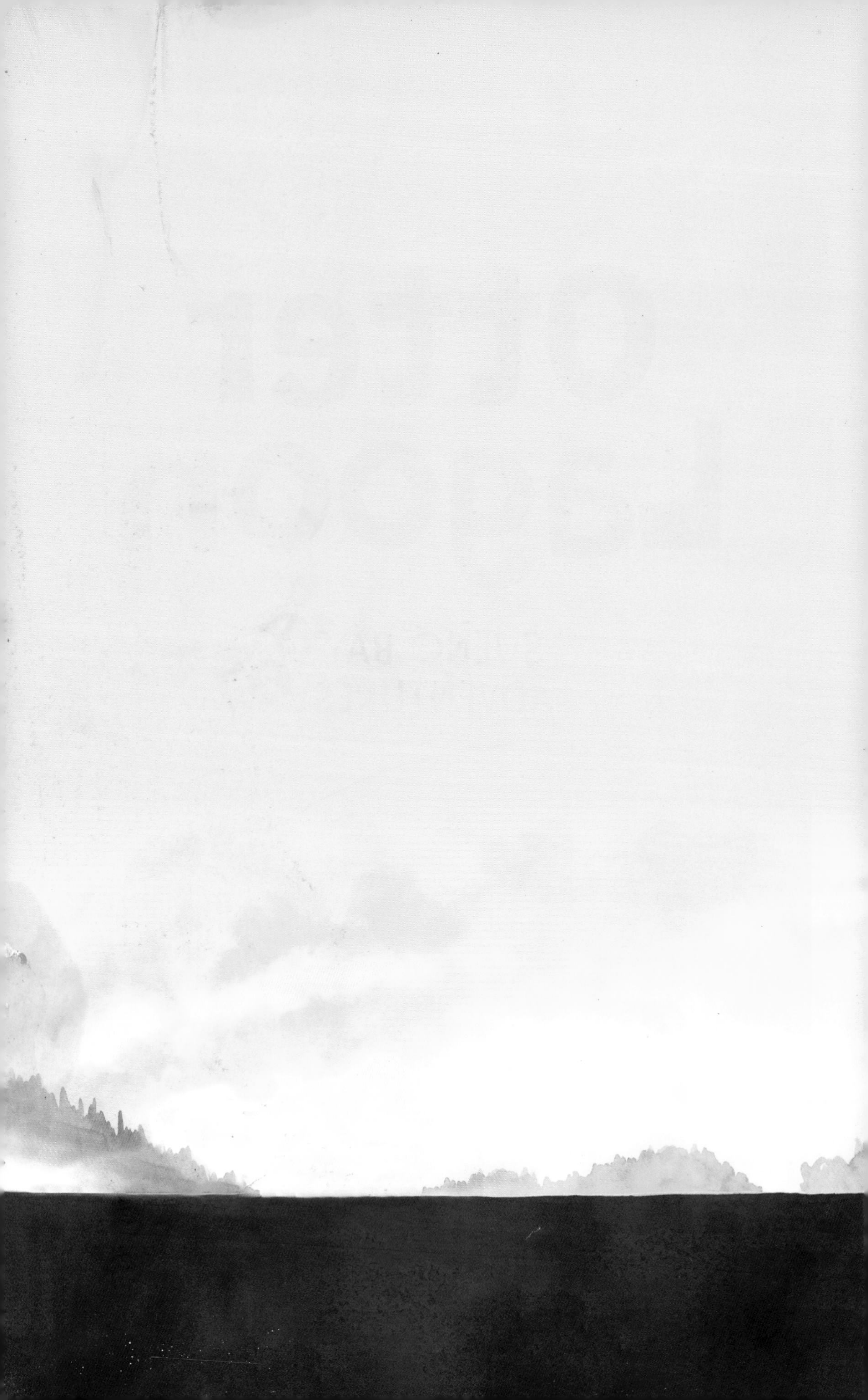

Otter Lagoon

SUEÑO BAY ADVENTURES  2

MIKE DEAS AND NANCY DEAS

ORCA BOOK PUBLISHERS

Published in Canada and the United States in 2021 by Orca Book Publishers.
orcabook.com

Library and Archives Canada Cataloguing in Publication
Title: Otter Lagoon / Mike Deas and Nancy Deas.
Names: Deas, Mike, 1982- author. | Deas, Nancy, author.
Series: Deas, Mike, 1982- Sueño Bay adventures ; 2.
Description: Series statement: Sueño Bay adventures ; 2
Identifiers: Canadiana (print) 20200330713 | Canadiana (ebook) 20200330748 |
ISBN 9781459819641 (softcover) | ISBN 9781459819665 (PDF) | ISBN 9781459819658 (EPUB)
Subjects: LCGFT: Graphic novels. | LCGFT: Action and adventure comics.
Classification: LCC PN6733.D43 O88 2021 | DDC j741.5/971—dc23

Library of Congress Control Number: 2020944958

Summary: In this graphic novel for early middle readers, a fearsome sea serpent
comes back to haunt an island in the Pacific Northwest after a 100-year reprieve.

Orca Book Publishers is committed to reducing the consumption of nonrenewable resources in
the making of our books. We make every effort to use materials that support a sustainable future.

Orca Book Publishers gratefully acknowledges the support for its publishing programs provided
by the following agencies: the Government of Canada, the Canada Council for the Arts and the
Province of British Columbia through the BC Arts Council and the Book Publishing Tax Credit.

Cover and interior illustrations by Mike Deas
Photos of Mike Deas and Nancy Deas by Billie Woods

Design by Jenn Playford
Layout by Dahlia Yuen
Edited by Liz Kemp

Printed and bound in China.

24 23 22 21 • 1 2 3 4

CHAPTER ONE

In Too Deep

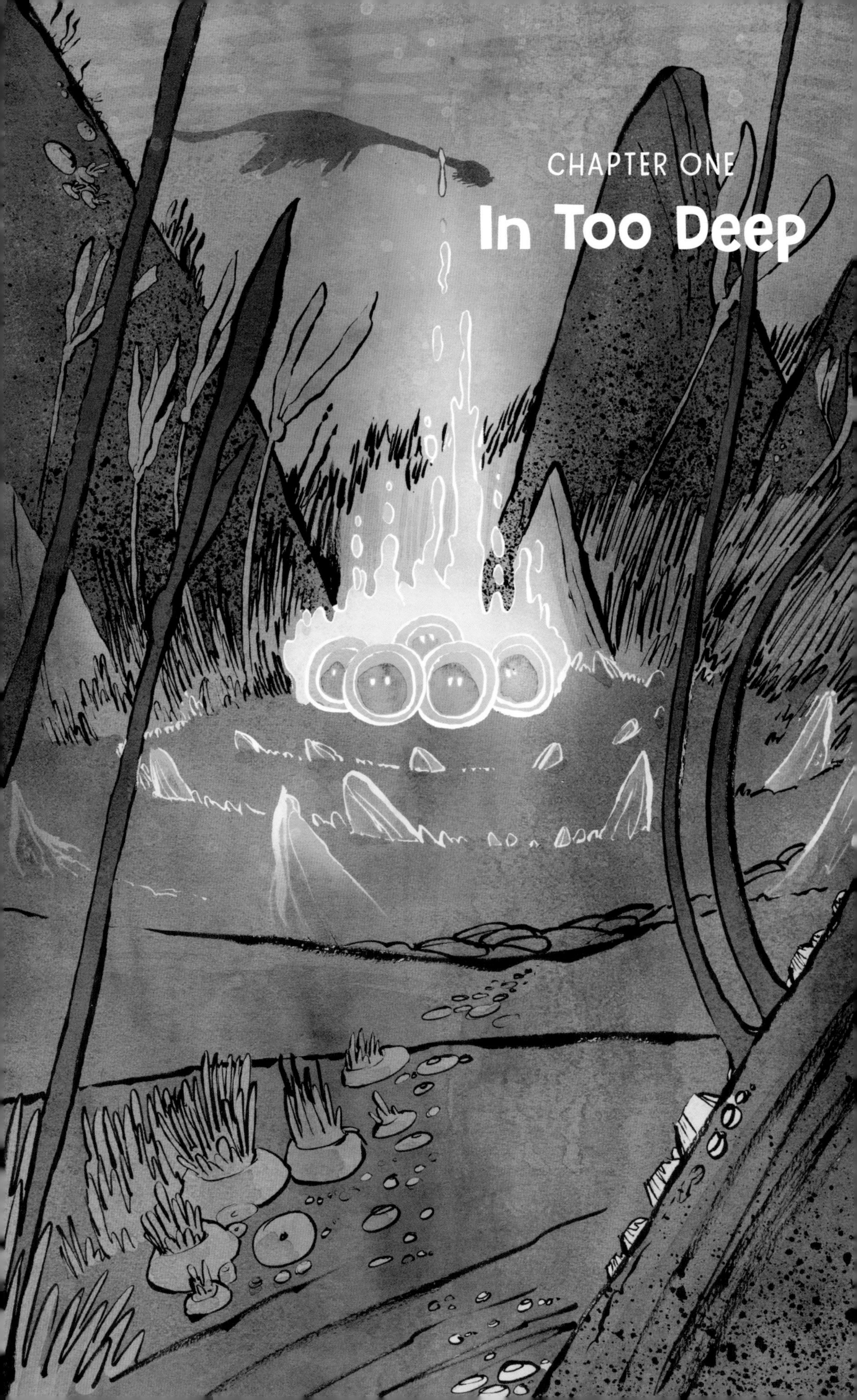

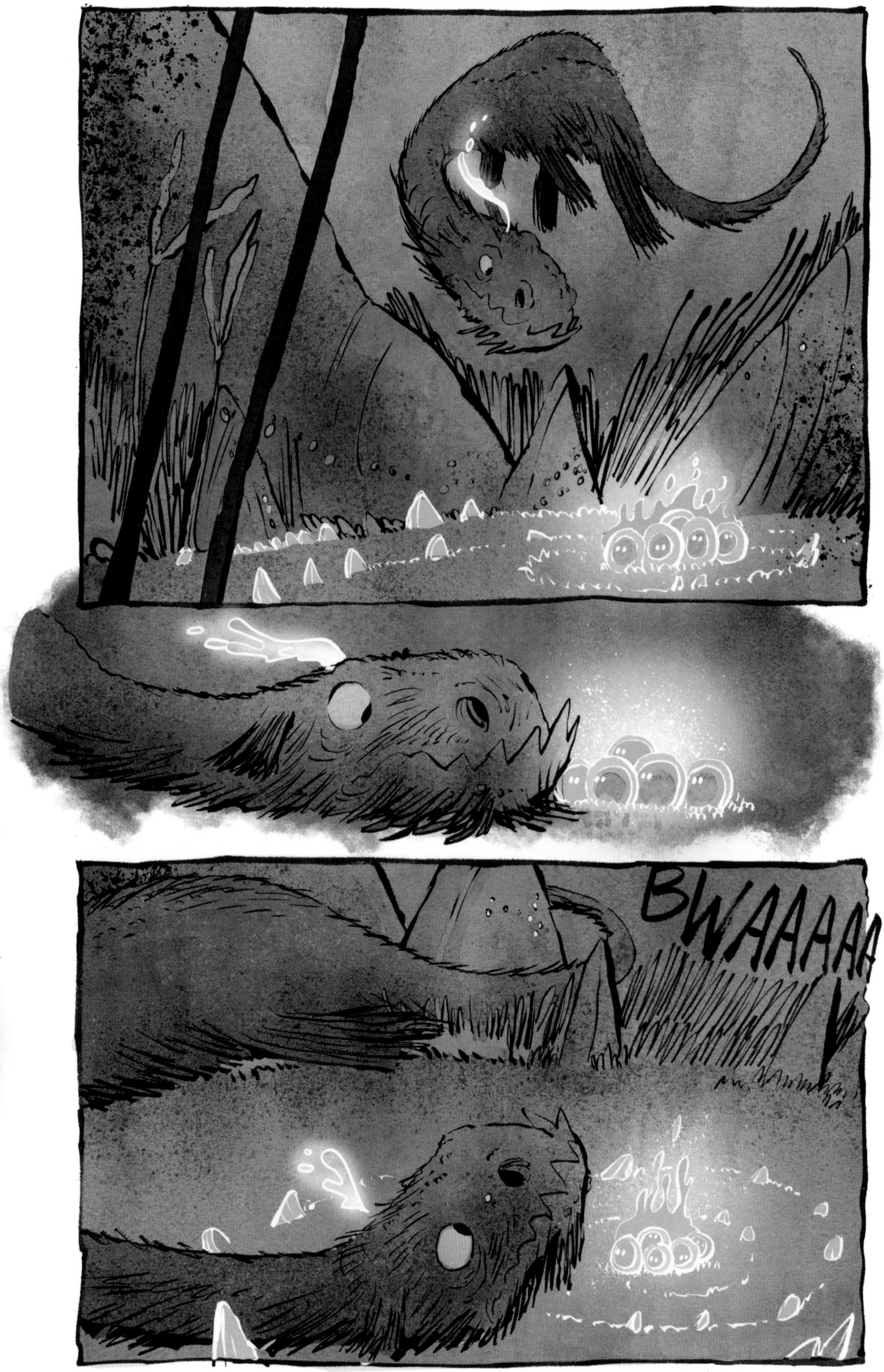
BWAAAAA

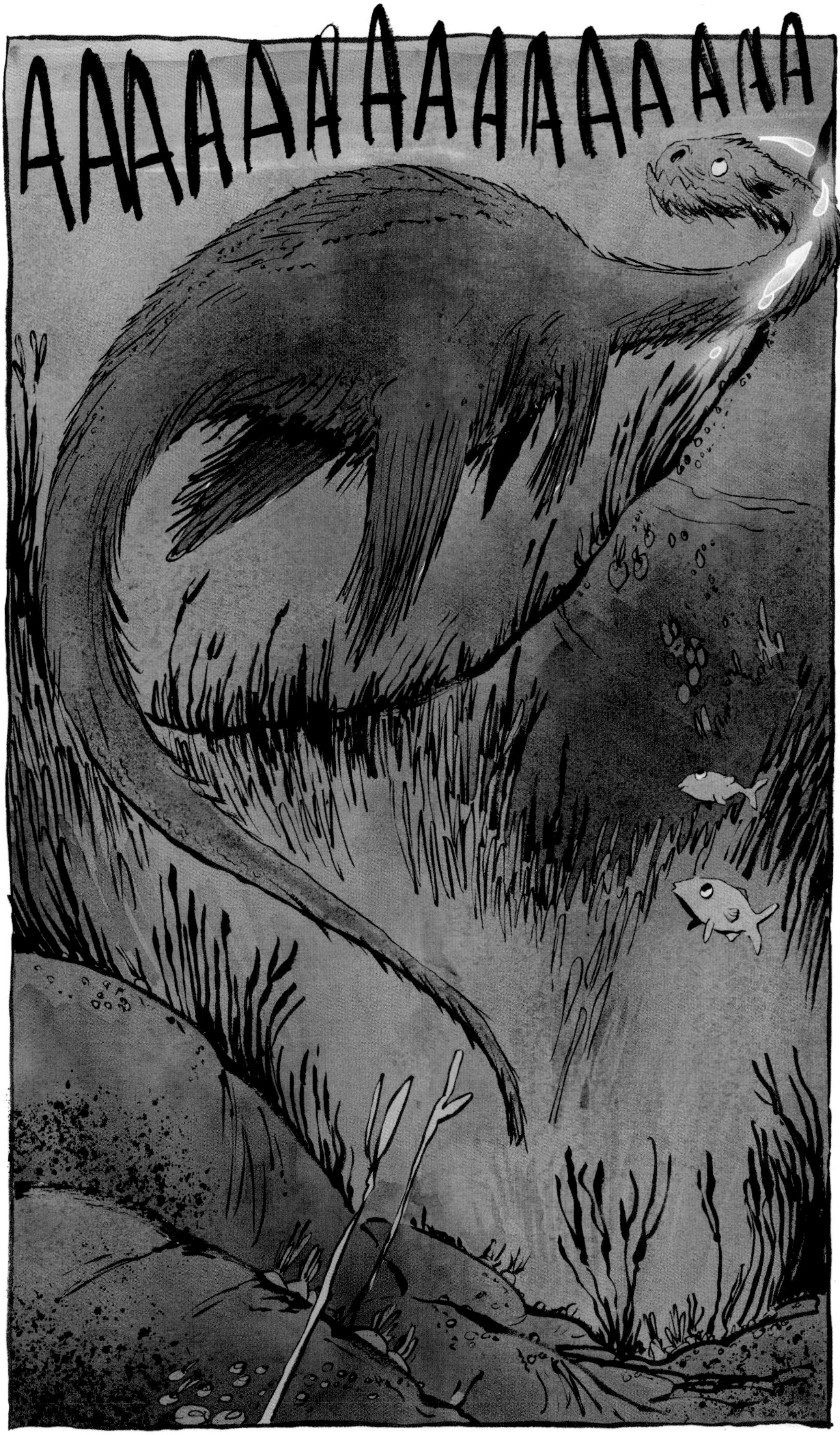
AAAAAAAAAAAAAAA

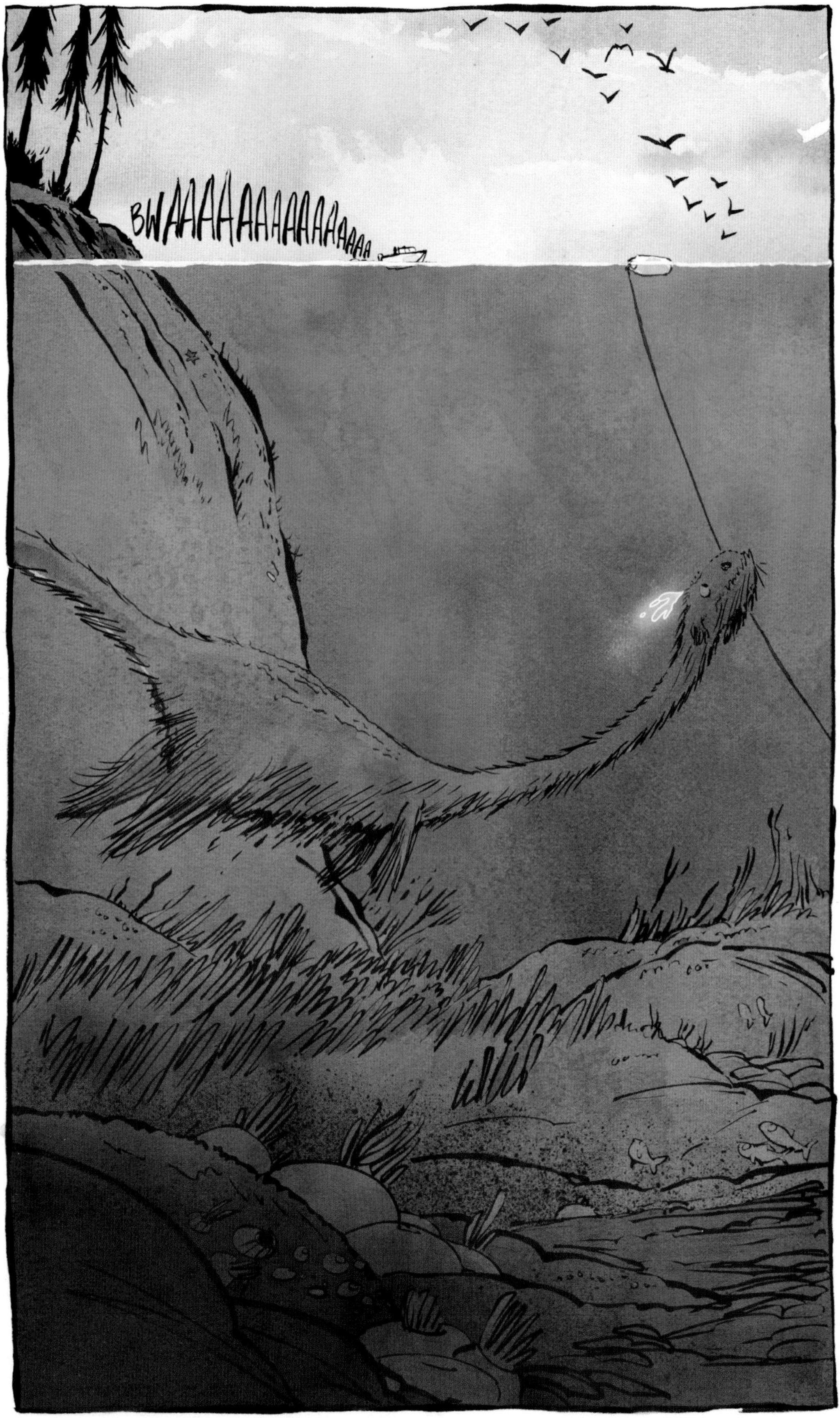
BWAAAAAAAAAAAAAAaaaa

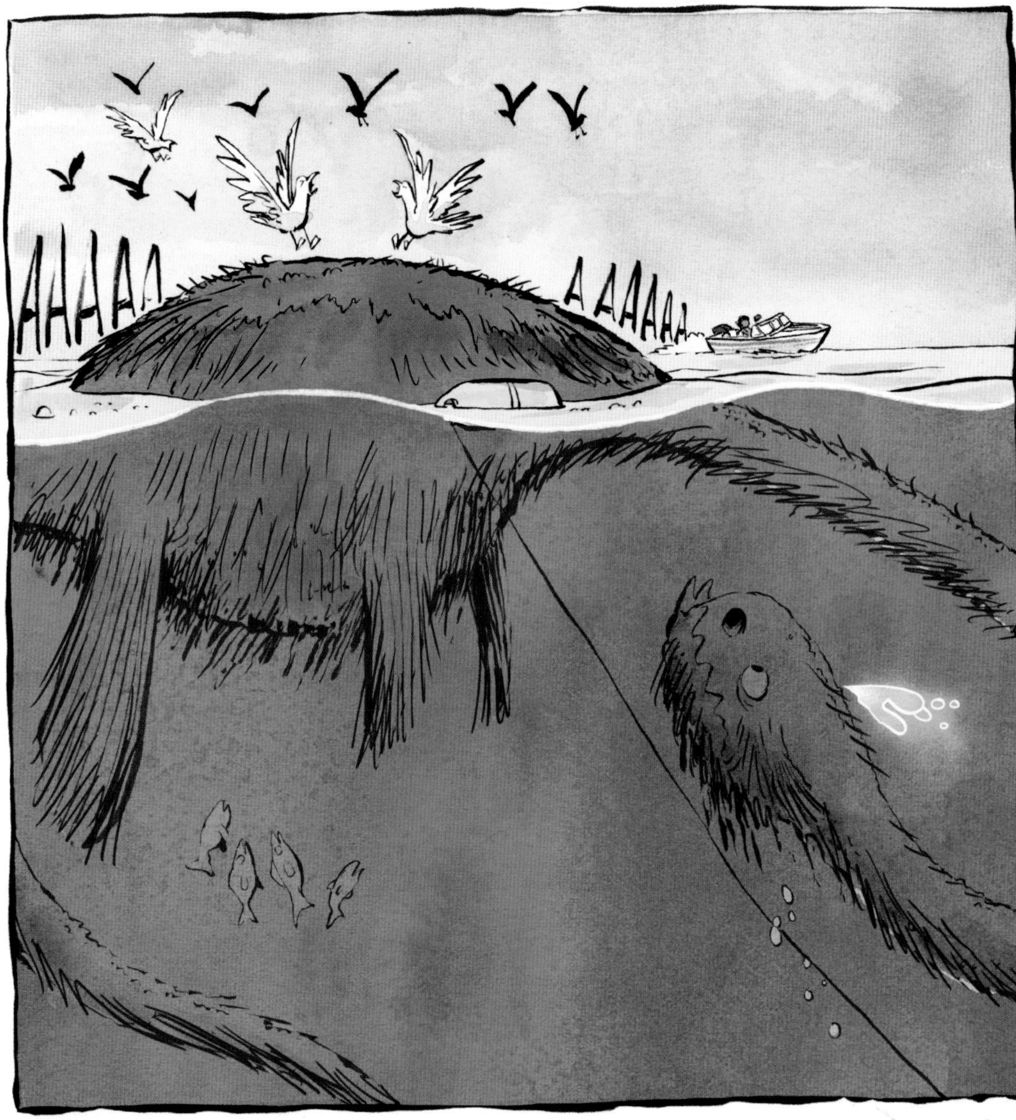
AAAAA
A AAAAA

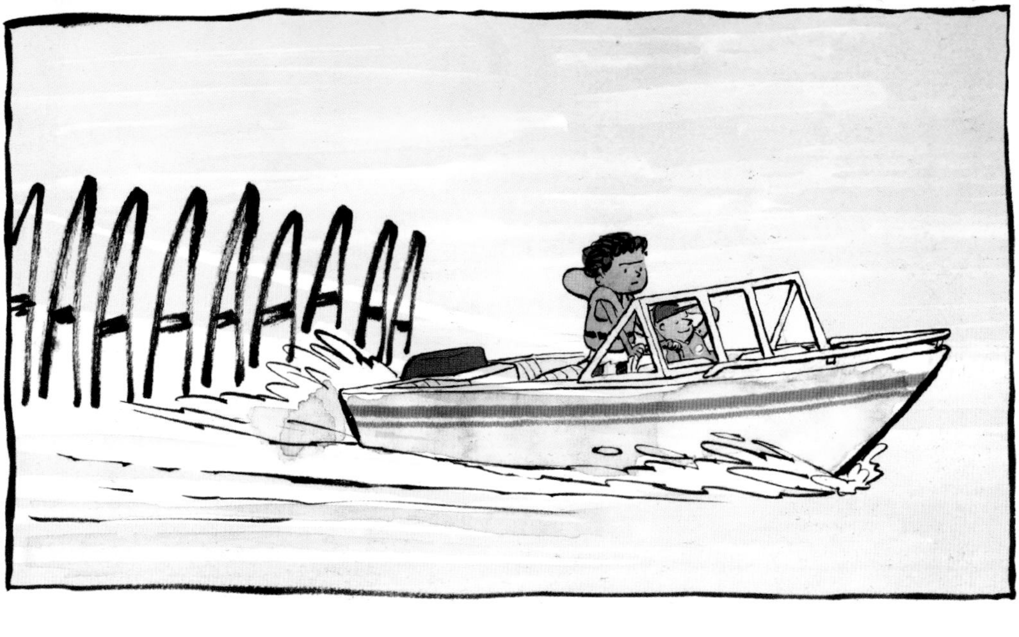
AAAAAAAAA

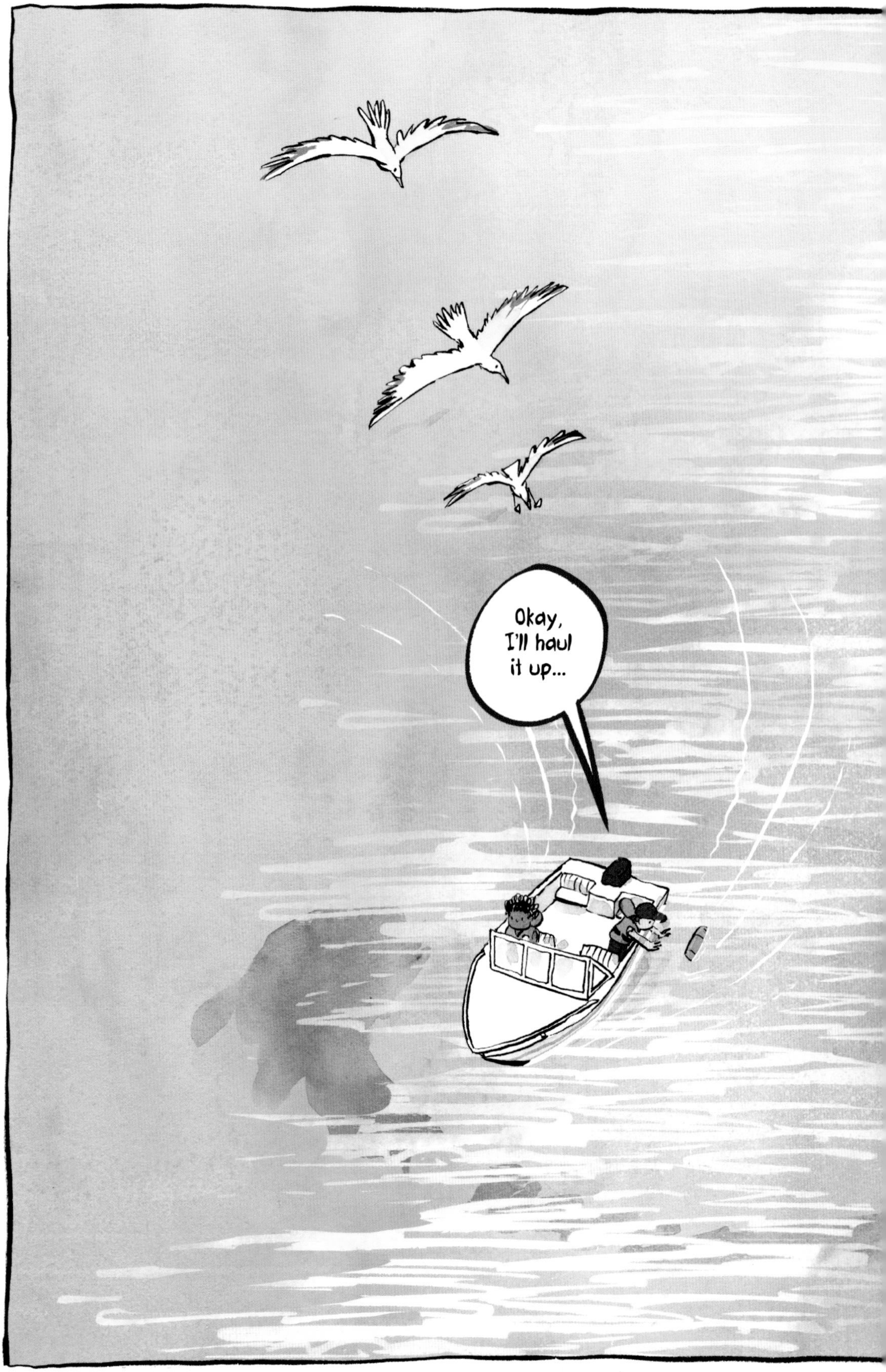
Okay, I'll haul it up...

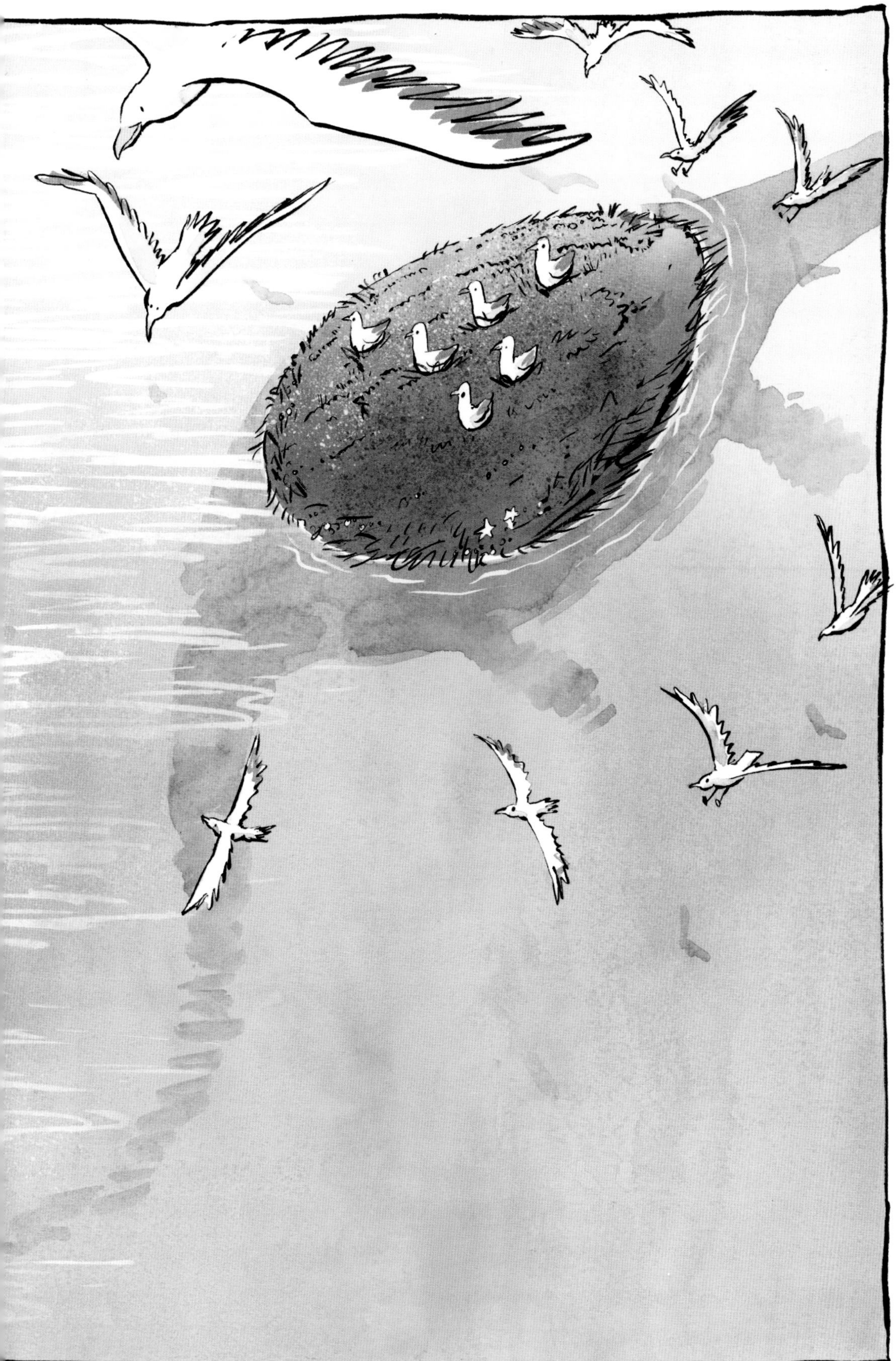

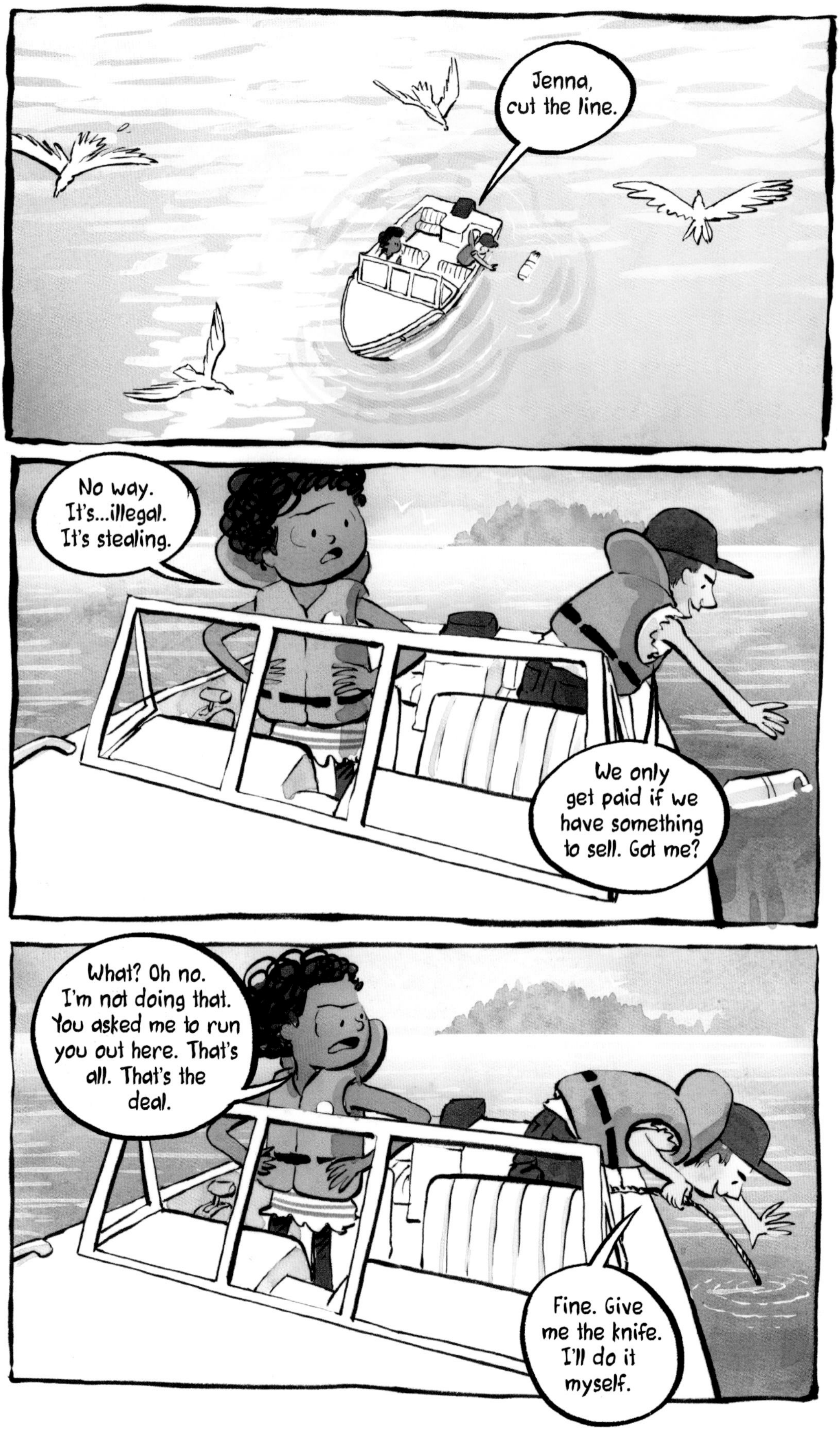
Jenna, cut the line.
No way. It's...illegal. It's stealing.
We only get paid if we have something to sell. Got me?
What? Oh no. I'm not doing that. You asked me to run you out here. That's all. That's the deal.
Fine. Give me the knife. I'll do it myself.

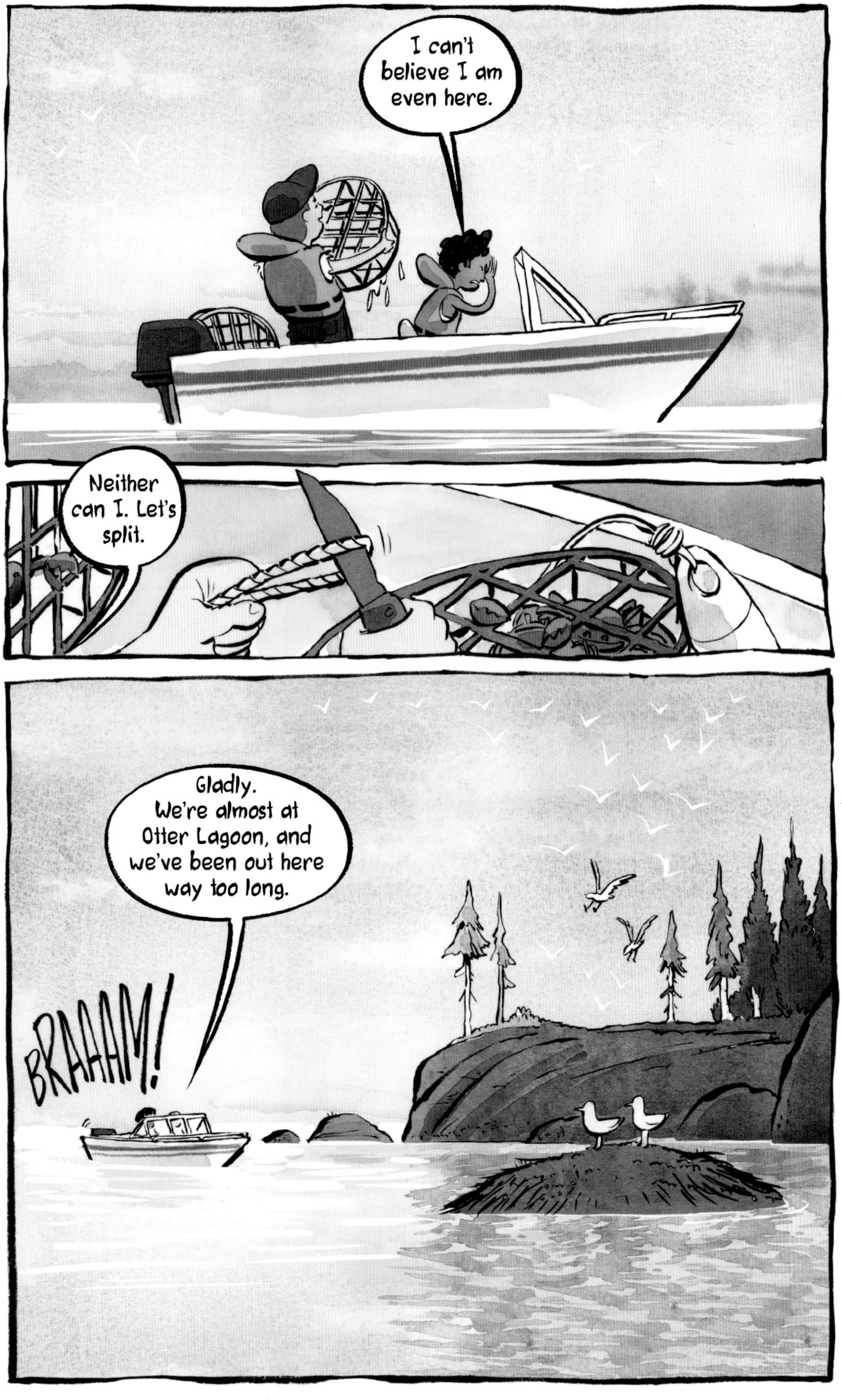
I can't believe I am even here.
Neither can I. Let's split.
Gladly. We're almost at Otter Lagoon, and we've been out here way too long.
BRAAAM!

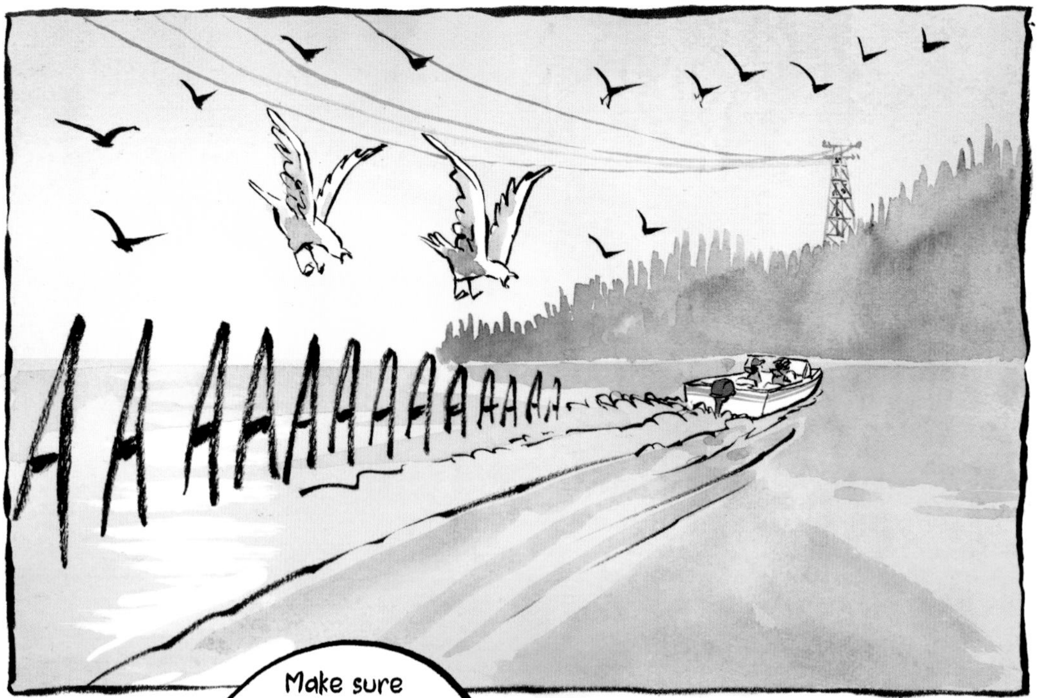
AAAAAAAAAAAA

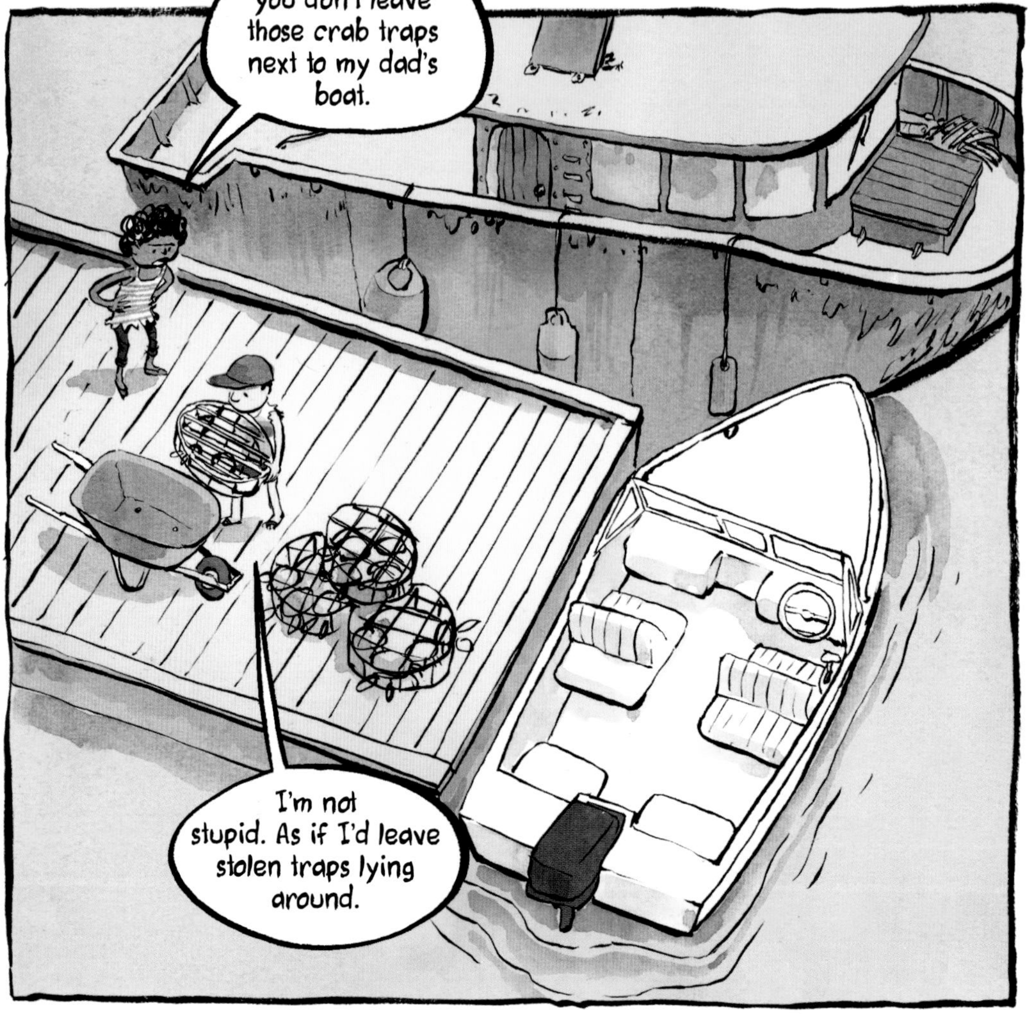
Make sure you don't leave those crab traps next to my dad's boat.
I'm not stupid. As if I'd leave stolen traps lying around.

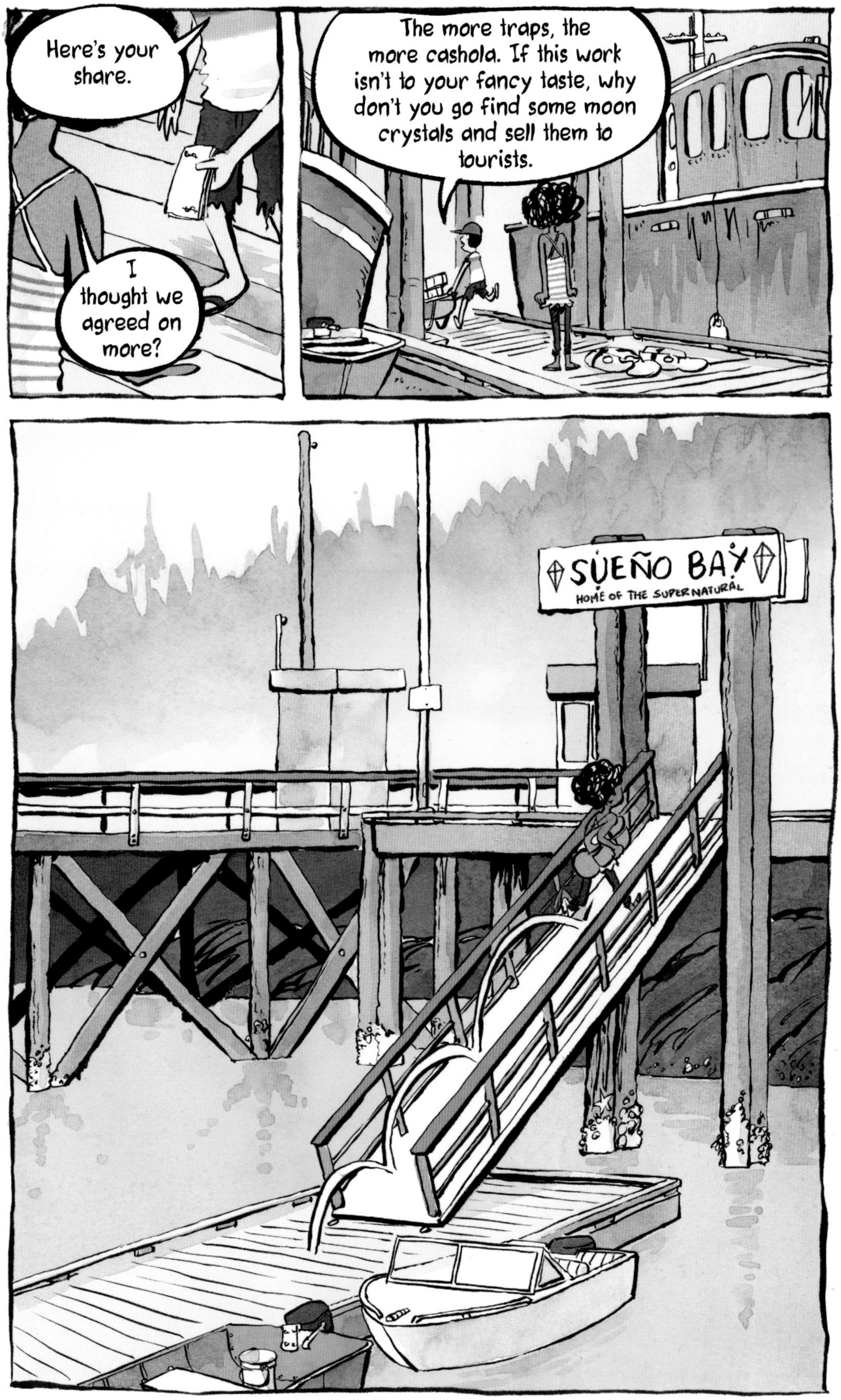
Here's your share.
I thought we agreed on more?
The more traps, the more cashola. If this work isn't to your fancy taste, why don't you go find some moon crystals and sell them to tourists.
SUEÑO BAY
HOME OF THE SUPERNATURAL

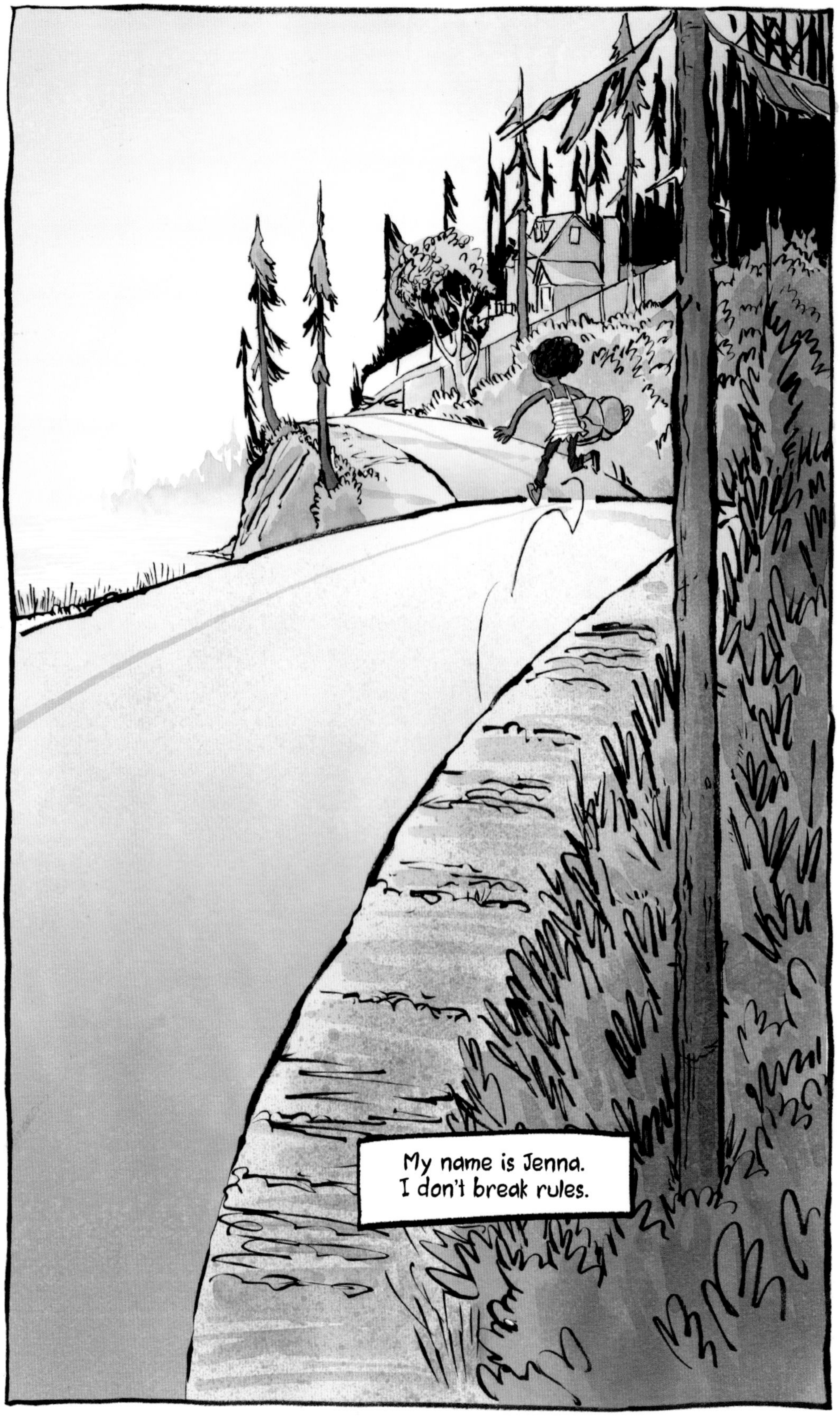
My name is Jenna.
I don't break rules.

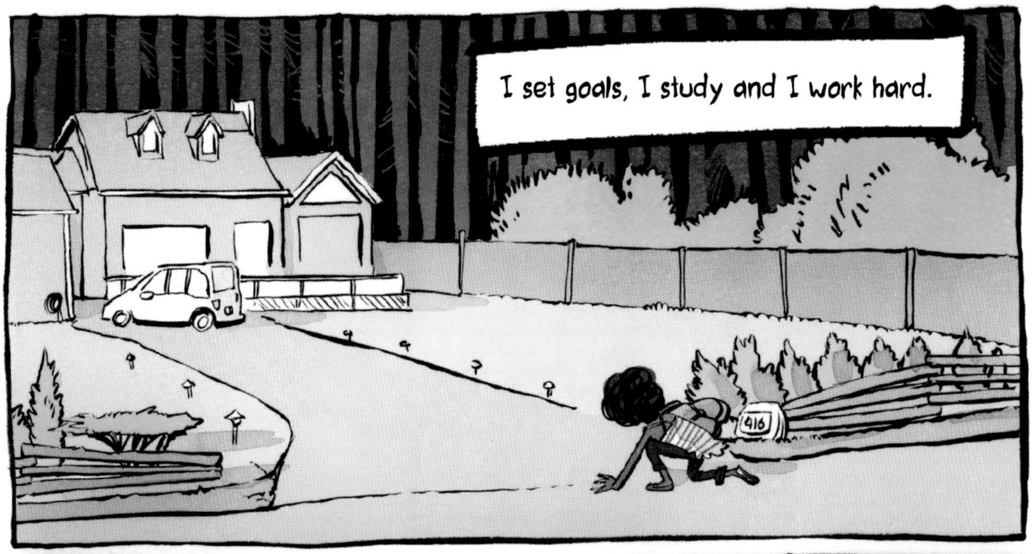
I set goals, I study and I work hard.
416

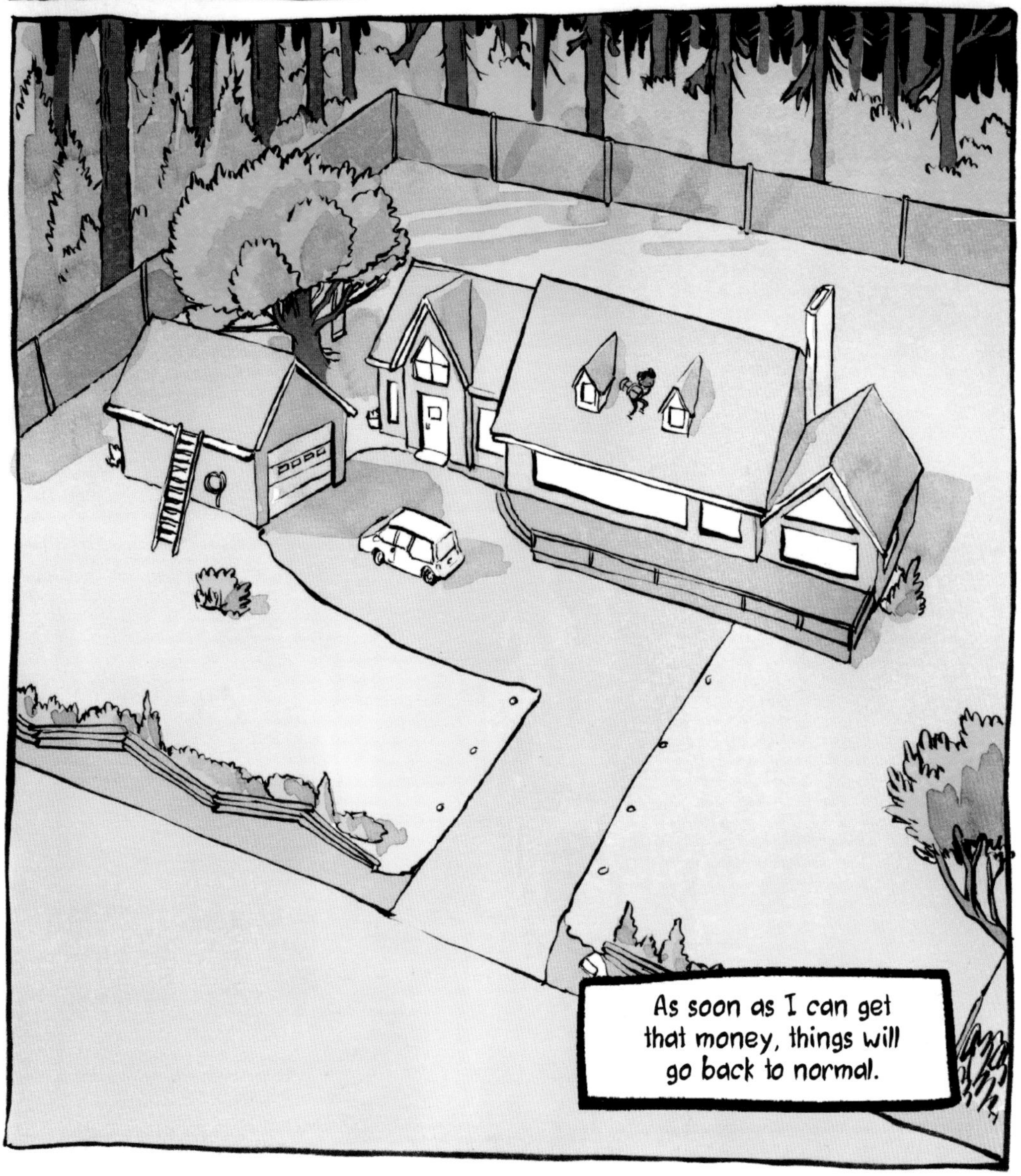
As soon as I can get that money, things will go back to normal.

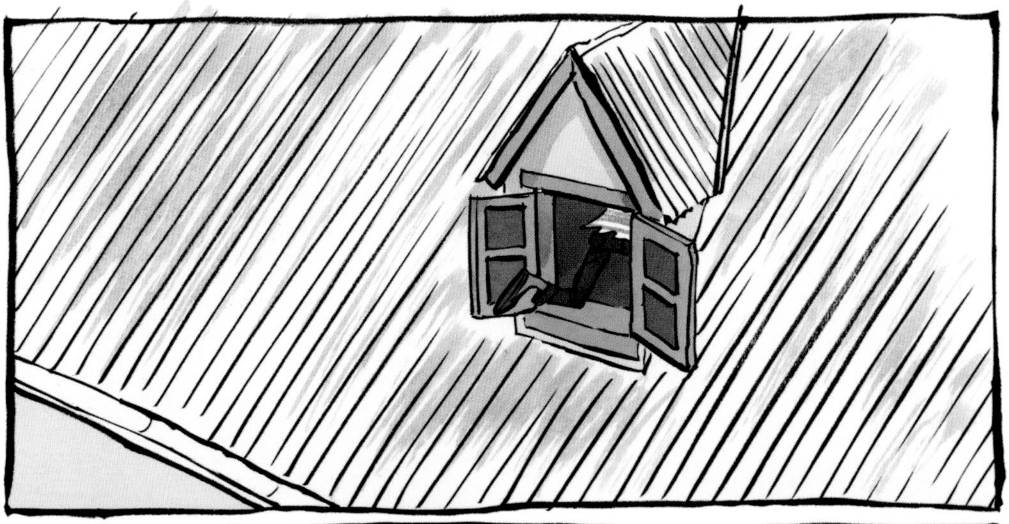

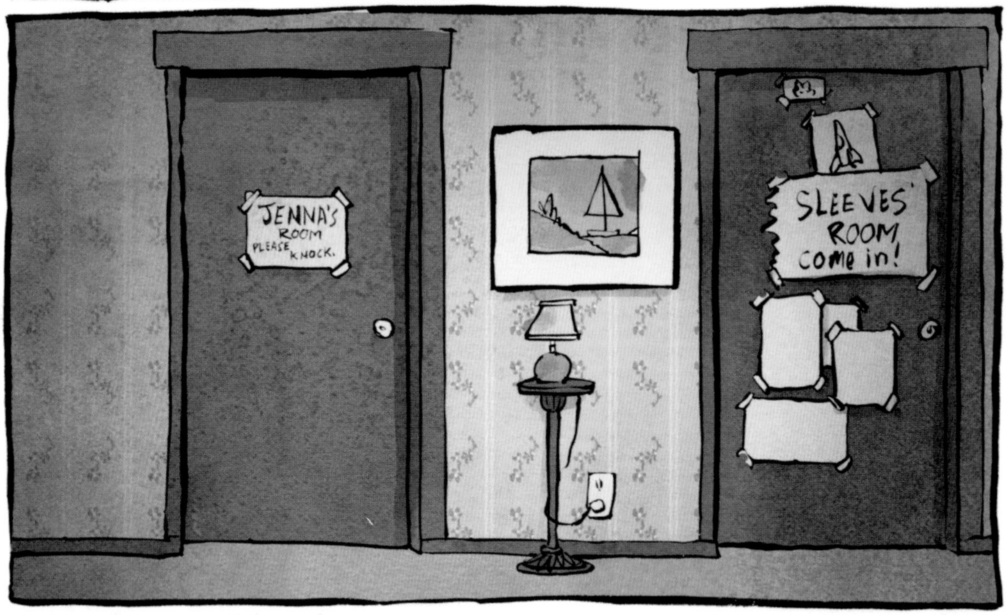
JENNA'S ROOM PLEASE KNOCK.
SLEEVES' ROOM come in!

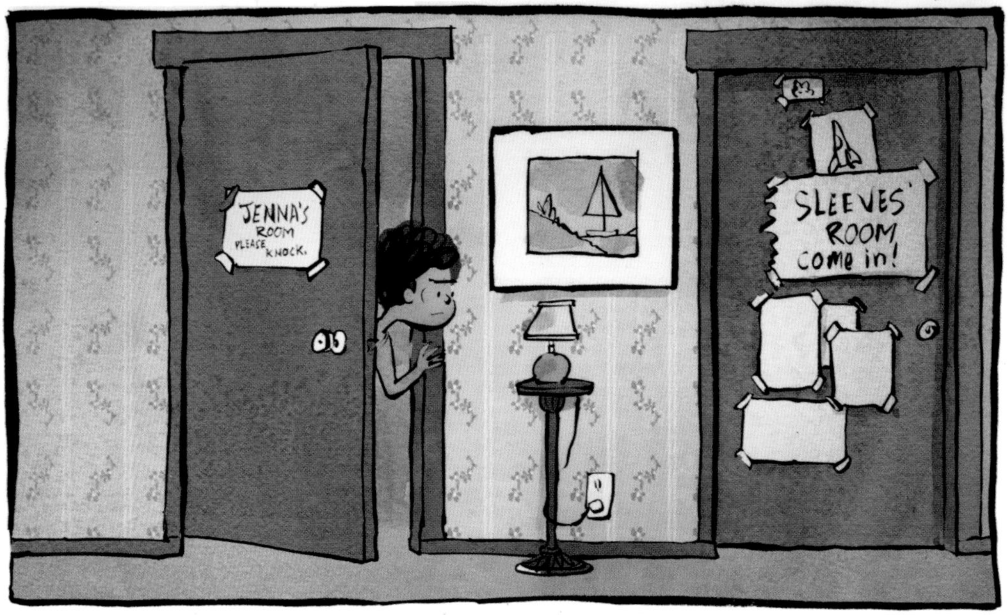
JENNA'S ROOM PLEASE KNOCK.
SLEEVES' ROOM come in!

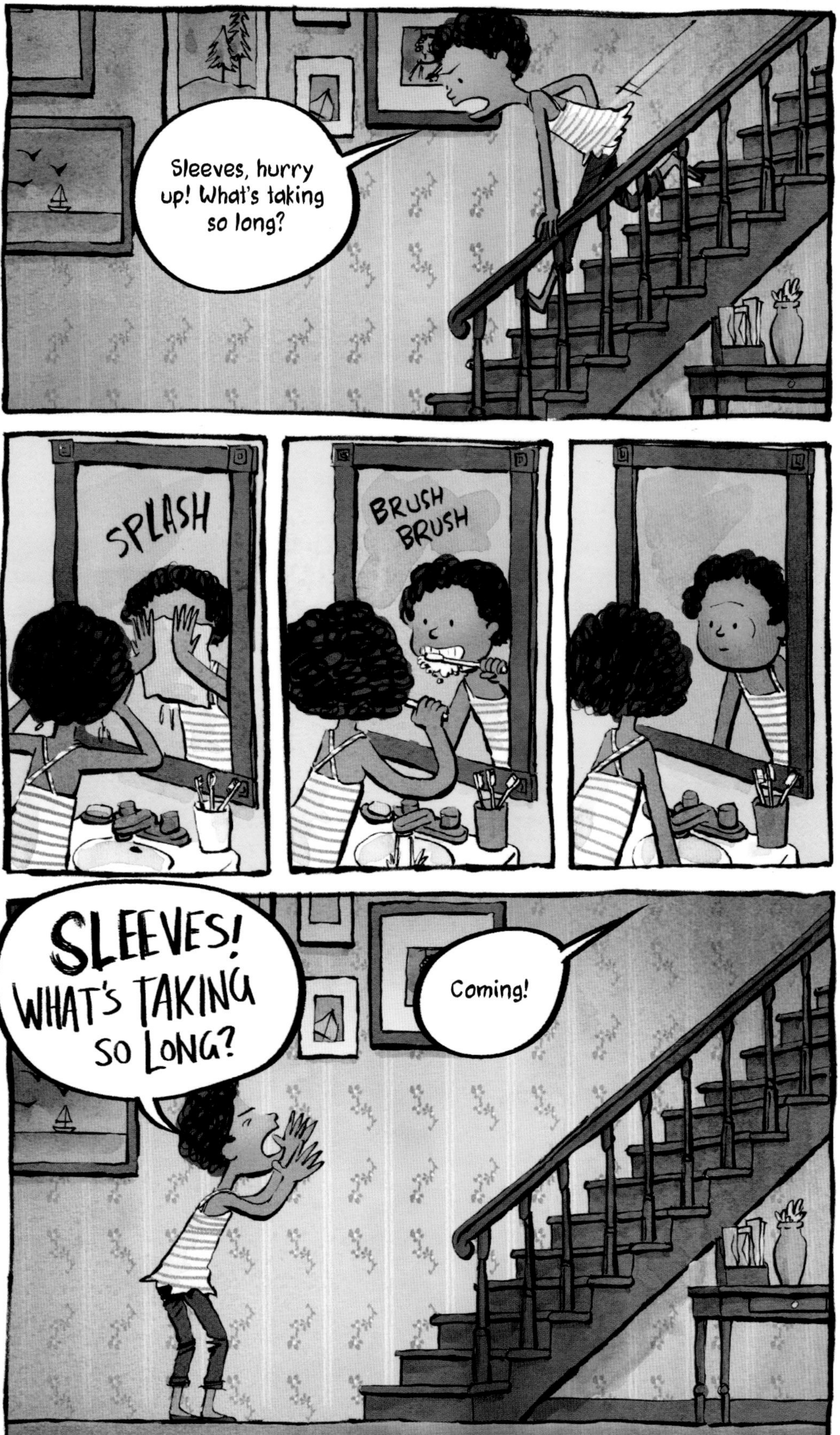
Sleeves, hurry up! What's taking so long?
SPLASH
BRUSH BRUSH
SLEEVES! WHAT'S TAKING SO LONG?
Coming!

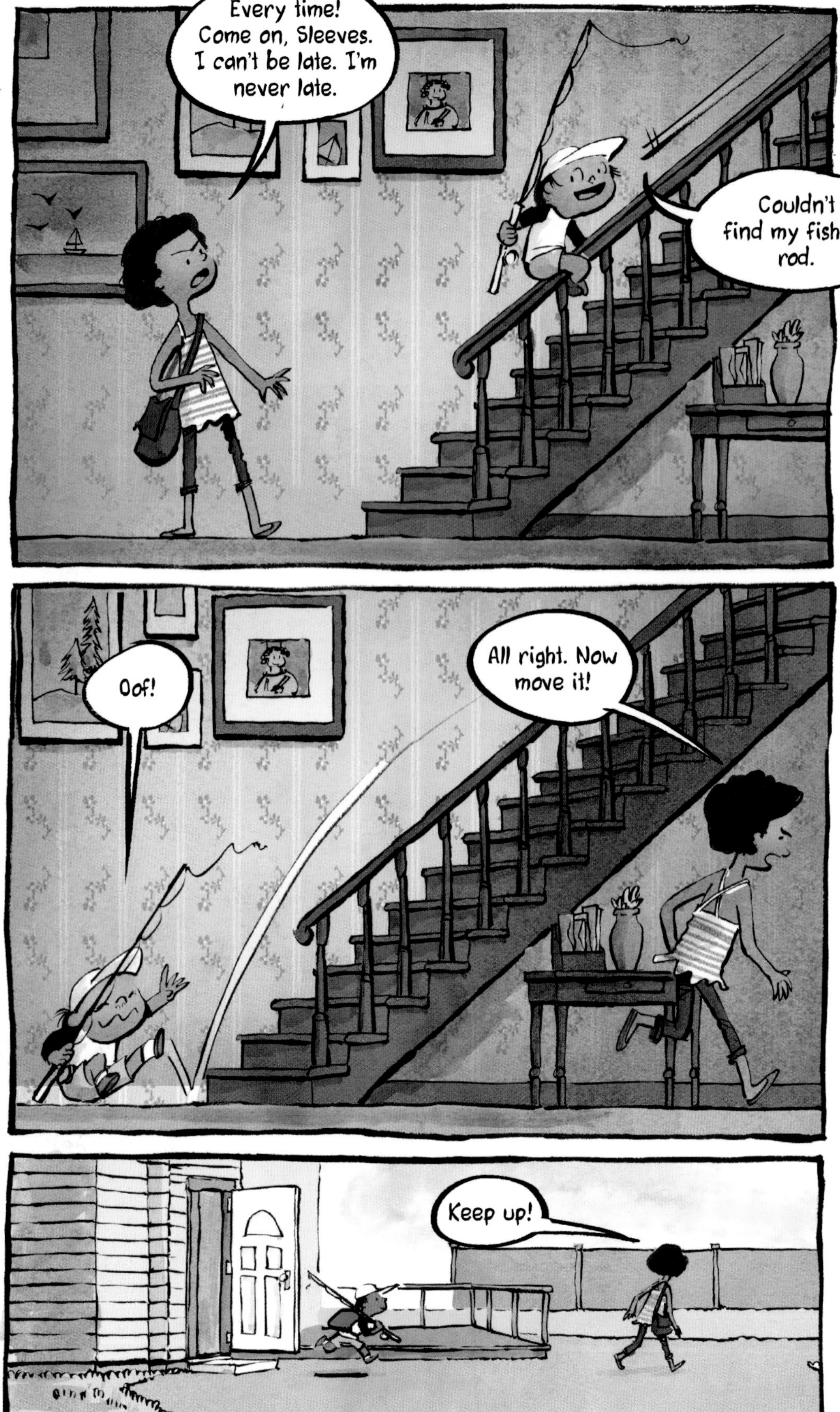
Every time! Come on, Sleeves. I can't be late. I'm never late.
Couldn't find my fishing rod.
Oof!
All right. Now move it!
Keep up!

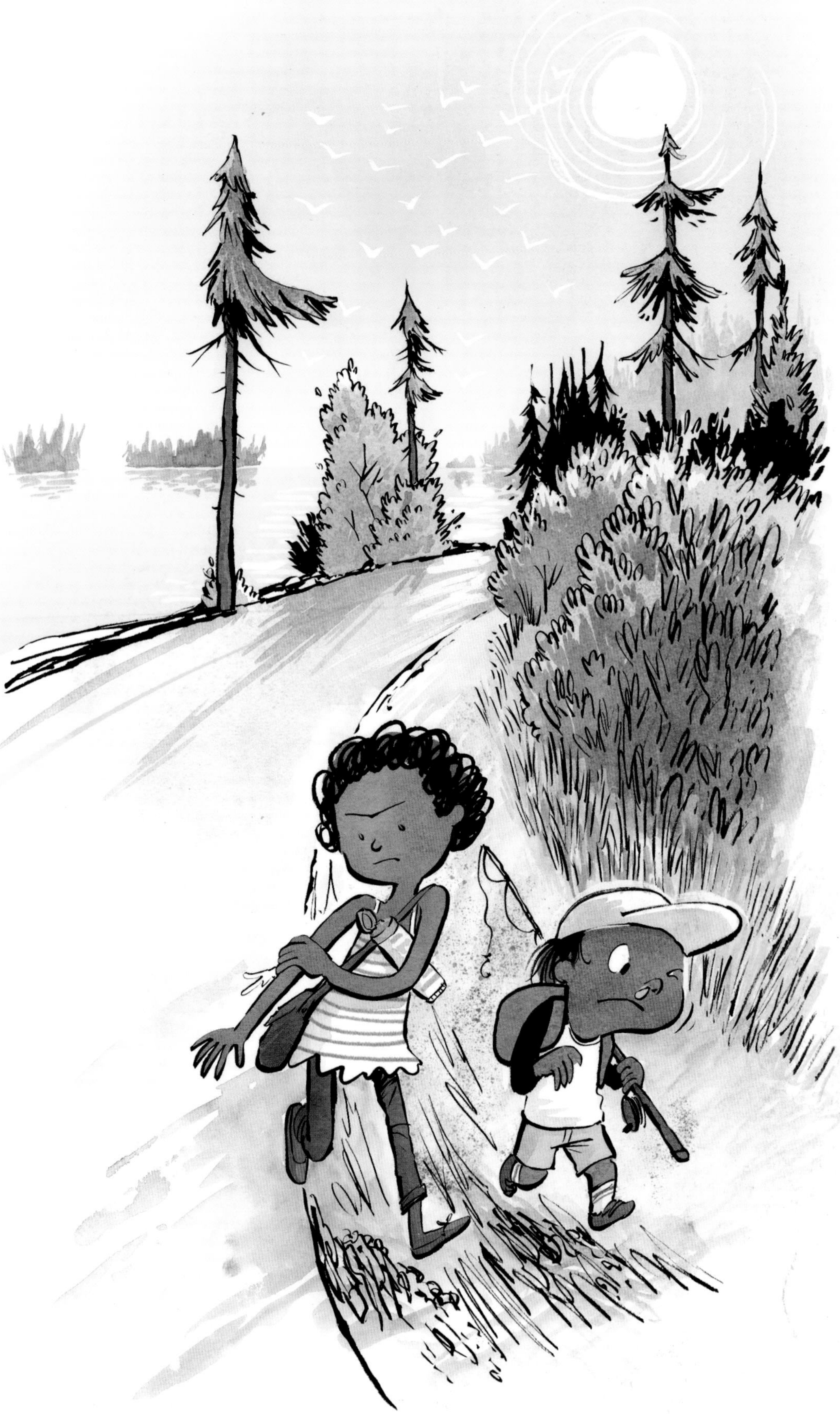

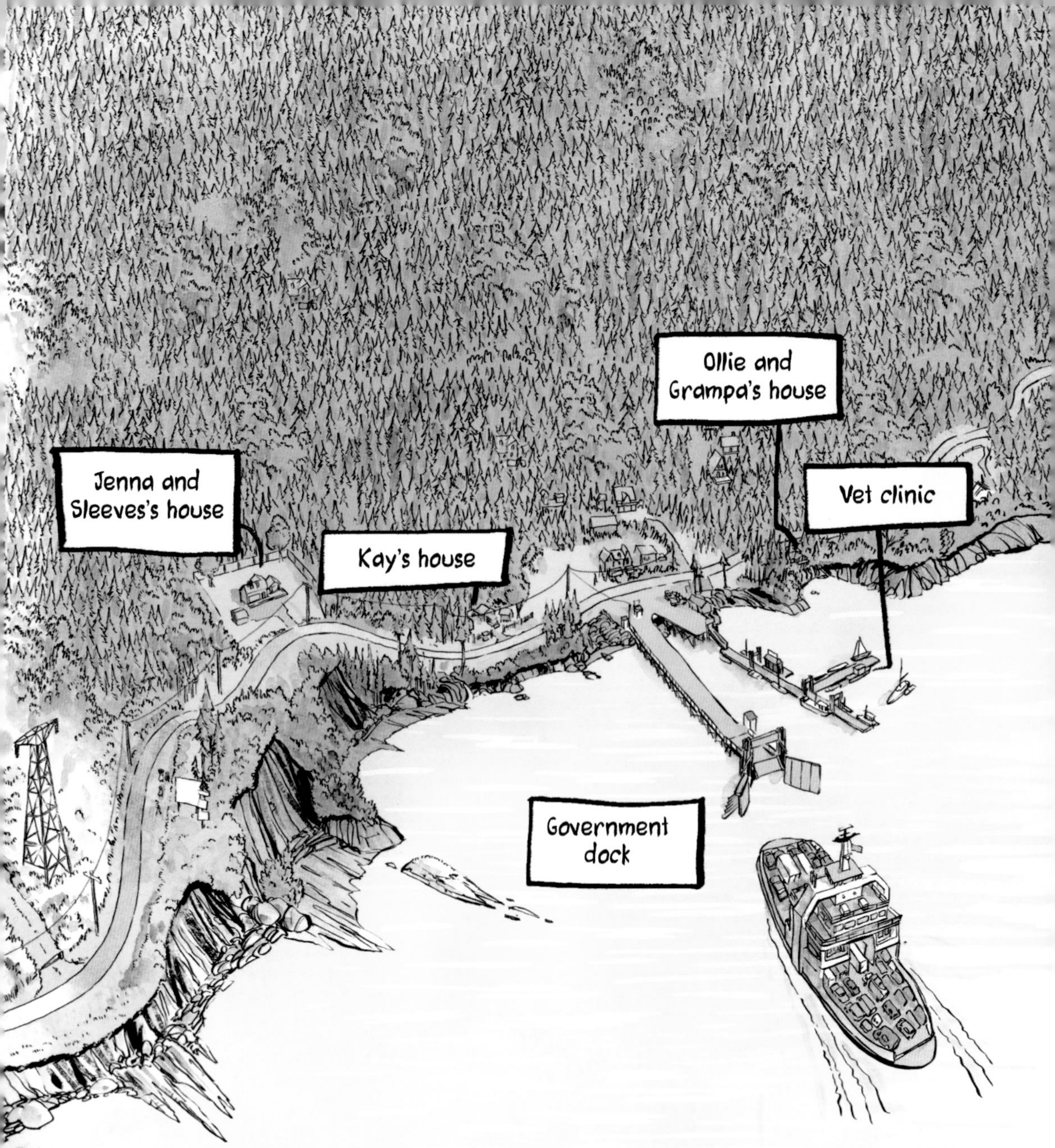
Ollie and Grampa's house
Jenna and Sleeves's house
Vet clinic
Kay's house
Government dock

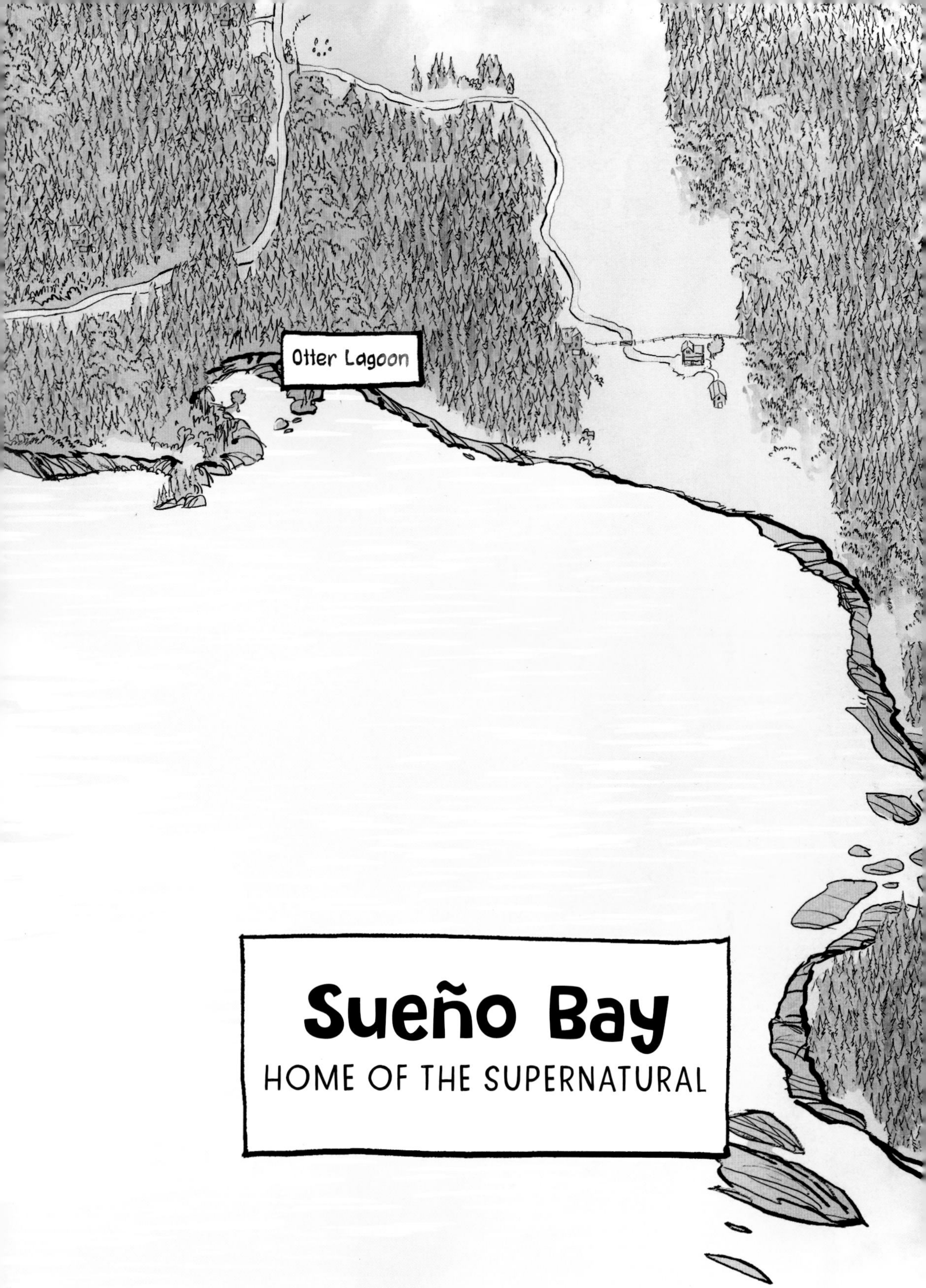
Otter Lagoon
Sueño Bay
HOME OF THE SUPERNATURAL

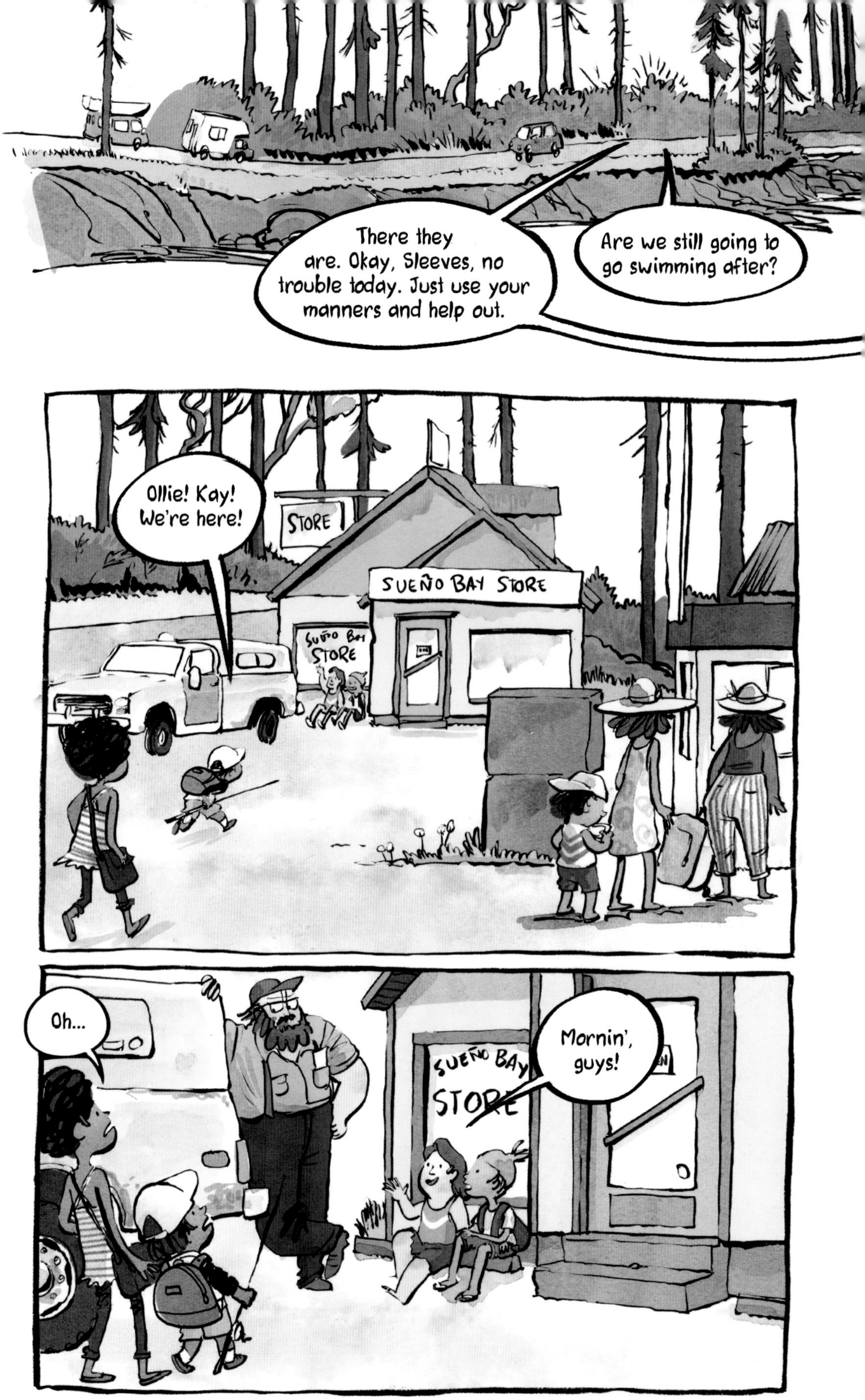
There they are. Okay, Sleeves, no trouble today. Just use your manners and help out.
Are we still going to go swimming after?
Ollie! Kay! We're here!
STORE
SUEÑO BAY STORE
SUEÑO BAY STORE
Oh...
SUEÑO BAY STORE
Mornin', guys!

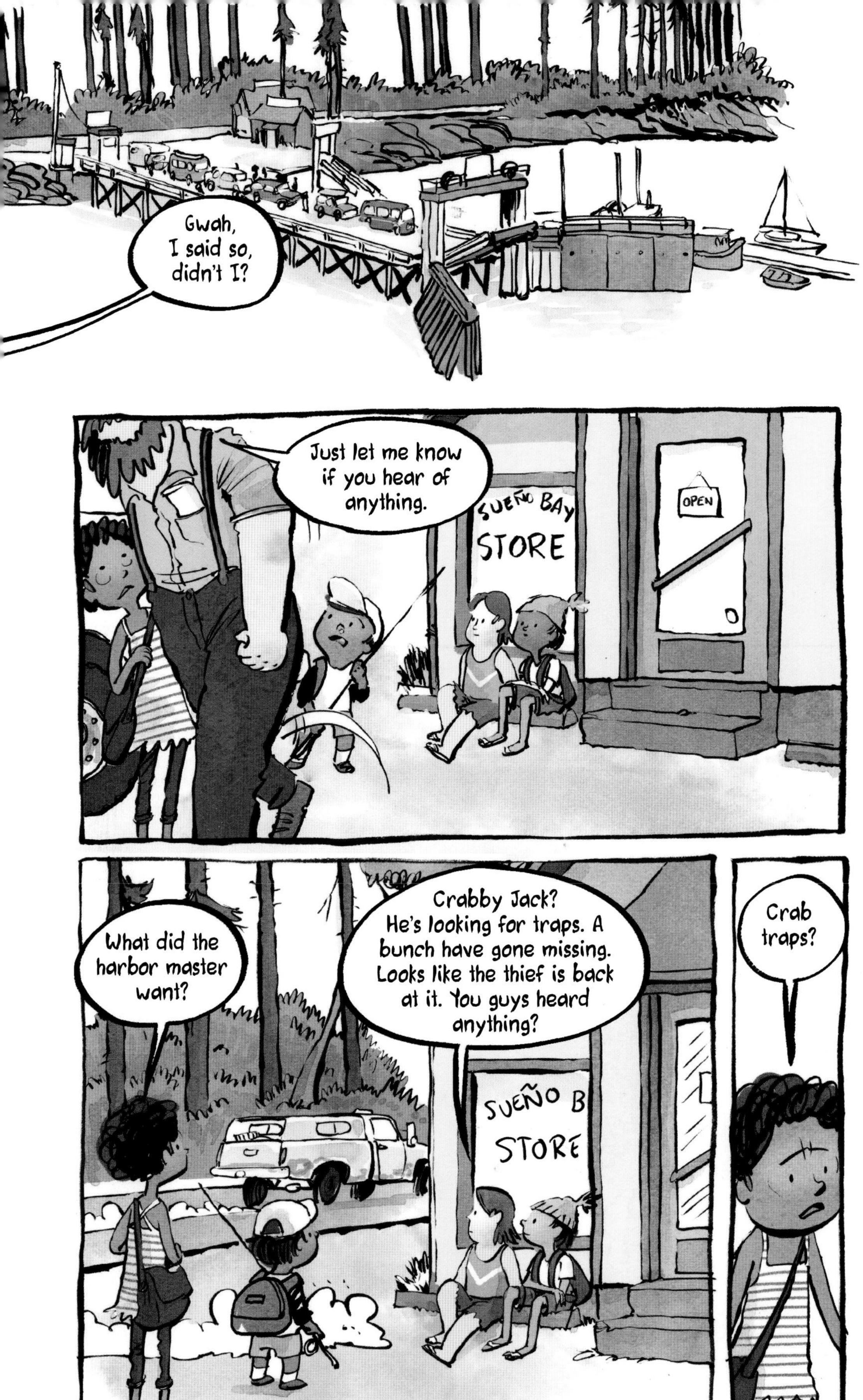
Gwah, I said so, didn't I?
Just let me know if you hear of anything.
SUEÑO BAY STORE
OPEN
What did the harbor master want?
Crabby Jack? He's looking for traps. A bunch have gone missing. Looks like the thief is back at it. You guys heard anything?
SUEÑO B STORE
Crab traps?

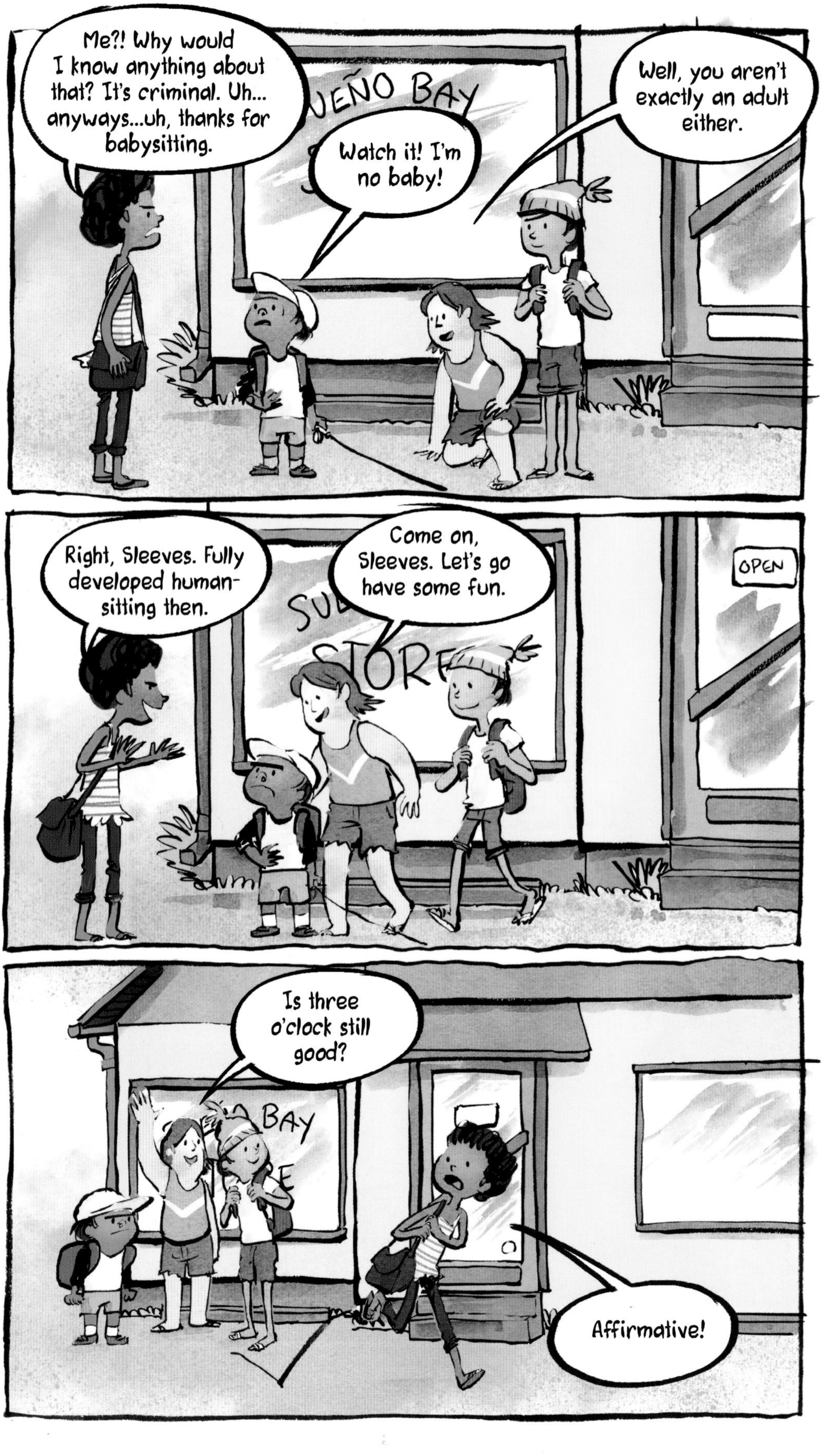
Me?! Why would I know anything about that? It's criminal. Uh... anyways...uh, thanks for babysitting.
Watch it! I'm no baby!
Well, you aren't exactly an adult either.
Right, Sleeves. Fully developed human-sitting then.
Come on, Sleeves. Let's go have some fun.
OPEN
Is three o'clock still good?
Affirmative!

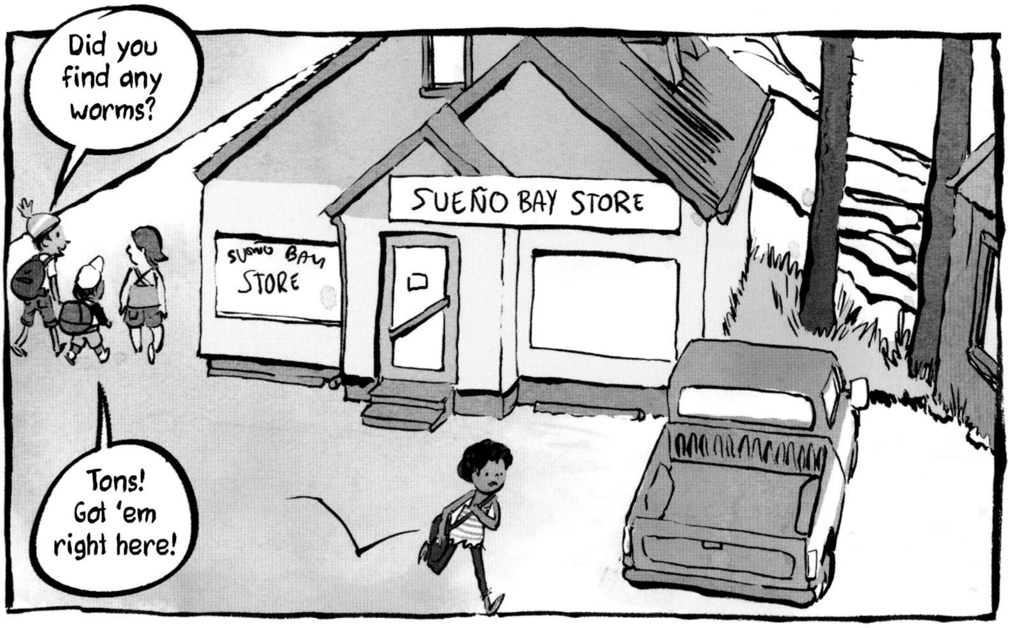
Did you find any worms?
SUEÑO BAY STORE
SUEÑO BAY STORE
Tons! Got 'em right here!

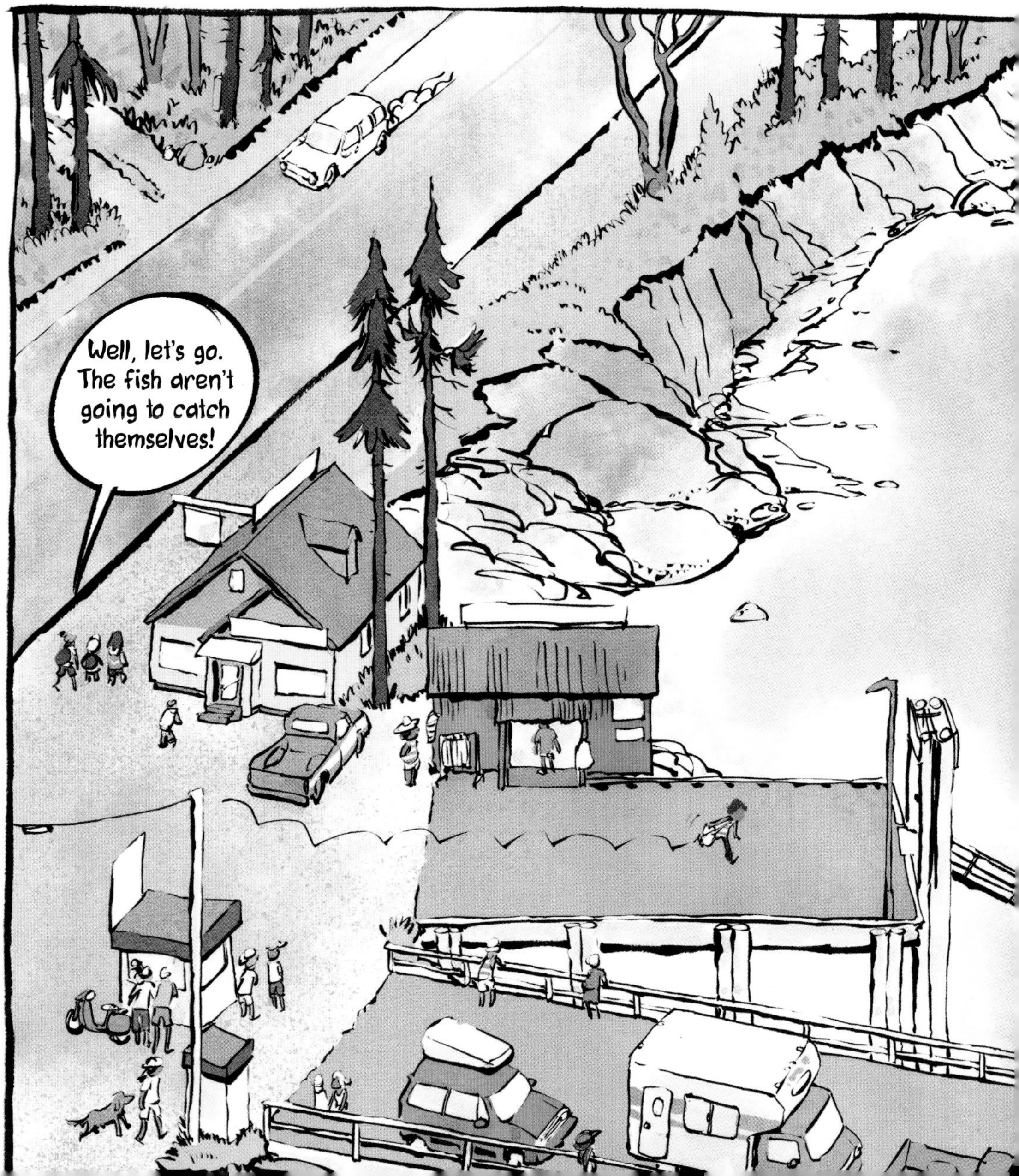
Well, let's go. The fish aren't going to catch themselves!

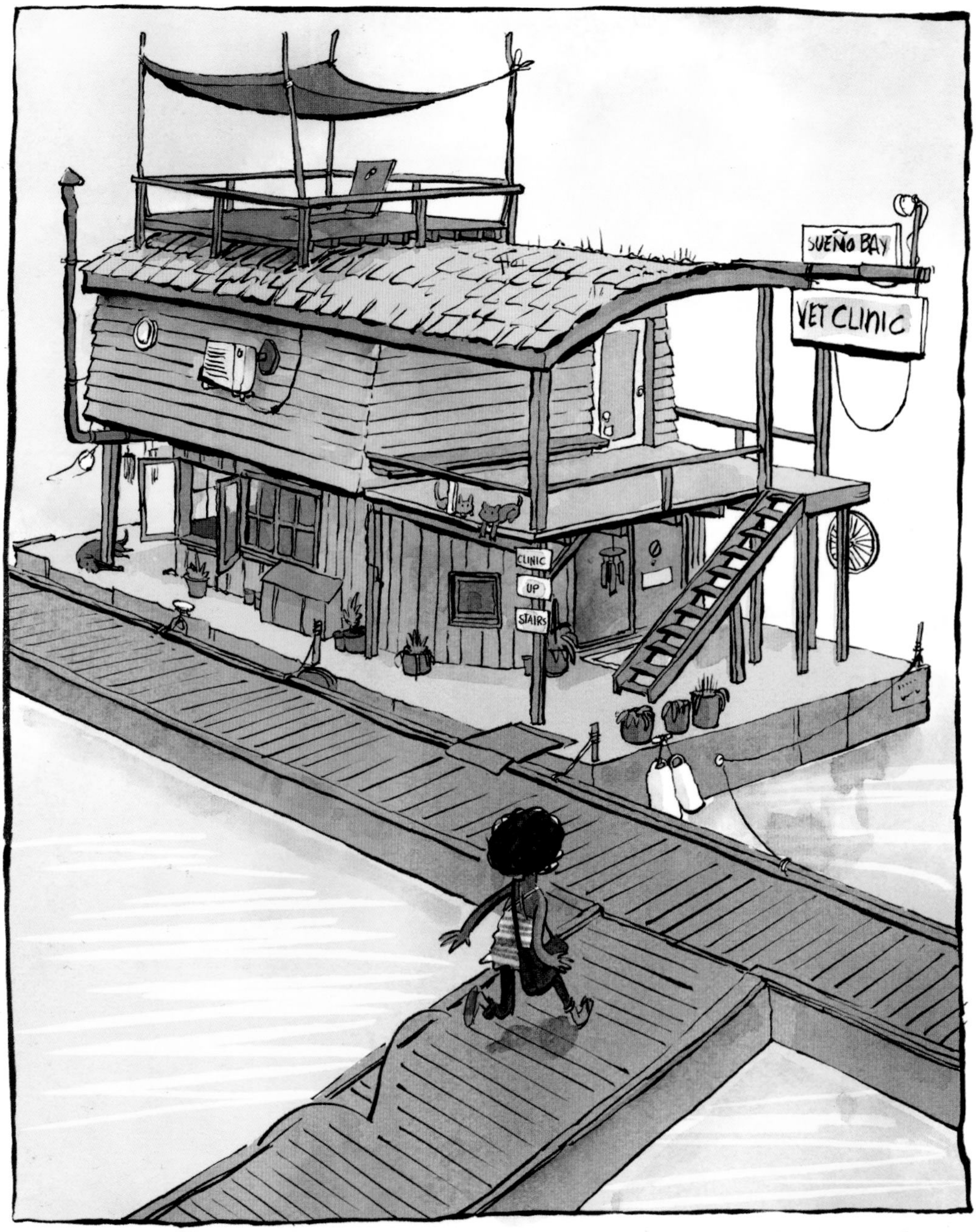
SUEÑO BAY
VET CLINIC
CLINIC
UP
STAIRS

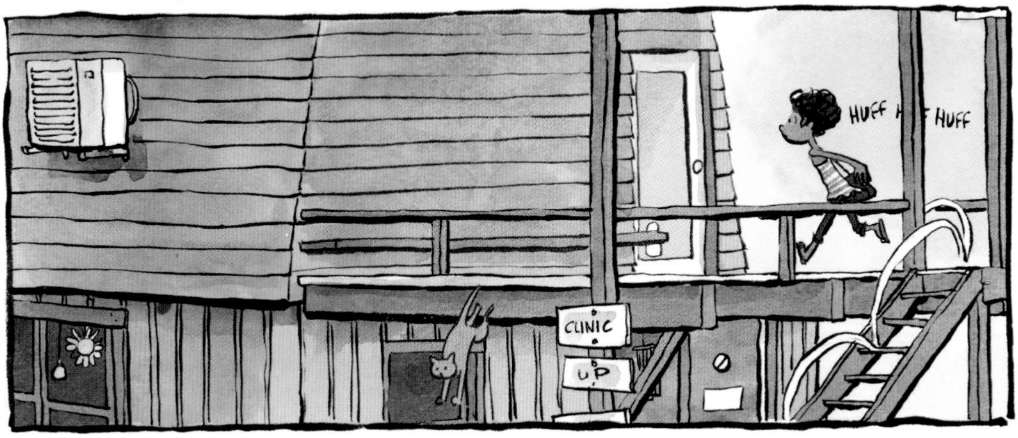
HUFF
HUFF
CLINIC
UP

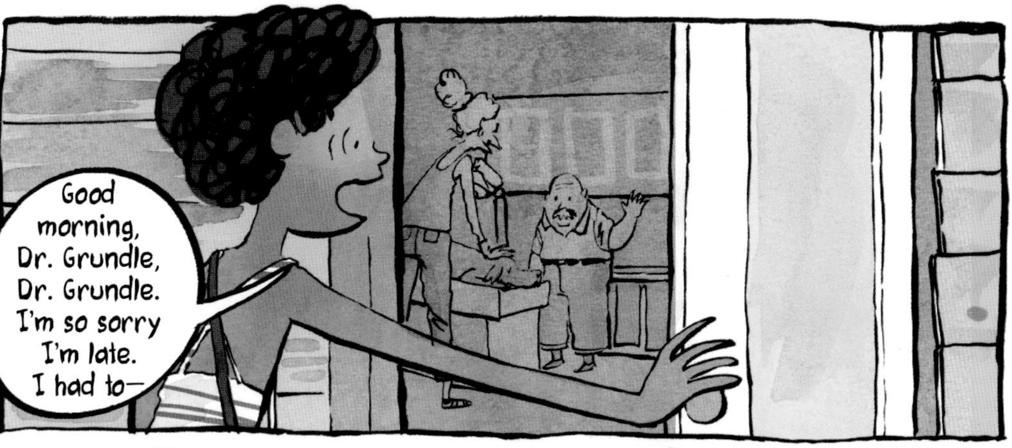
Good morning, Dr. Grundle, Dr. Grundle. I'm so sorry I'm late. I had to—

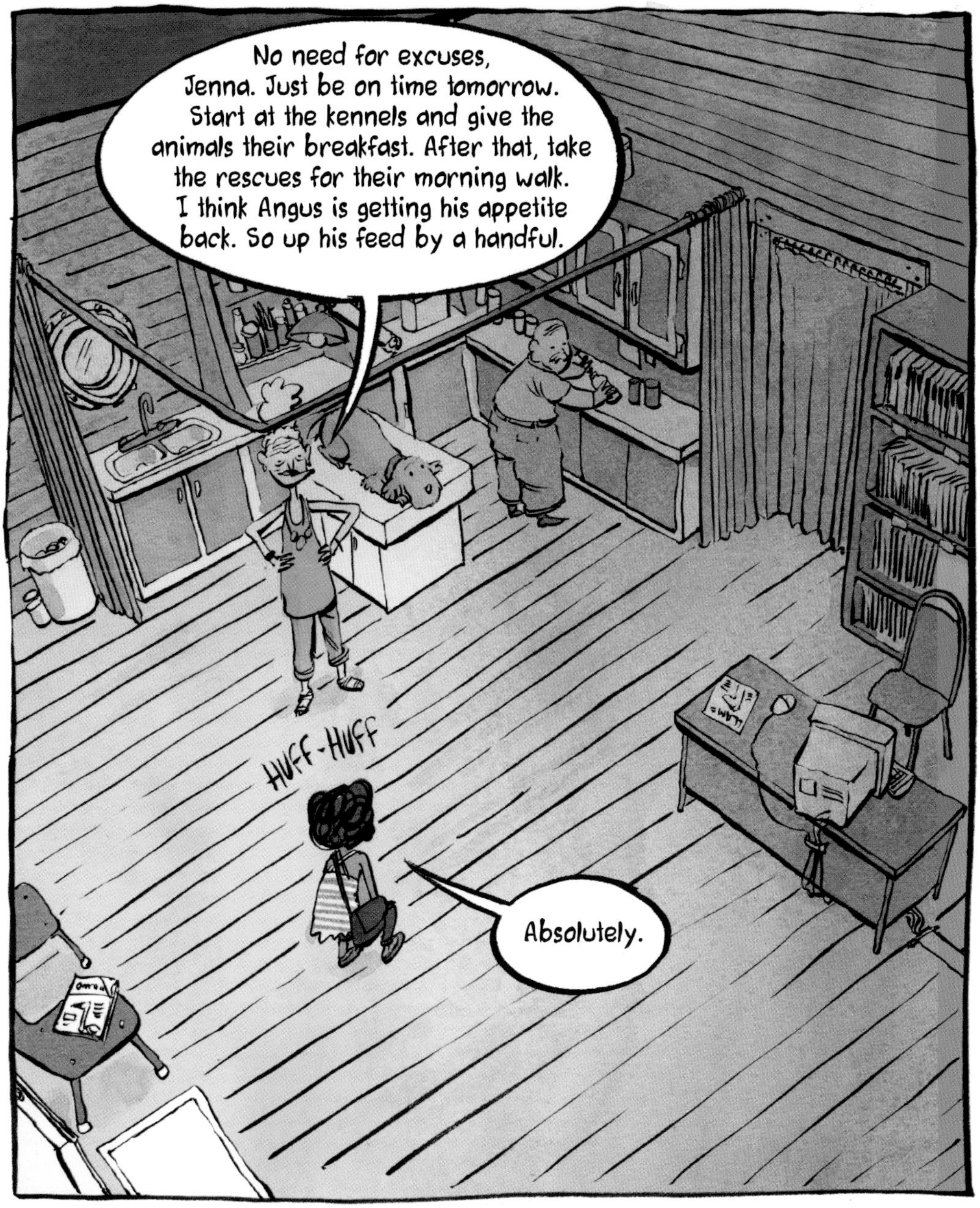
No need for excuses, Jenna. Just be on time tomorrow. Start at the kennels and give the animals their breakfast. After that, take the rescues for their morning walk. I think Angus is getting his appetite back. So up his feed by a handful.
HUFF-HUFF
Absolutely.

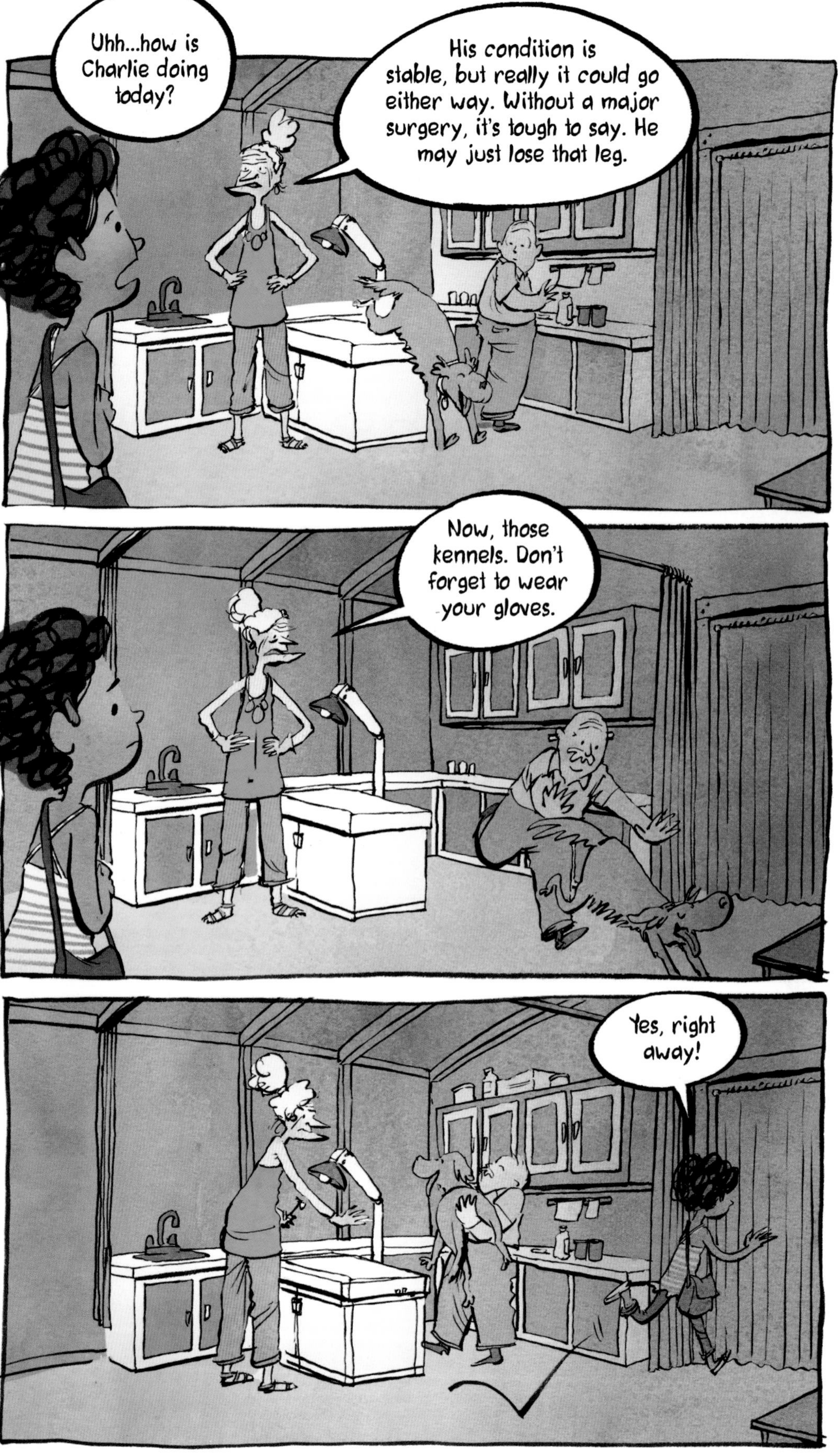
Uhh...how is Charlie doing today?
His condition is stable, but really it could go either way. Without a major surgery, it's tough to say. He may just lose that leg.
Now, those kennels. Don't forget to wear your gloves.
Yes, right away!

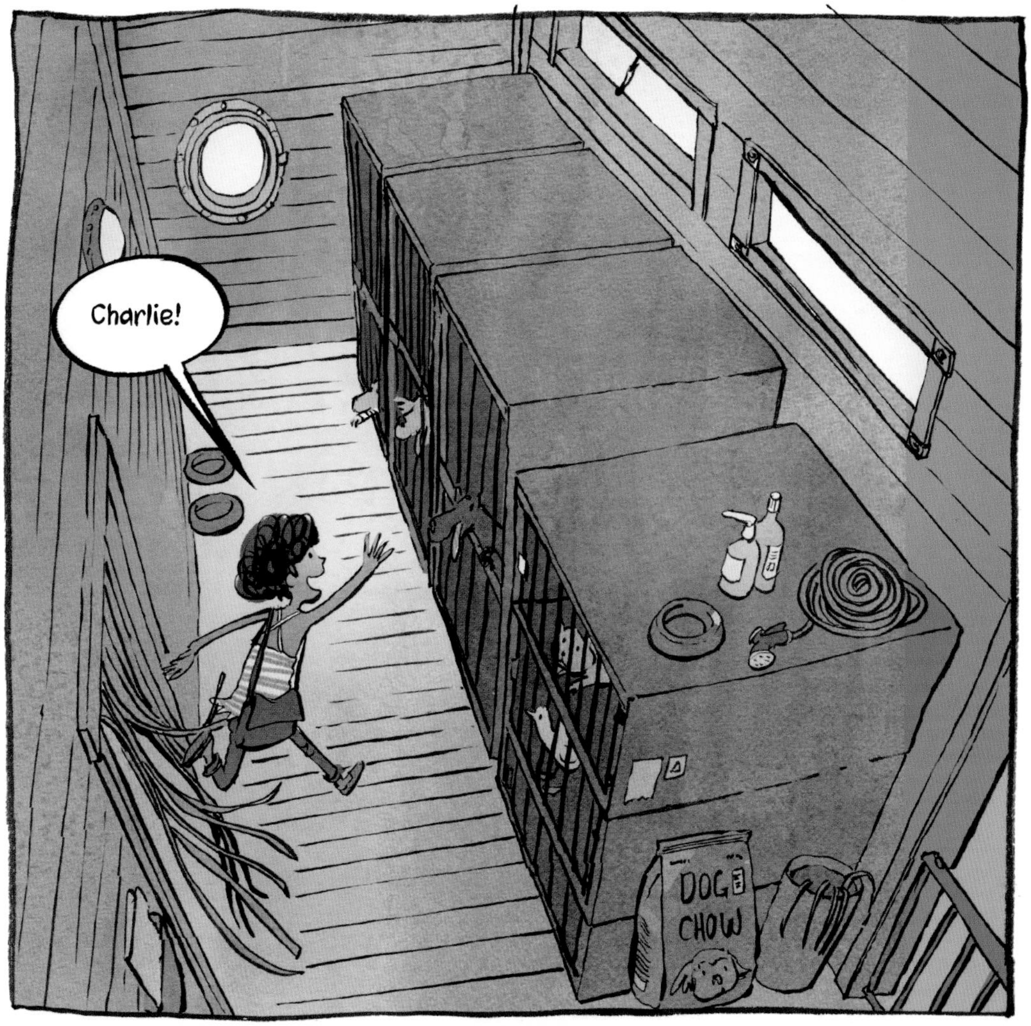
Charlie!
DOG CHOW

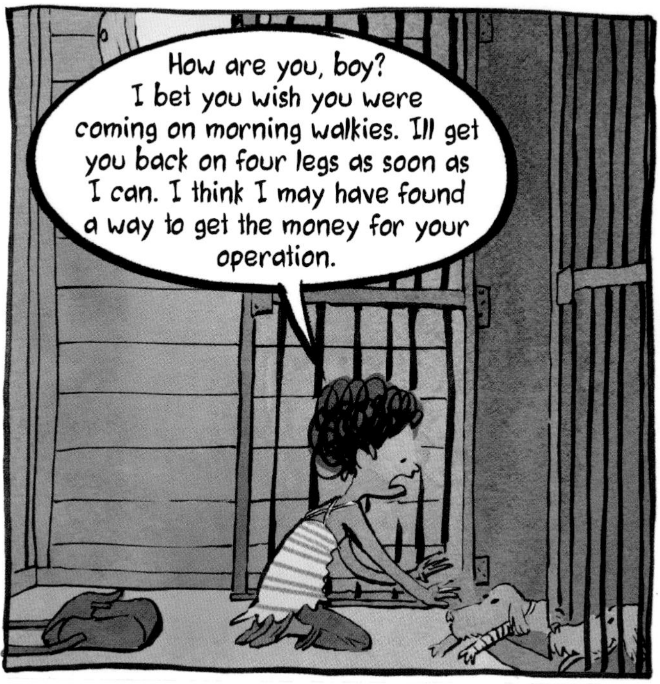
How are you, boy? I bet you wish you were coming on morning walkies. Ill get you back on four legs as soon as I can. I think I may have found a way to get the money for your operation.

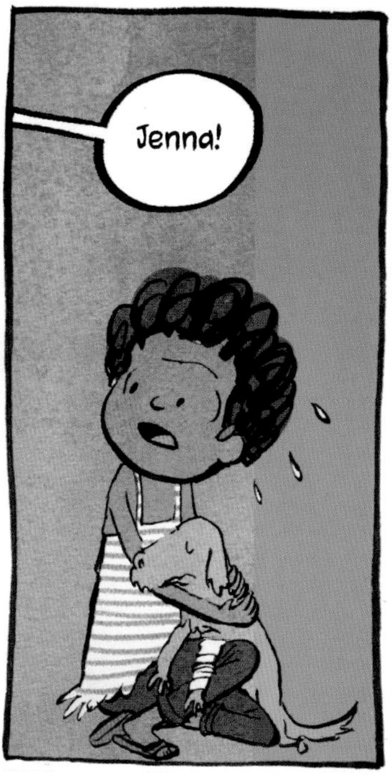
Jenna!

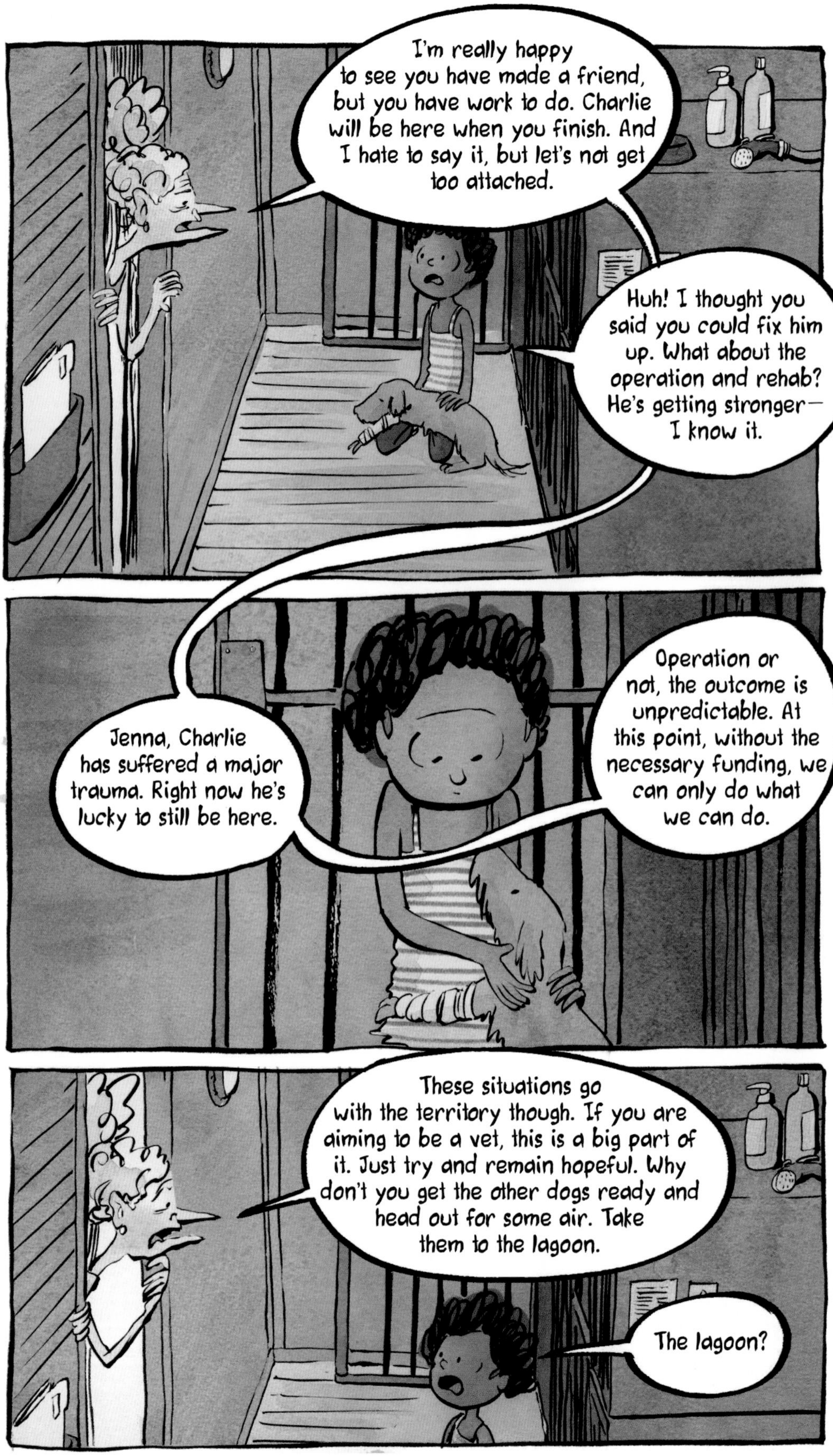
I'm really happy to see you have made a friend, but you have work to do. Charlie will be here when you finish. And I hate to say it, but let's not get too attached.
Huh! I thought you said you could fix him up. What about the operation and rehab? He's getting stronger—I know it.
Jenna, Charlie has suffered a major trauma. Right now he's lucky to still be here.
Operation or not, the outcome is unpredictable. At this point, without the necessary funding, we can only do what we can do.
These situations go with the territory though. If you are aiming to be a vet, this is a big part of it. Just try and remain hopeful. Why don't you get the other dogs ready and head out for some air. Take them to the lagoon.
The lagoon?

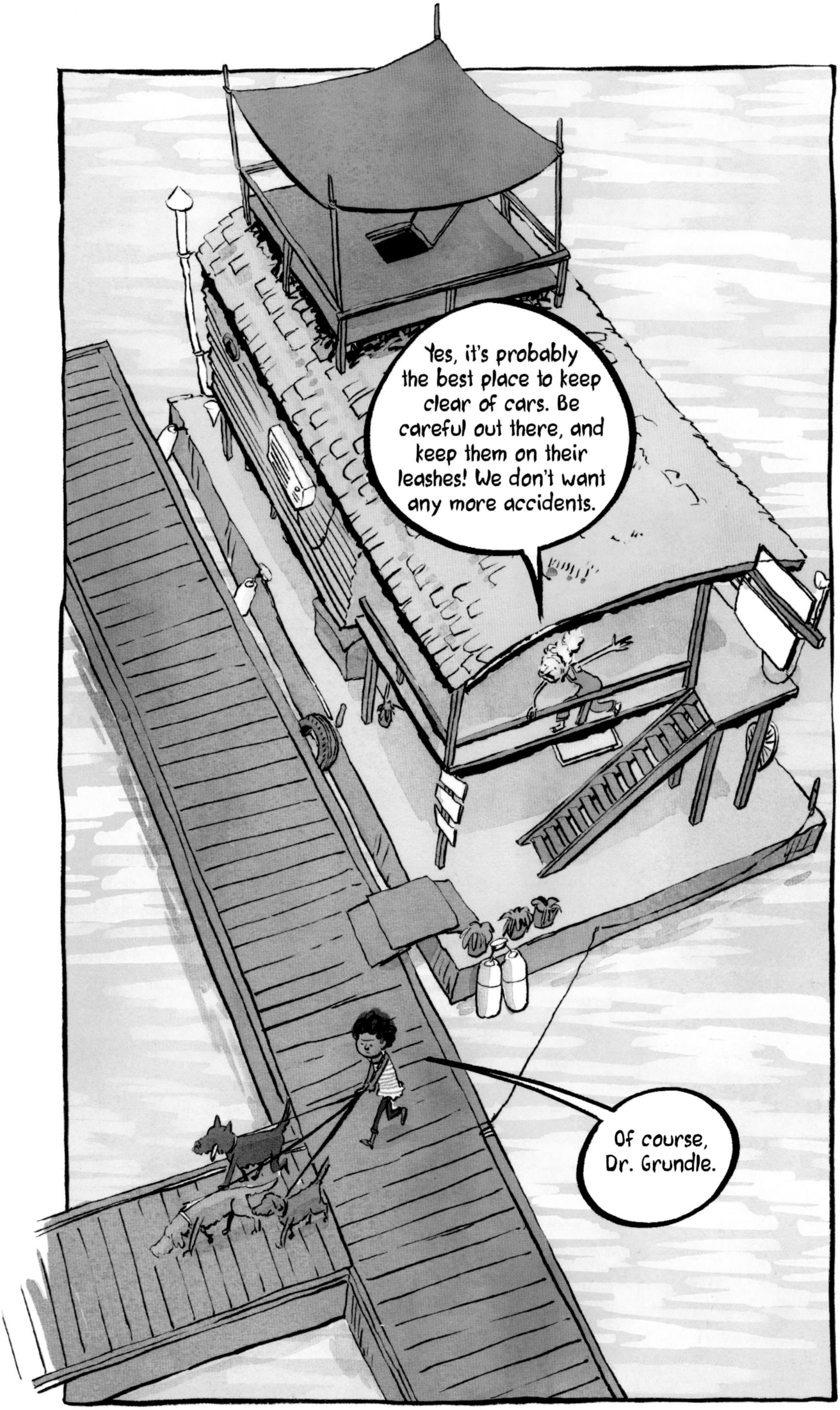
Yes, it's probably the best place to keep clear of cars. Be careful out there, and keep them on their leashes! We don't want any more accidents.
Of course, Dr. Grundle.

CHAPTER TWO

Lunar Serpentis

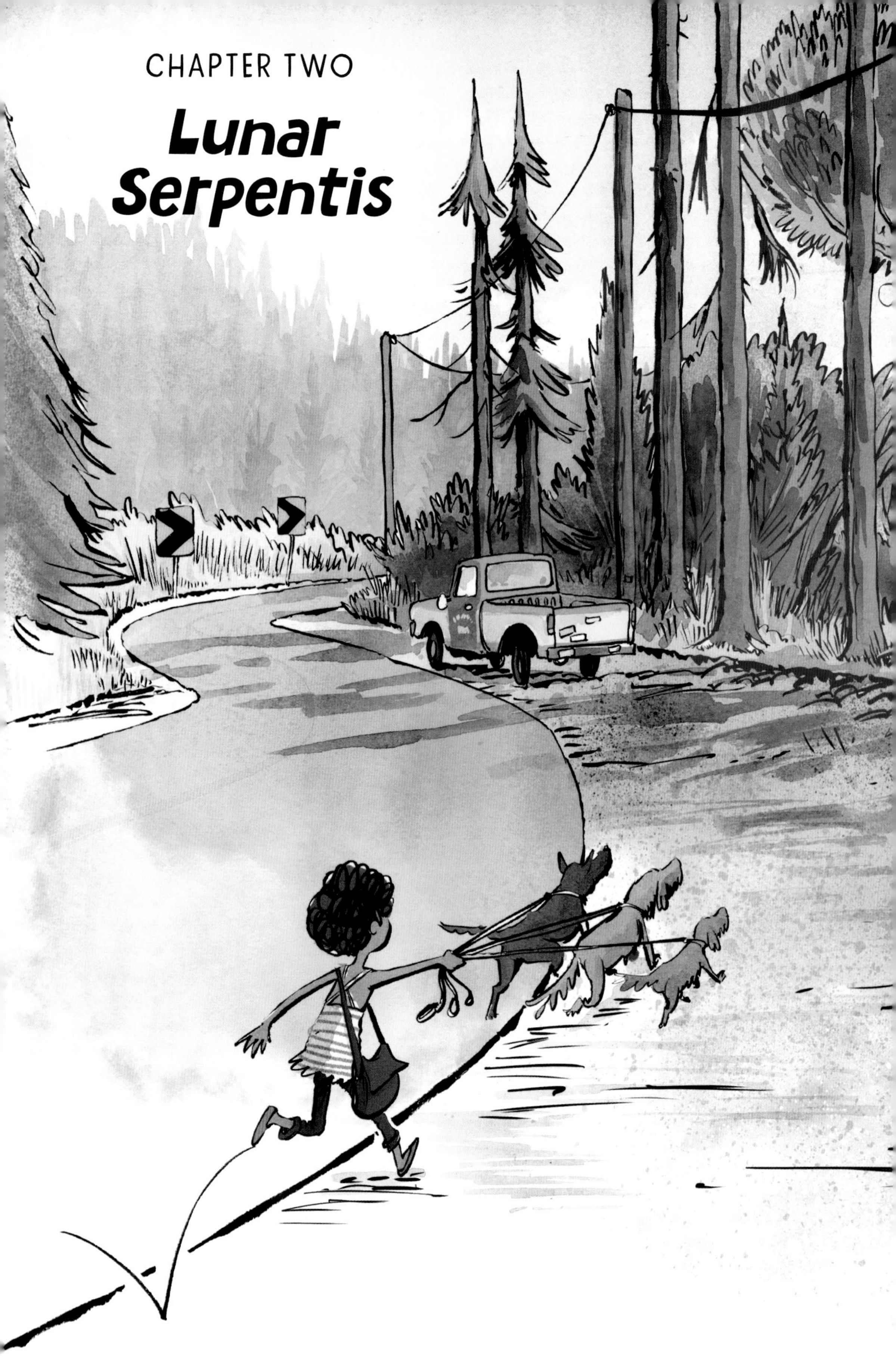

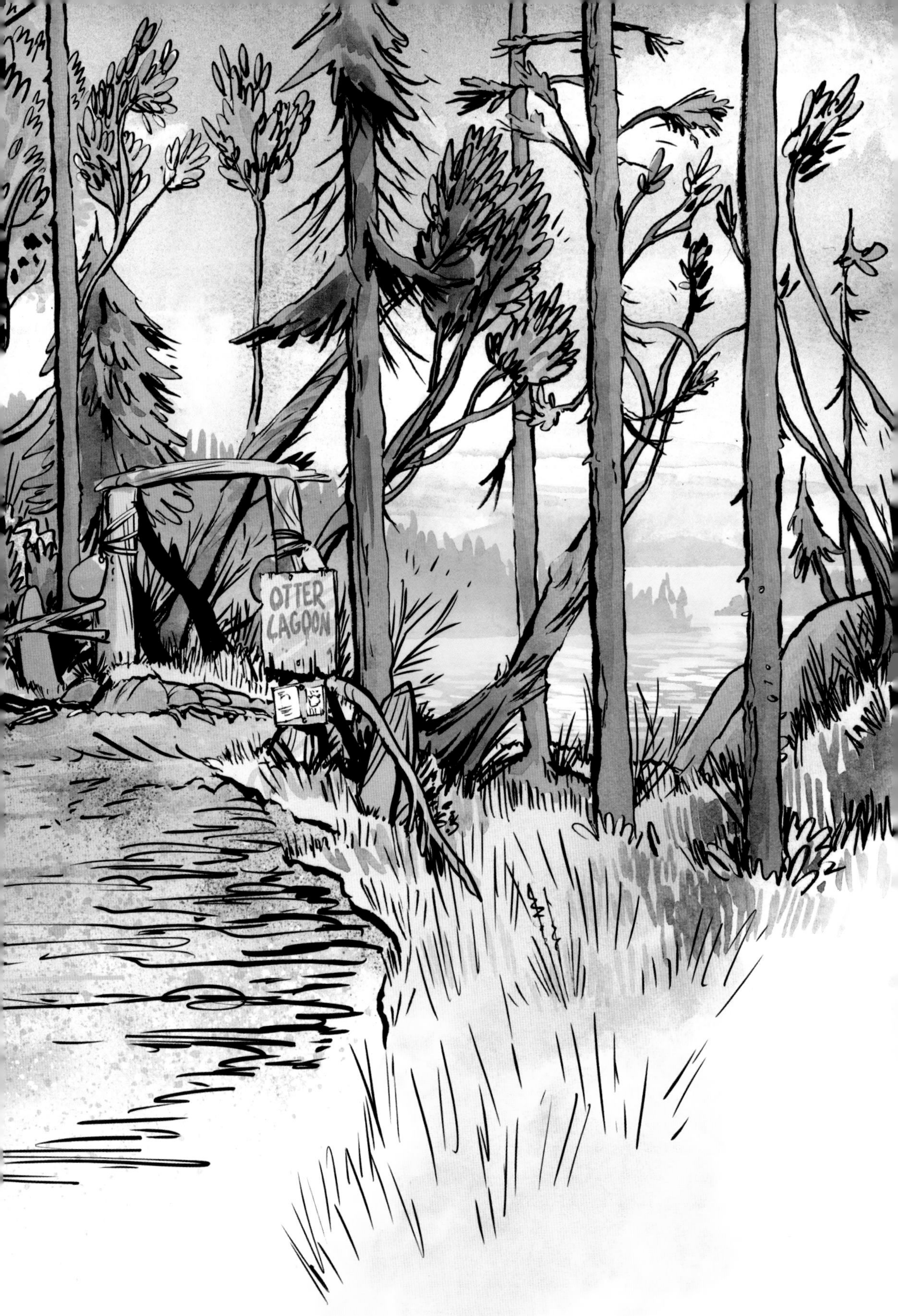
OTTER
LAGOON

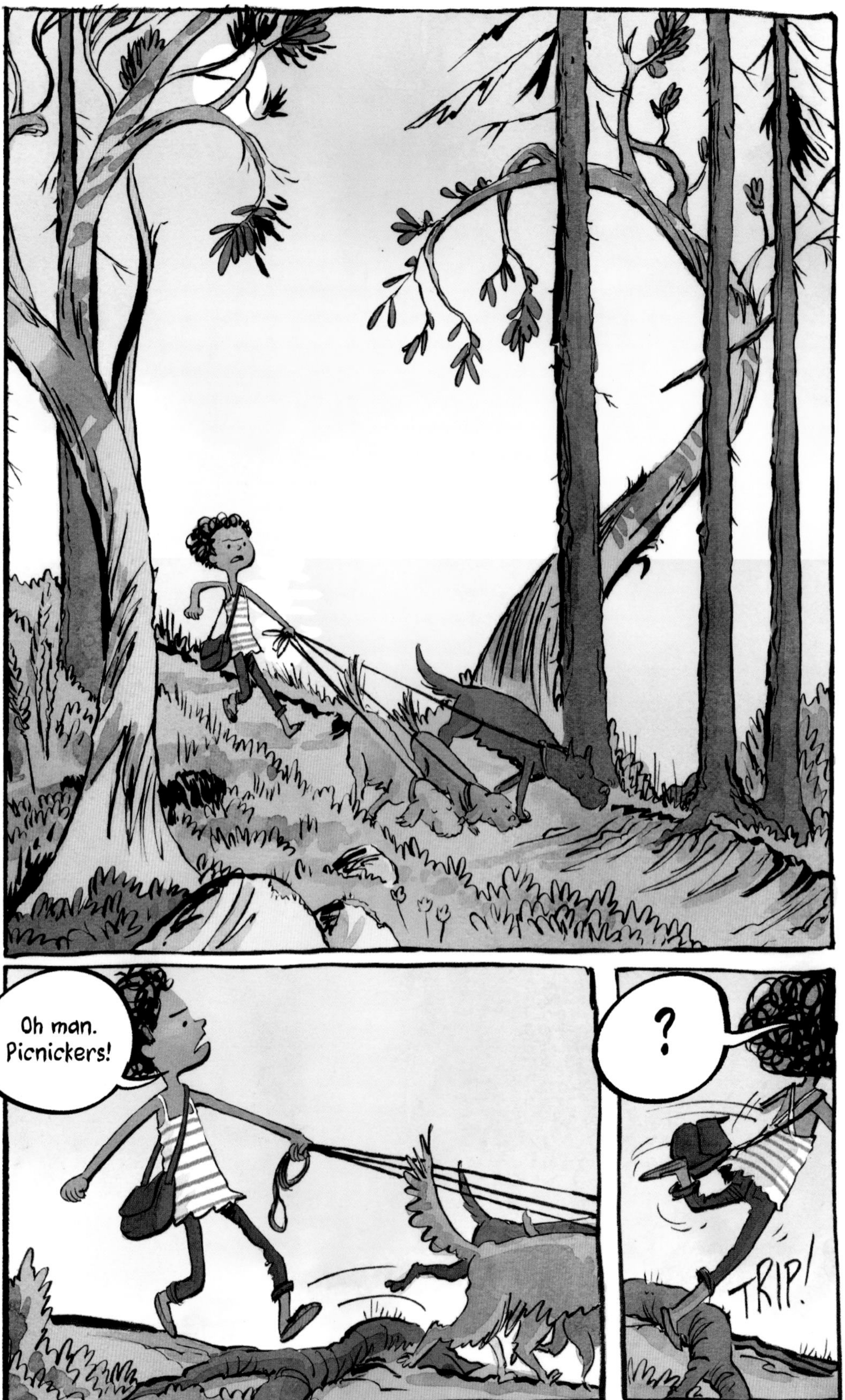
Oh man. Picnickers!
?
TRIP!

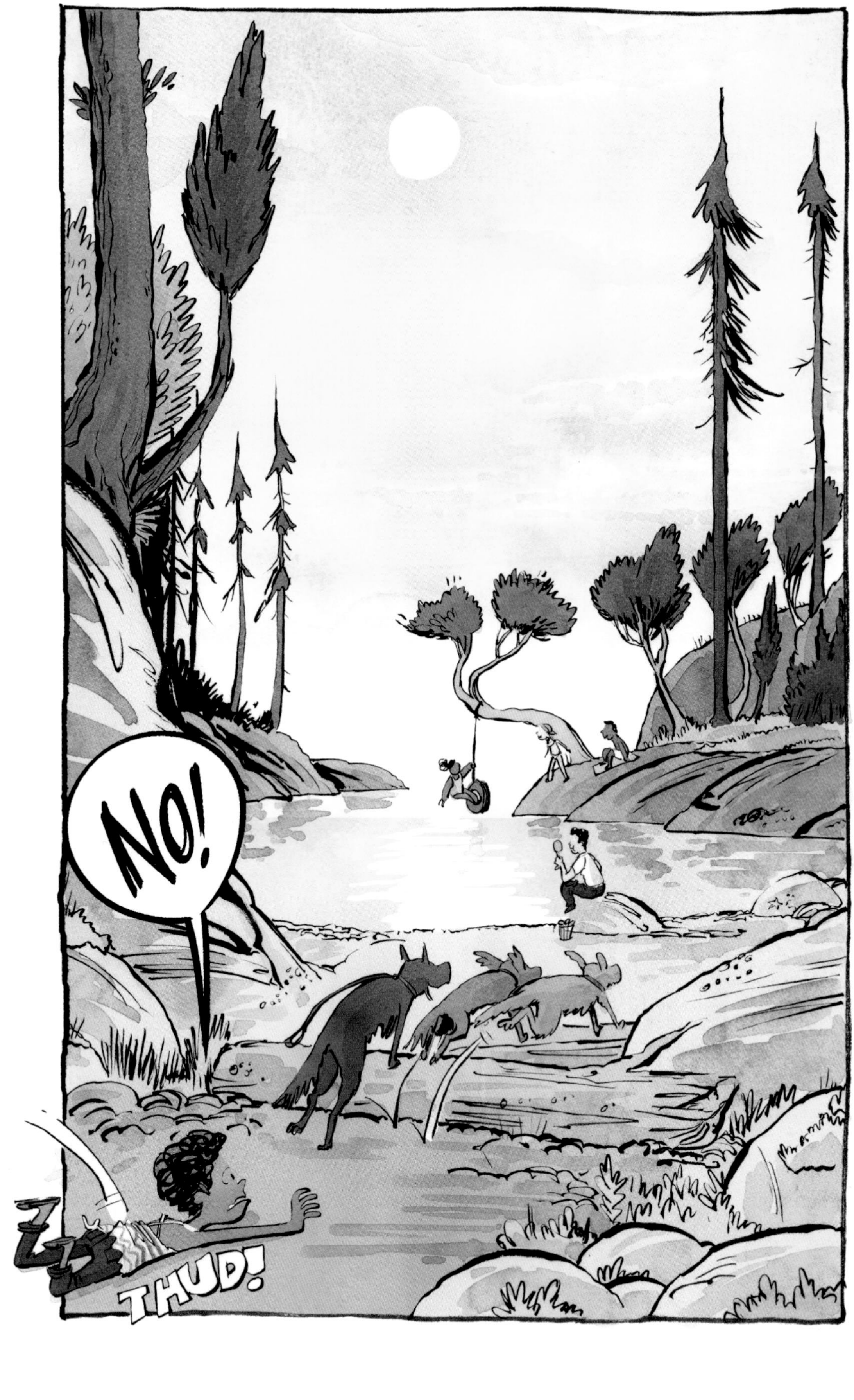
NO!
THUD!

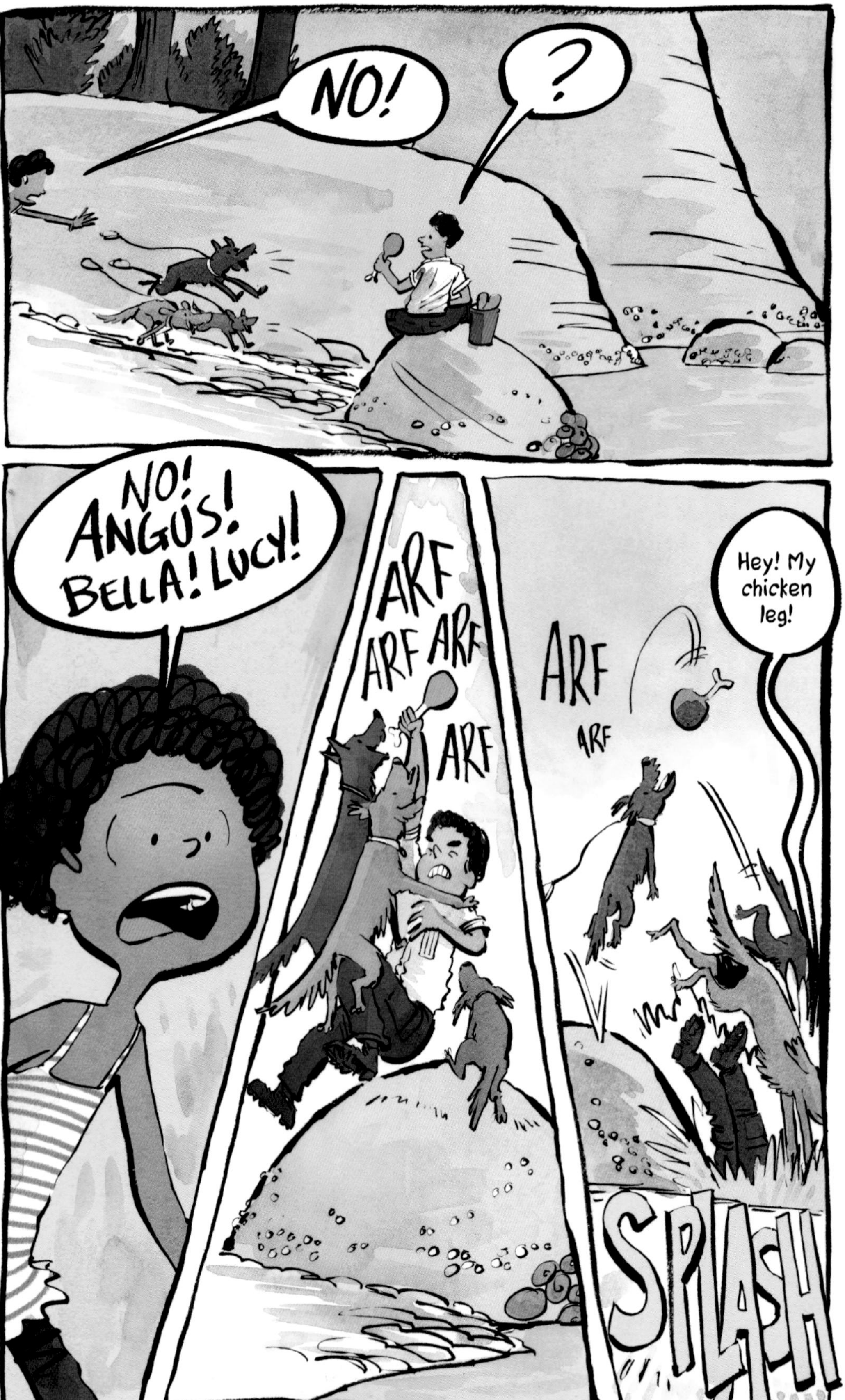
NO!
?
NO! ANGUS! BELLA! LUCY!
ARF ARF ARF ARF
ARF
ARF
Hey! My chicken leg!
SPLASH

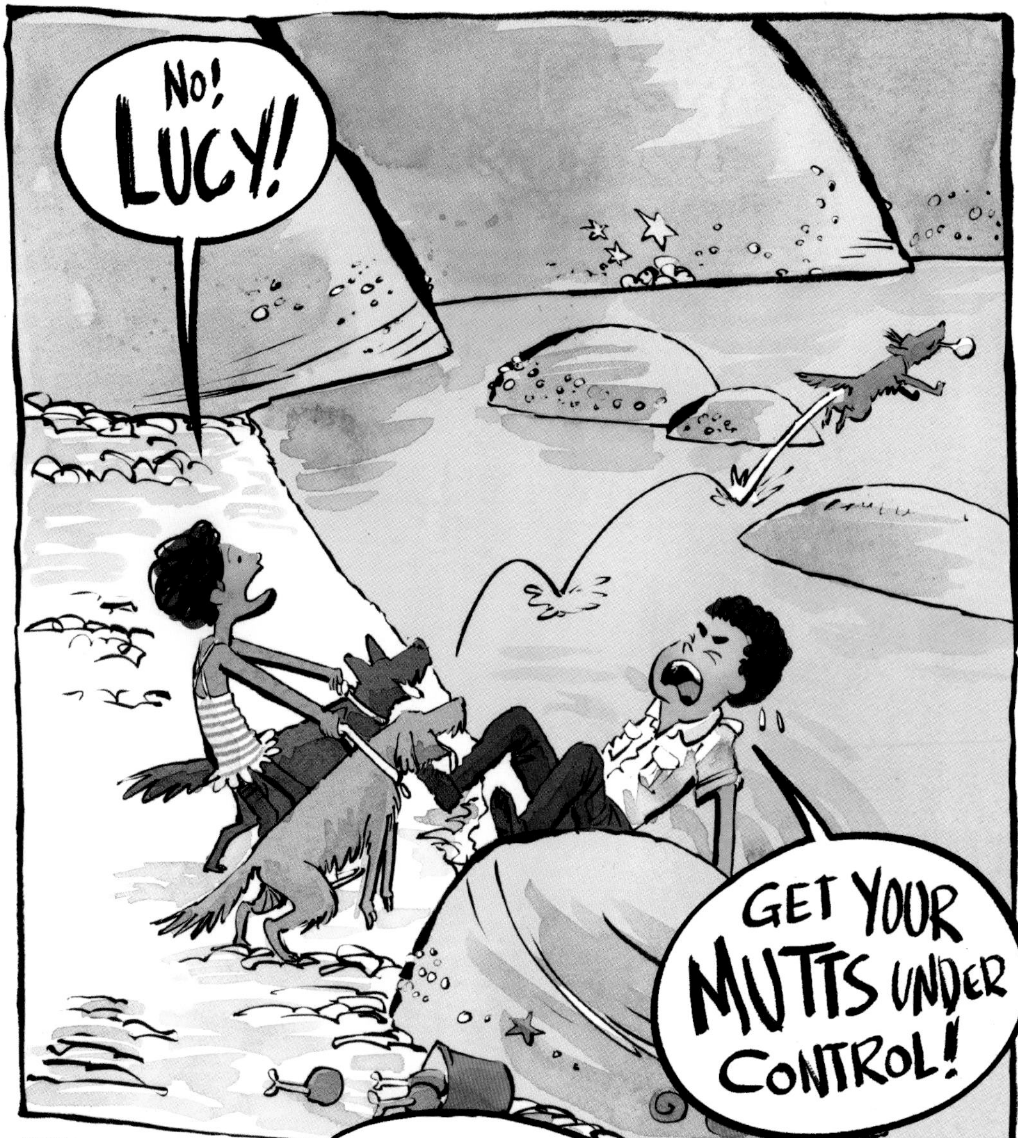
No! LUCY!
GET YOUR MUTTS UNDER CONTROL!

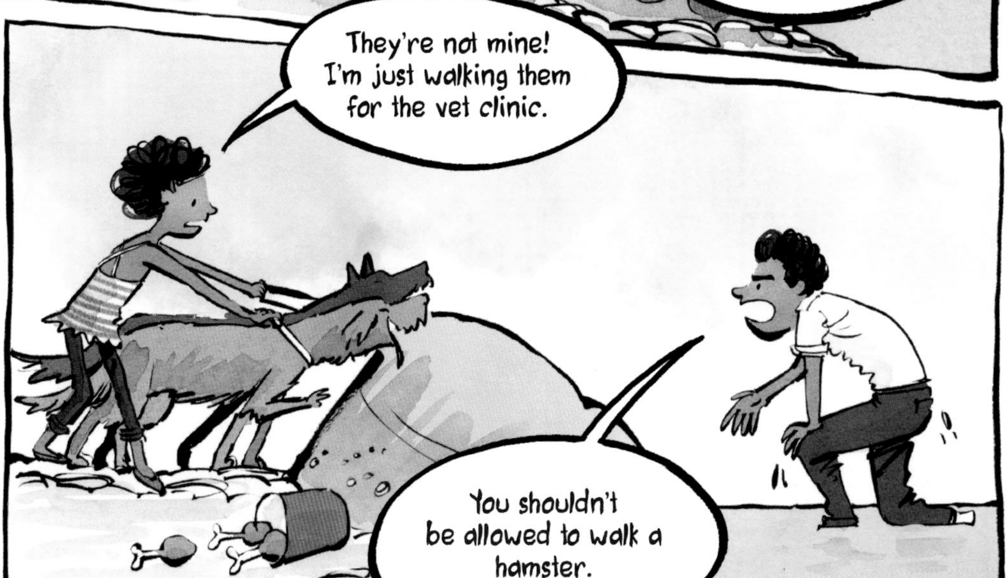
They're not mine! I'm just walking them for the vet clinic.
You shouldn't be allowed to walk a hamster.

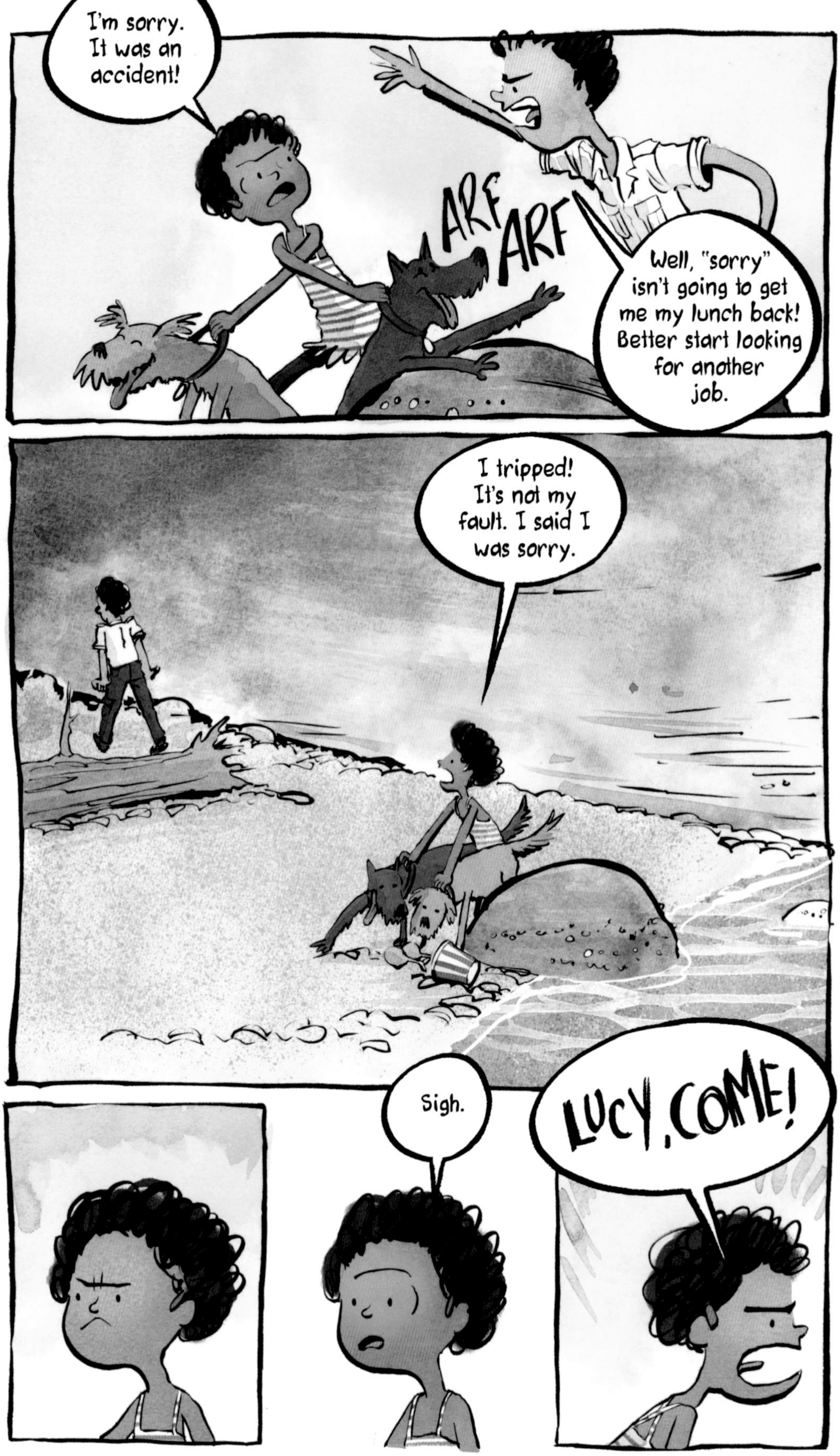
I'm sorry.
It was an accident!
ARF ARF
Well, "sorry" isn't going to get me my lunch back! Better start looking for another job.
I tripped! It's not my fault. I said I was sorry.
Sigh.
LUCY, COME!

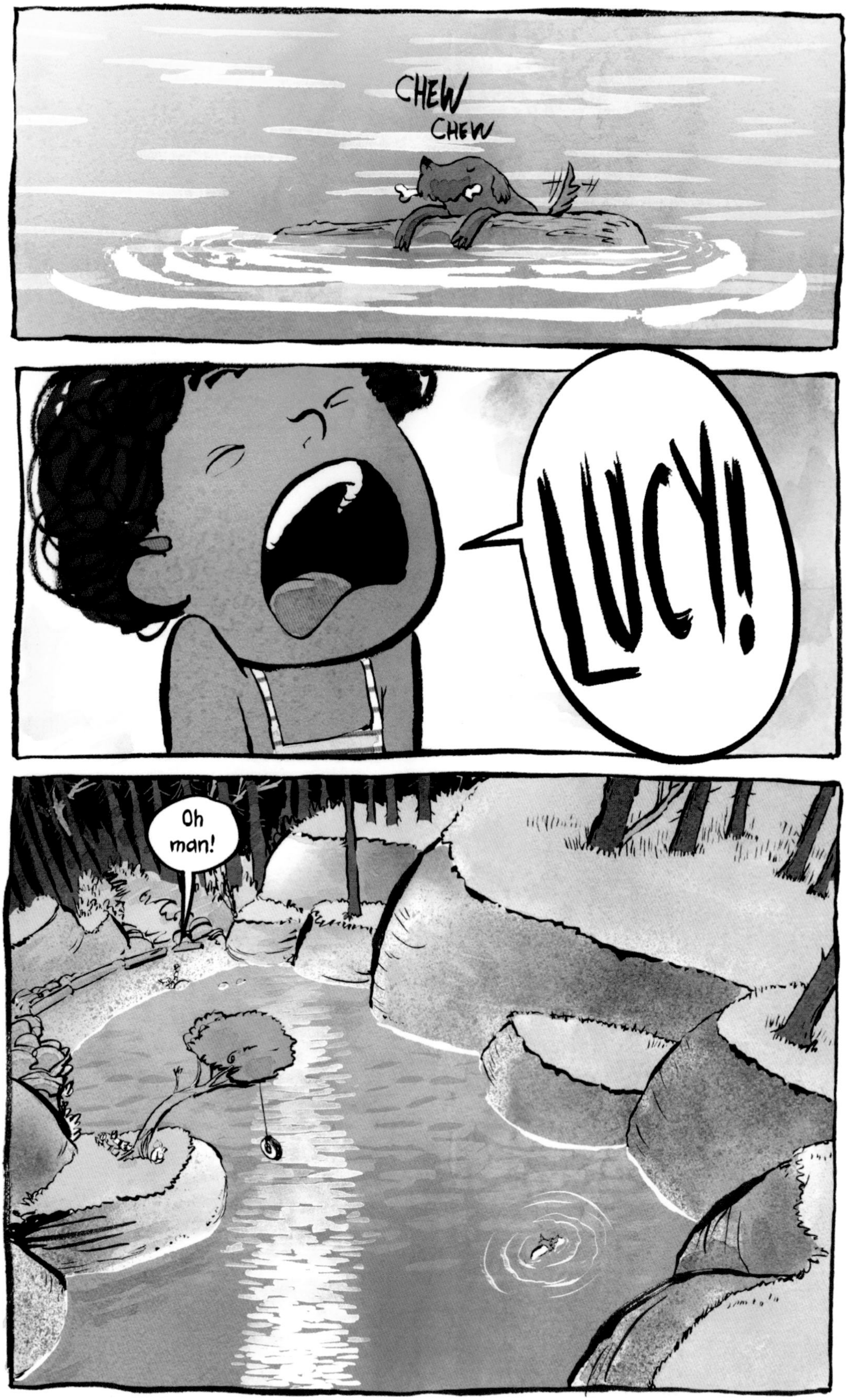
CHEW
CHEW
LUCY!
Oh man!

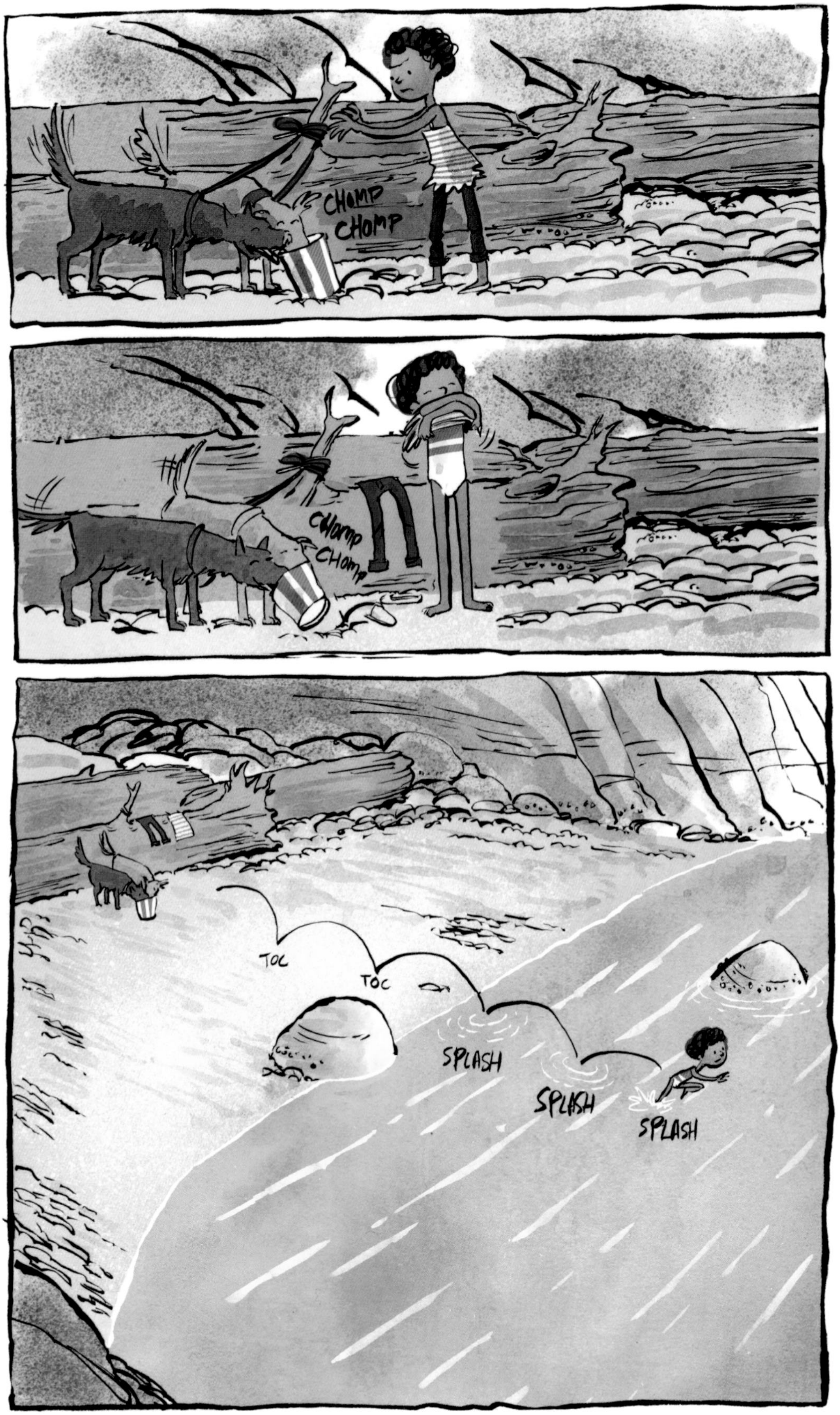
CHOMP
CHOMP
CHOMP
CHOMP
TOC
TOC
SPLASH
SPLASH
SPLASH

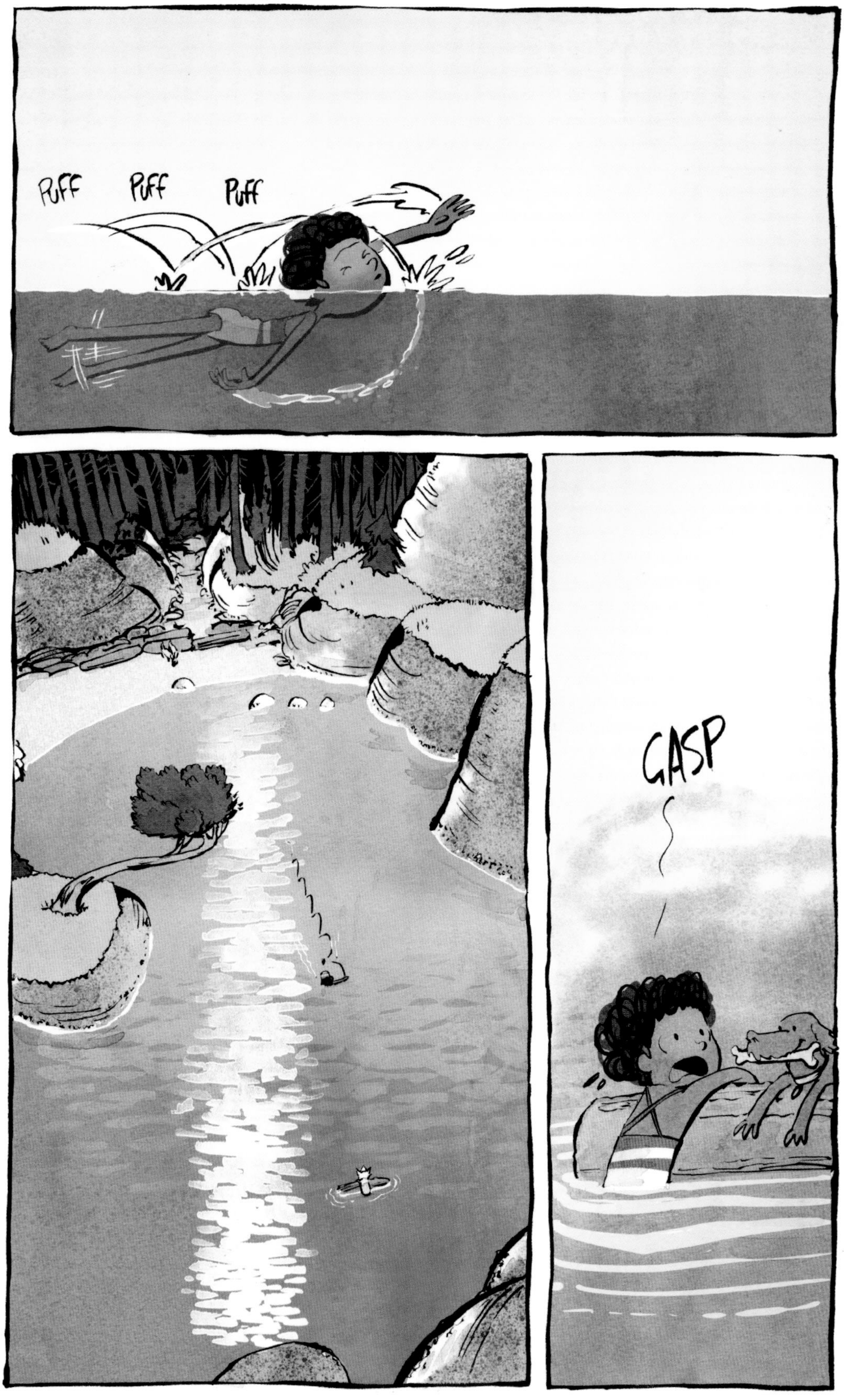
PUFF
PUFF
PUFF
GASP

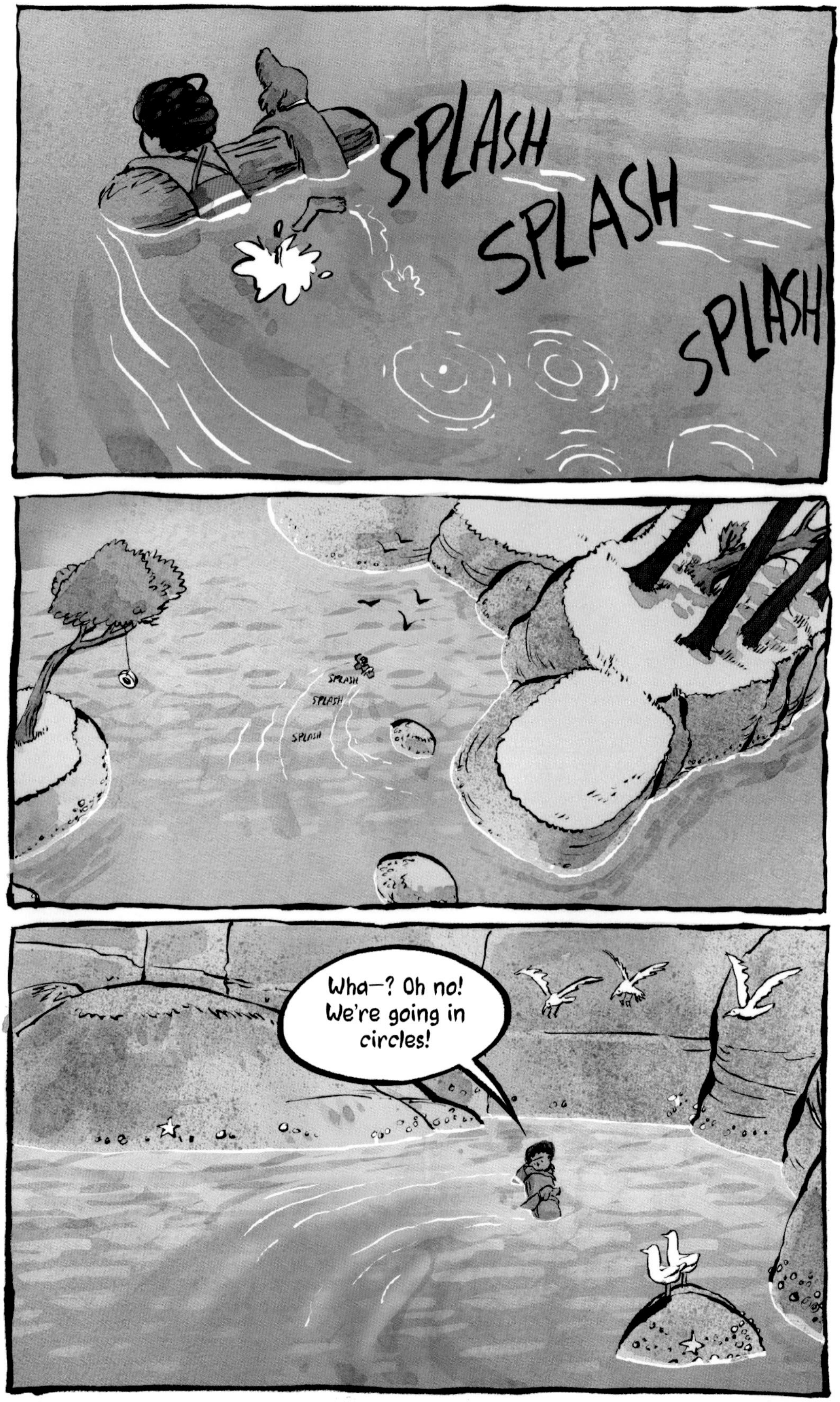
SPLASH
SPLASH
SPLASH
SPLASH
SPLASH
SPLASH
Wha–? Oh no! We're going in circles!

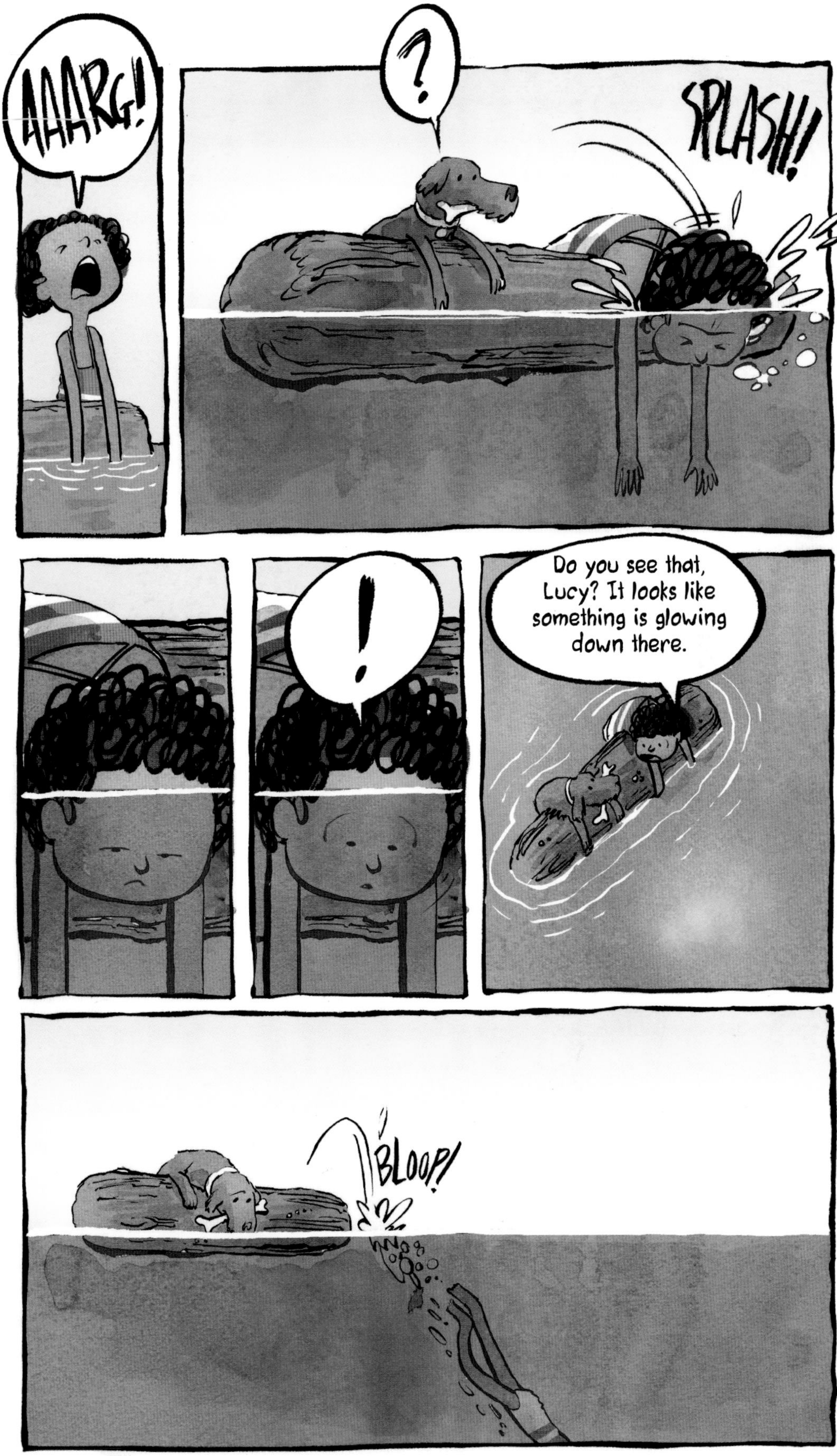
AAARG!
?
SPLASH!!
!
Do you see that, Lucy? It looks like something is glowing down there.
BLOOP!

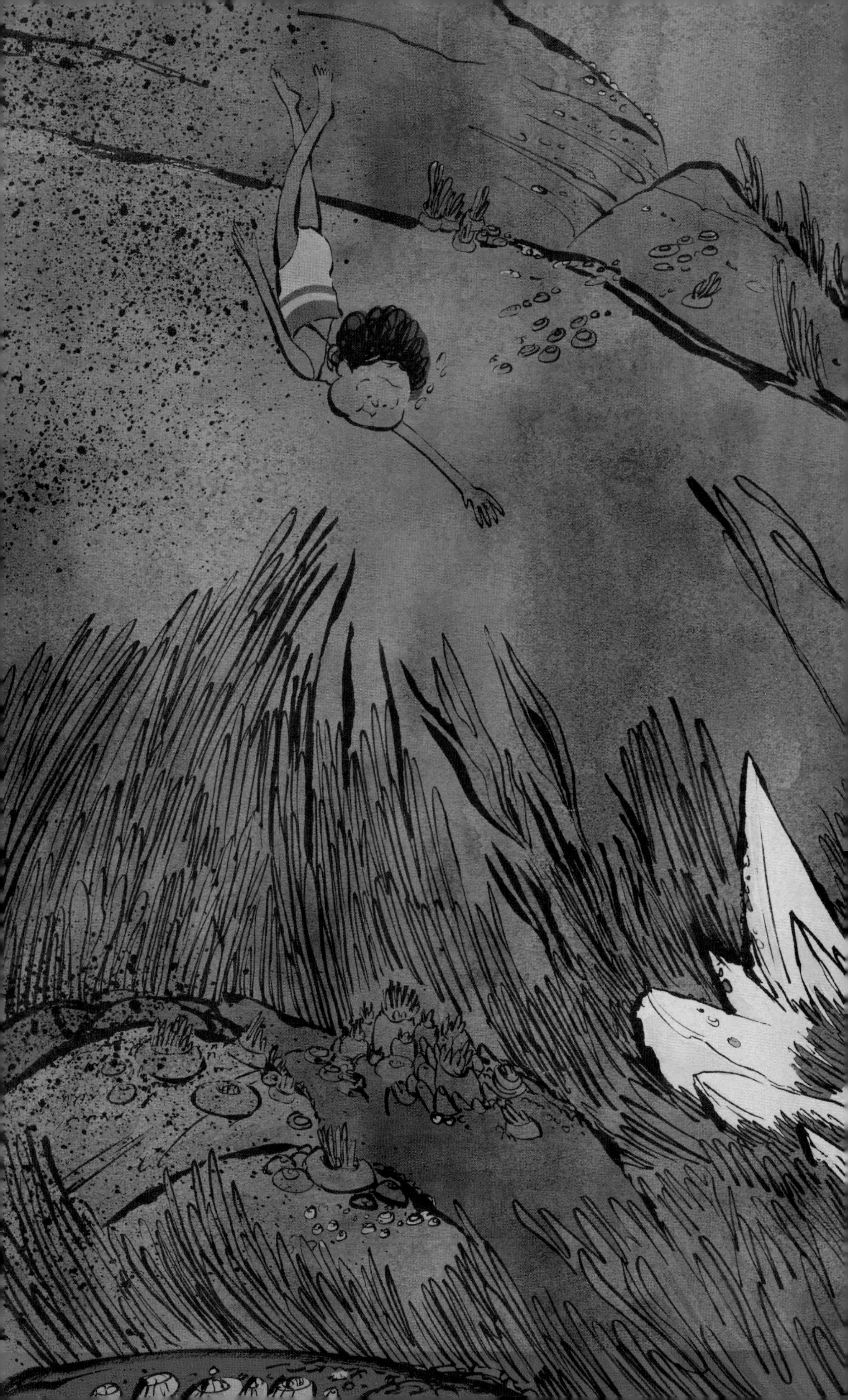

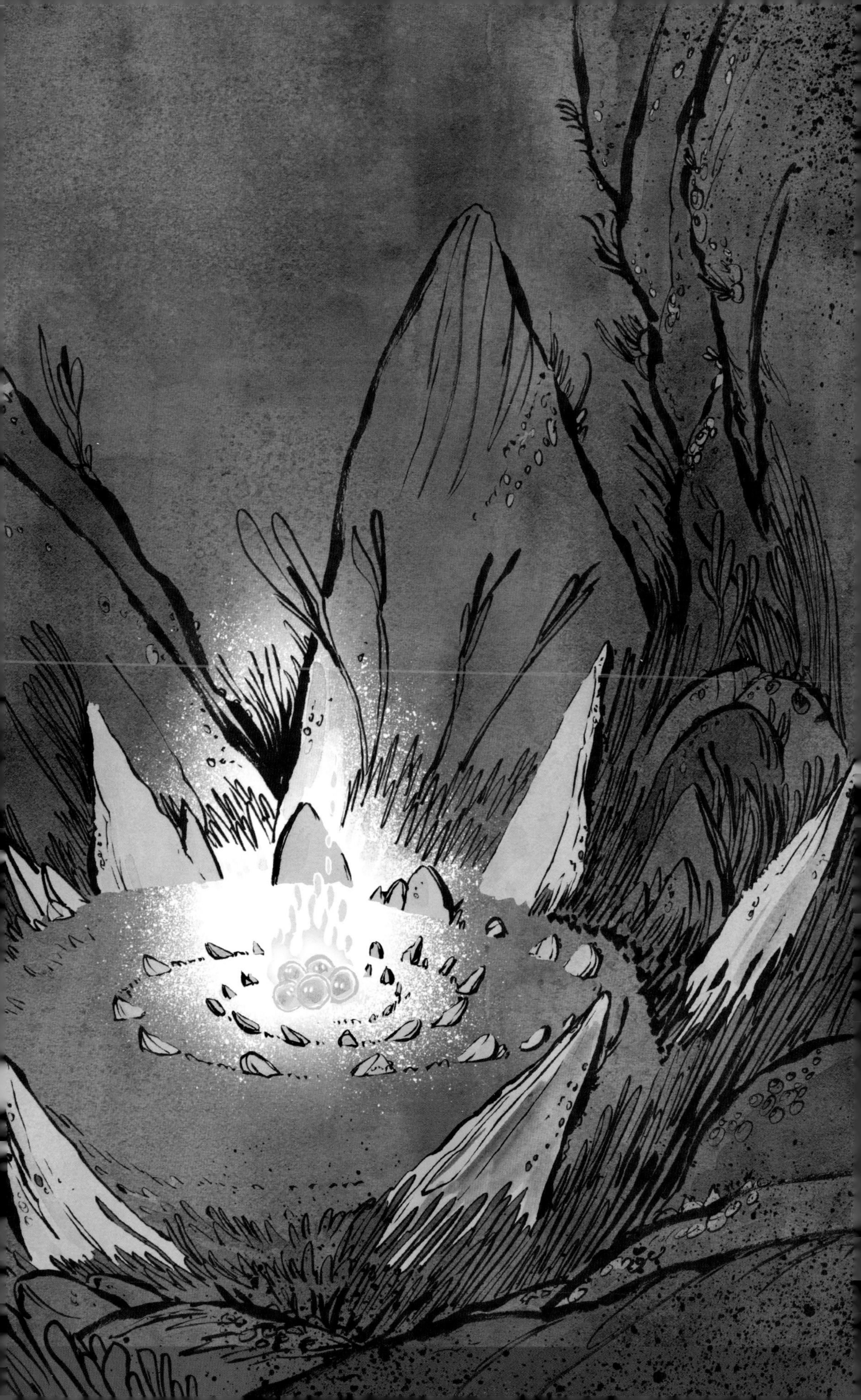

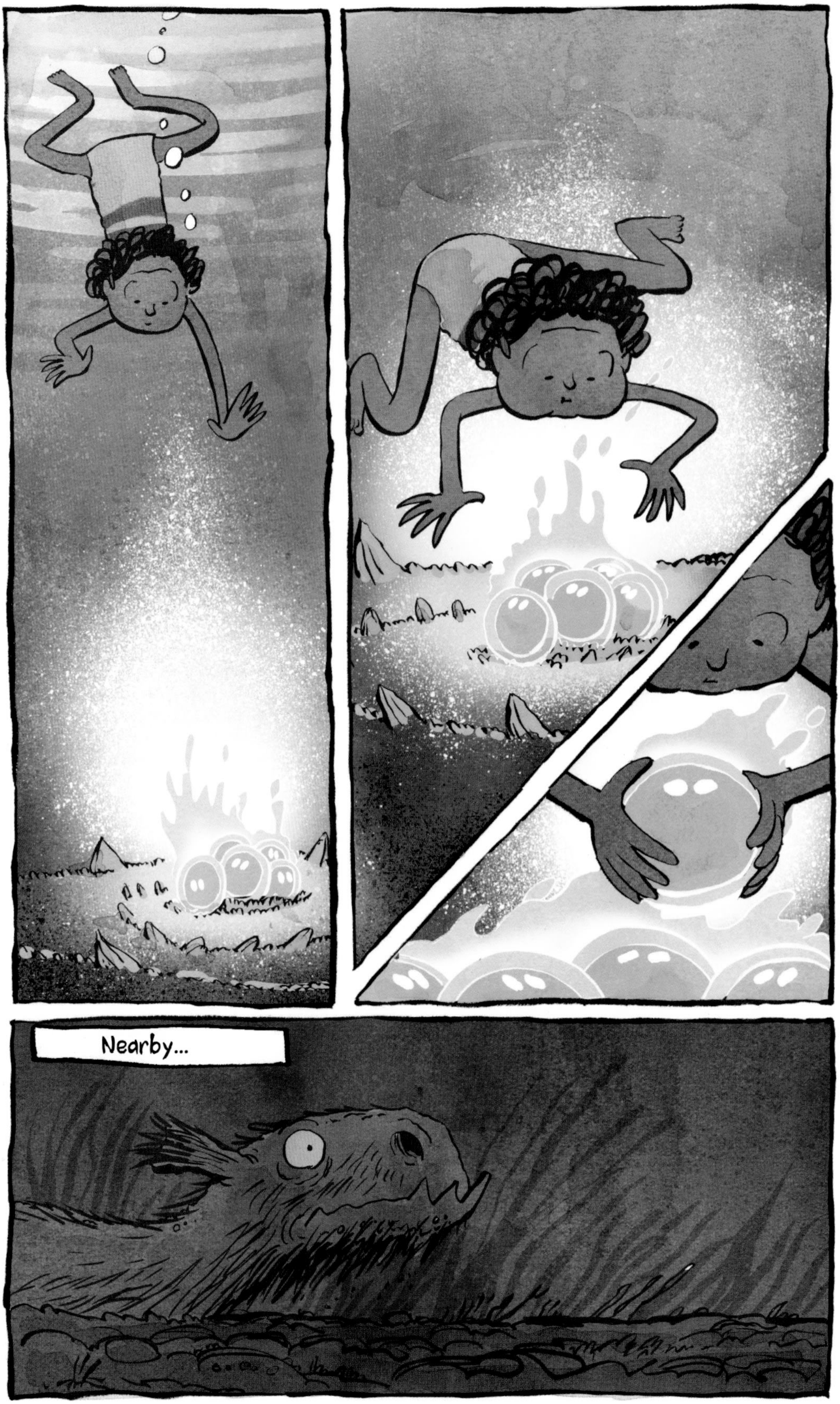
Nearby...

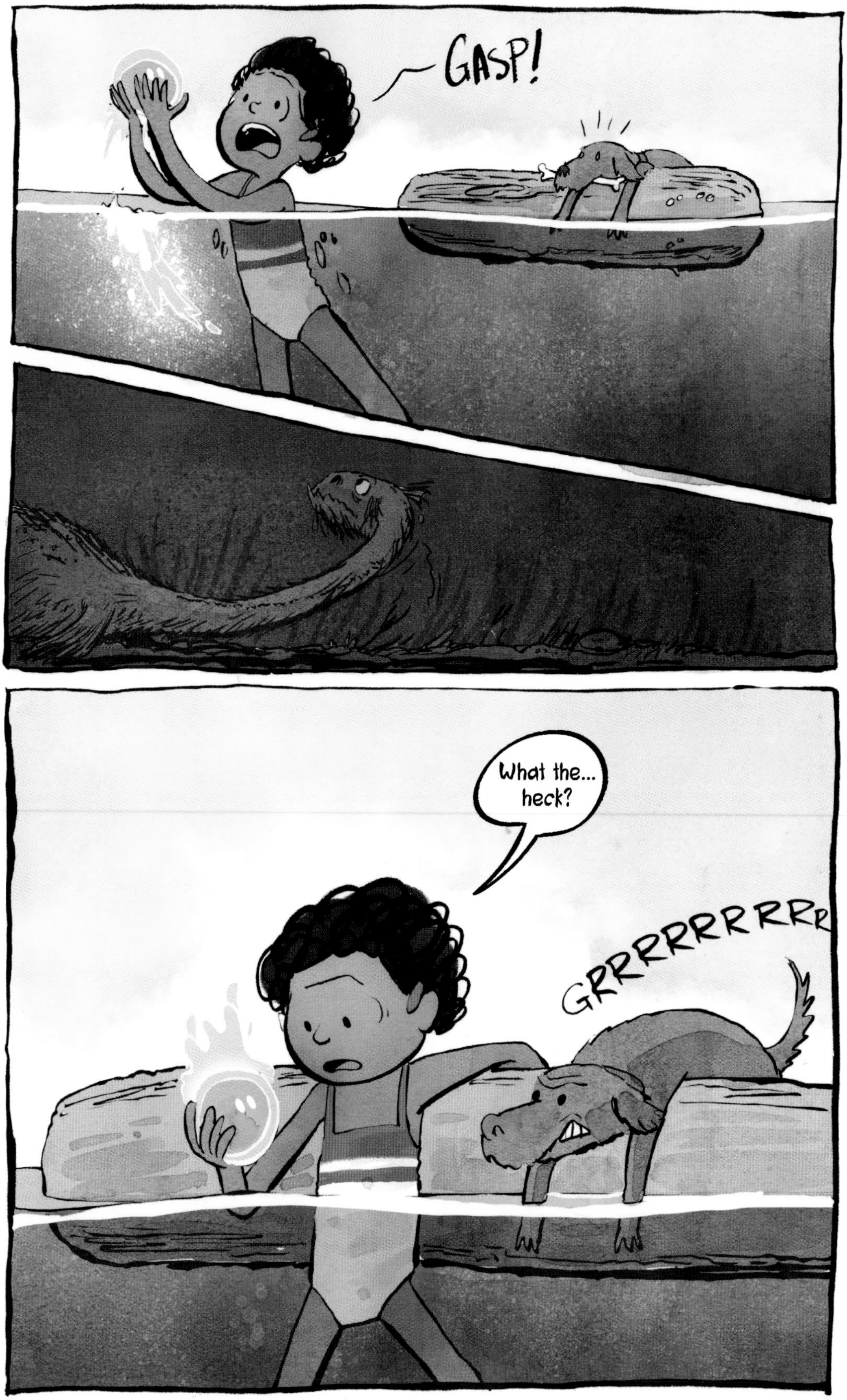
GASP!
What the... heck?
GRRRRRRRRRR

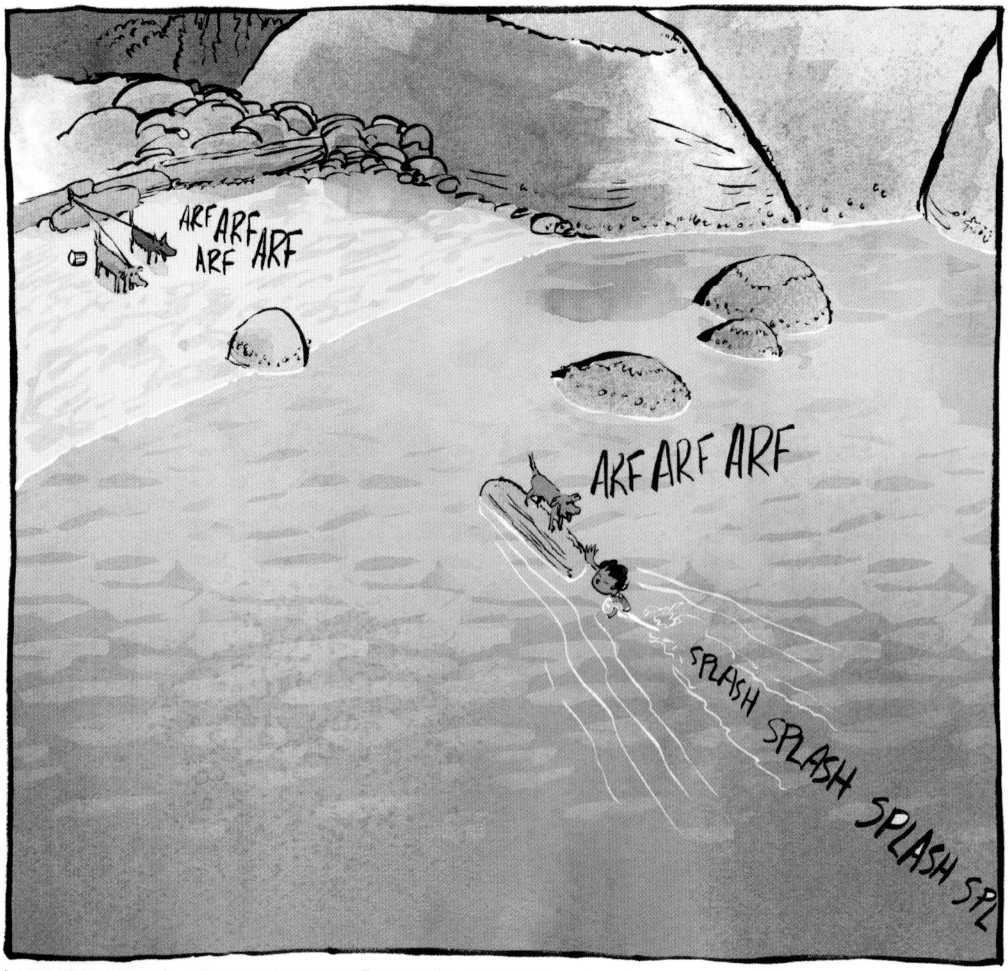
ARF ARF ARF
ARF ARF
ARF ARF ARF
SPLASH SPLASH SPLASH SPL

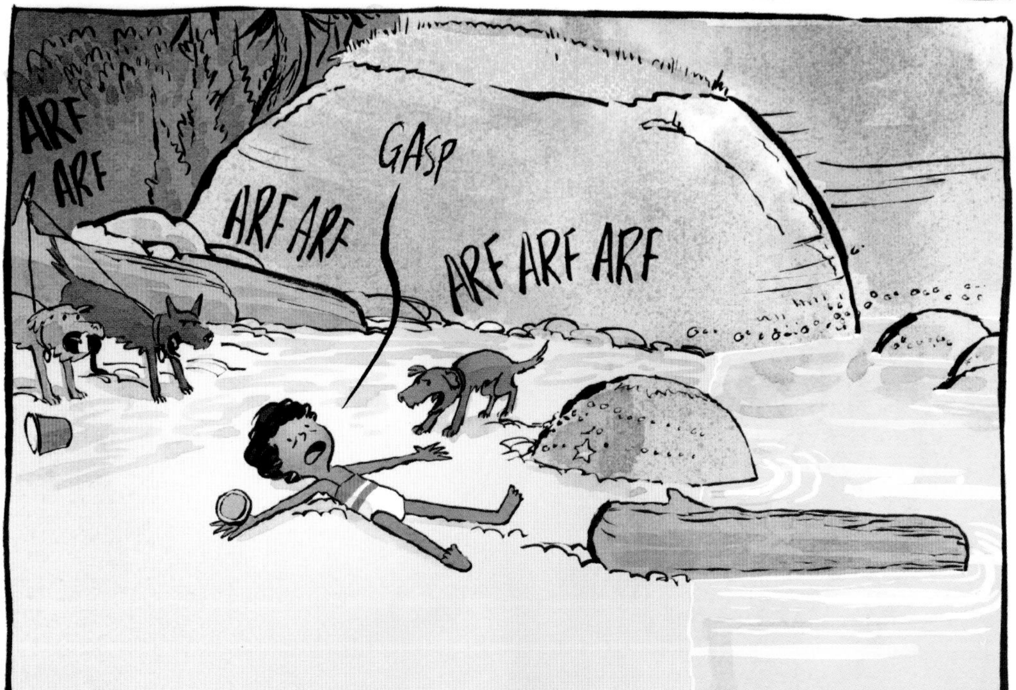
ARF ARF
ARF ARF
GASP
ARF ARF ARF

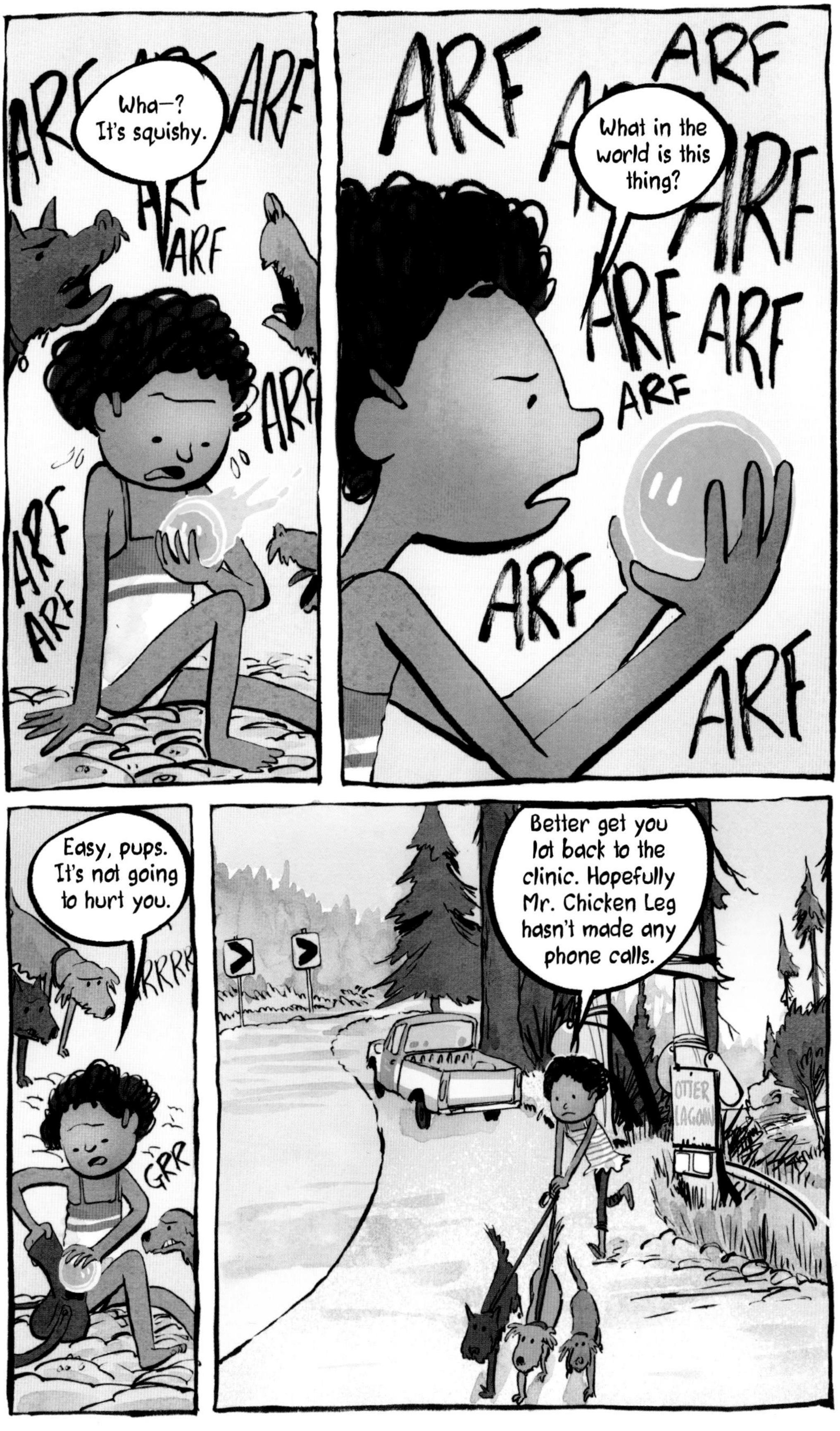
ARF
Wha–?
It's squishy.
ARF
ARF
ARF
ARF
ARF
ARF
ARF
ARF
What in the world is this thing?
ARF
ARF
ARF
ARF
ARF
ARF
Easy, pups. It's not going to hurt you.
RRRR
GRR
Better get you lot back to the clinic. Hopefully Mr. Chicken Leg hasn't made any phone calls.
OTTER LAGOON

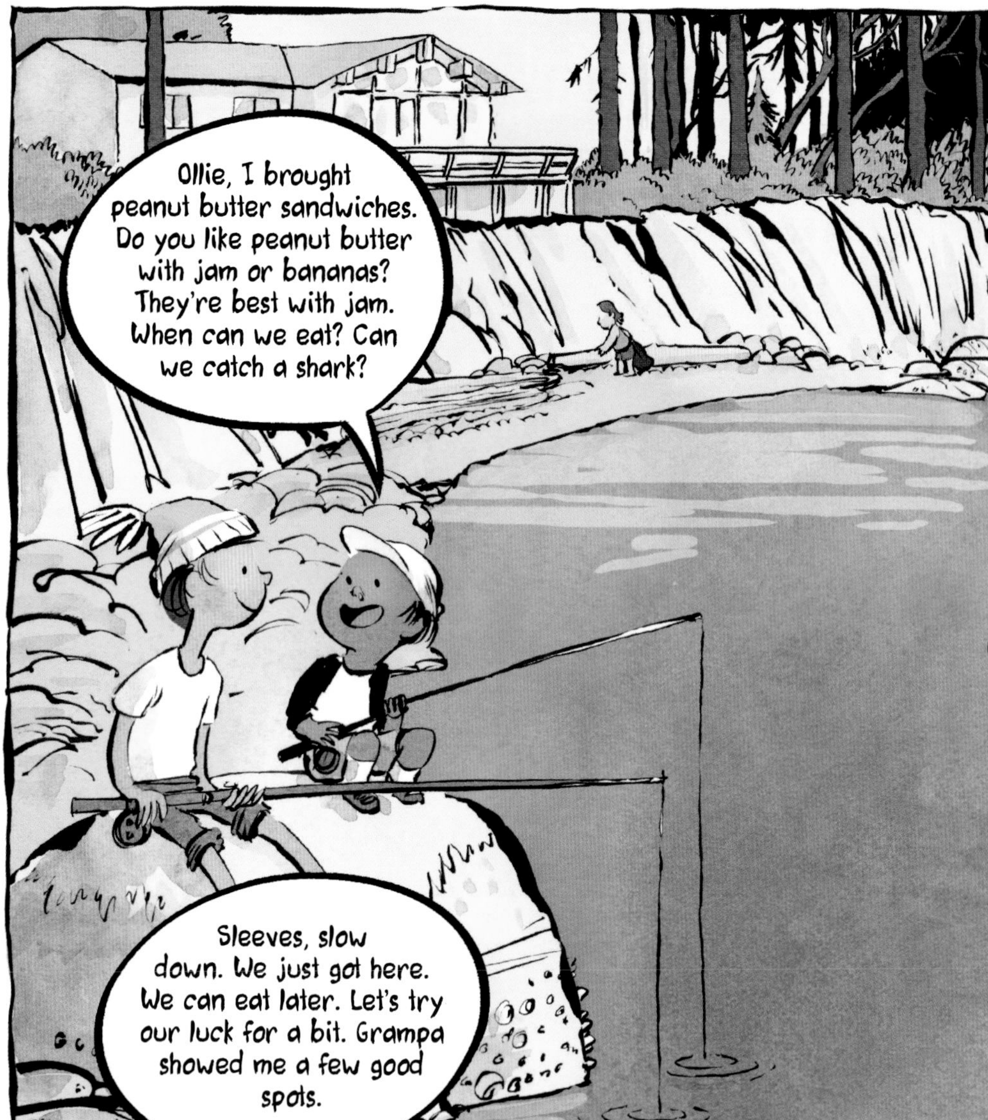
Ollie, I brought peanut butter sandwiches. Do you like peanut butter with jam or bananas? They're best with jam. When can we eat? Can we catch a shark?
Sleeves, slow down. We just got here. We can eat later. Let's try our luck for a bit. Grampa showed me a few good spots.

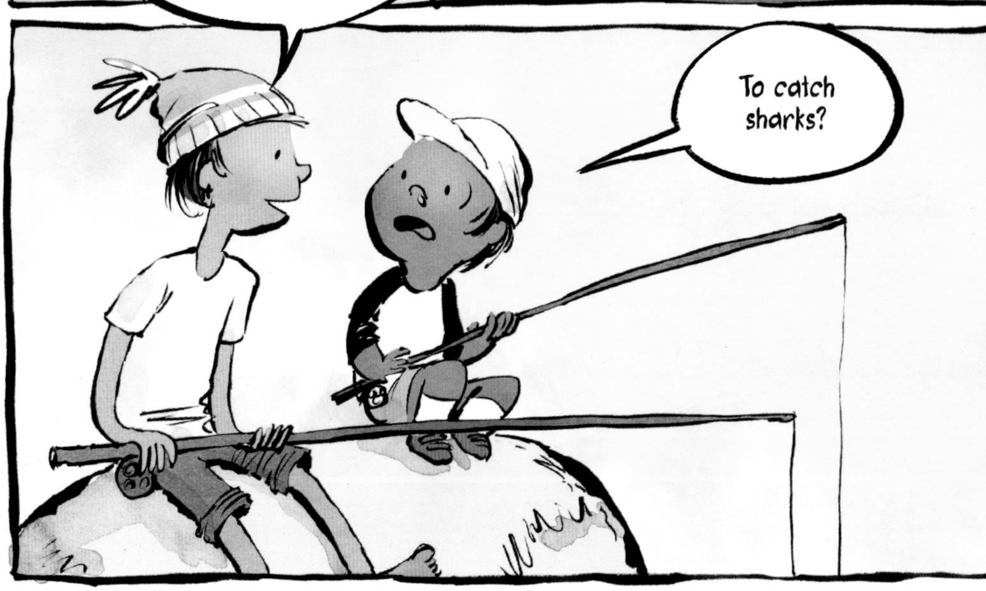
To catch sharks?

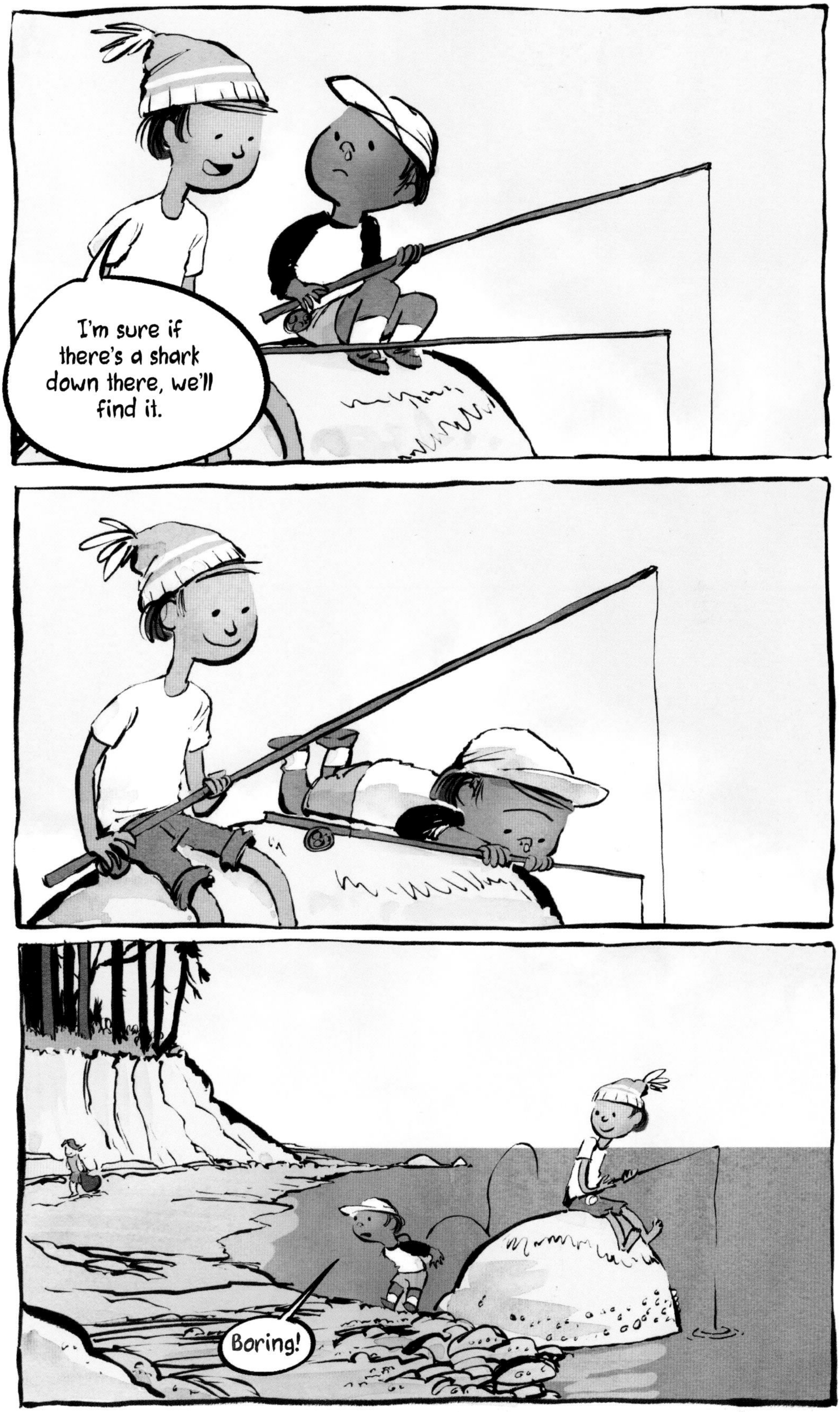
I'm sure if there's a shark down there, we'll find it.
Boring!

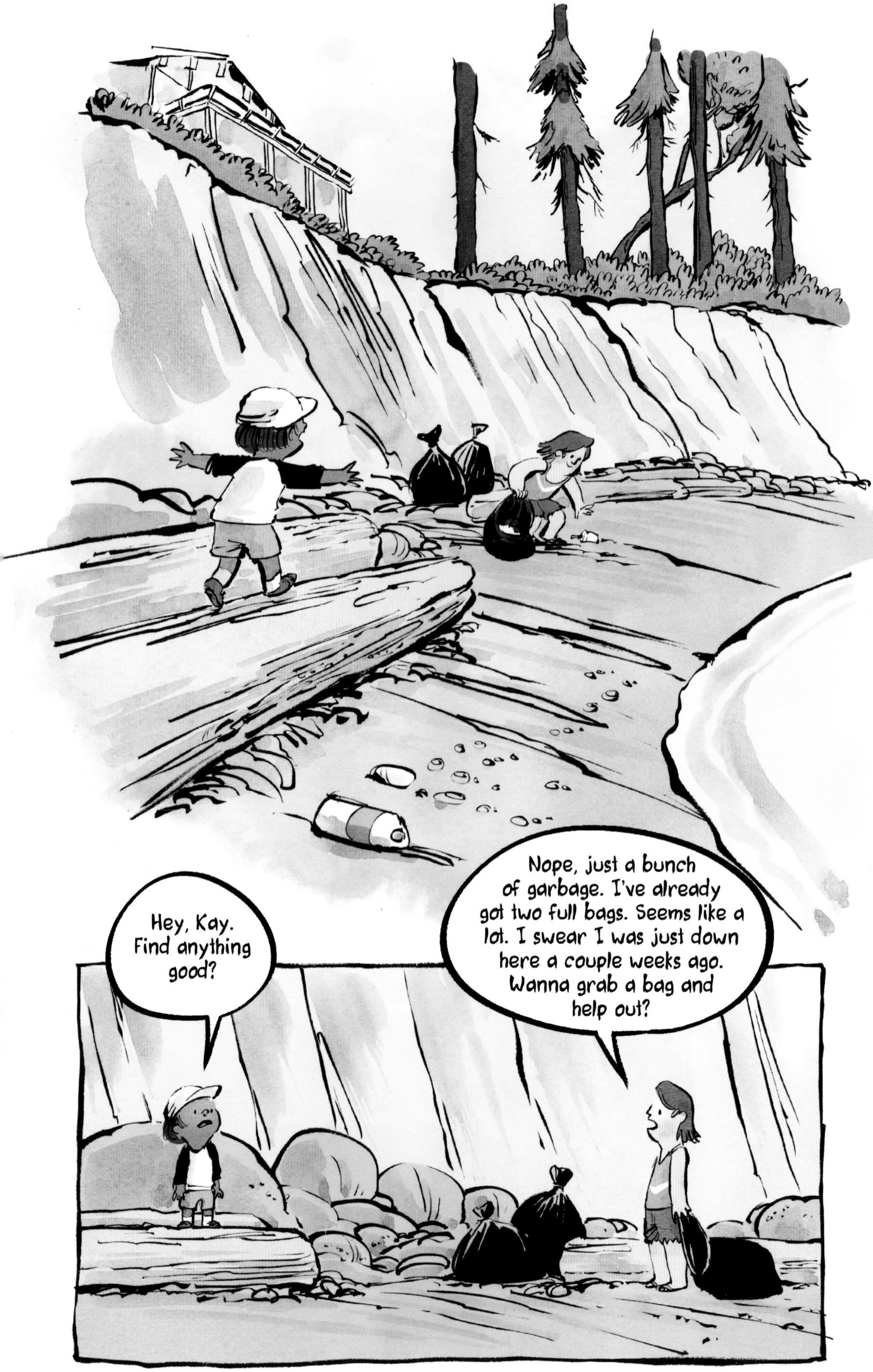
Hey, Kay. Find anything good?
Nope, just a bunch of garbage. I've already got two full bags. Seems like a lot. I swear I was just down here a couple weeks ago. Wanna grab a bag and help out?

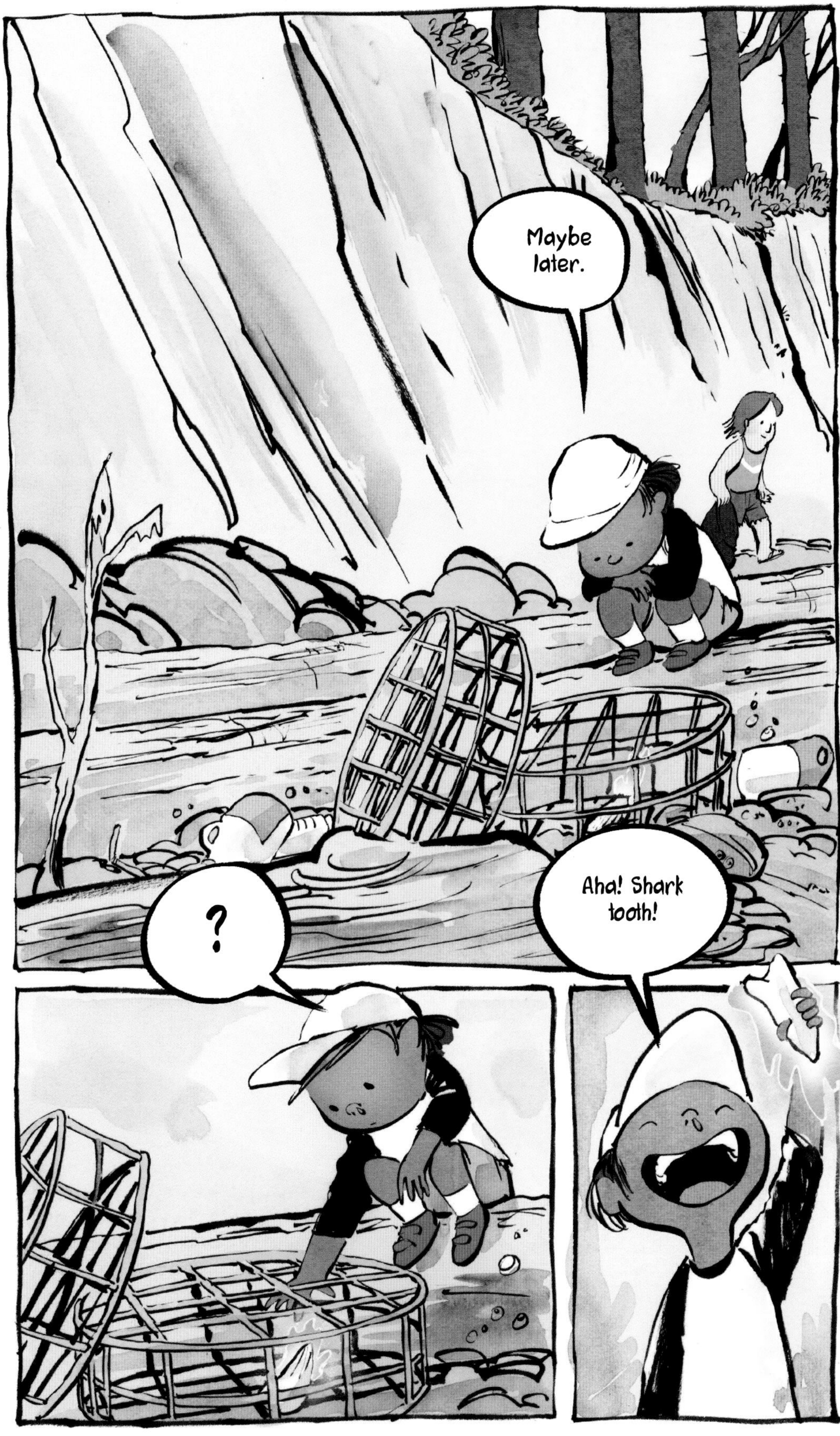
Maybe later.
?
Aha! Shark tooth!

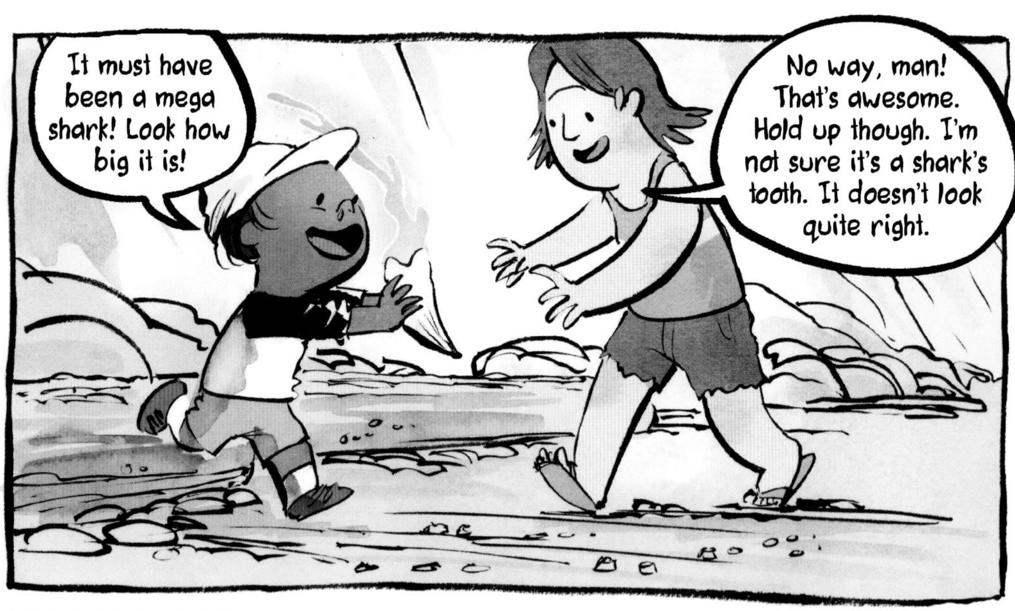
It must have been a mega shark! Look how big it is!
No way, man! That's awesome. Hold up though. I'm not sure it's a shark's tooth. It doesn't look quite right.

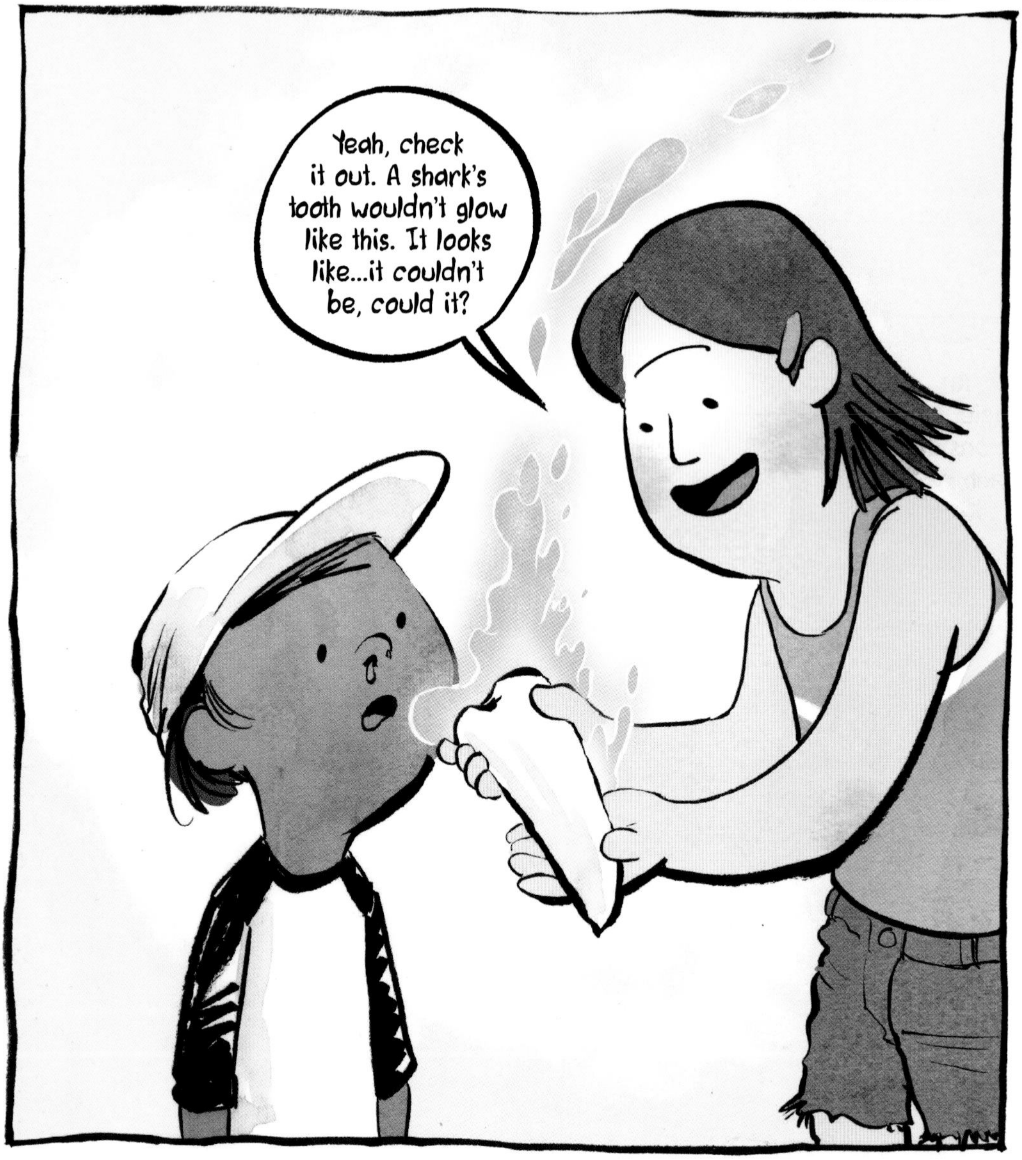
Yeah, check it out. A shark's tooth wouldn't glow like this. It looks like...it couldn't be, could it?

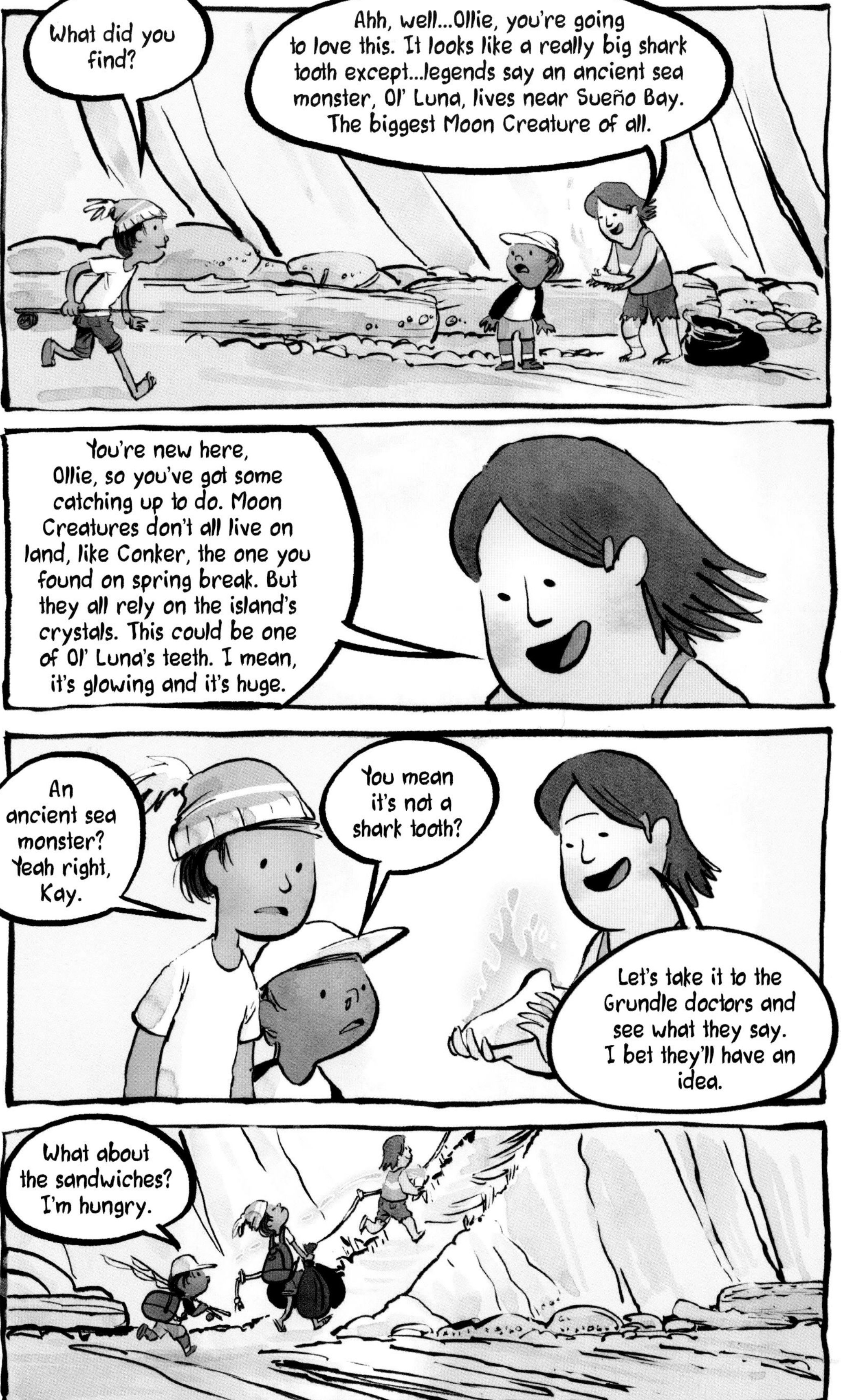
What did you find?
Ahh, well...Ollie, you're going to love this. It looks like a really big shark tooth except...legends say an ancient sea monster, Ol' Luna, lives near Sueño Bay. The biggest Moon Creature of all.
You're new here, Ollie, so you've got some catching up to do. Moon Creatures don't all live on land, like Conker, the one you found on spring break. But they all rely on the island's crystals. This could be one of Ol' Luna's teeth. I mean, it's glowing and it's huge.
An ancient sea monster? Yeah right, Kay.
You mean it's not a shark tooth?
Let's take it to the Grundle doctors and see what they say. I bet they'll have an idea.
What about the sandwiches? I'm hungry.

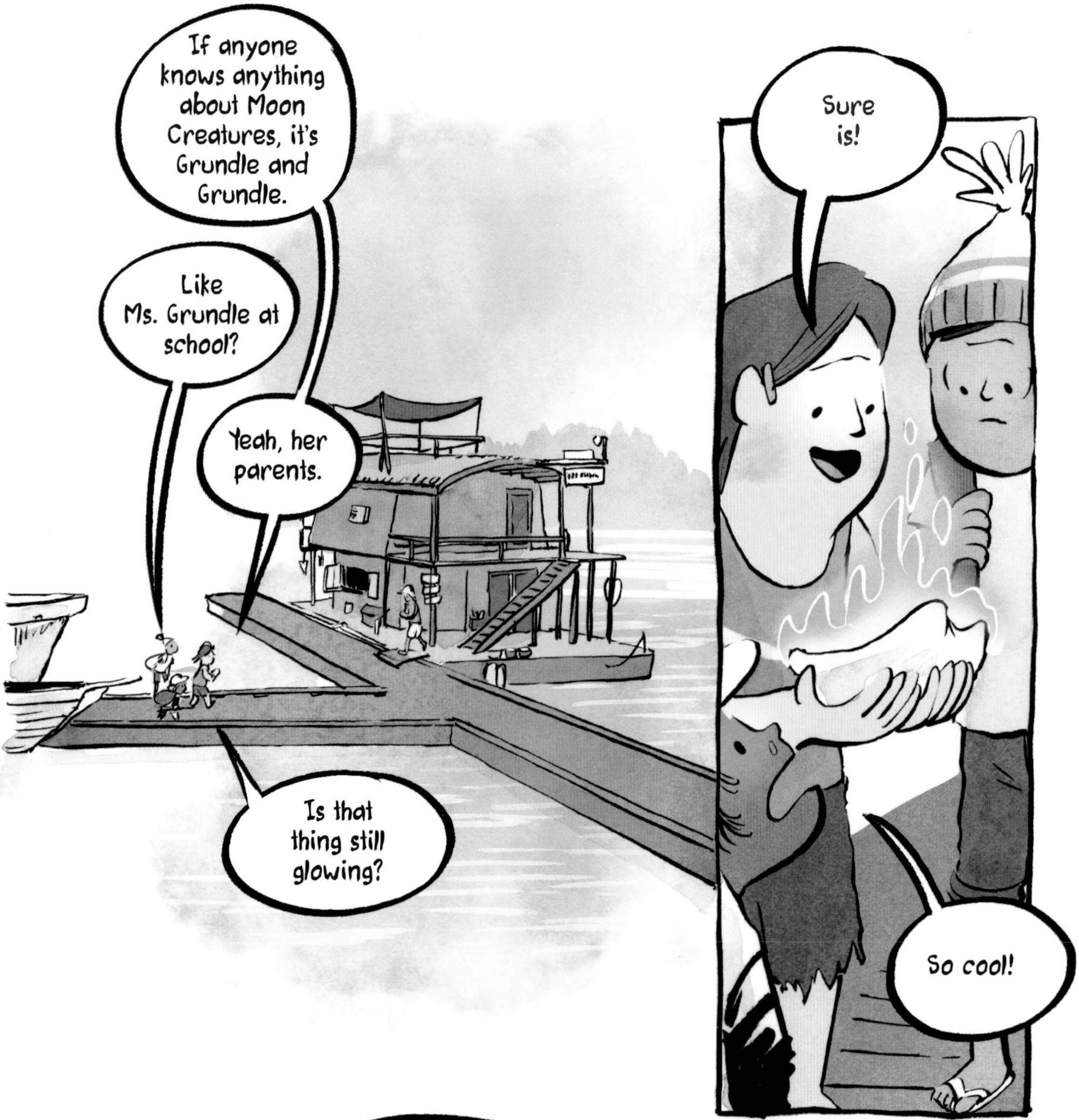
If anyone knows anything about Moon Creatures, it's Grundle and Grundle.
Like Ms. Grundle at school?
Yeah, her parents.
Is that thing still glowing?
Sure is!
So cool!

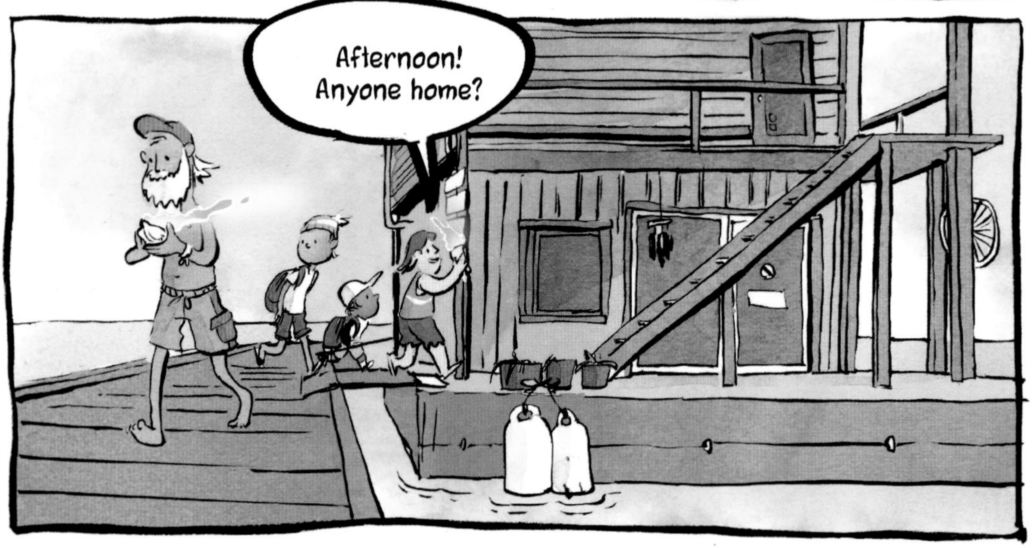
Afternoon! Anyone home?

Kay, nice to see you!

Another raccoon need rescue?

Nope, not today. Just curious if you've ever seen one of these before. We pulled it off a junked crab trap.

You're not the only ones who've been by today. We've had people all morning with strange stuff they've found on the beach.

Well, let's have a look.

It glows?

I mean, I have a theory.

She thinks it's from an ancient sea monster.

Ancient sea monster... probably not. Hmm...maybe a Moon Creature of sorts.

57

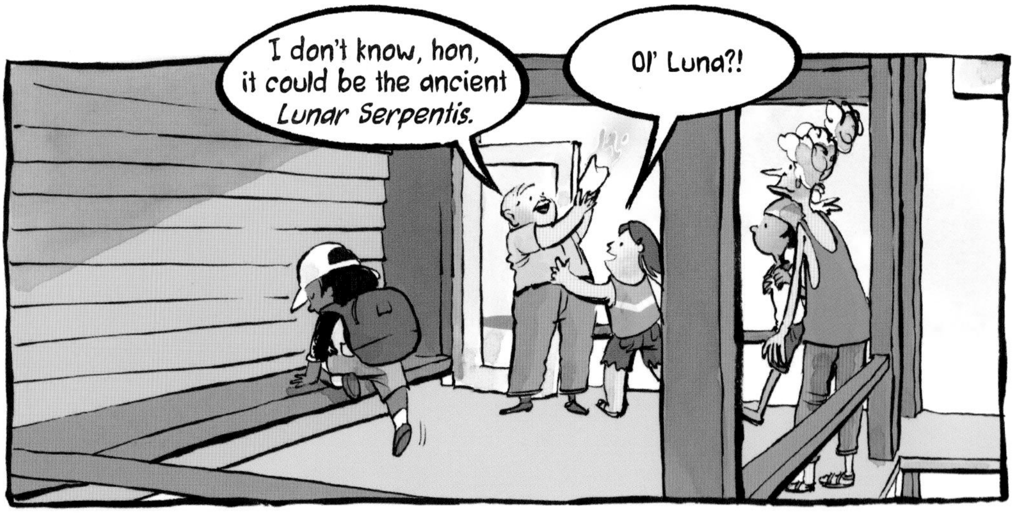
I don't know, hon, it could be the ancient *Lunar Serpentis.*
Ol' Luna?!

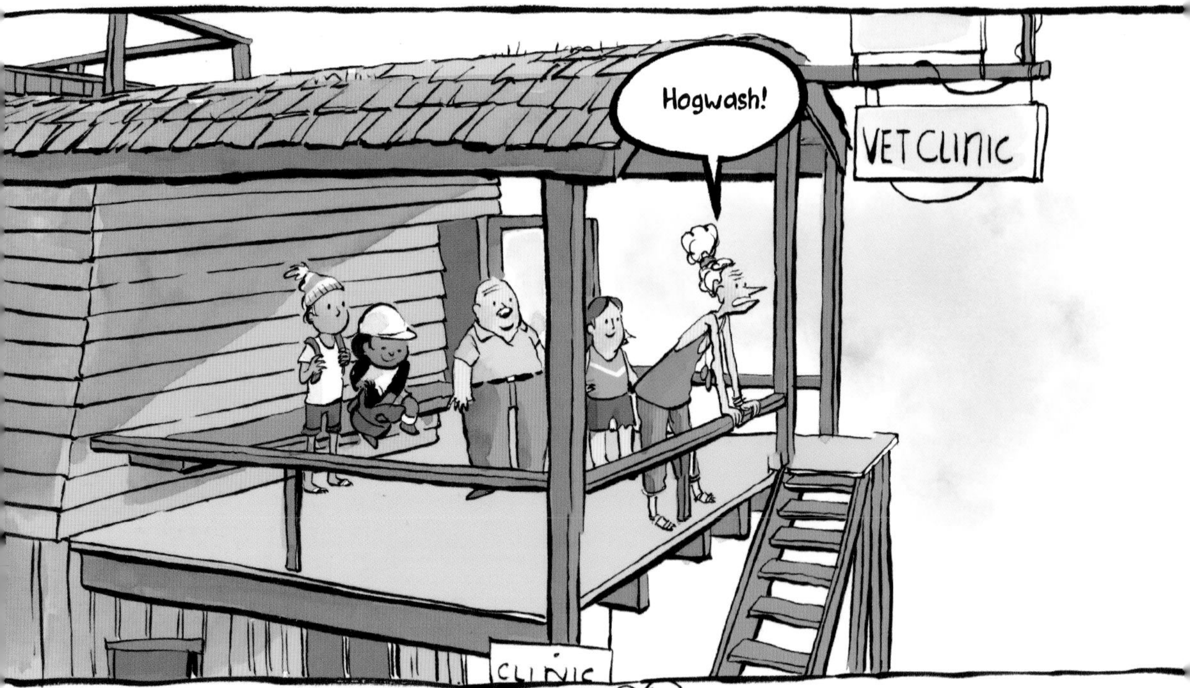
Hogwash!
VET CLINIC

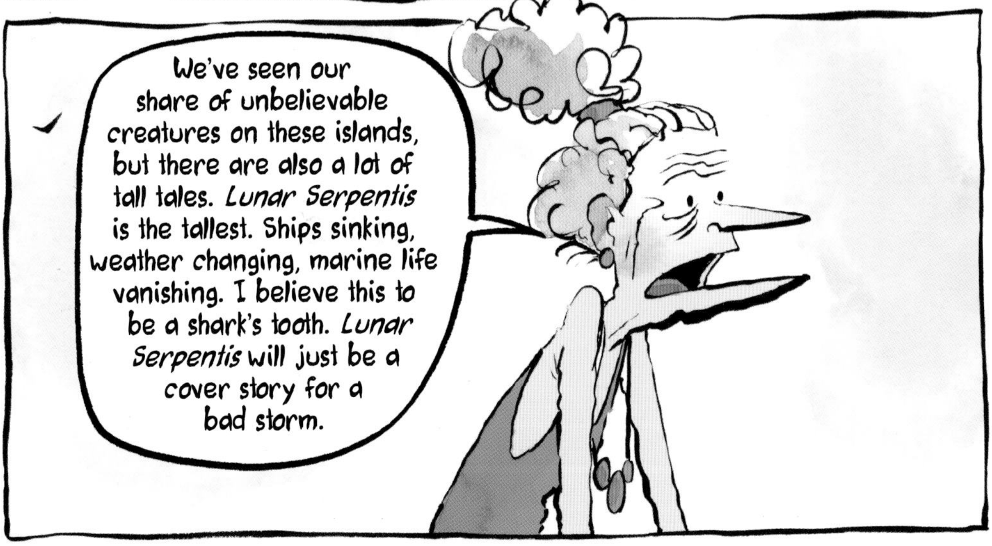
We've seen our share of unbelievable creatures on these islands, but there are also a lot of tall tales. *Lunar Serpentis* is the tallest. Ships sinking, weather changing, marine life vanishing. I believe this to be a shark's tooth. *Lunar Serpentis* will just be a cover story for a bad storm.

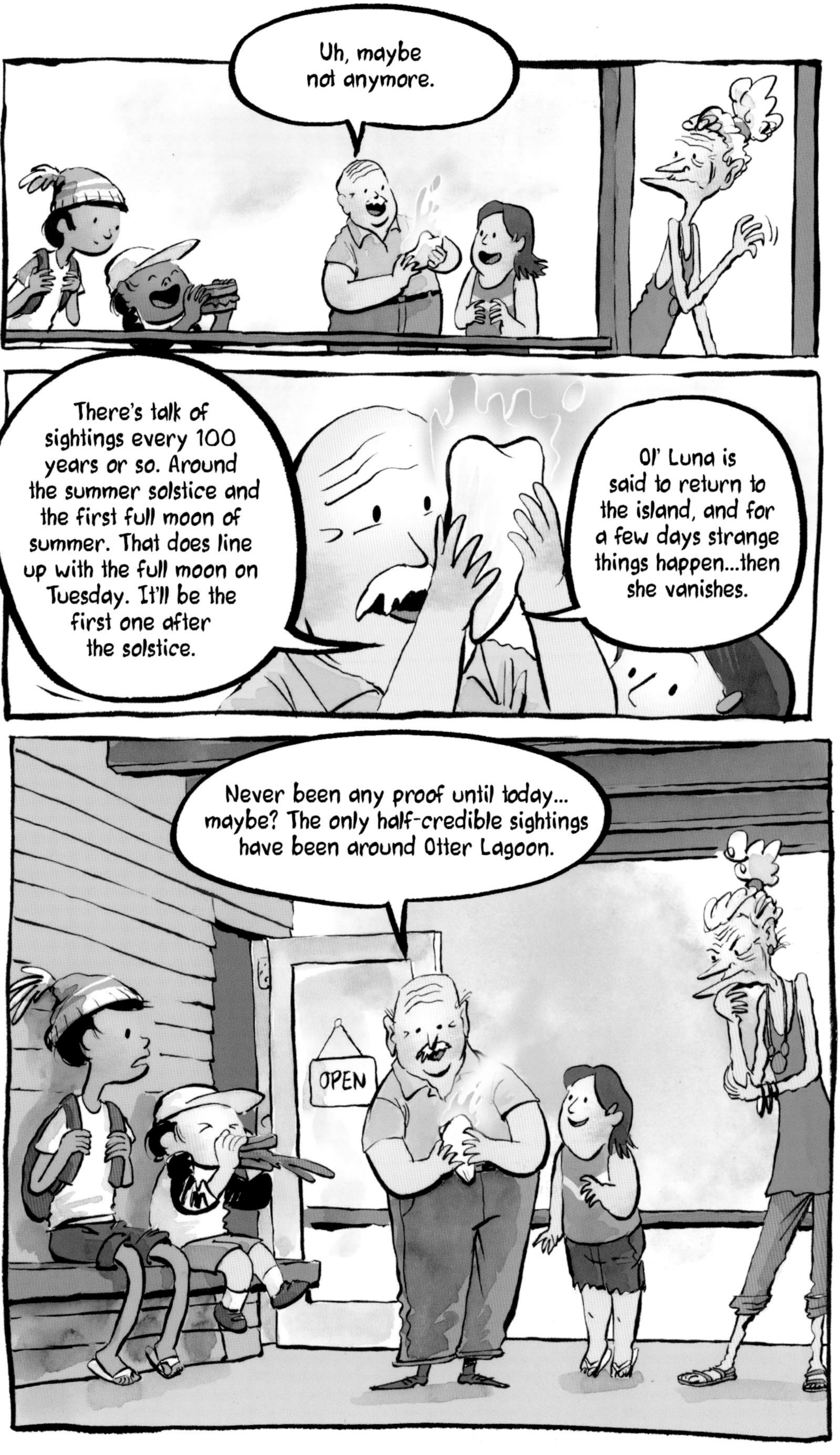
Uh, maybe not anymore.
There's talk of sightings every 100 years or so. Around the summer solstice and the first full moon of summer. That does line up with the full moon on Tuesday. It'll be the first one after the solstice.
Ol' Luna is said to return to the island, and for a few days strange things happen...then she vanishes.
Never been any proof until today... maybe? The only half-credible sightings have been around Otter Lagoon.
OPEN

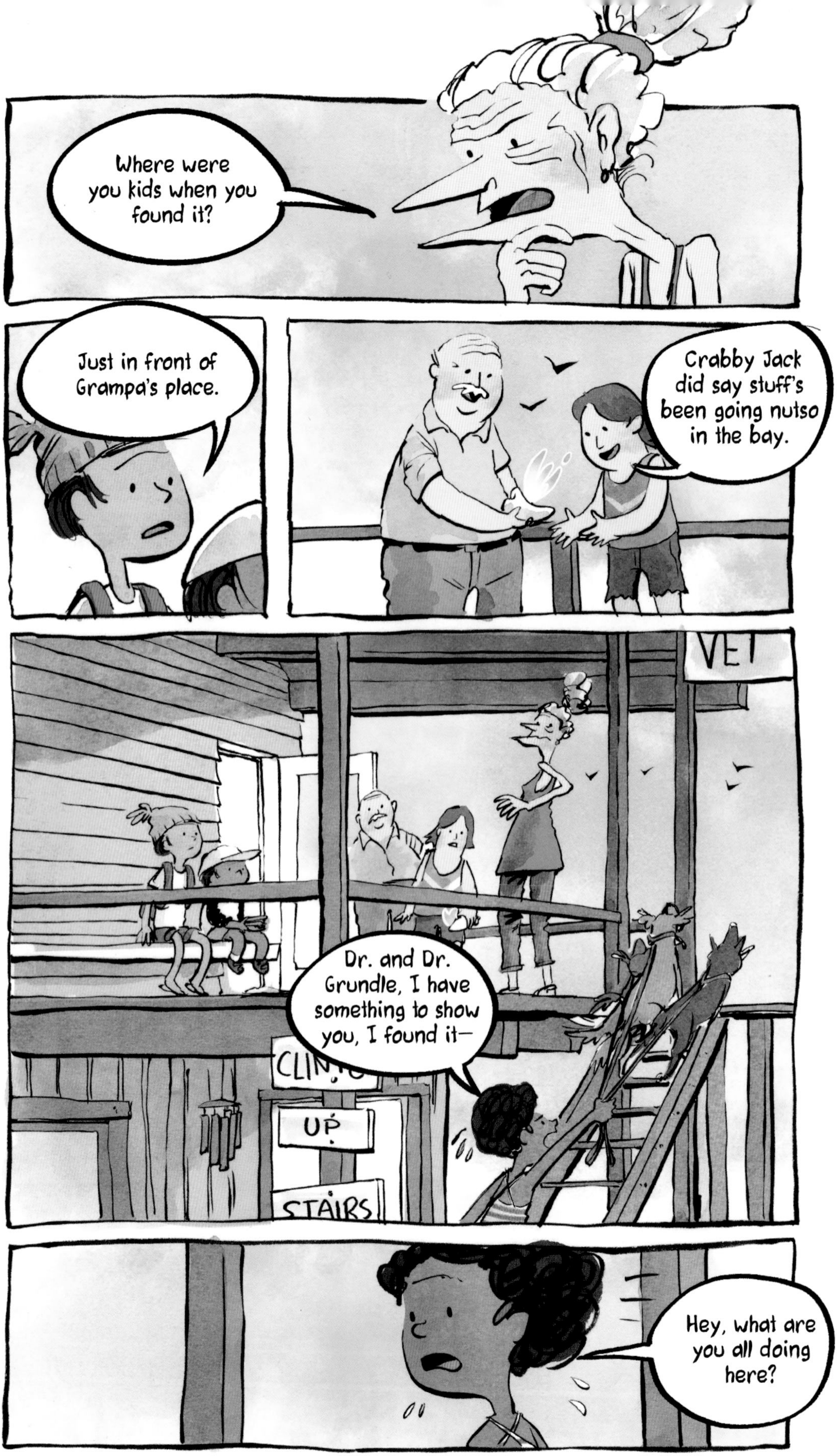
Where were you kids when you found it?
Just in front of Grampa's place.
Crabby Jack did say stuff's been going nutso in the bay.
VET
Dr. and Dr. Grundle, I have something to show you, I found it—
UP
STAIRS
Hey, what are you all doing here?

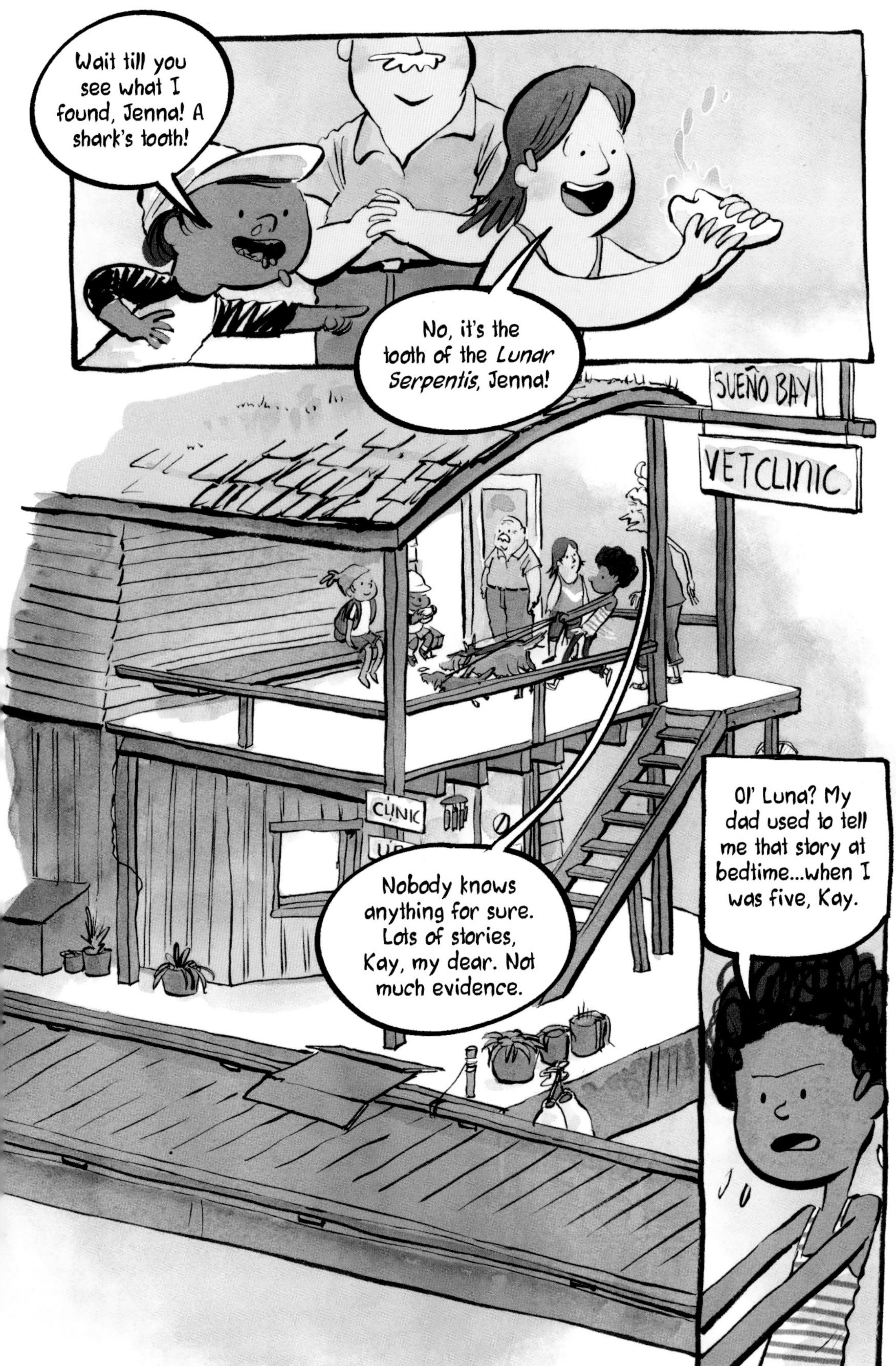
Wait till you see what I found, Jenna! A shark's tooth!
No, it's the tooth of the *Lunar Serpentis*, Jenna!
SUEÑO BAY
VETCLINIC
CLINIC
Nobody knows anything for sure. Lots of stories, Kay, my dear. Not much evidence.
Ol' Luna? My dad used to tell me that story at bedtime...when I was five, Kay.

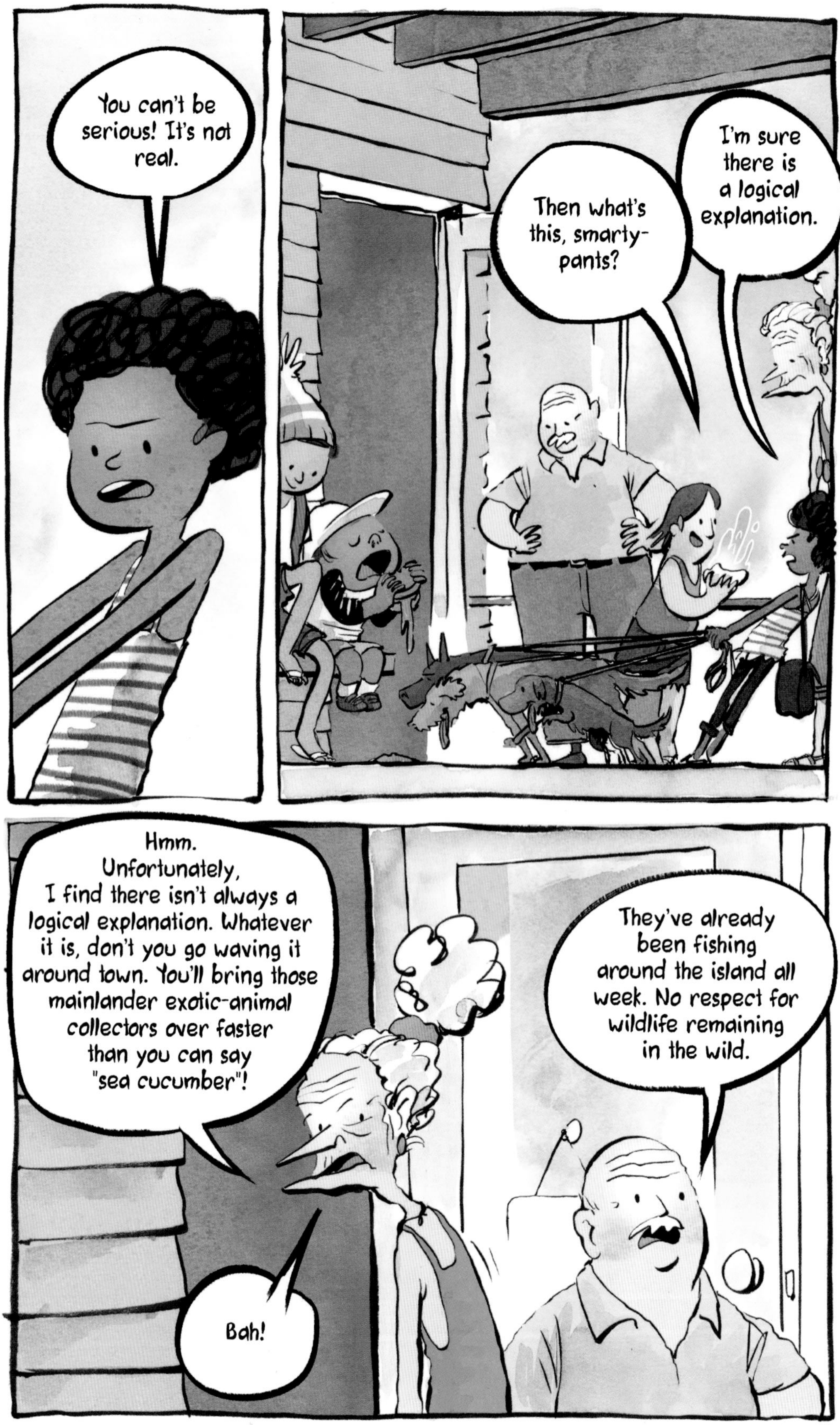
You can't be serious! It's not real.
Then what's this, smarty-pants?
I'm sure there is a logical explanation.
Hmm. Unfortunately, I find there isn't always a logical explanation. Whatever it is, don't you go waving it around town. You'll bring those mainlander exotic-animal collectors over faster than you can say "sea cucumber"!
They've already been fishing around the island all week. No respect for wildlife remaining in the wild.
Bah!

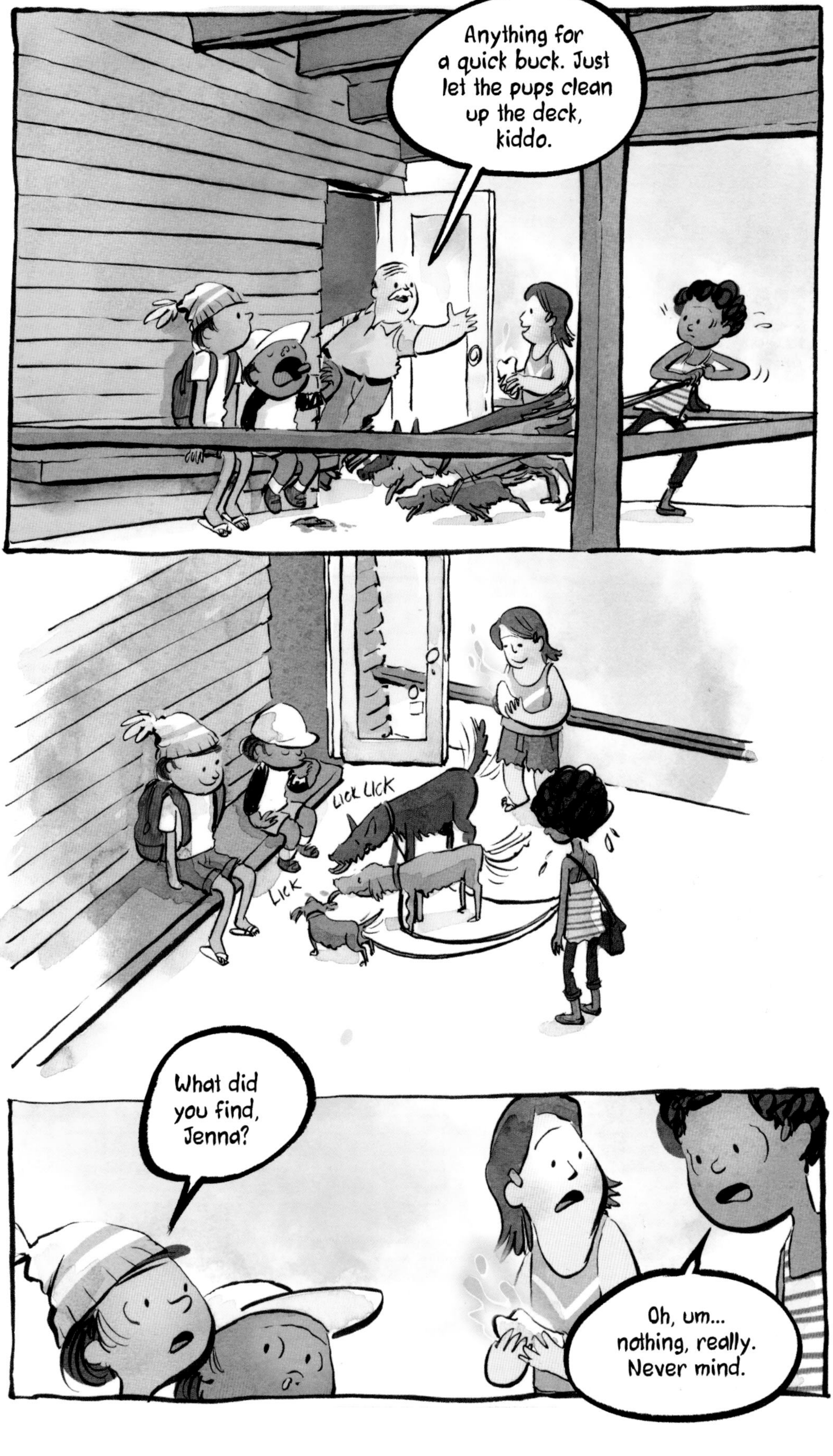
Anything for a quick buck. Just let the pups clean up the deck, kiddo.
LICK LICK
LICK
What did you find, Jenna?
Oh, um... nothing, really. Never mind.

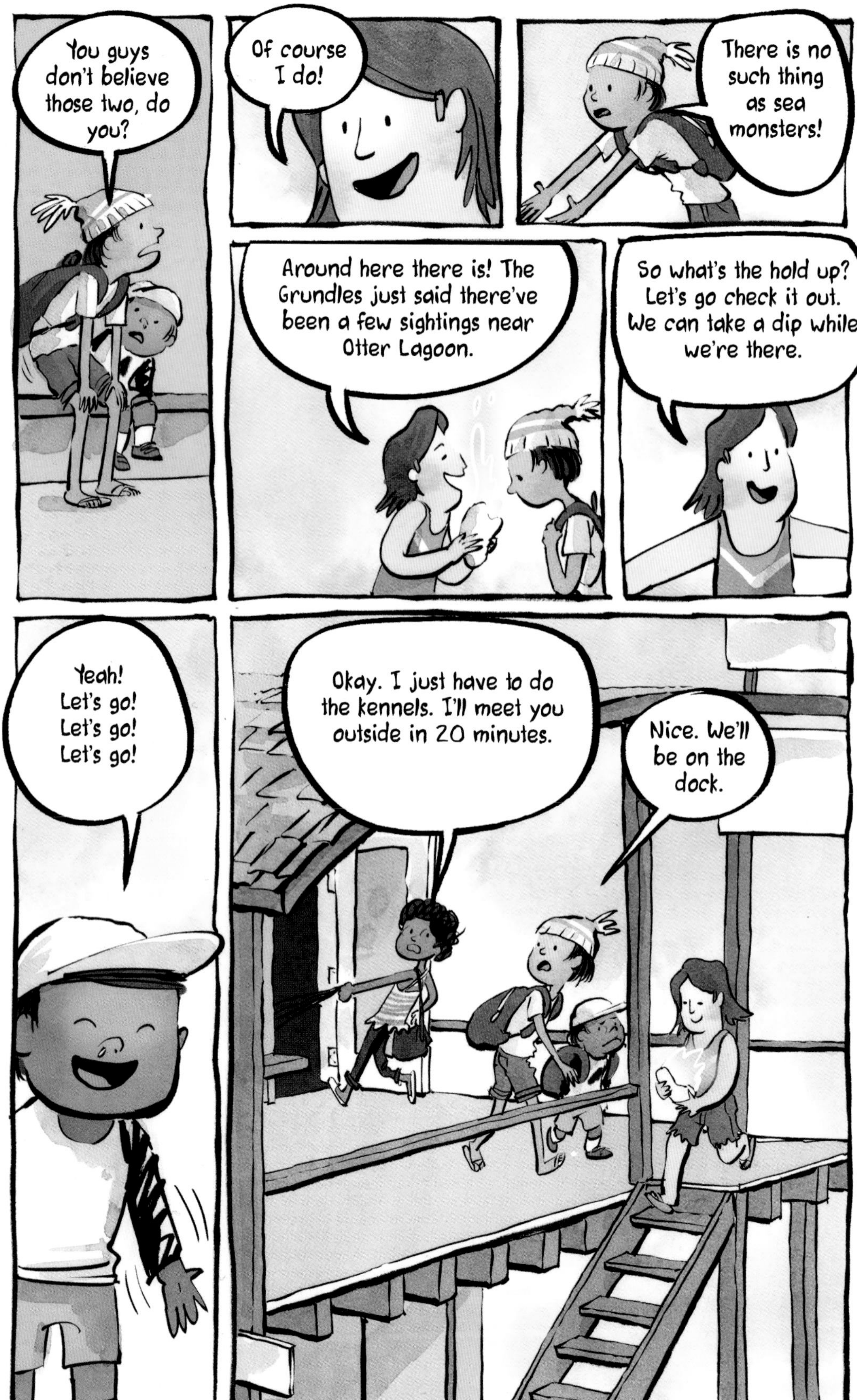
You guys don't believe those two, do you?
Of course I do!
There is no such thing as sea monsters!
Around here there is! The Grundles just said there've been a few sightings near Otter Lagoon.
So what's the hold up? Let's go check it out. We can take a dip while we're there.
Yeah! Let's go! Let's go! Let's go!
Okay. I just have to do the kennels. I'll meet you outside in 20 minutes.
Nice. We'll be on the dock.

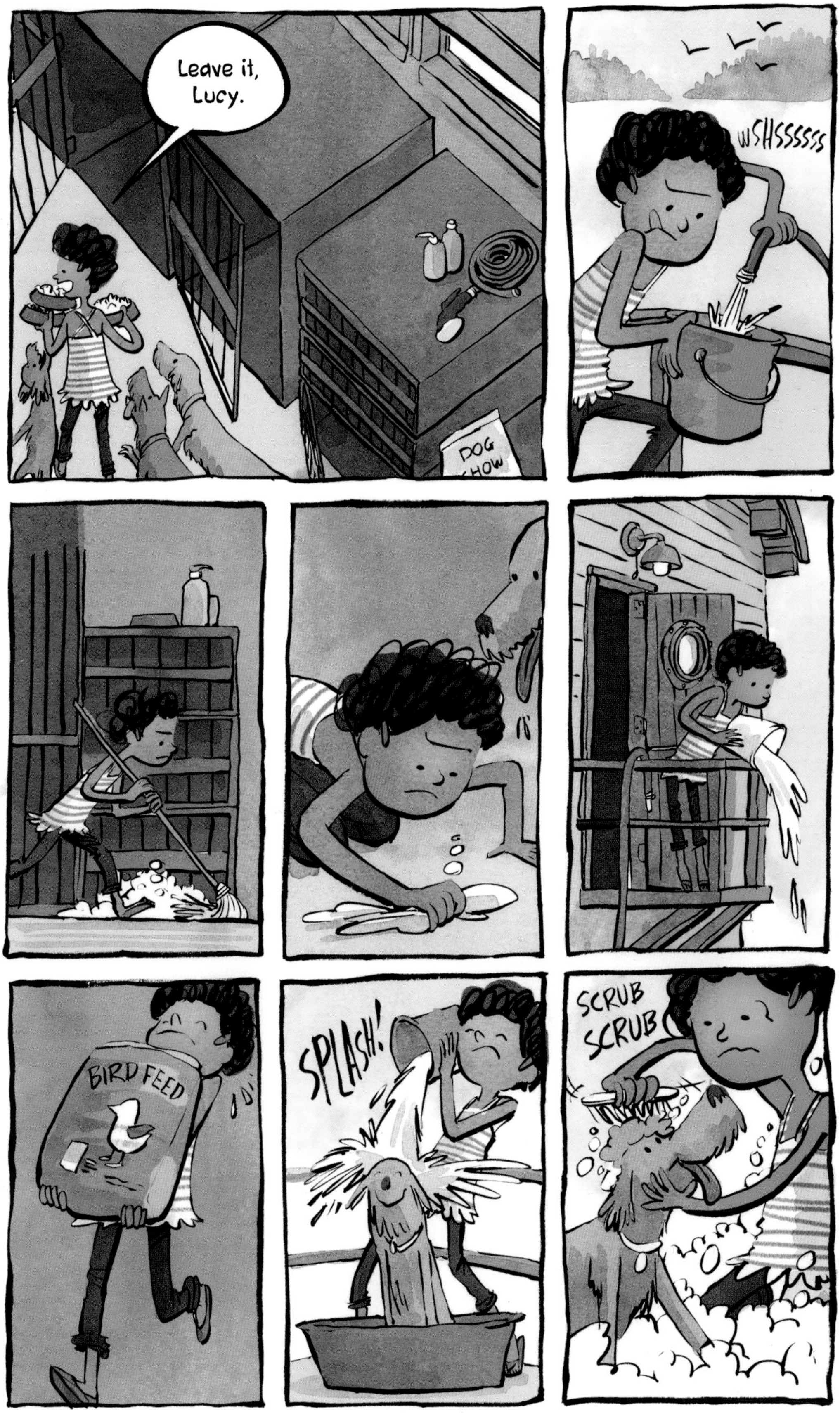
Leave it,
Lucy.
DOG
SHOW
WSHSSSSSS
BIRD FEED
SPLASH!
SCRUB
SCRUB

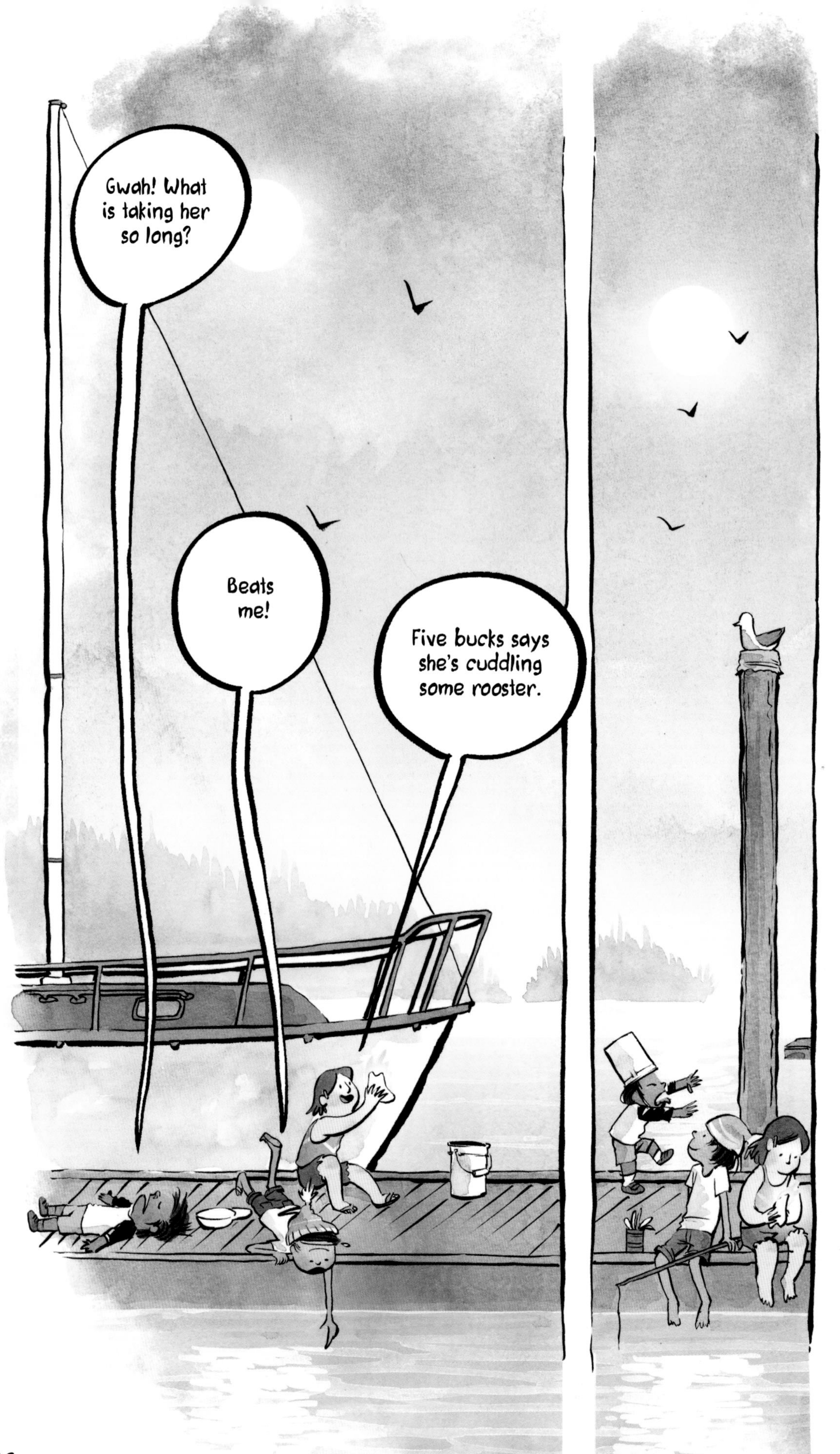
Gwah! What is taking her so long?
Beats me!
Five bucks says she's cuddling some rooster.

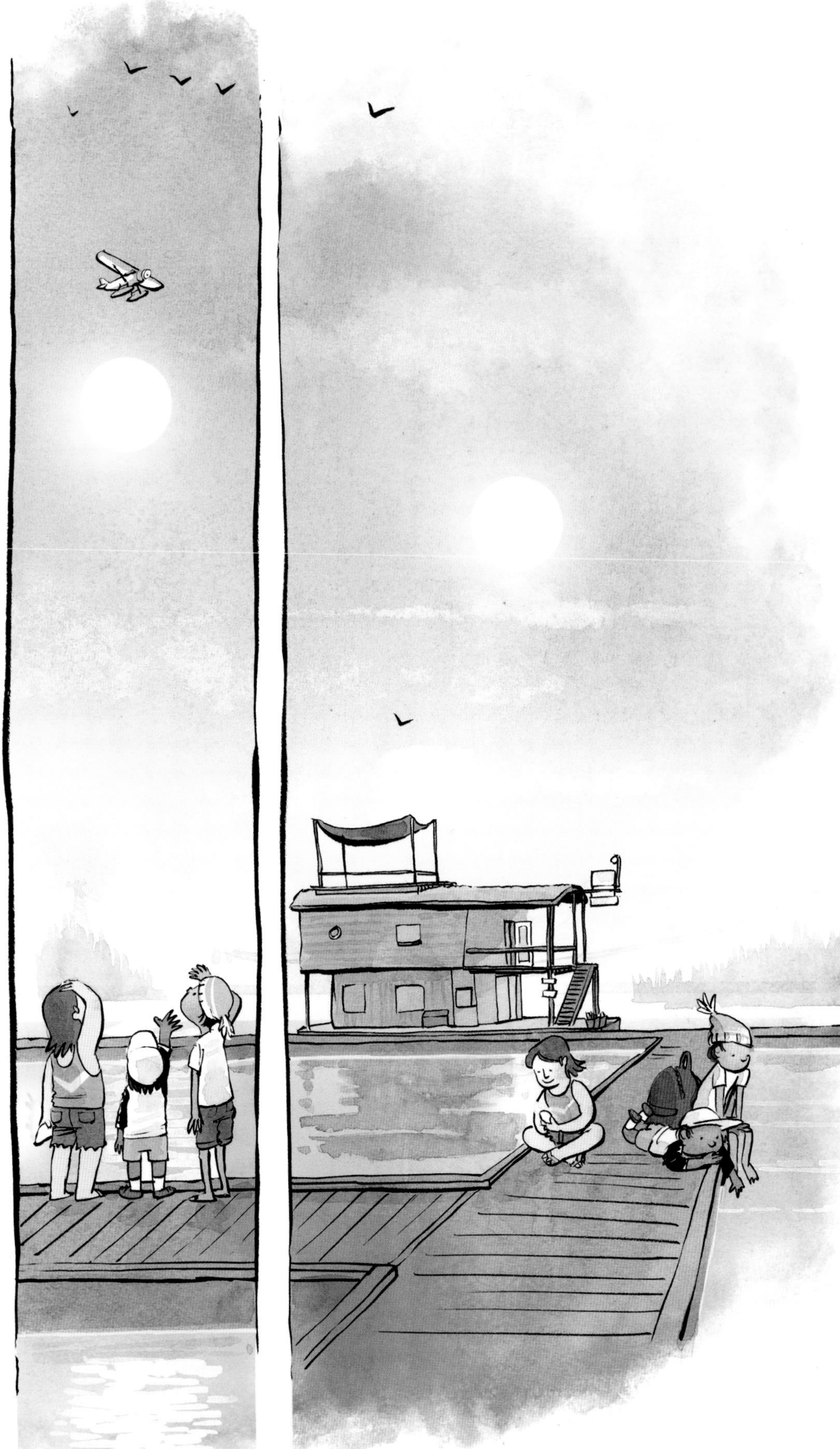

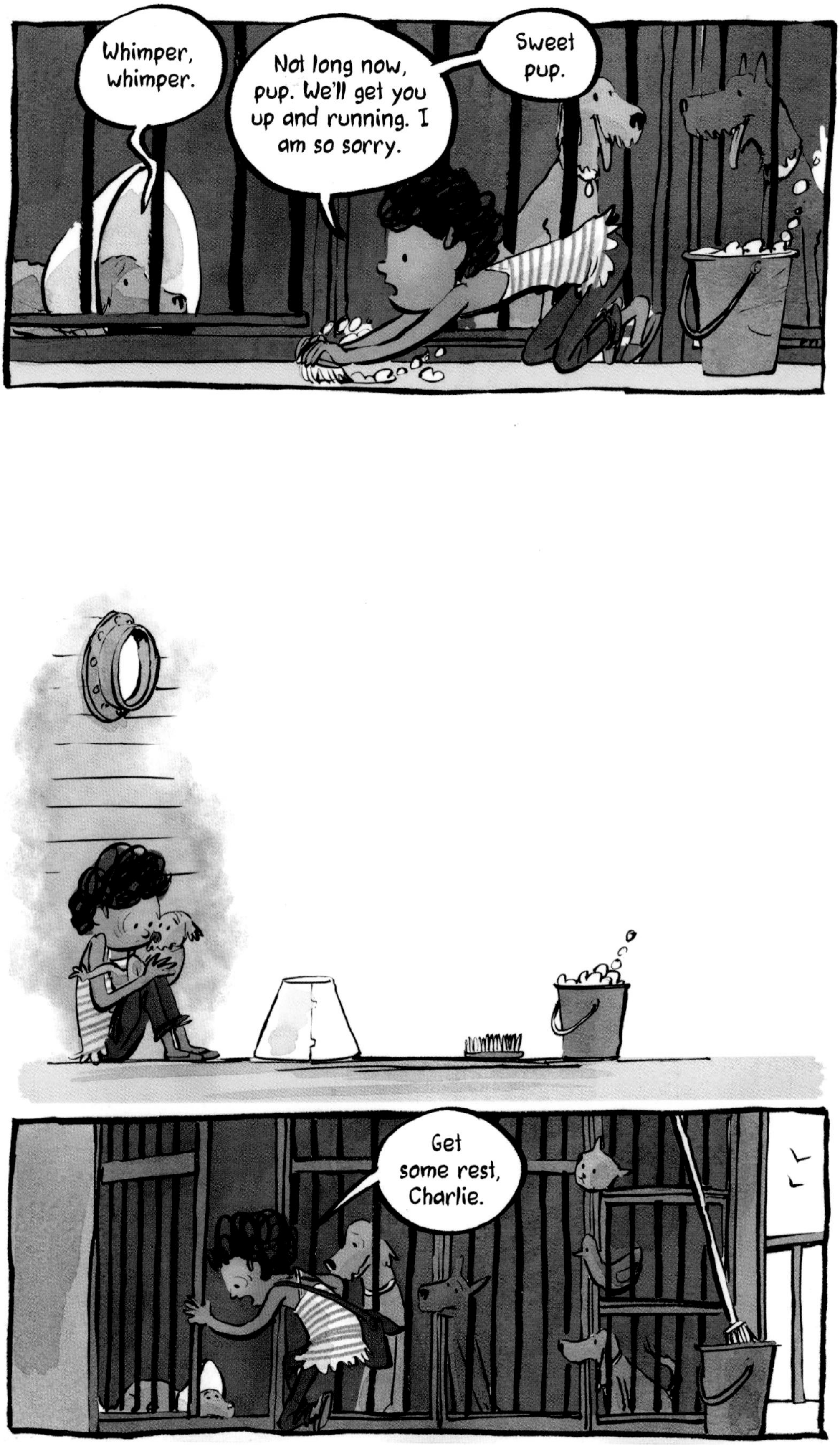
Whimper, whimper.
Not long now, pup. We'll get you up and running. I am so sorry.
Sweet pup.
Get some rest, Charlie.

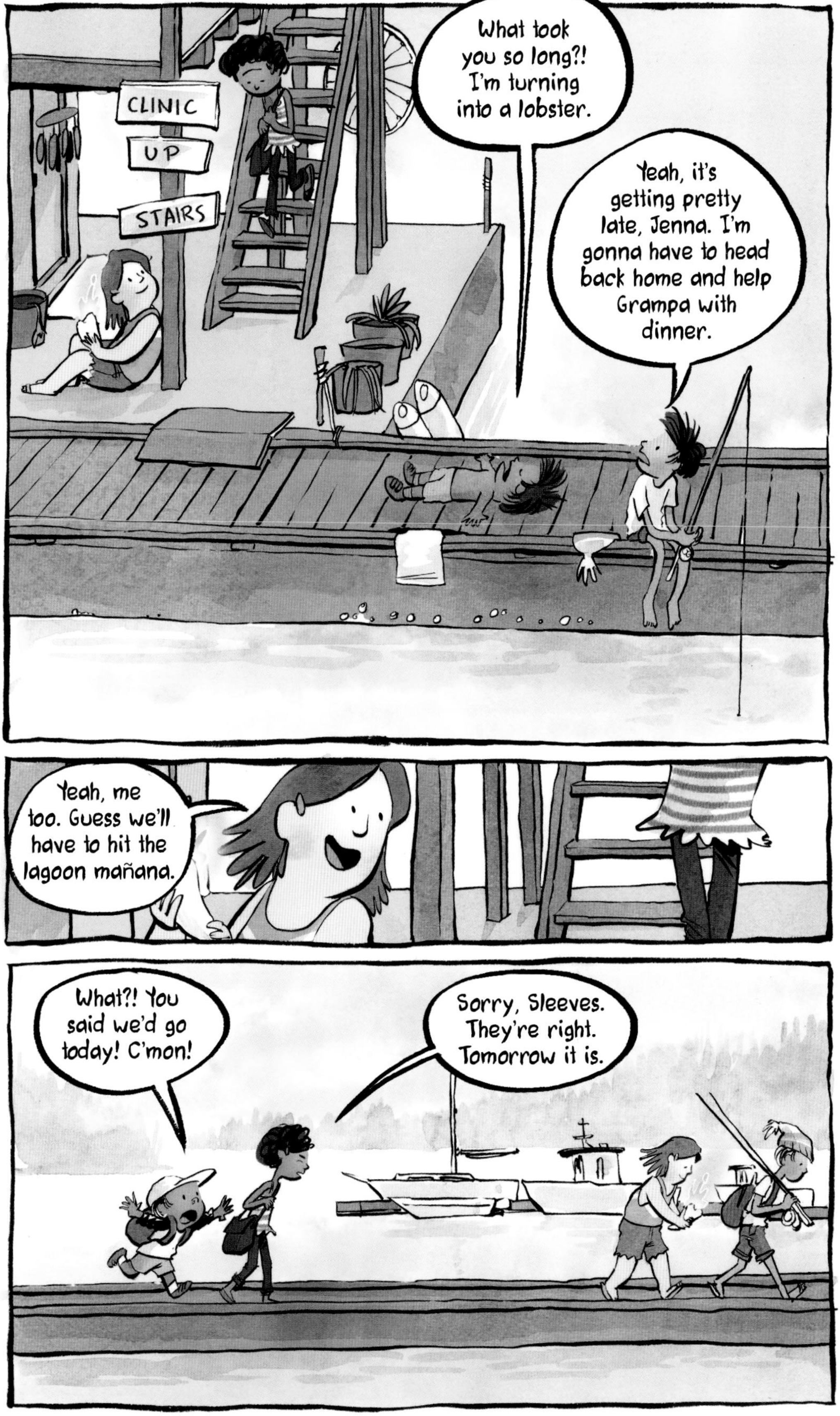
CLINIC
UP
STAIRS
What took you so long?! I'm turning into a lobster.
Yeah, it's getting pretty late, Jenna. I'm gonna have to head back home and help Grampa with dinner.
Yeah, me too. Guess we'll have to hit the lagoon mañana.
What?! You said we'd go today! C'mon!
Sorry, Sleeves. They're right. Tomorrow it is.

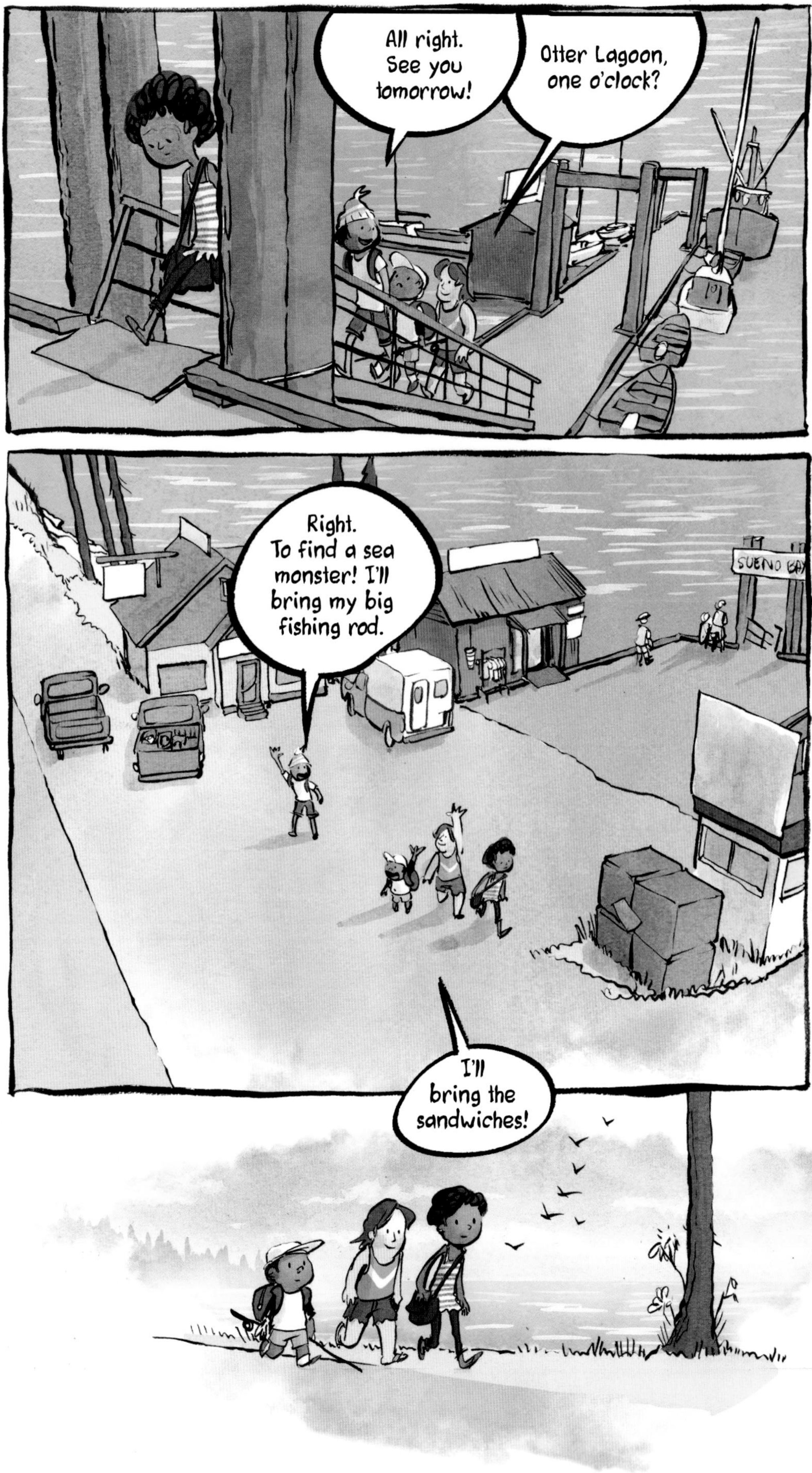
All right. See you tomorrow!
Otter Lagoon, one o'clock?
SUENO BAY
Right. To find a sea monster! I'll bring my big fishing rod.
I'll bring the sandwiches!

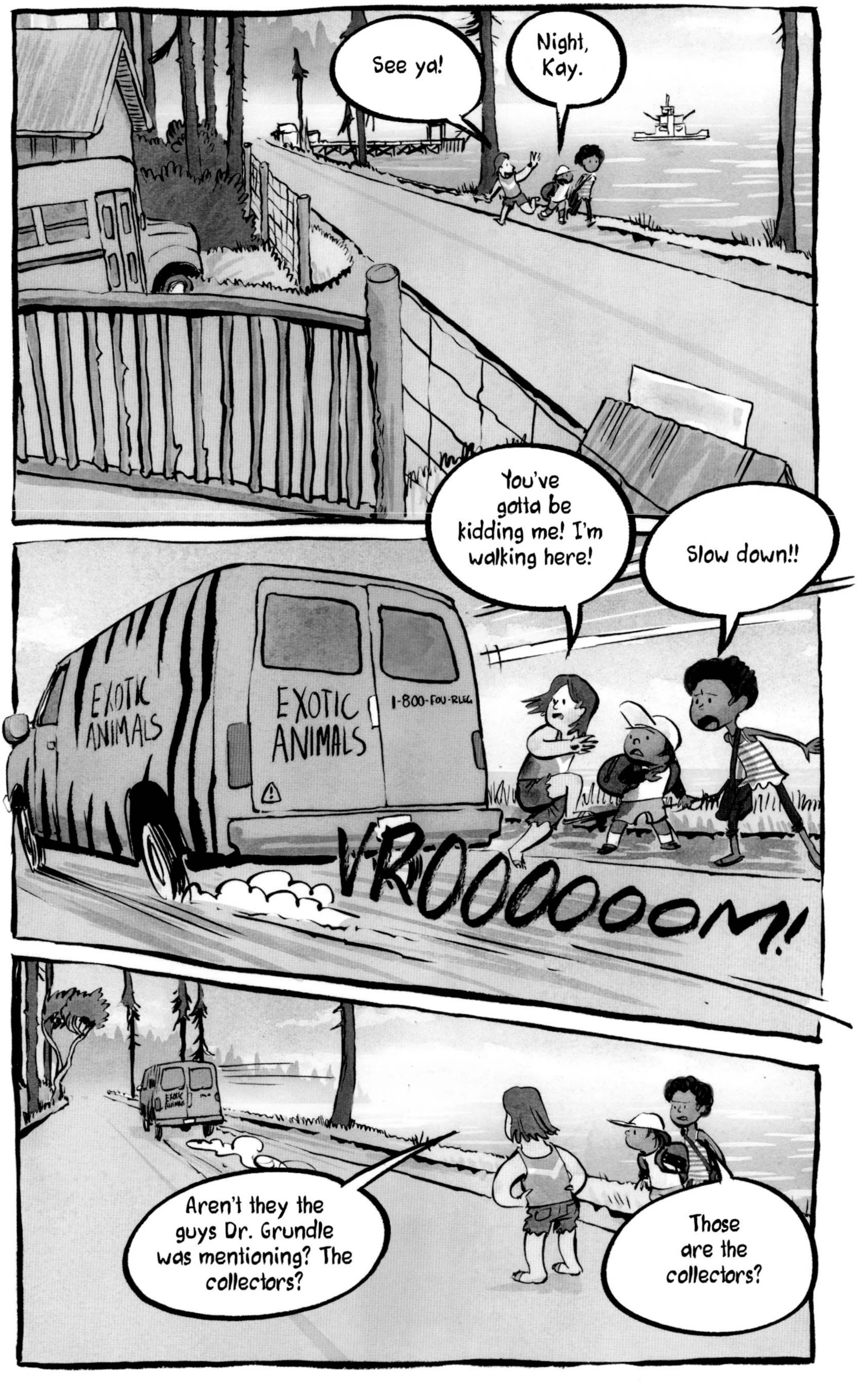
See ya!
Night, Kay.
You've gotta be kidding me! I'm walking here!
Slow down!!
EXOTIC ANIMALS
EXOTIC ANIMALS
1-800-FOU-RLEG
VROOOOOOOM!
Aren't they the guys Dr. Grundle was mentioning? The collectors?
Those are the collectors?

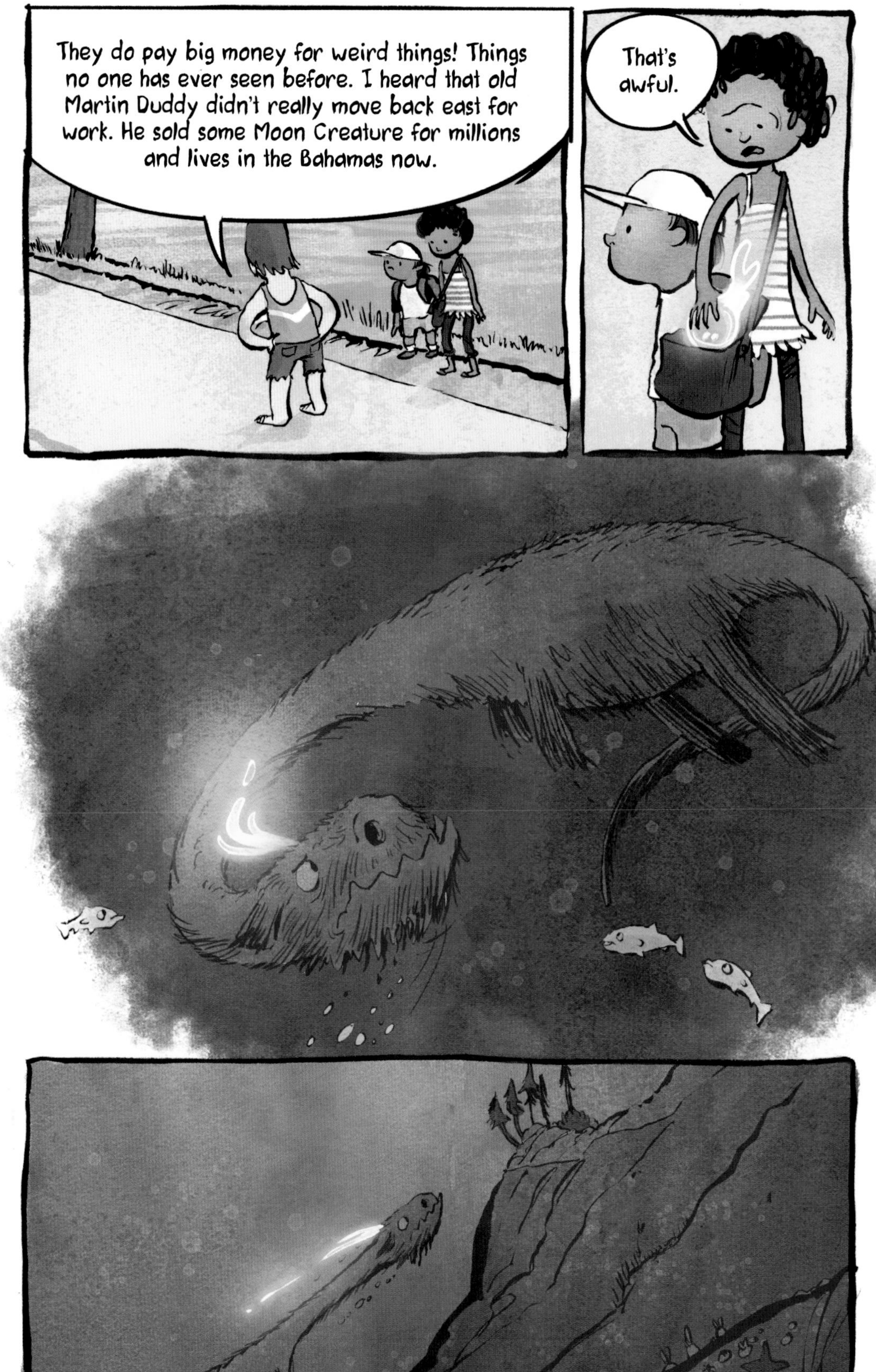

They do pay big money for weird things! Things no one has ever seen before. I heard that old Martin Duddy didn't really move back east for work. He sold some Moon Creature for millions and lives in the Bahamas now.
That's awful.

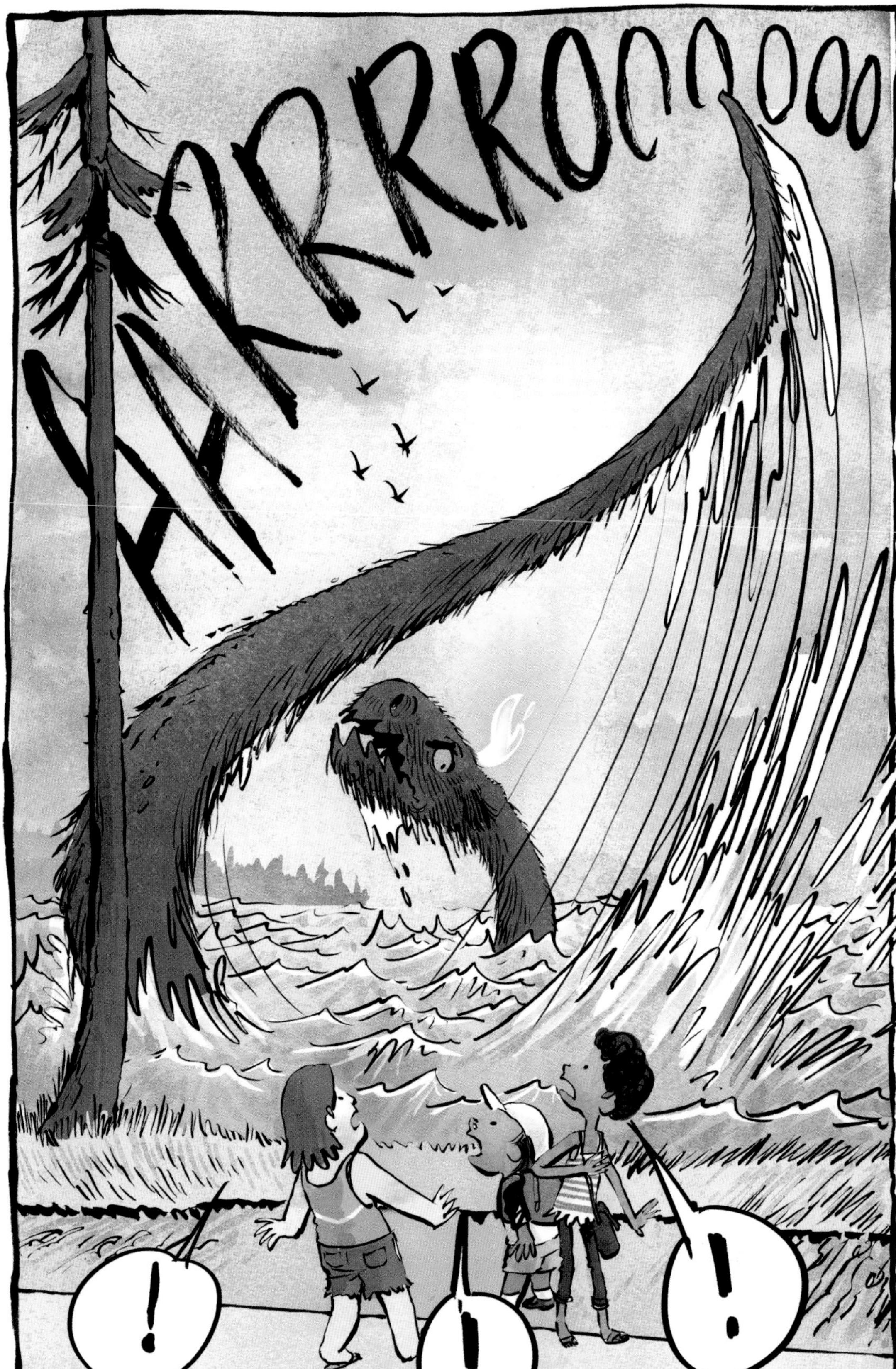
HARRRROOOOOO
!
!
!

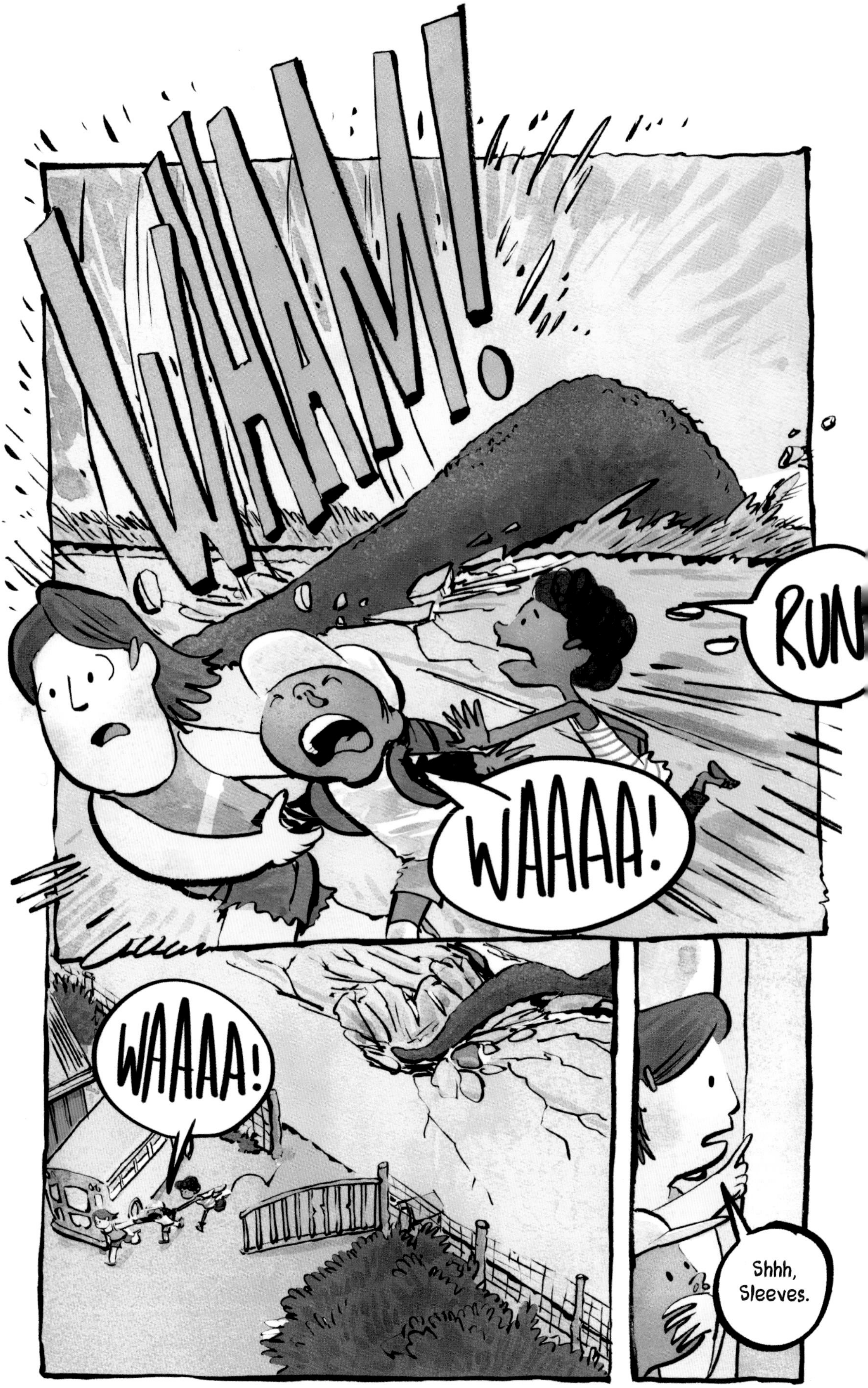
WHAM!
RUN
WAAAA!
WAAAA!
Shhh, Sleeves.

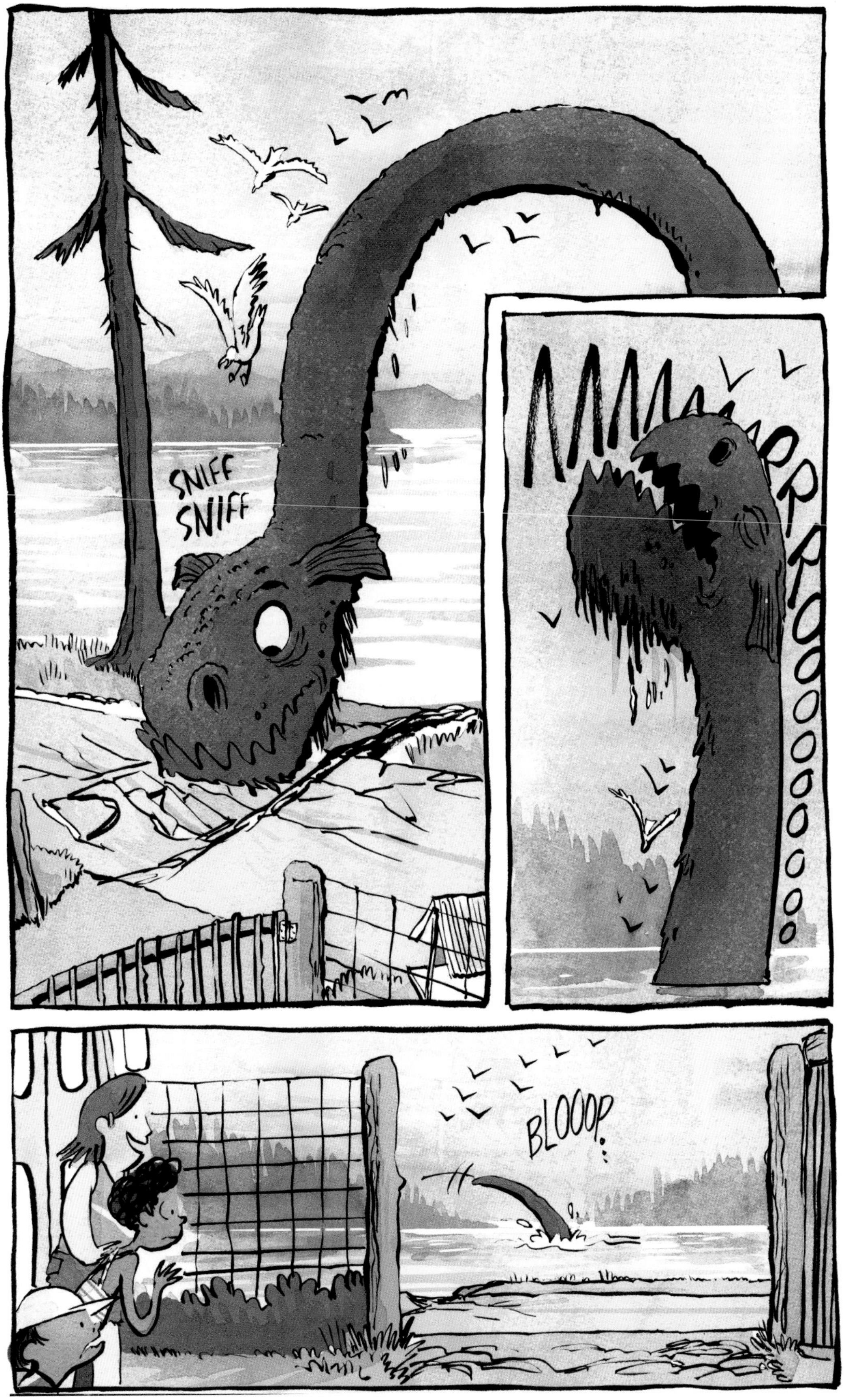
SNIFF
SNIFF
MMMMRRROOOOOOOOOOOO
BLOOOP...

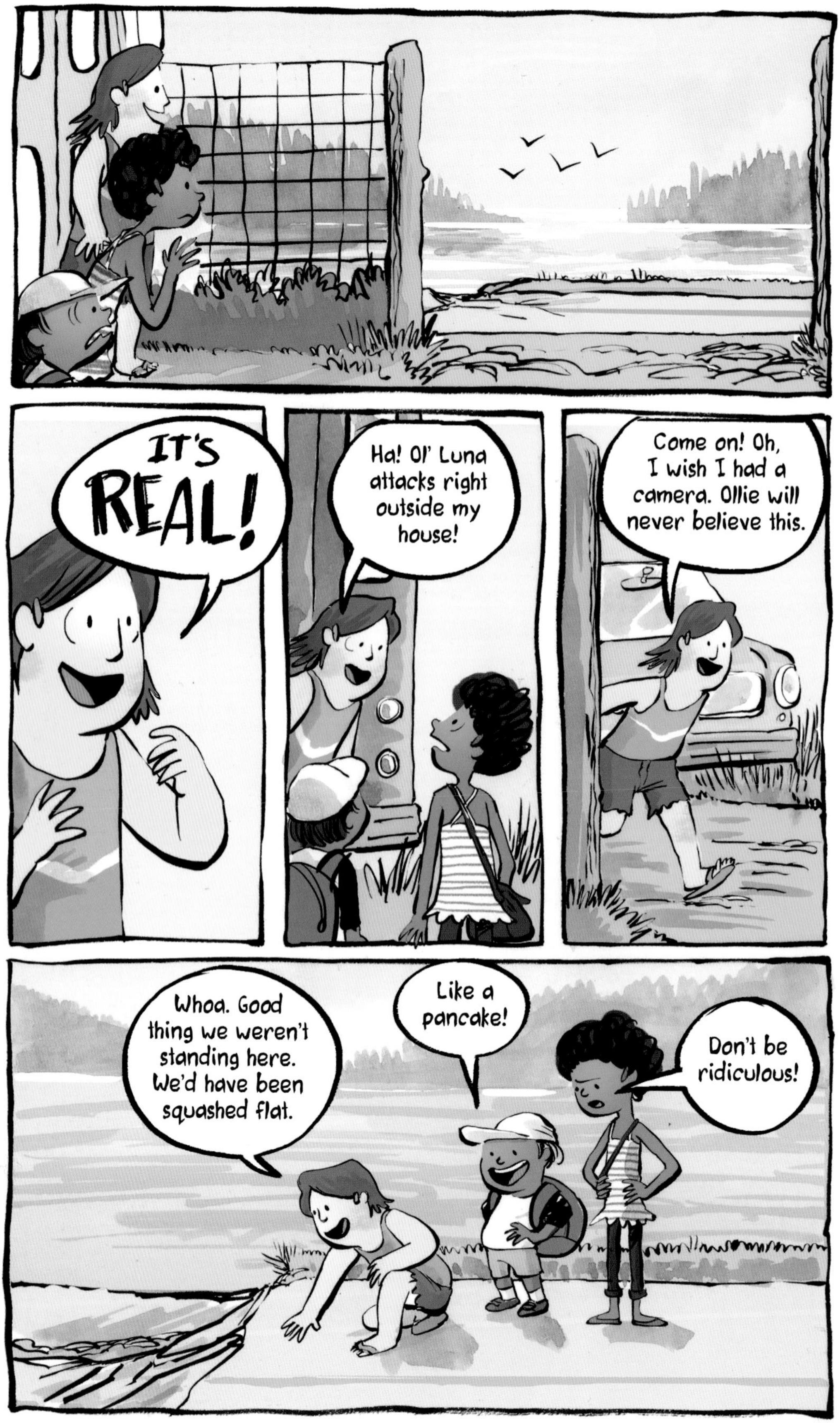
IT'S REAL!
Ha! Ol' Luna attacks right outside my house!
Come on! Oh, I wish I had a camera. Ollie will never believe this.
Whoa. Good thing we weren't standing here. We'd have been squashed flat.
Like a pancake!
Don't be ridiculous!

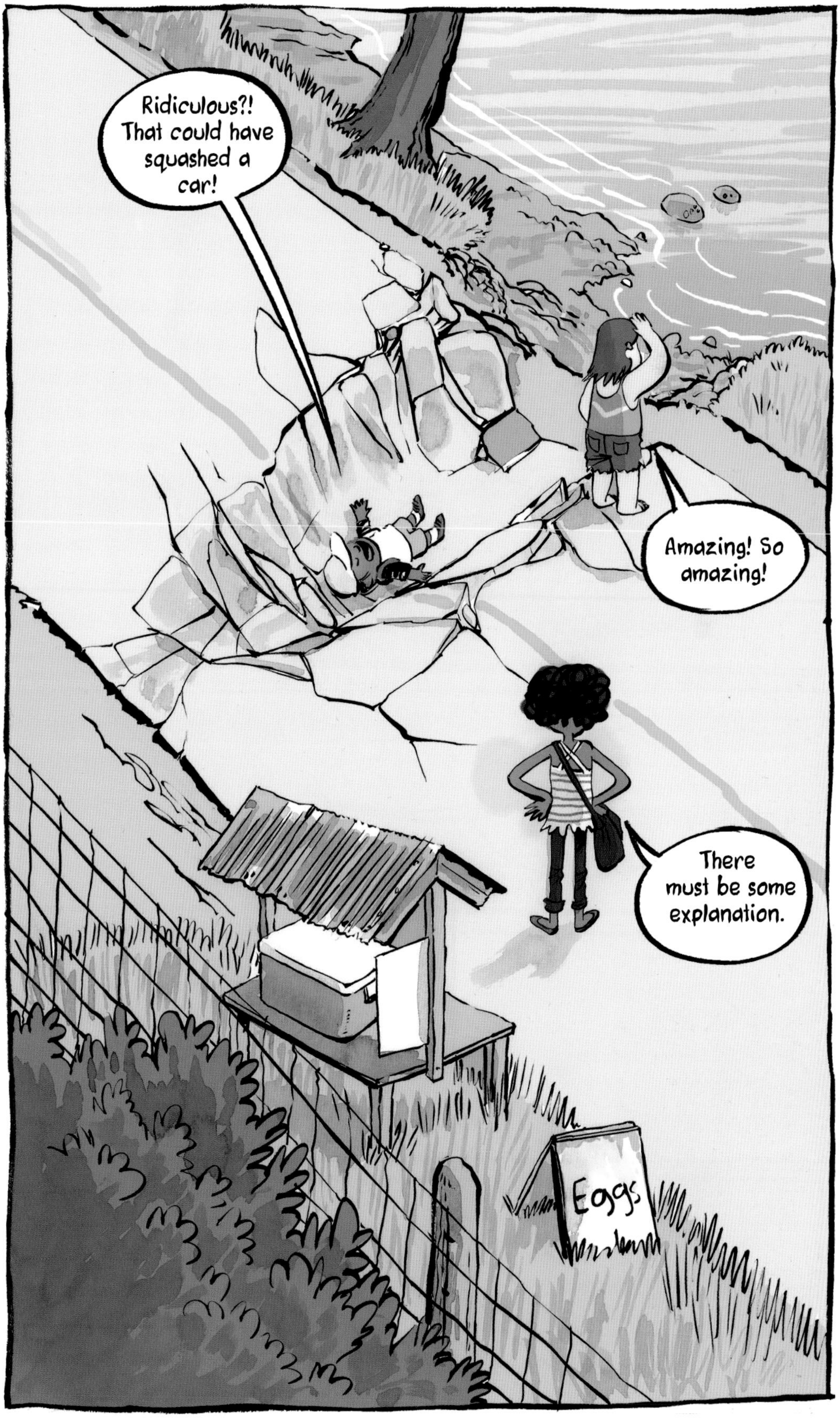

Ridiculous?! That could have squashed a car!
Amazing! So amazing!
There must be some explanation.
Eggs

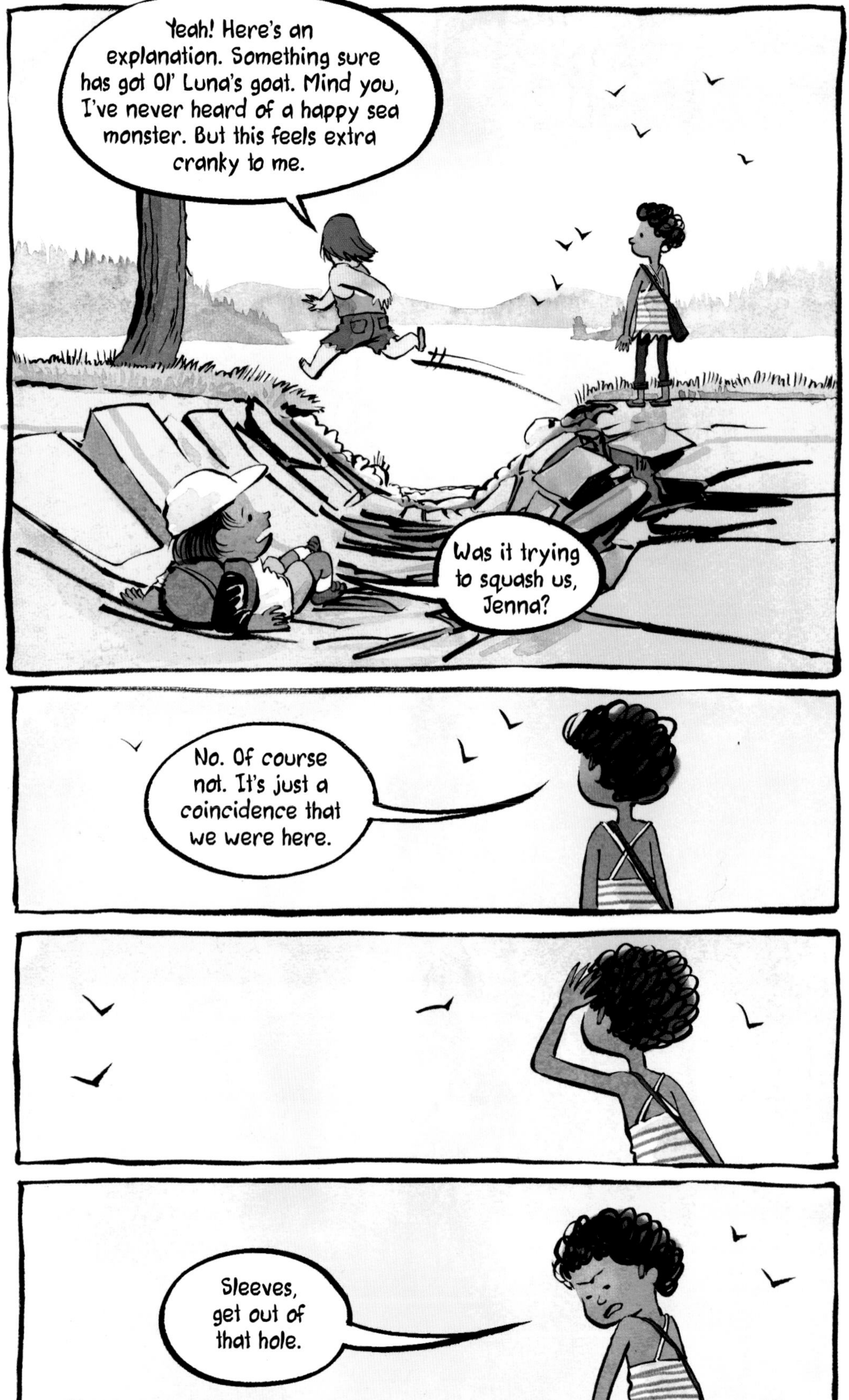
Yeah! Here's an explanation. Something sure has got Ol' Luna's goat. Mind you, I've never heard of a happy sea monster. But this feels extra cranky to me.
Was it trying to squash us, Jenna?
No. Of course not. It's just a coincidence that we were here.
Sleeves, get out of that hole.

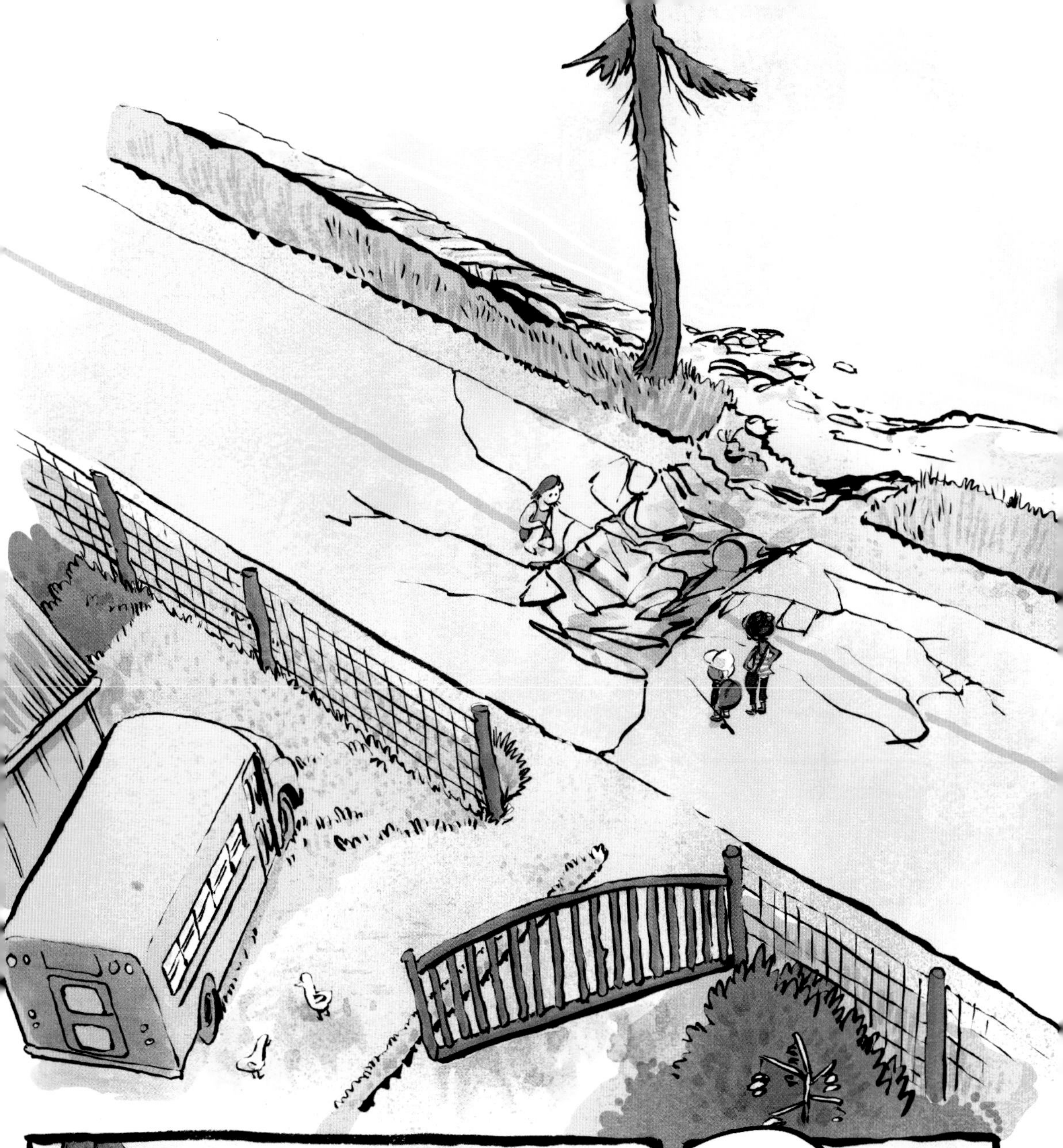
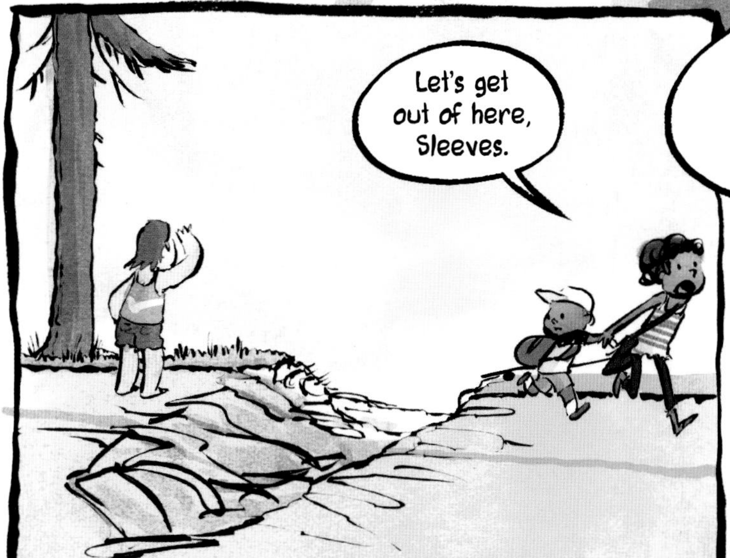
Let's get out of here, Sleeves.
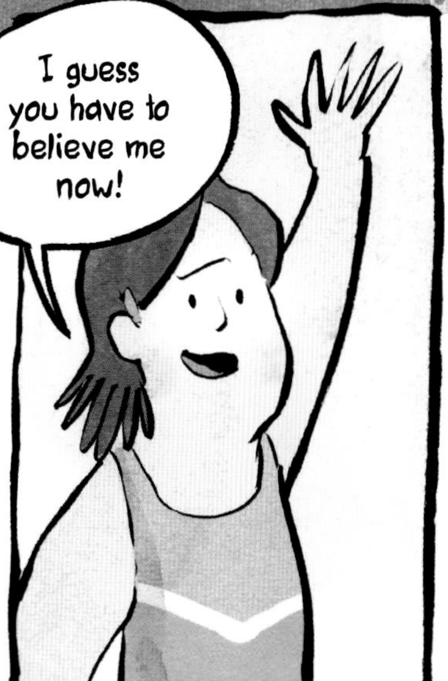
I guess you have to believe me now!

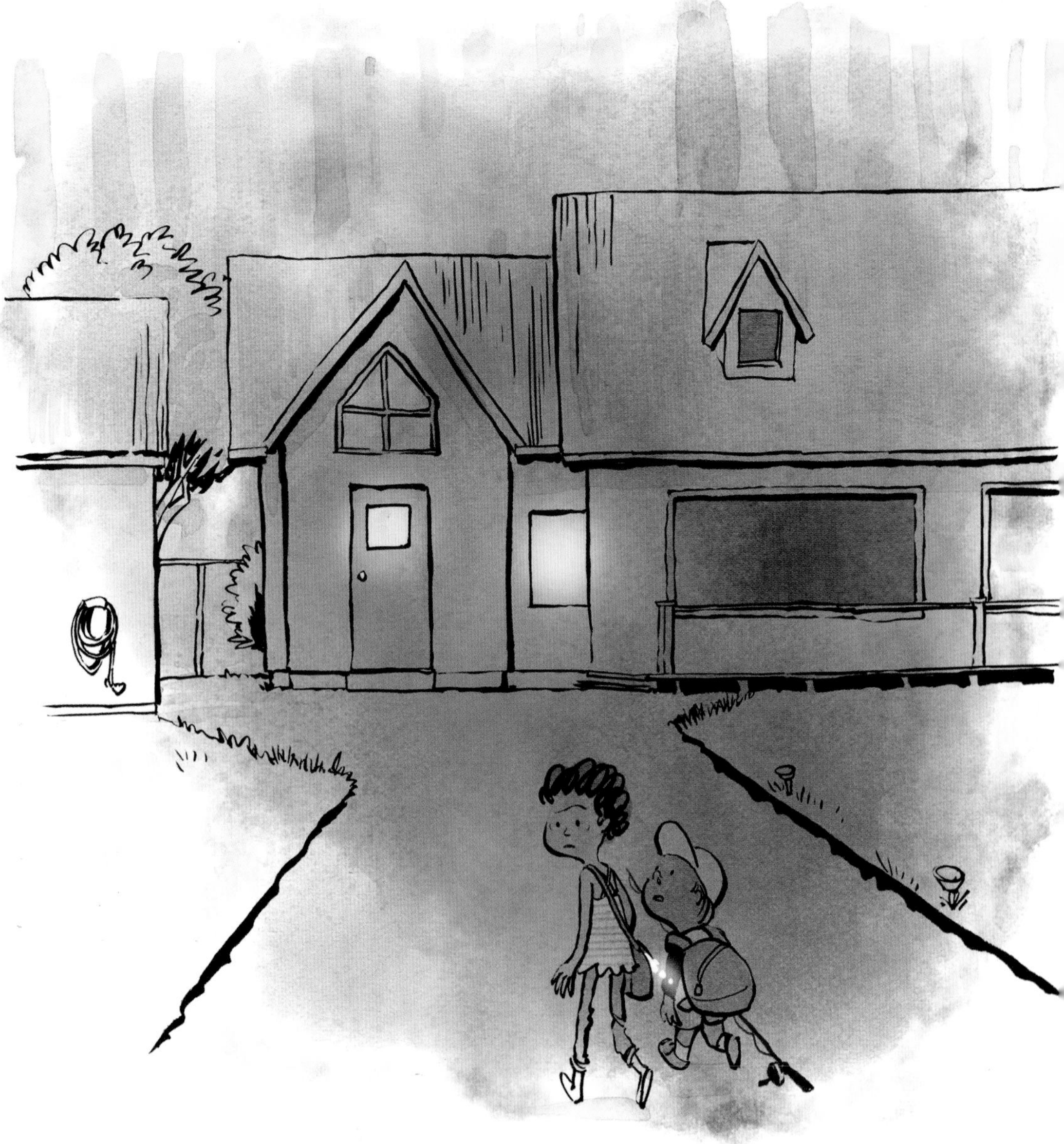

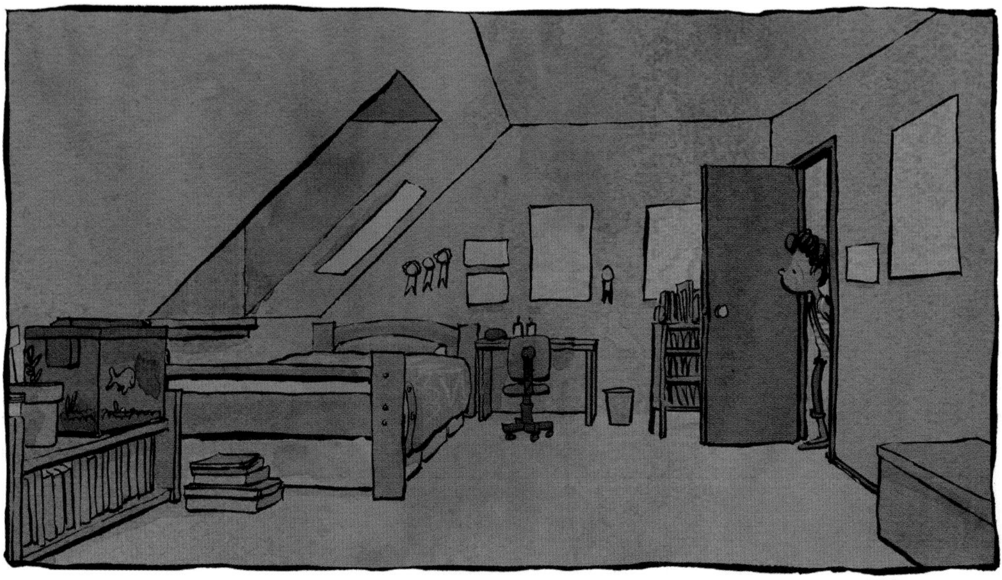

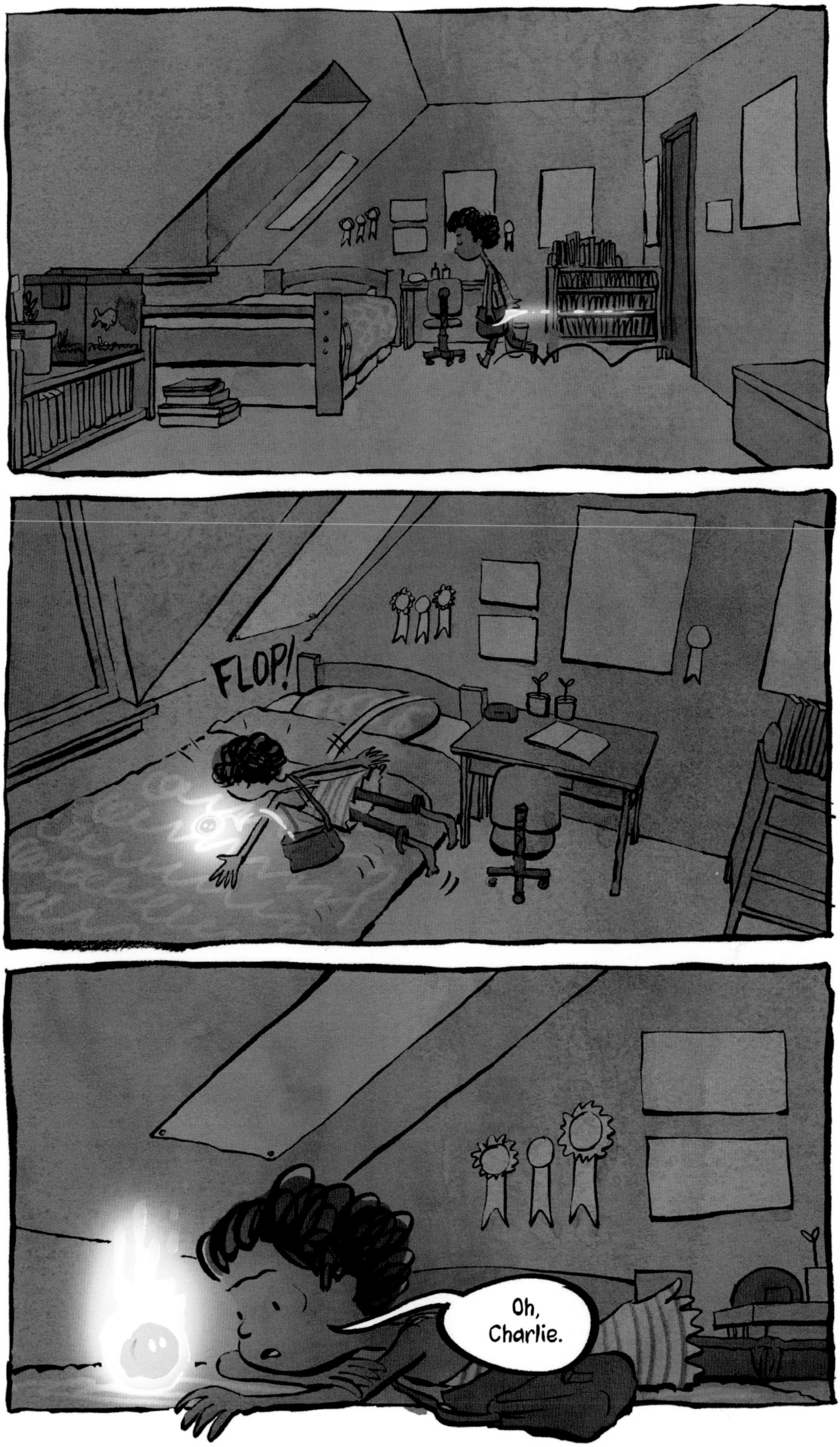
FLOP!
Oh, Charlie.

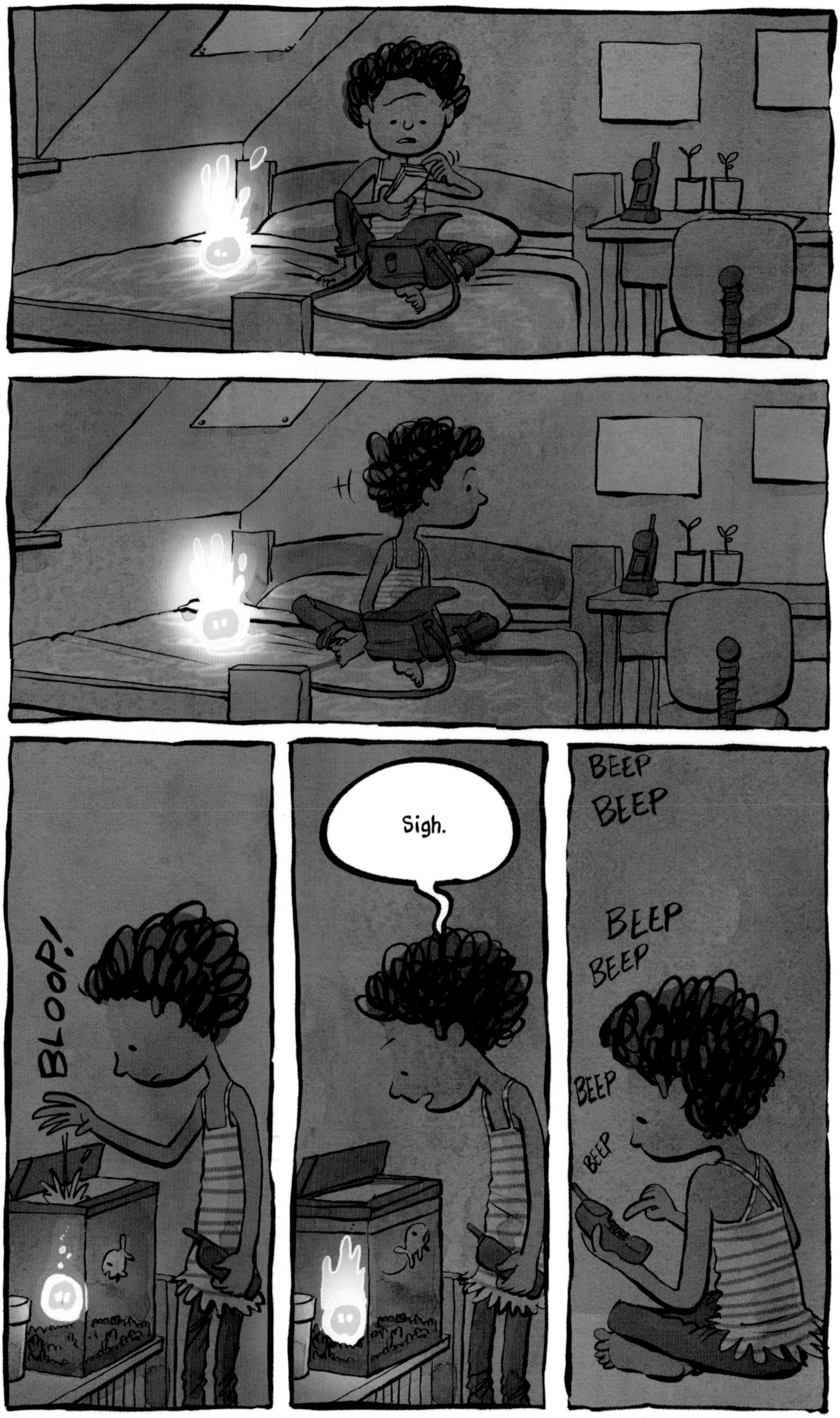
BLOOP!
Sigh.
BEEP
BEEP
BEEP
BEEP
BEEP
BEEP

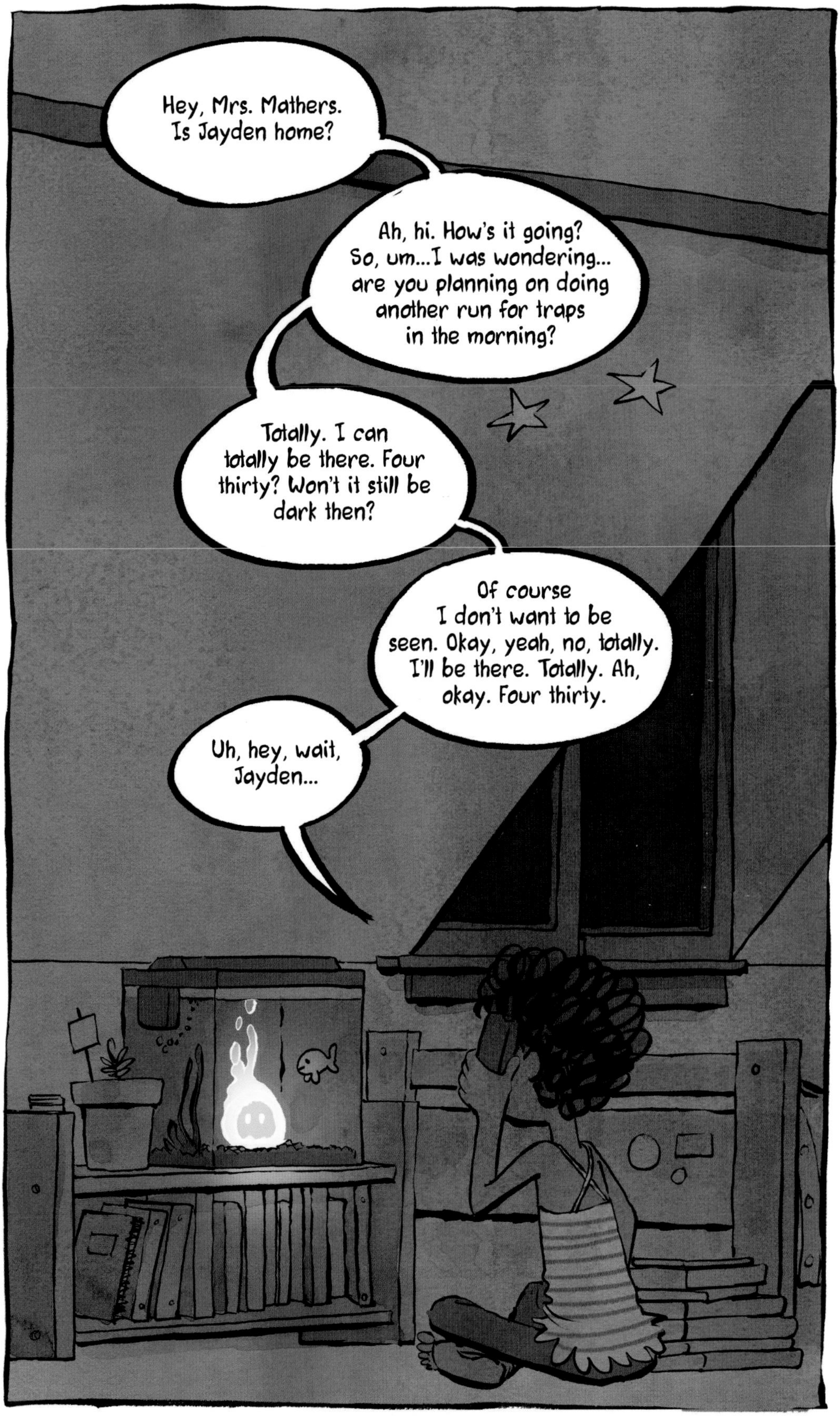
Hey, Mrs. Mathers. Is Jayden home?
Ah, hi. How's it going? So, um...I was wondering... are you planning on doing another run for traps in the morning?
Totally. I can totally be there. Four thirty? Won't it still be dark then?
Of course I don't want to be seen. Okay, yeah, no, totally. I'll be there. Totally. Ah, okay. Four thirty.
Uh, hey, wait, Jayden...

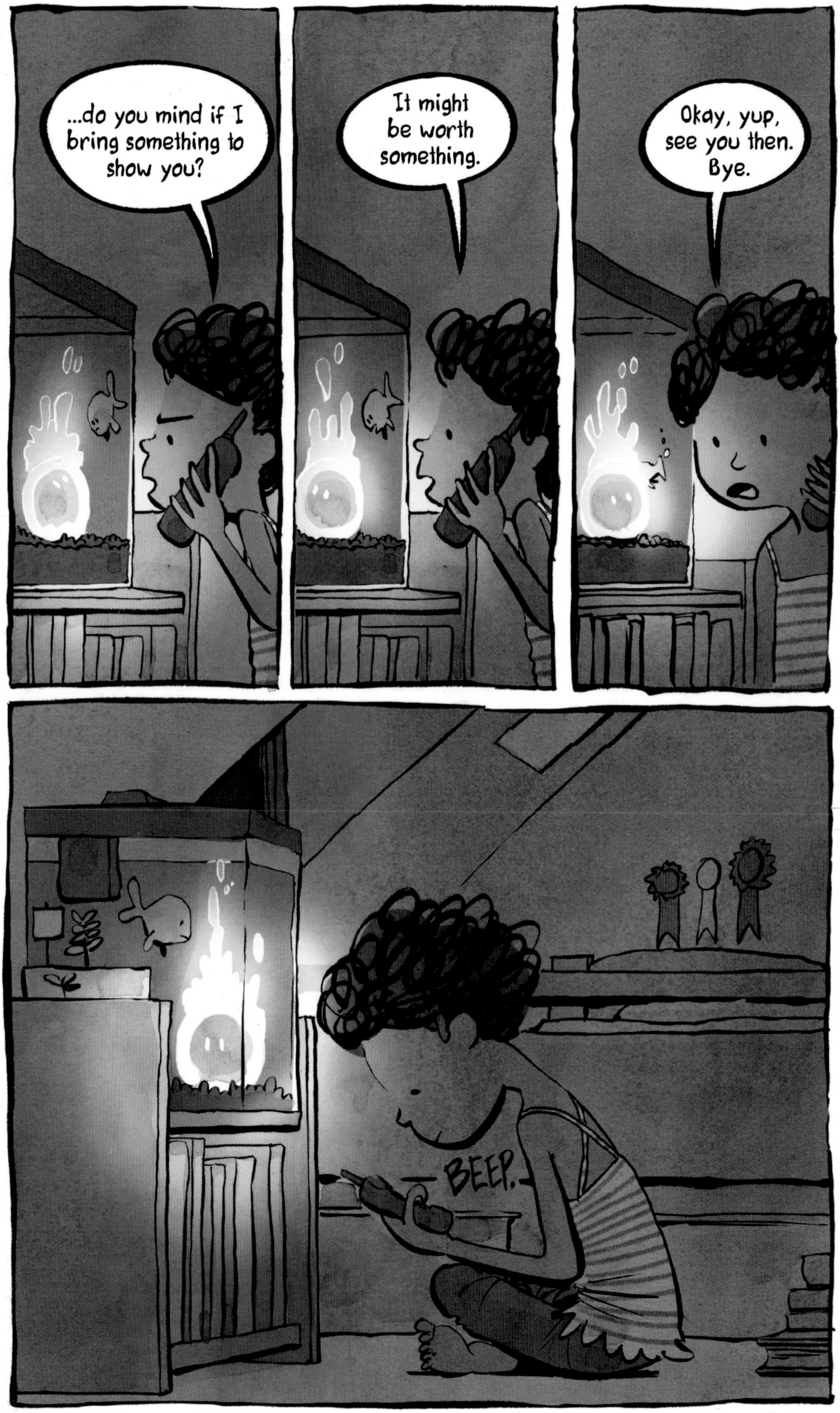
...do you mind if I bring something to show you?
It might be worth something.
Okay, yup, see you then. Bye.
BEEP.

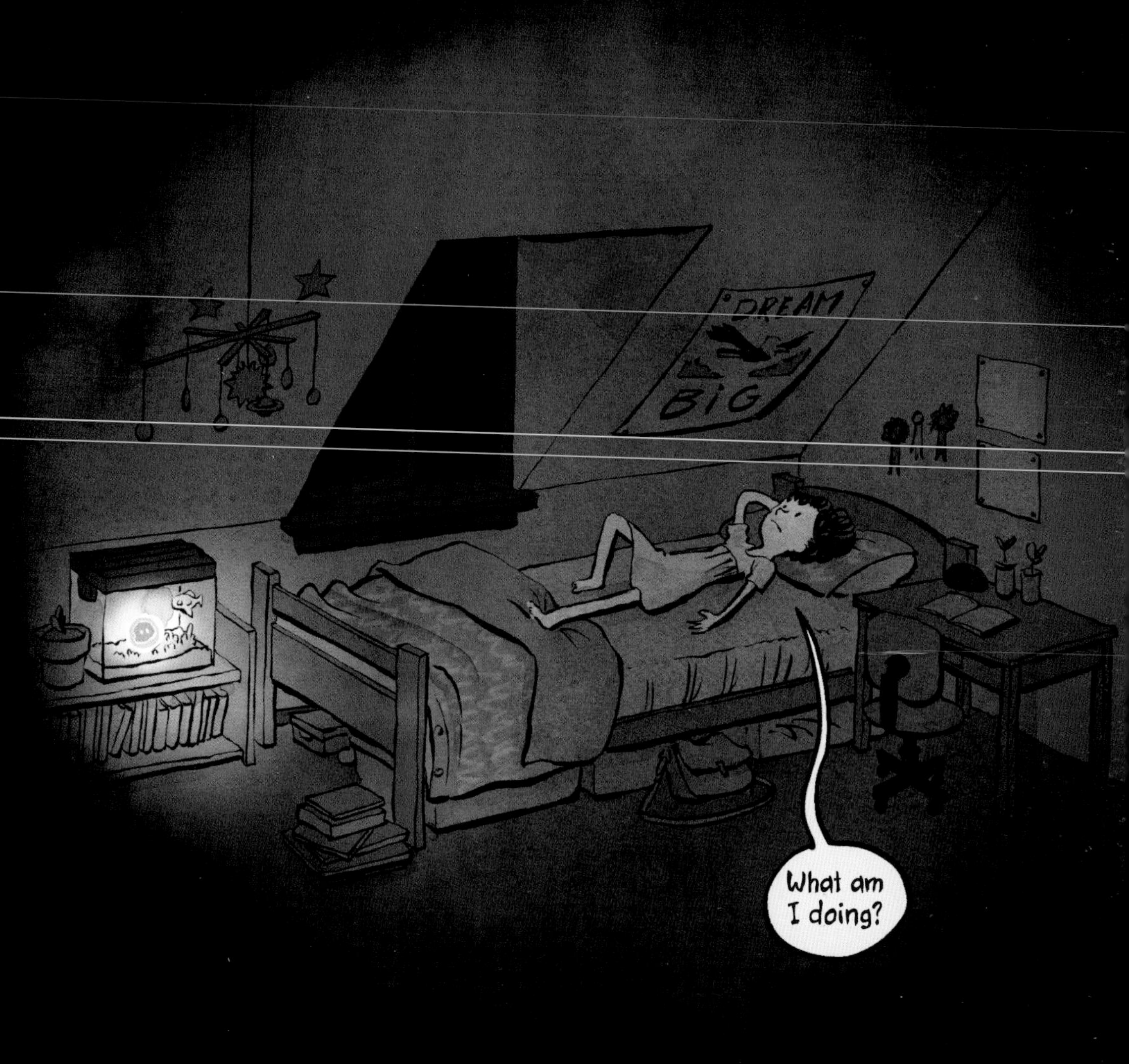
DREAM
BIG
What am I doing?

CHAPTER THREE

It's None of Your Business

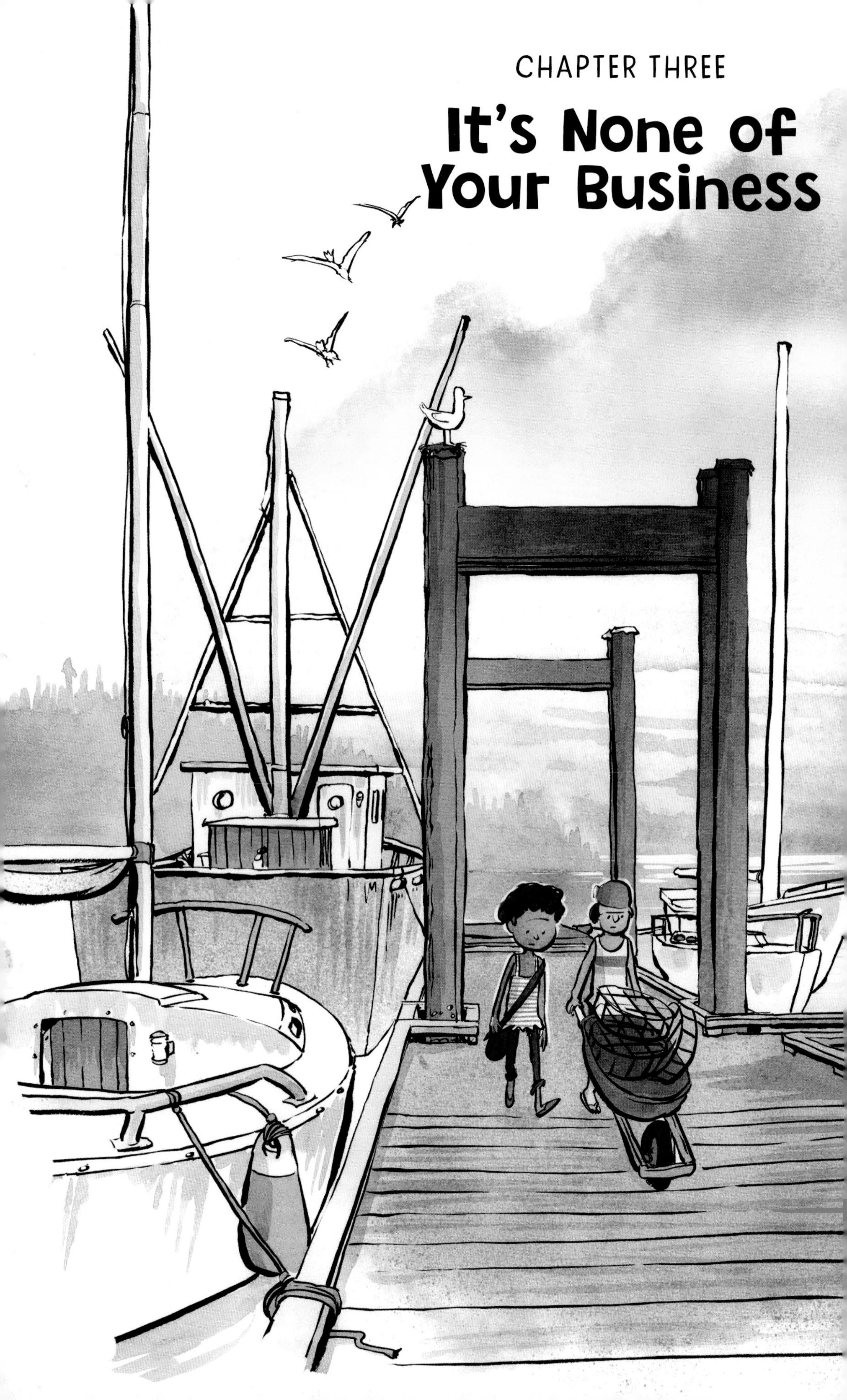

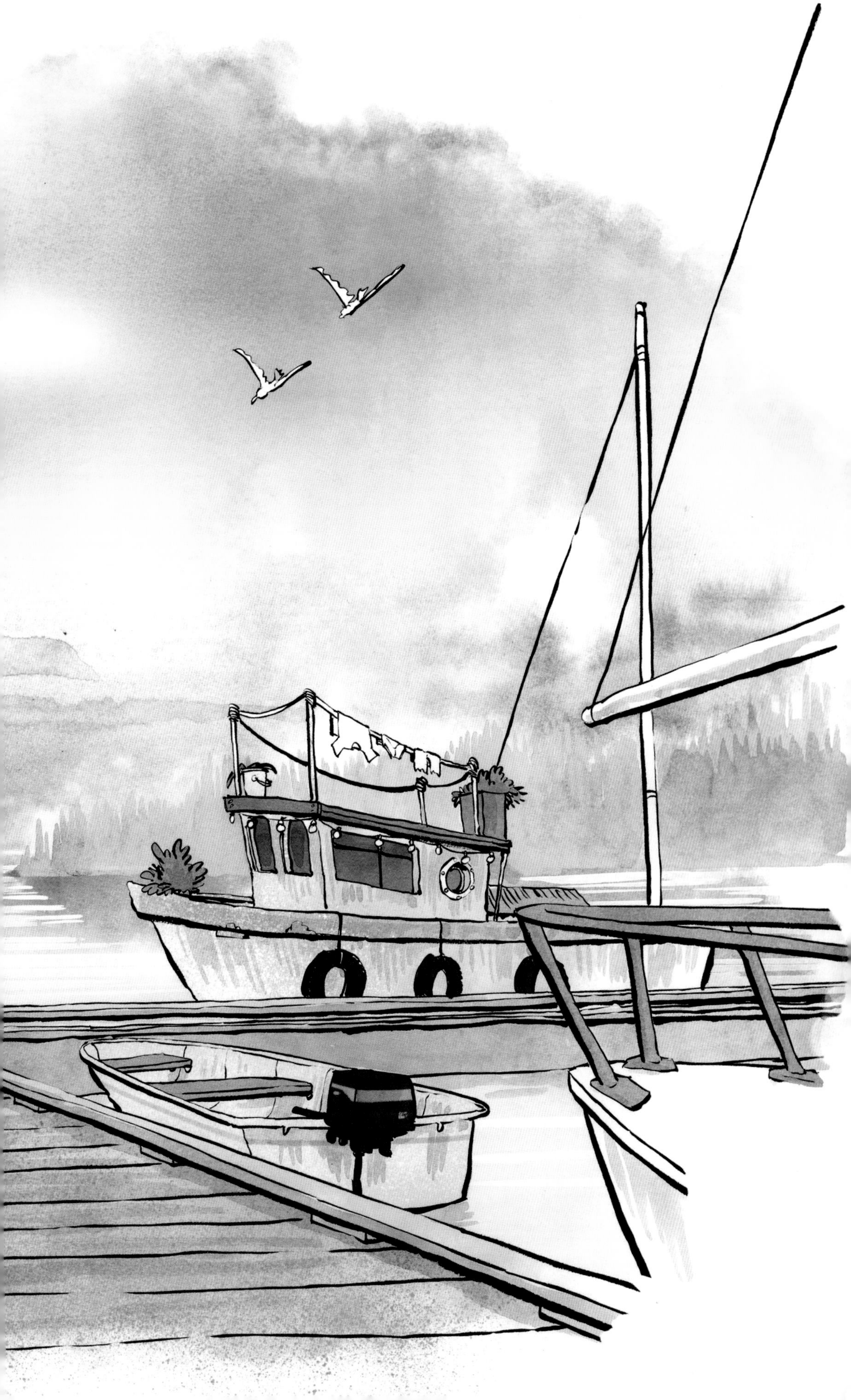

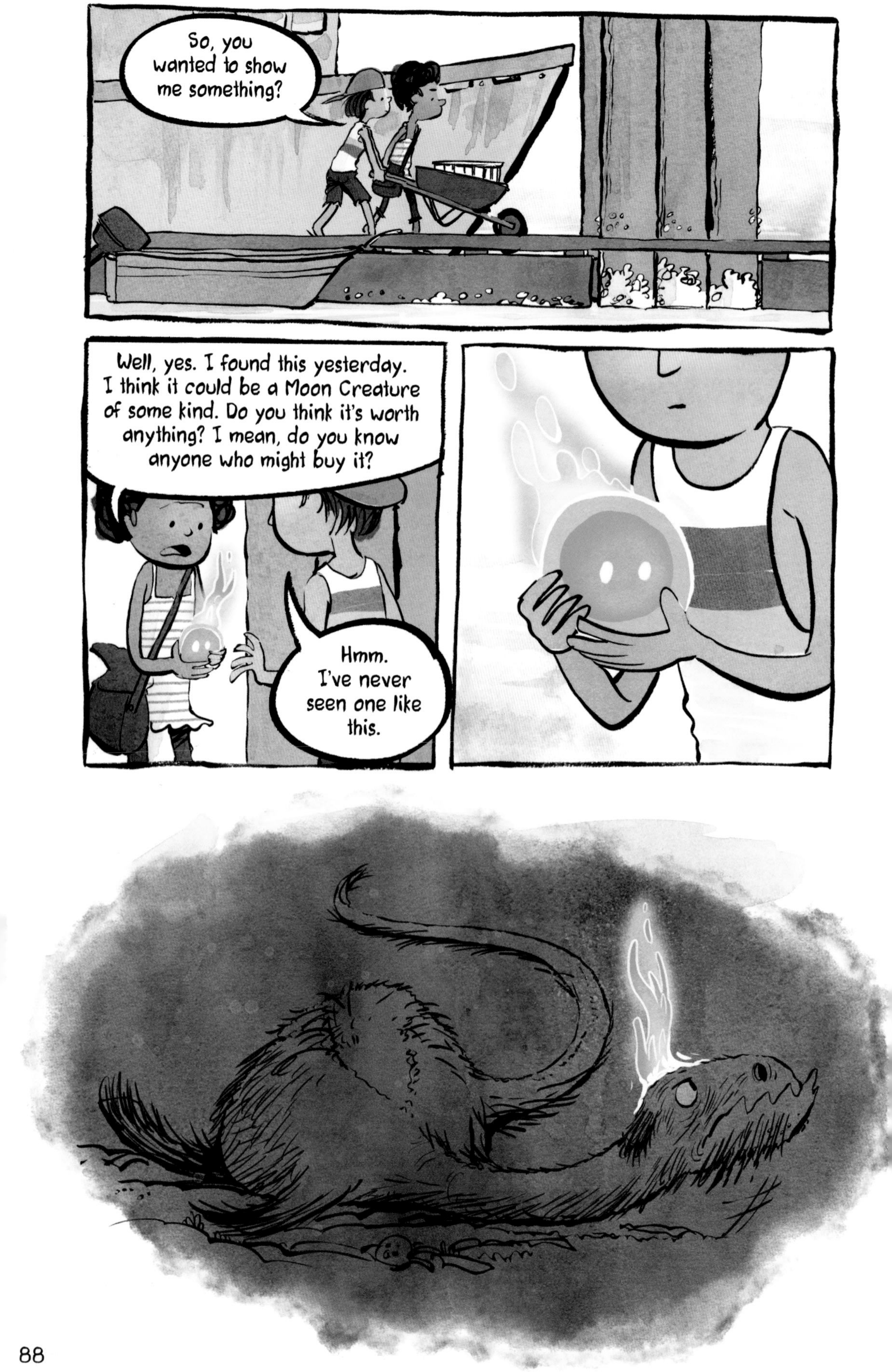
So, you wanted to show me something?
Well, yes. I found this yesterday. I think it could be a Moon Creature of some kind. Do you think it's worth anything? I mean, do you know anyone who might buy it?
Hmm. I've never seen one like this.

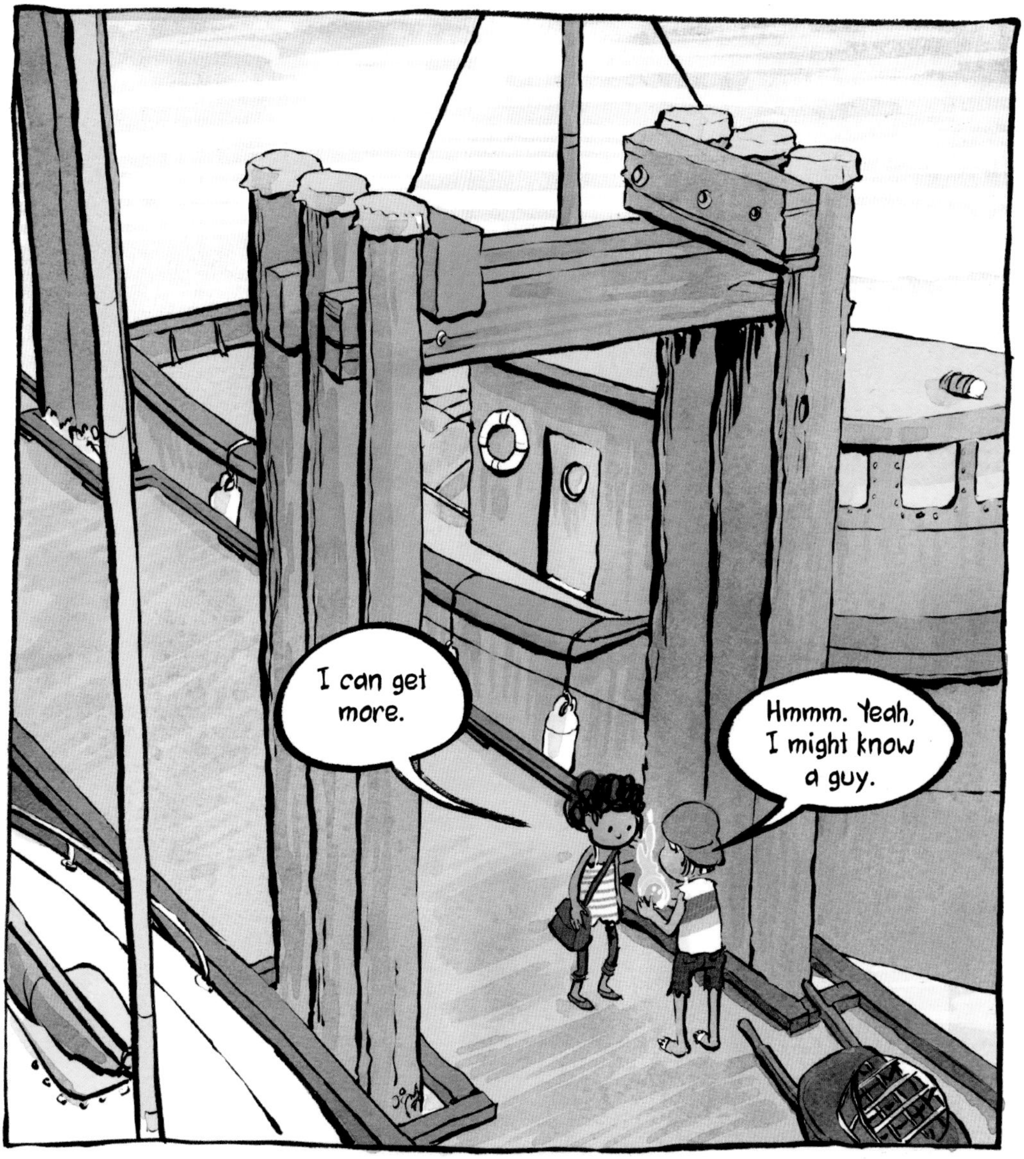
I can get more.
Hmmm. Yeah, I might know a guy.

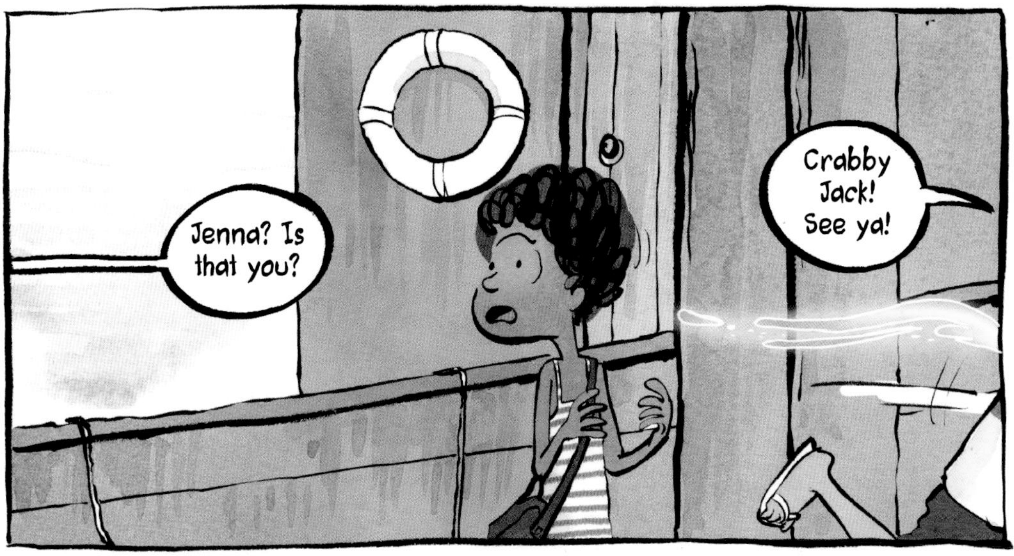
Jenna? Is that you?
Crabby Jack! See ya!

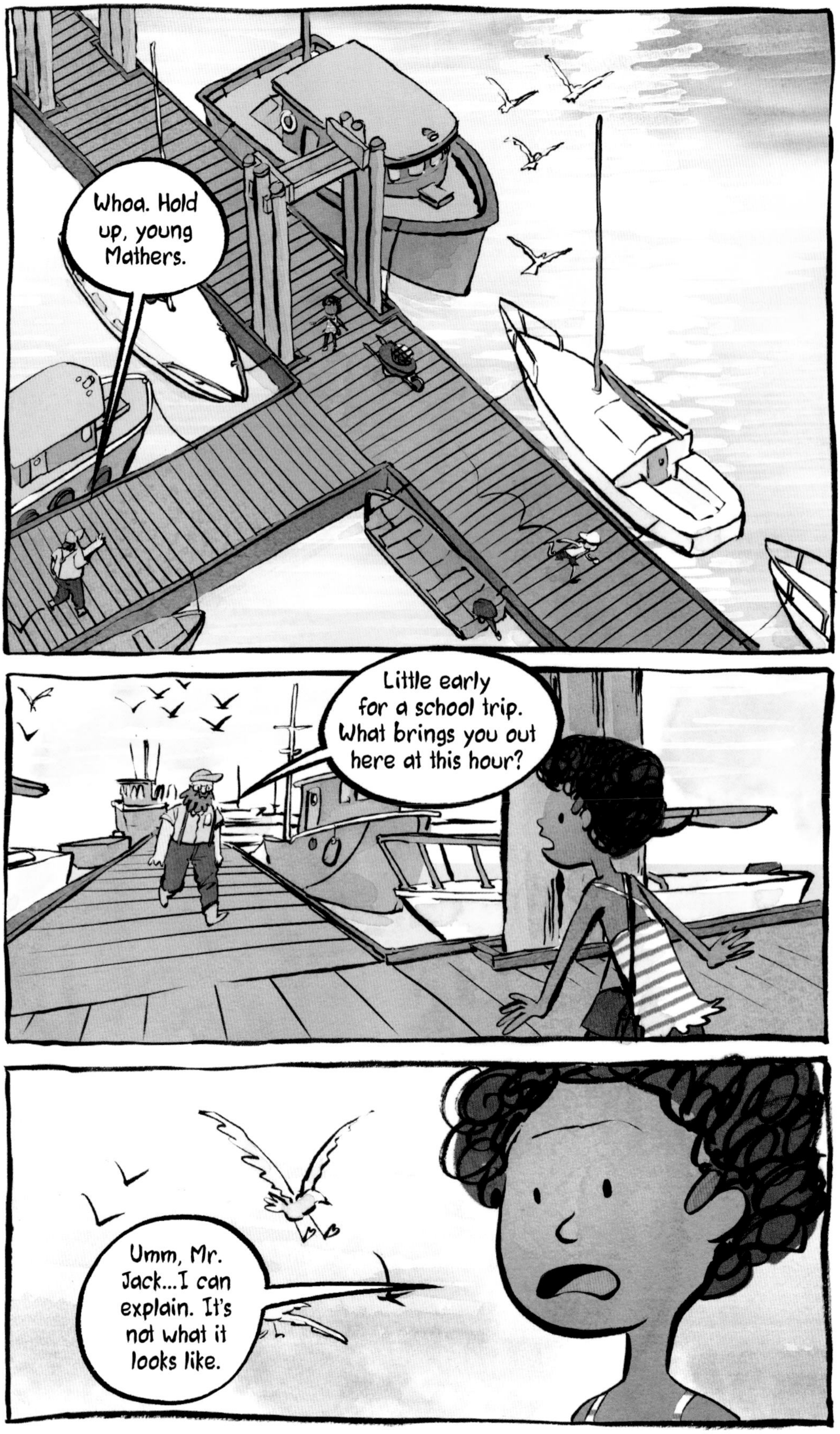
Whoa. Hold up, young Mathers.
Little early for a school trip. What brings you out here at this hour?
Umm, Mr. Jack...I can explain. It's not what it looks like.

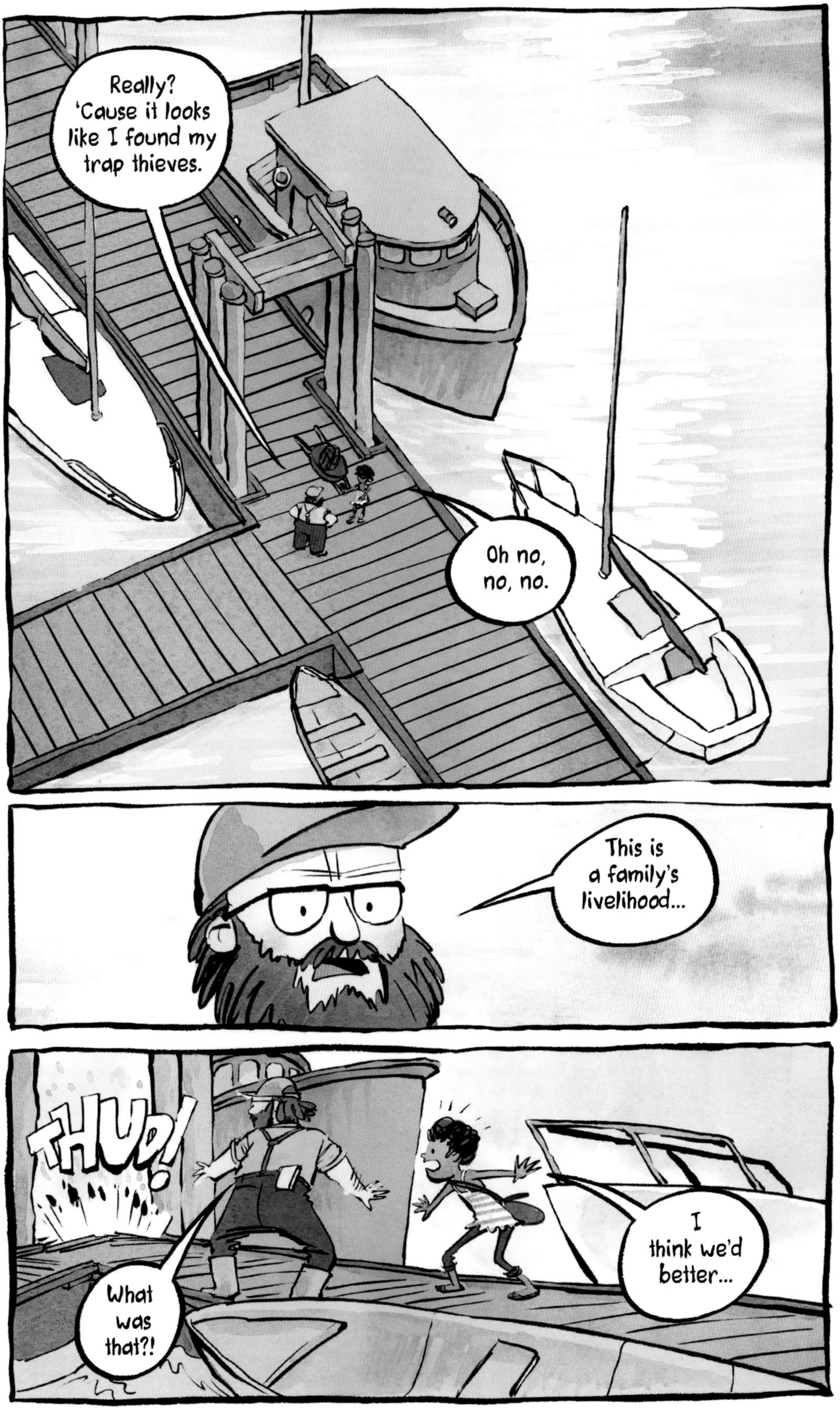
Really? 'Cause it looks like I found my trap thieves.
Oh no, no, no.
This is a family's livelihood...
THUD!
What was that?!
I think we'd better...

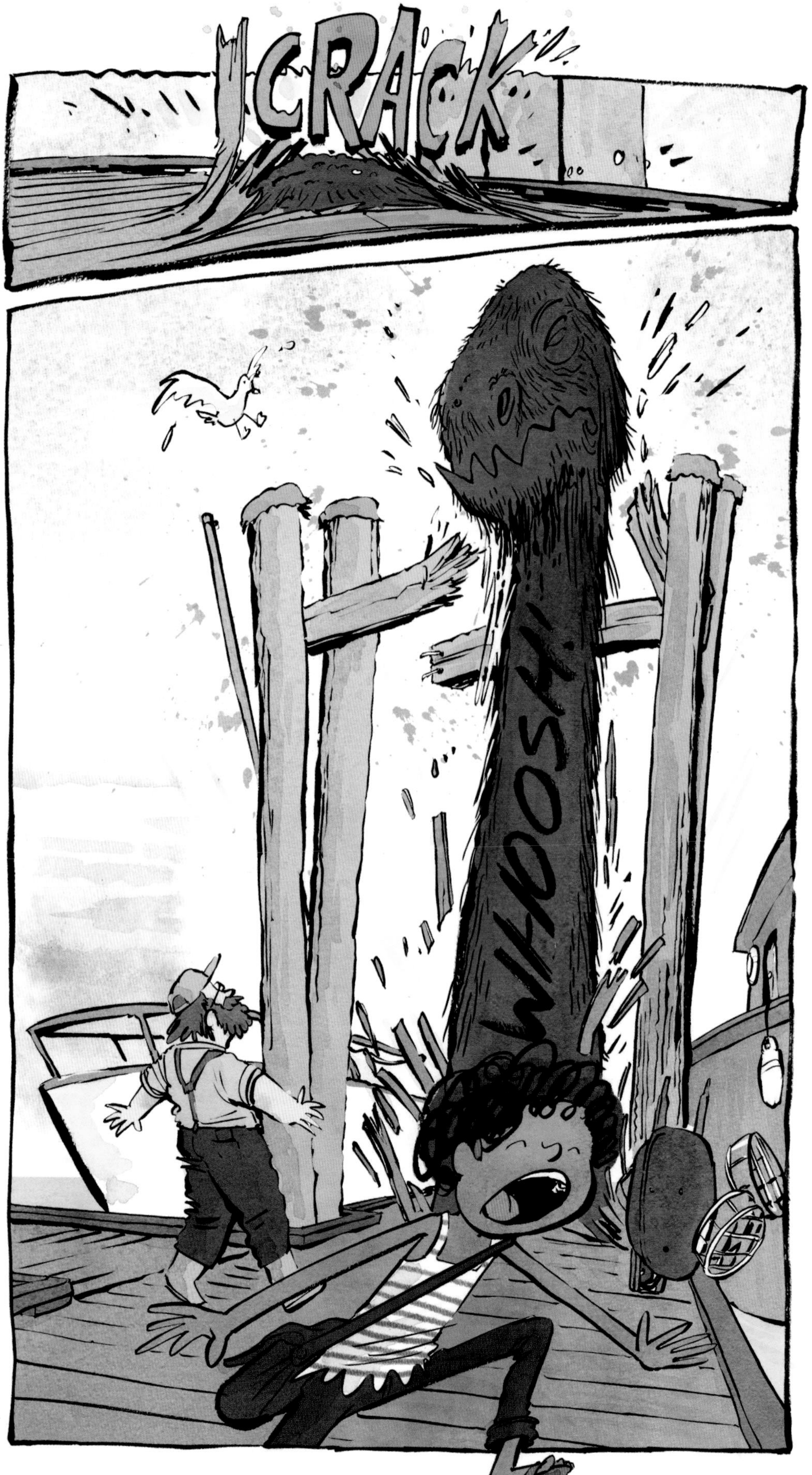
CRACK
WHOOSH!

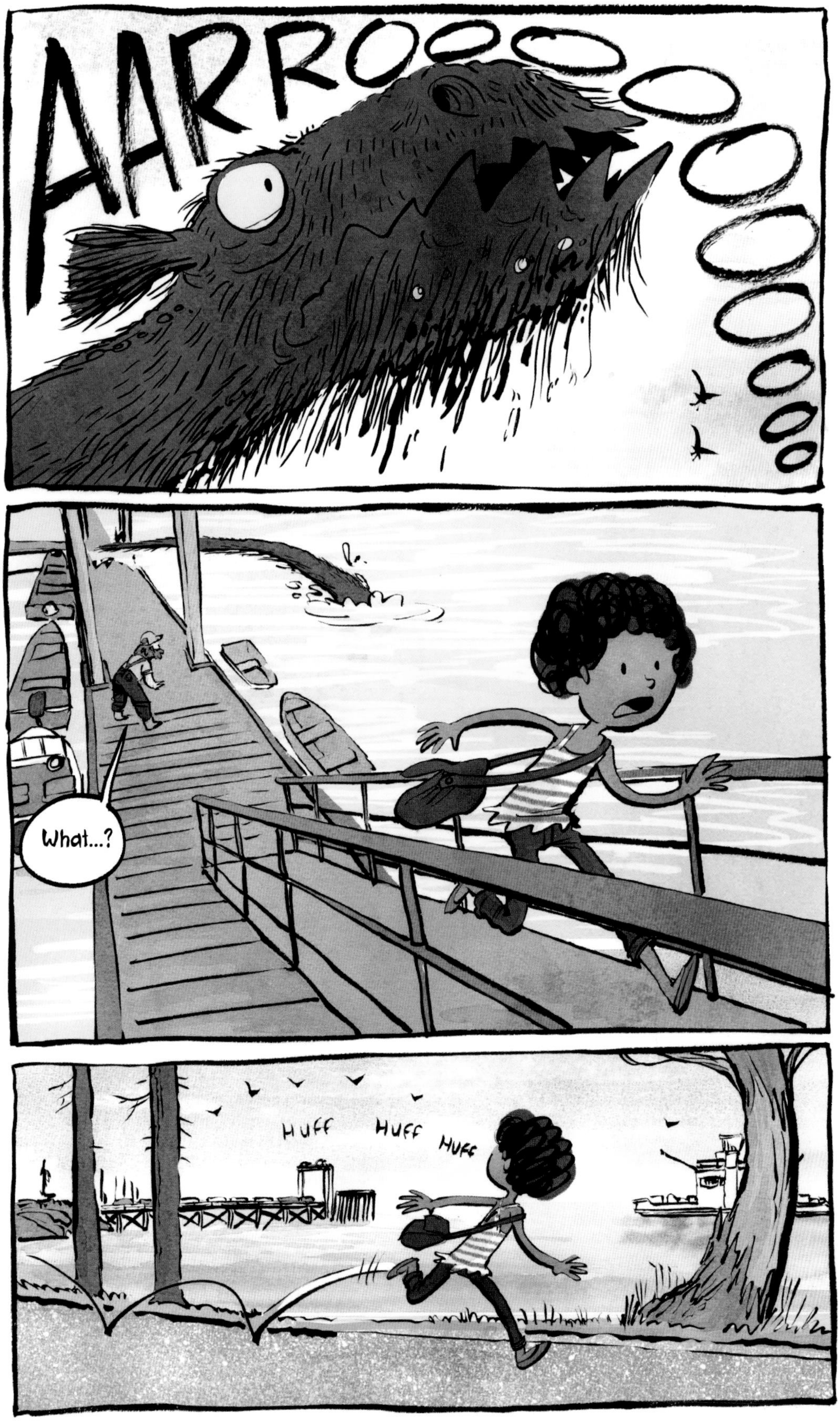
AARROOOOOOOOOOOOO
What...?
HUFF HUFF HUFF

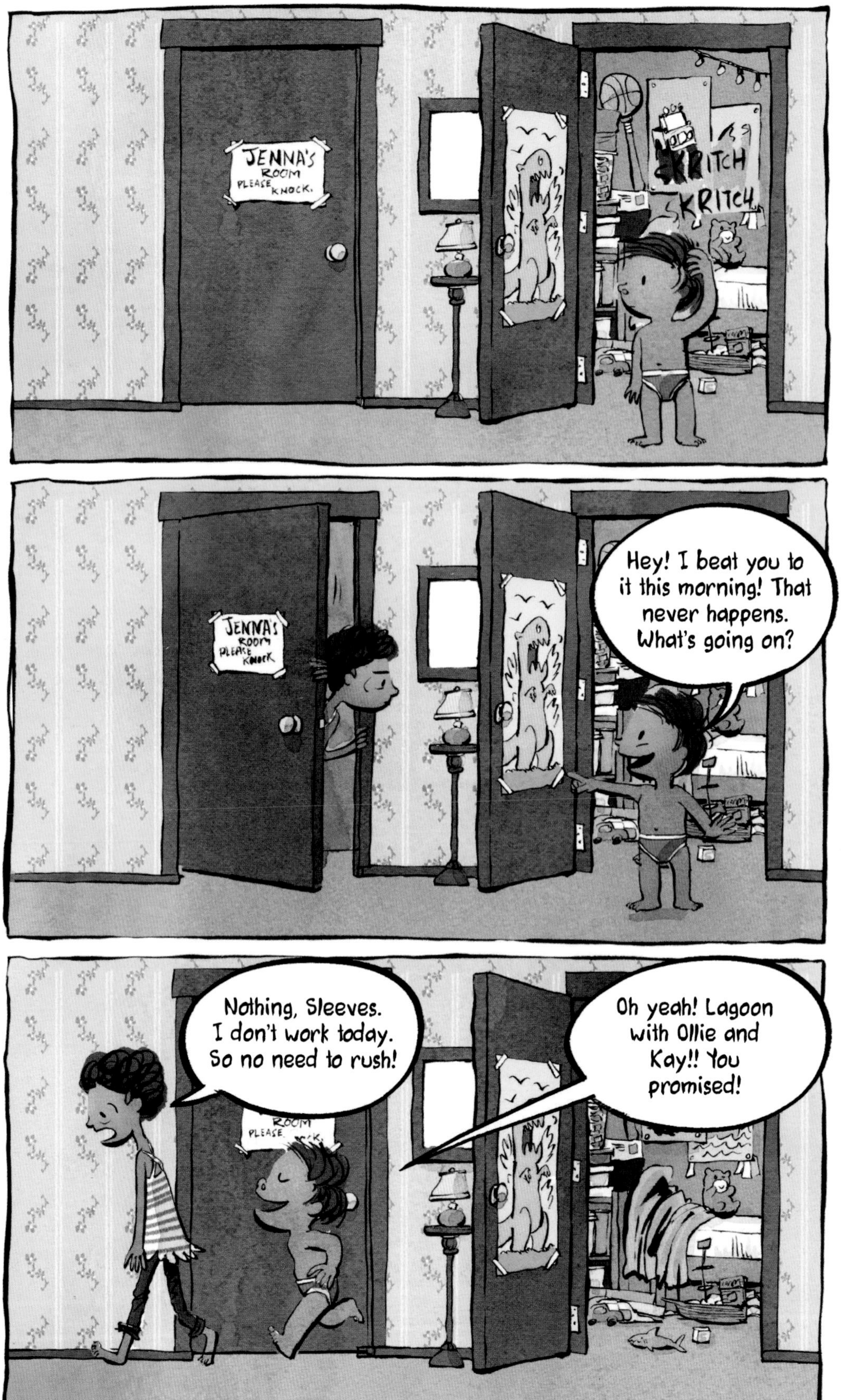
JENNA'S ROOM PLEASE KNOCK.
KRITCH KRITCH
Hey! I beat you to it this morning! That never happens. What's going on?
Nothing, Sleeves. I don't work today. So no need to rush!
Oh yeah! Lagoon with Ollie and Kay!! You promised!

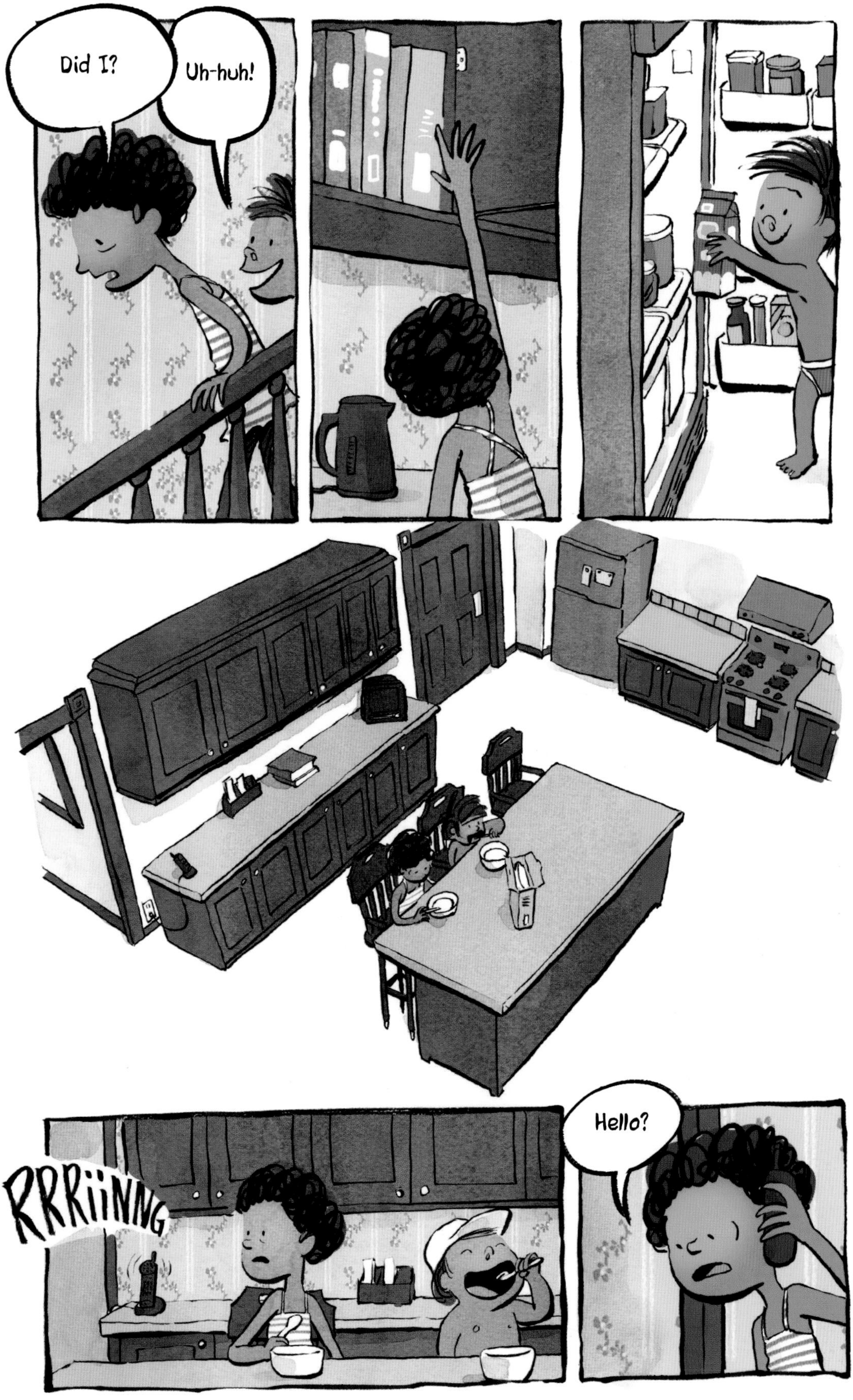
Did I?
Uh-huh!
RRRiiNNG
Hello?

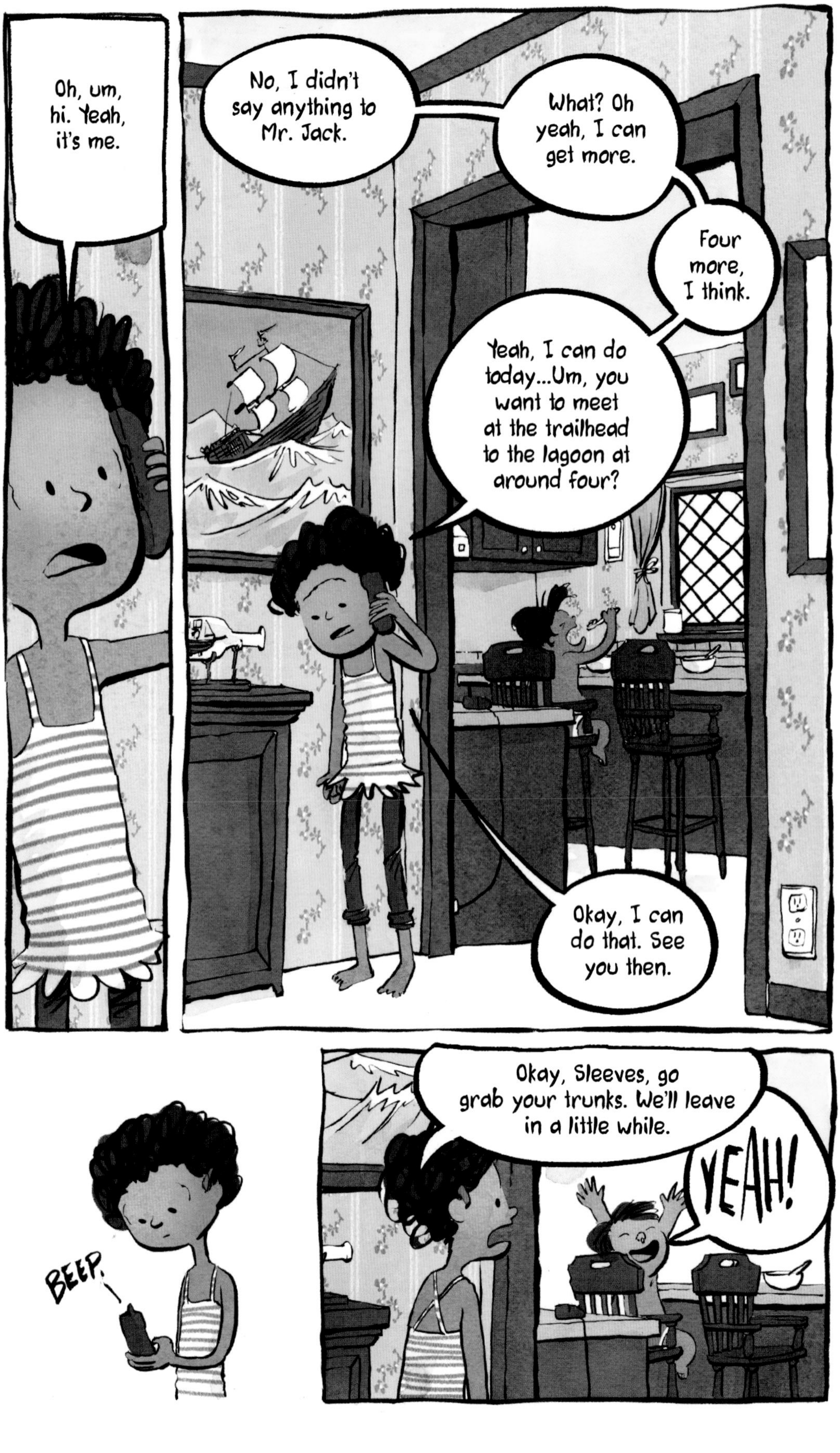
Oh, um, hi. Yeah, it's me.
No, I didn't say anything to Mr. Jack.
What? Oh yeah, I can get more.
Four more, I think.
Yeah, I can do today...Um, you want to meet at the trailhead to the lagoon at around four?
Okay, I can do that. See you then.
BEEP.
Okay, Sleeves, go grab your trunks. We'll leave in a little while.
YEAH!

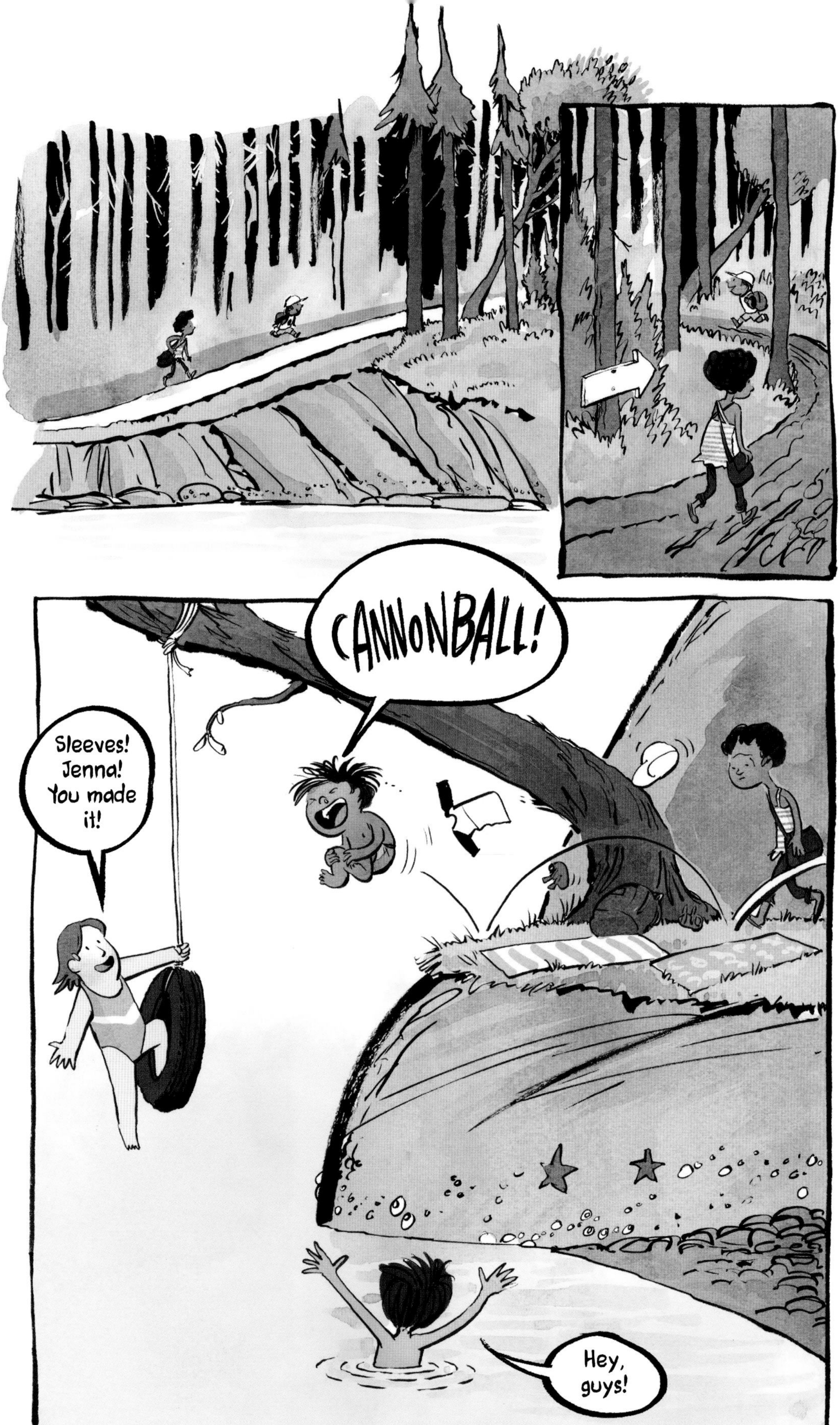
CANNONBALL!
Sleeves! Jenna! You made it!
Hey, guys!

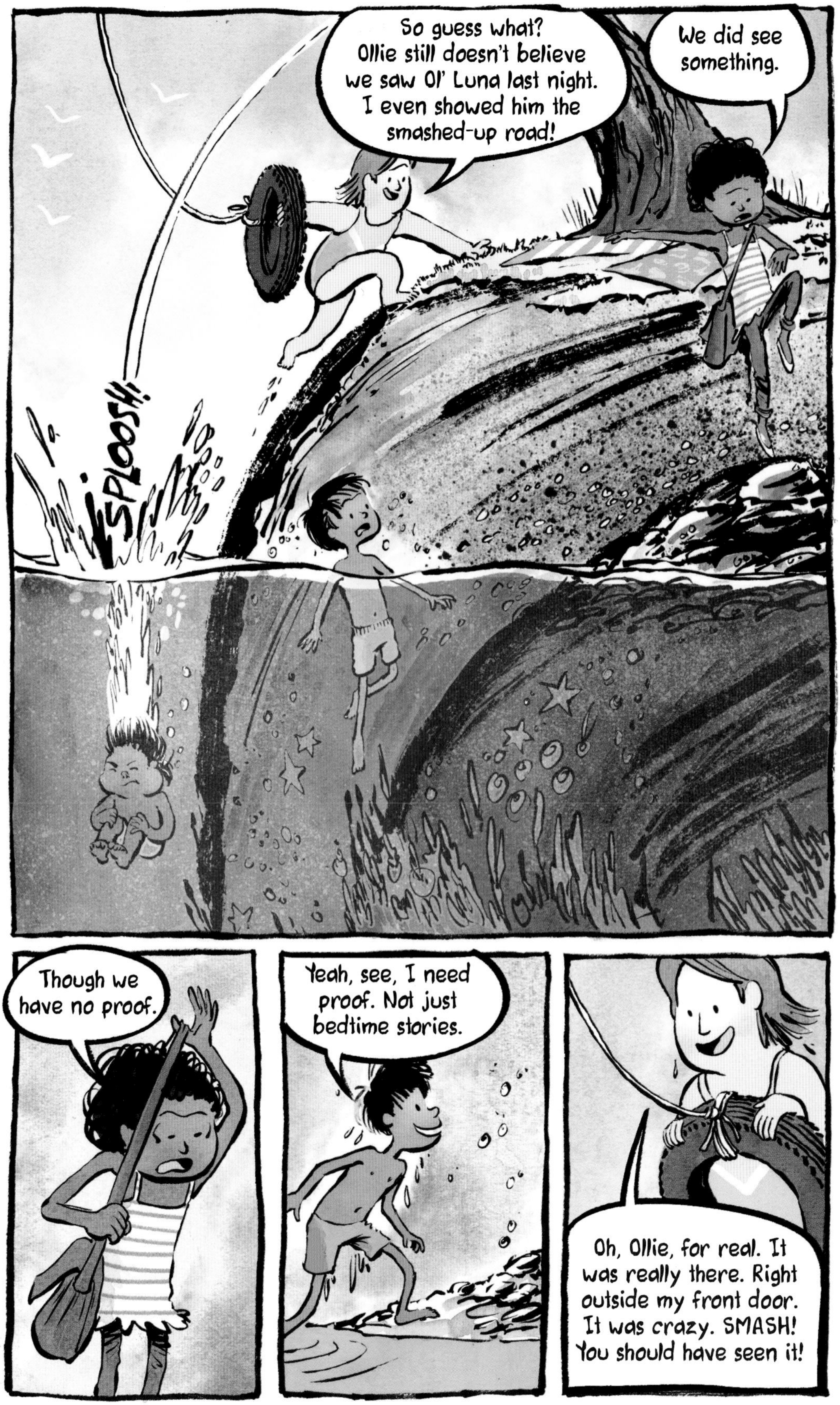
So guess what? Ollie still doesn't believe we saw Ol' Luna last night. I even showed him the smashed-up road!
We did see something.
SPLOOSH!
Though we have no proof.
Yeah, see, I need proof. Not just bedtime stories.
Oh, Ollie, for real. It was really there. Right outside my front door. It was crazy. SMASH! You should have seen it!

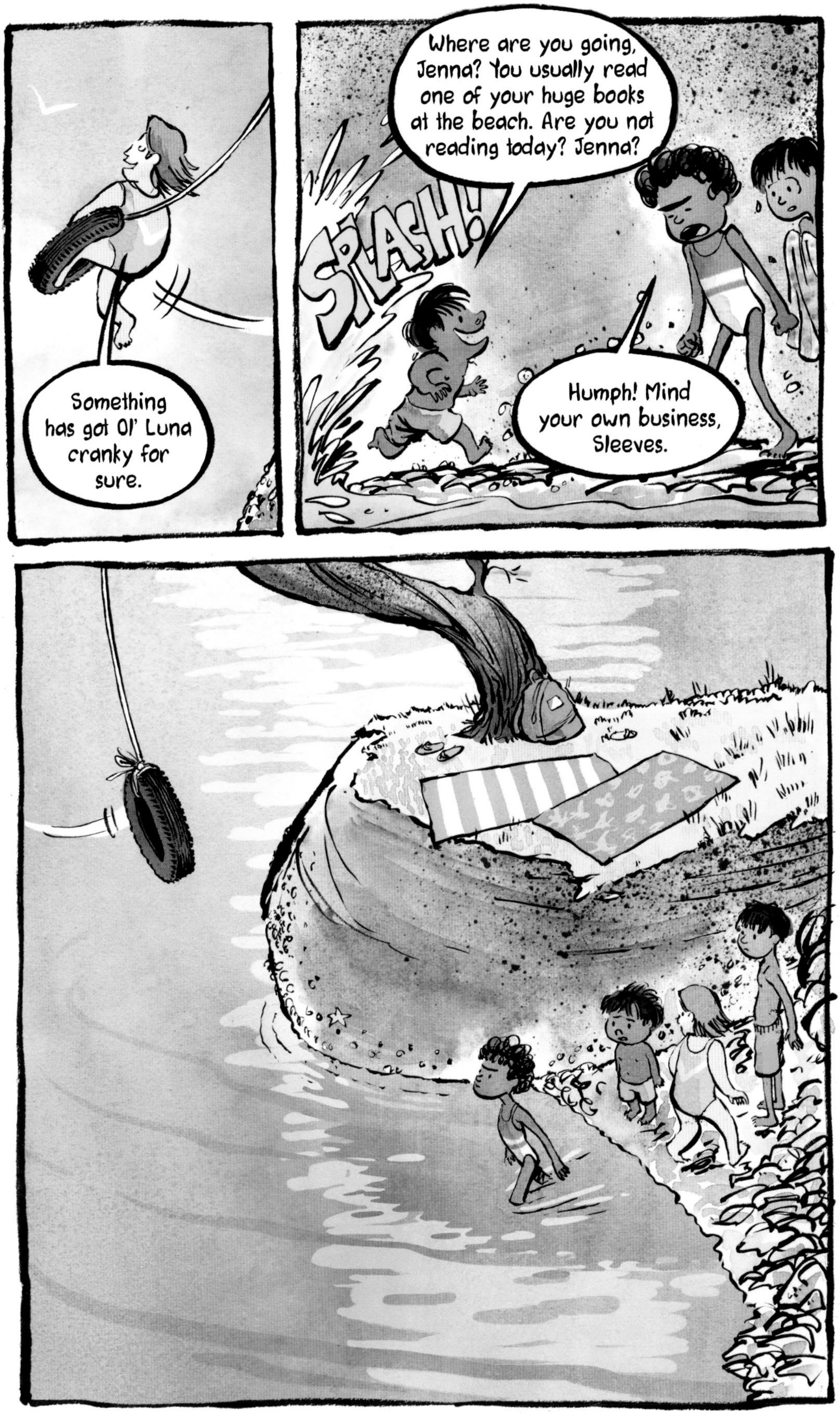

Something has got Ol' Luna cranky for sure.
Where are you going, Jenna? You usually read one of your huge books at the beach. Are you not reading today? Jenna?
SPLASH!
Humph! Mind your own business, Sleeves.

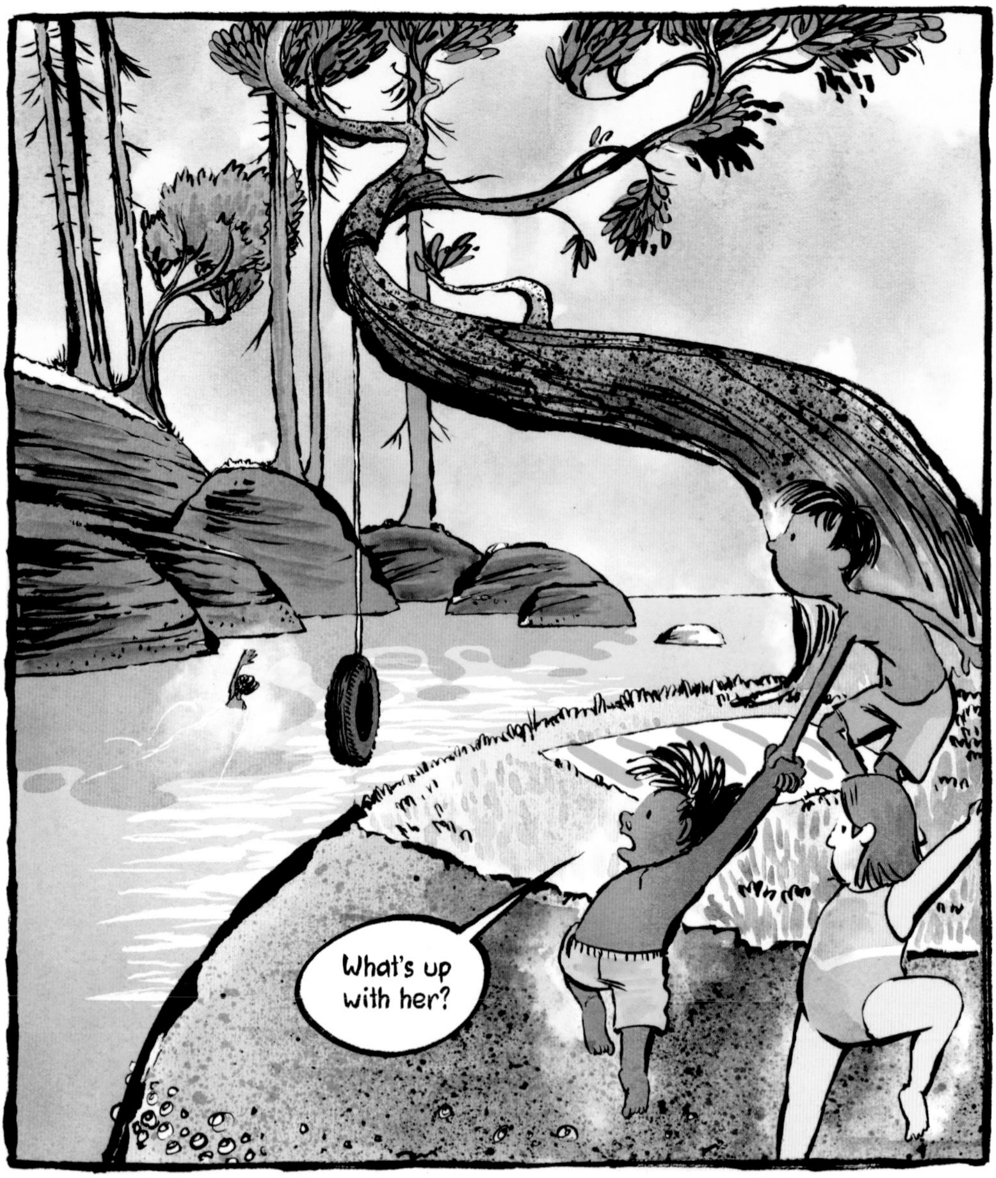
What's up with her?

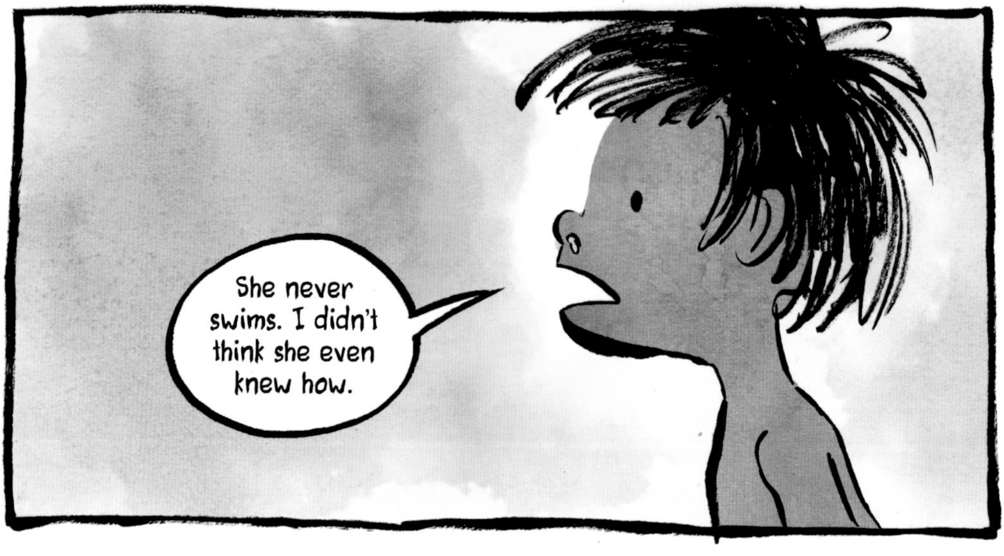
She never swims. I didn't think she even knew how.

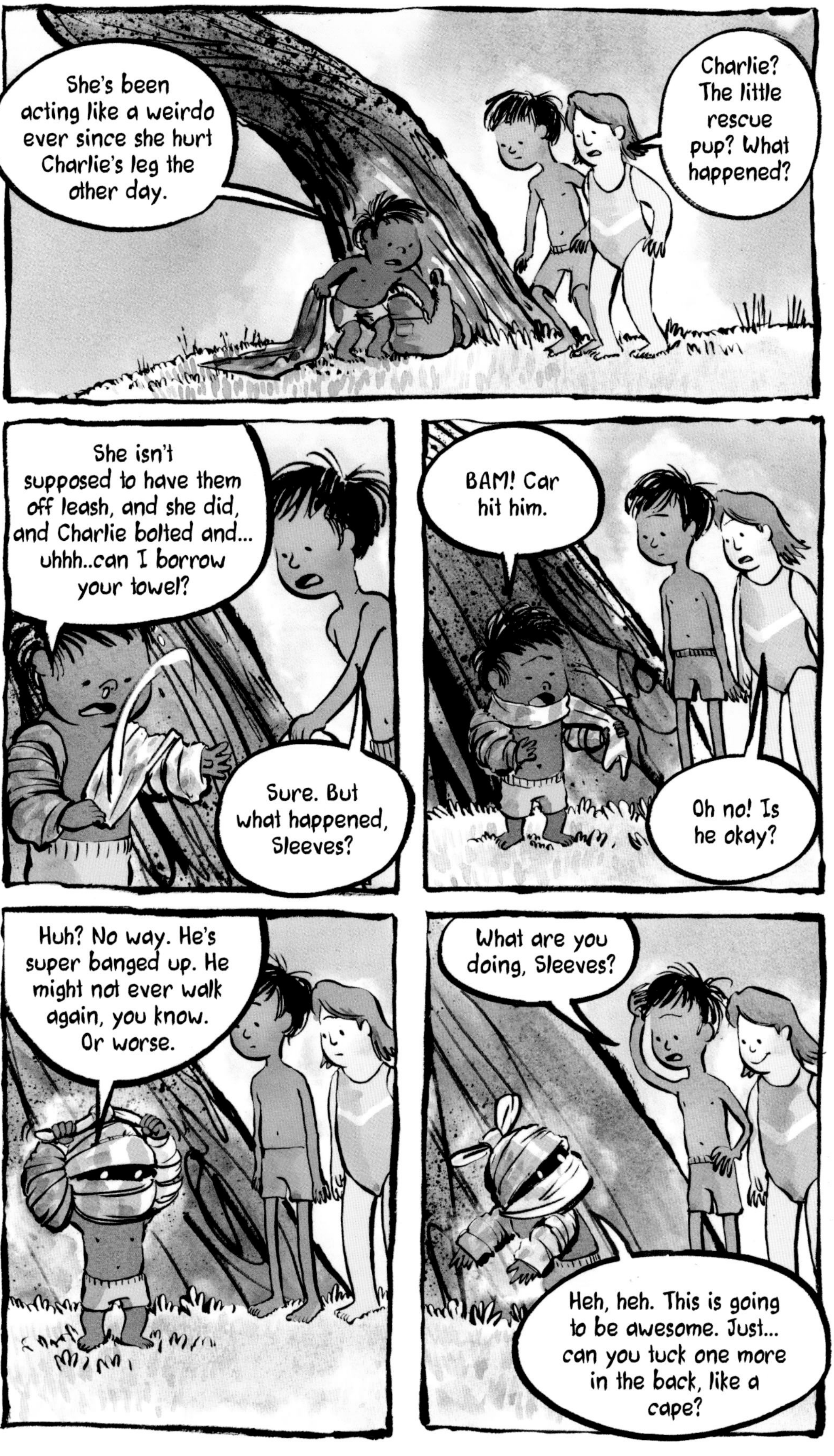

She's been acting like a weirdo ever since she hurt Charlie's leg the other day.
Charlie? The little rescue pup? What happened?
She isn't supposed to have them off leash, and she did, and Charlie bolted and... uhhh..can I borrow your towel?
Sure. But what happened, Sleeves?
BAM! Car hit him.
Oh no! Is he okay?
Huh? No way. He's super banged up. He might not ever walk again, you know. Or worse.
What are you doing, Sleeves?
Heh, heh. This is going to be awesome. Just... can you tuck one more in the back, like a cape?

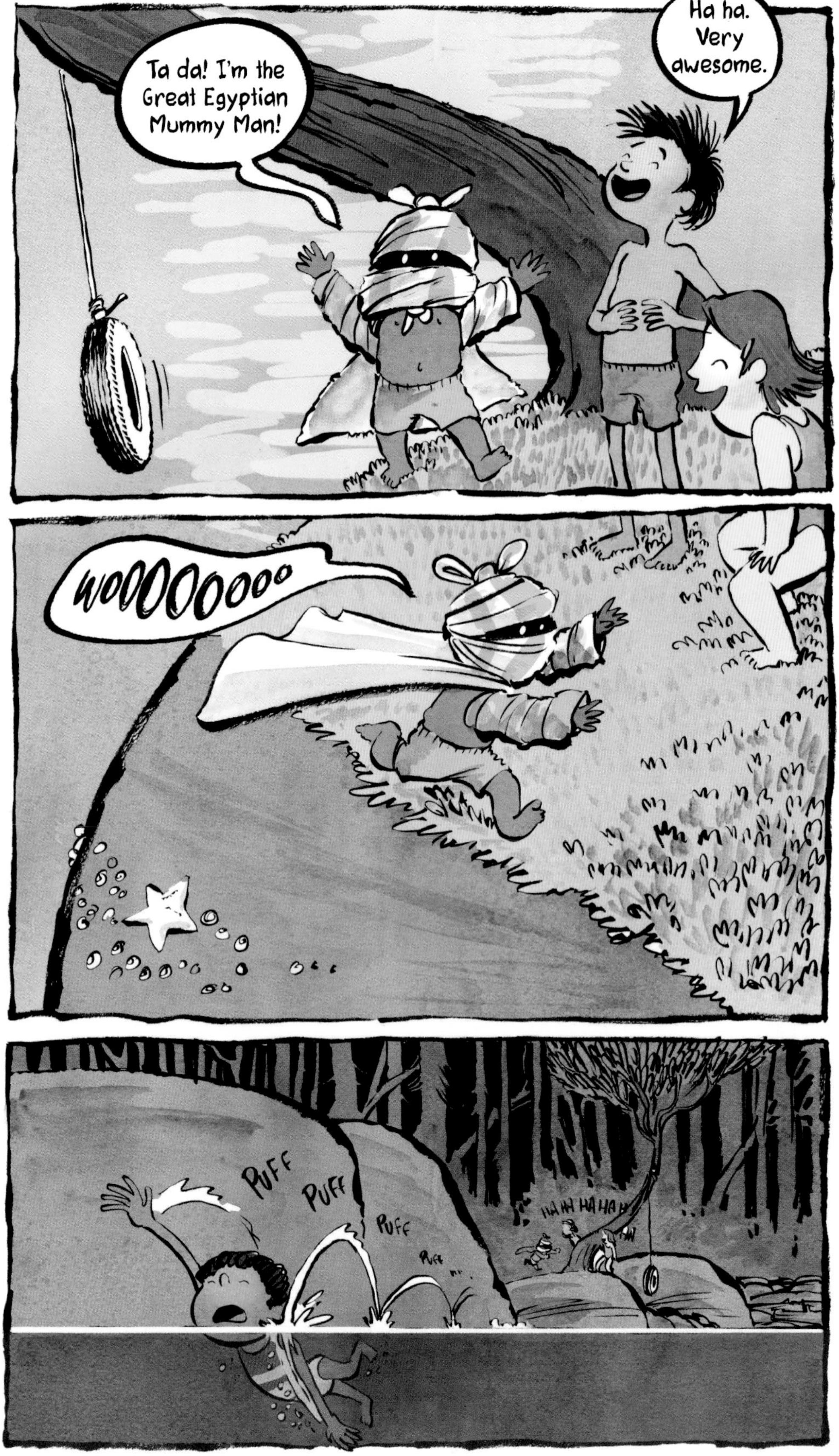
Ta da! I'm the Great Egyptian Mummy Man!
Ha ha. Very awesome.
WOOOOOOOo
PUFF
PUFF
PUFF
PUFF
HA HA HA HA

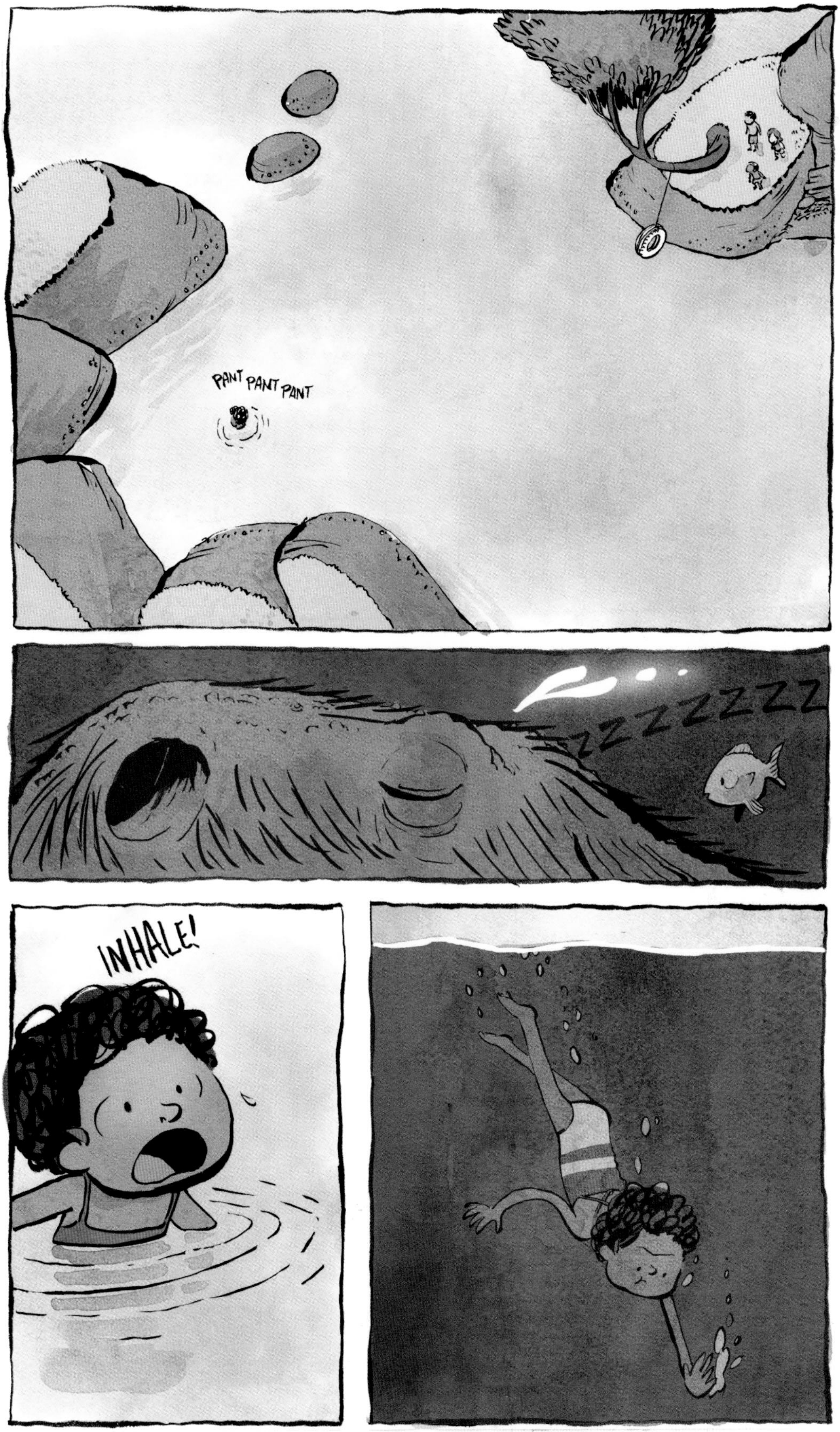
PANT PANT PANT
ZZZZZZZZZ
INHALE!

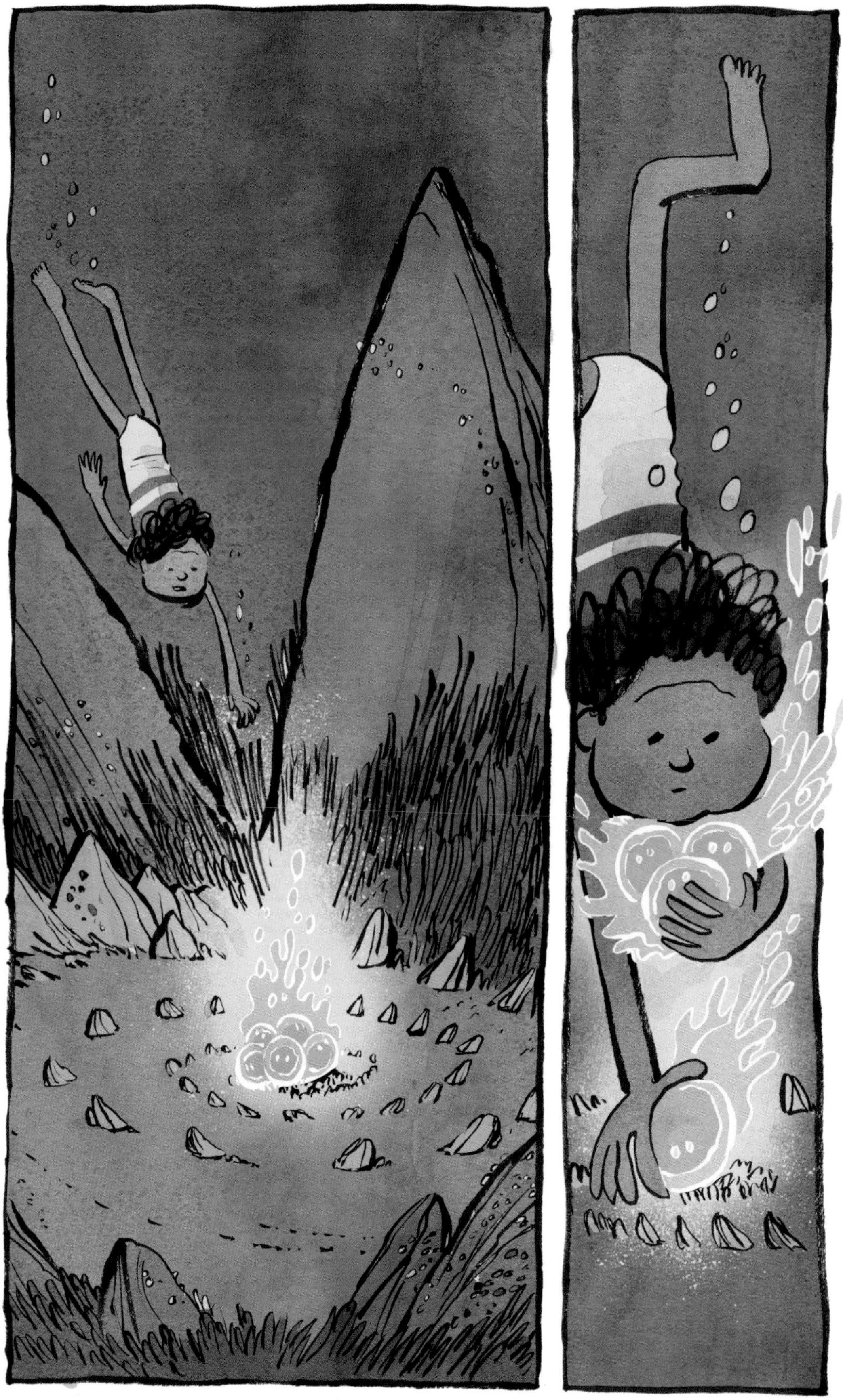

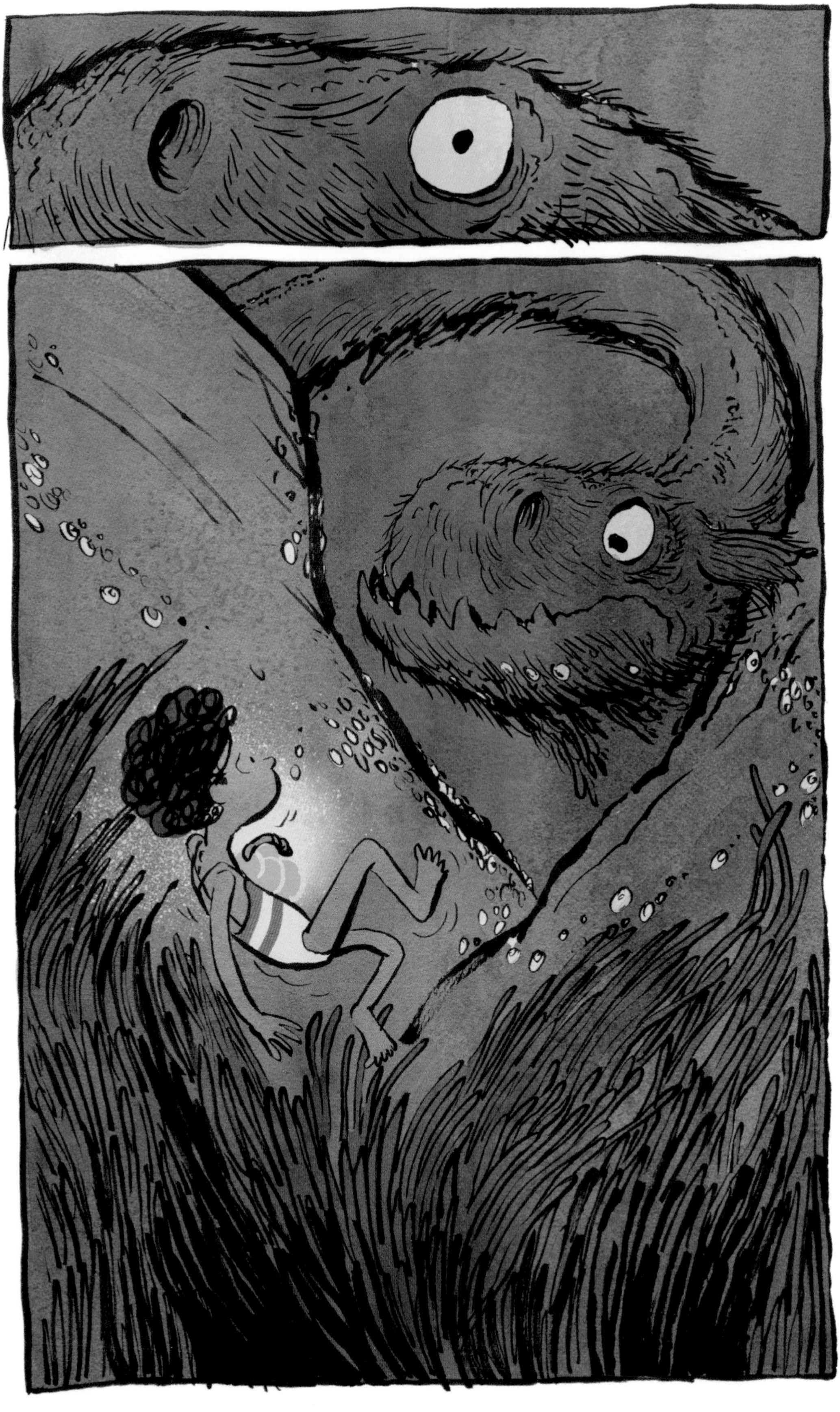

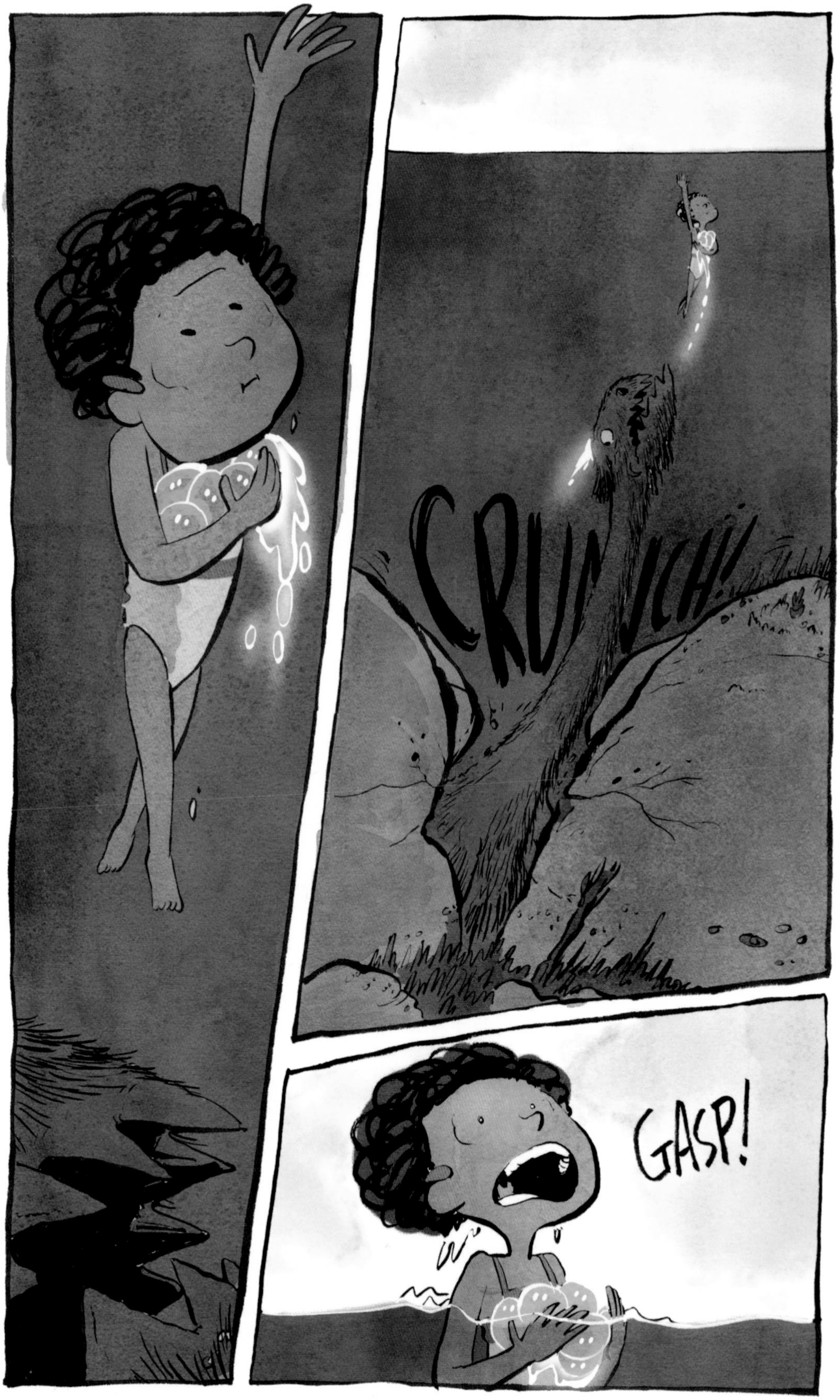
CRUNCH!
GASP!

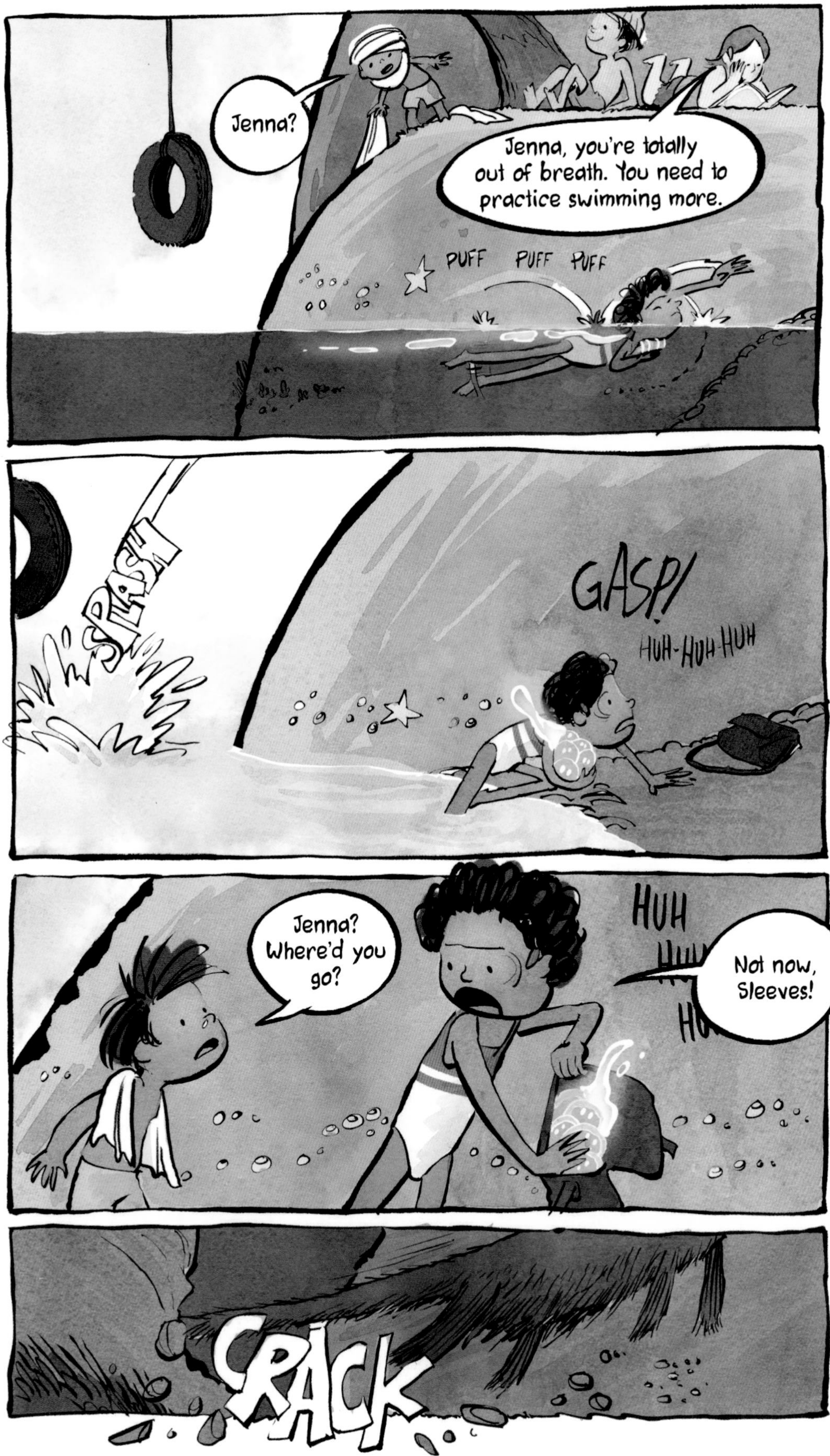

Jenna?
Jenna, you're totally out of breath. You need to practice swimming more.
PUFF PUFF PUFF
SPLASH
GASP!
HUH-HUH-HUH
Jenna? Where'd you go?
HUH
Not now, Sleeves!
CRACK

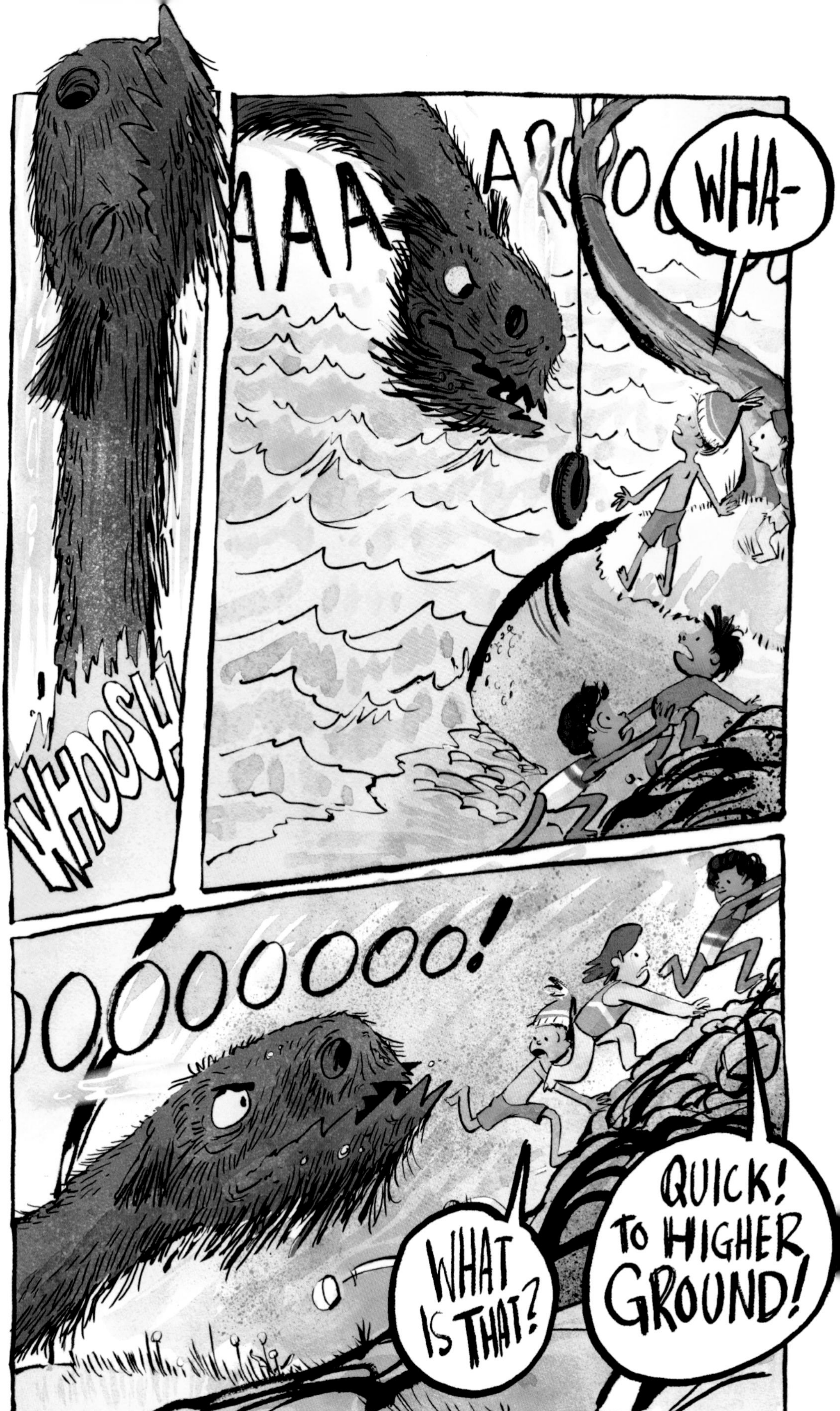
WHOOSH!
AAAAROOO
WHA-
OOOOOOOOOO!
WHAT IS THAT?
QUICK! TO HIGHER GROUND!

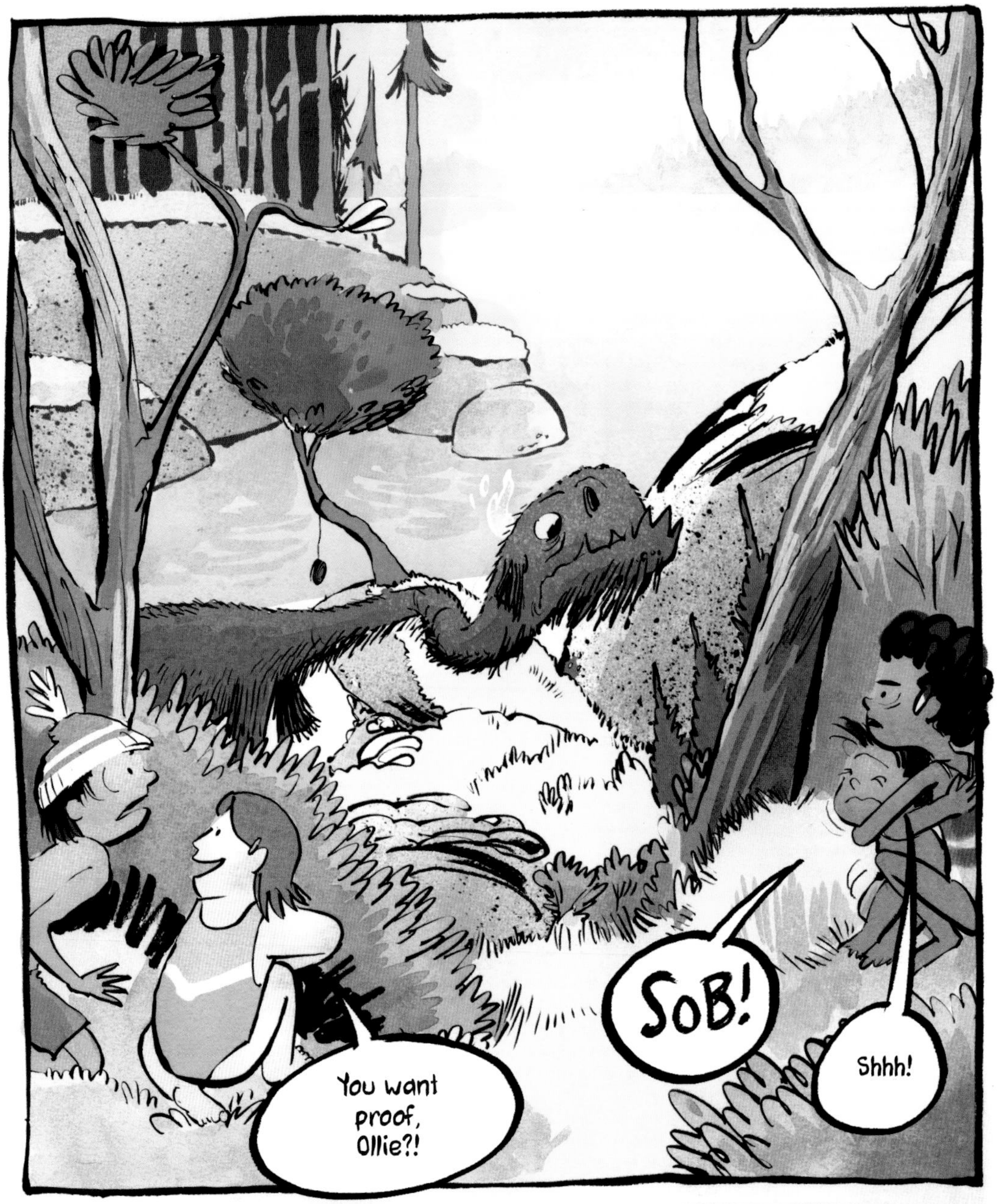
You want proof, Ollie?!
SOB!
Shhh!

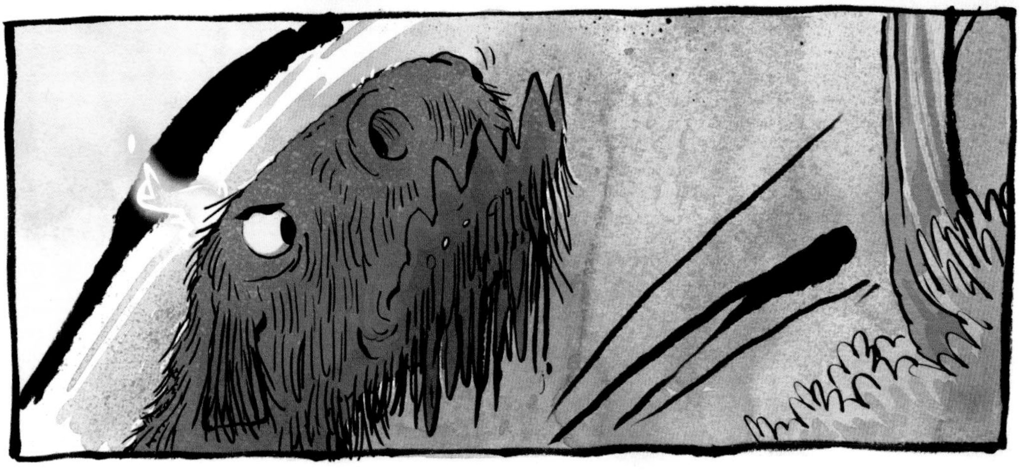

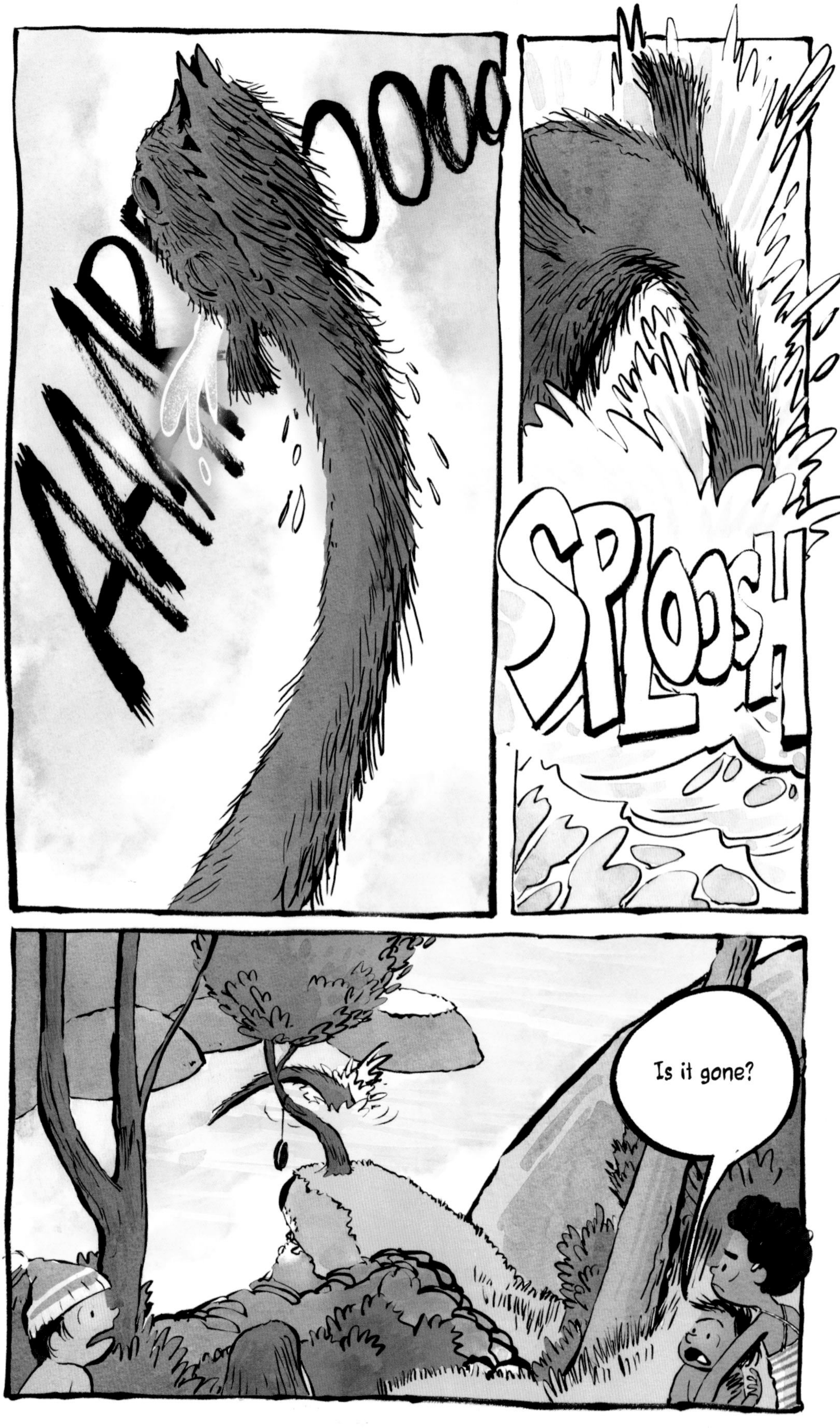
AHROOOOO
SPLOOSH
Is it gone?

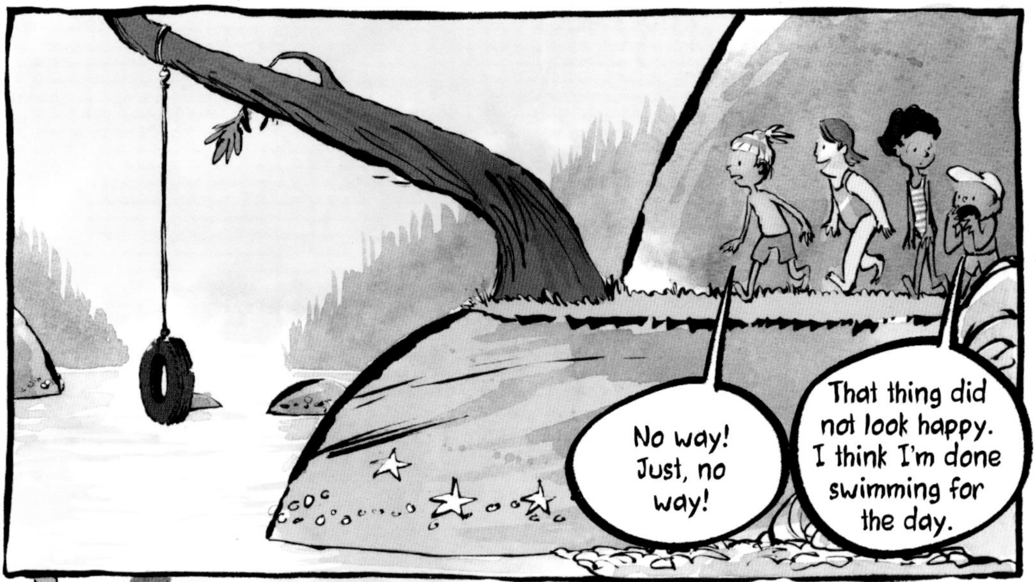
No way! Just, no way!
That thing did not look happy. I think I'm done swimming for the day.

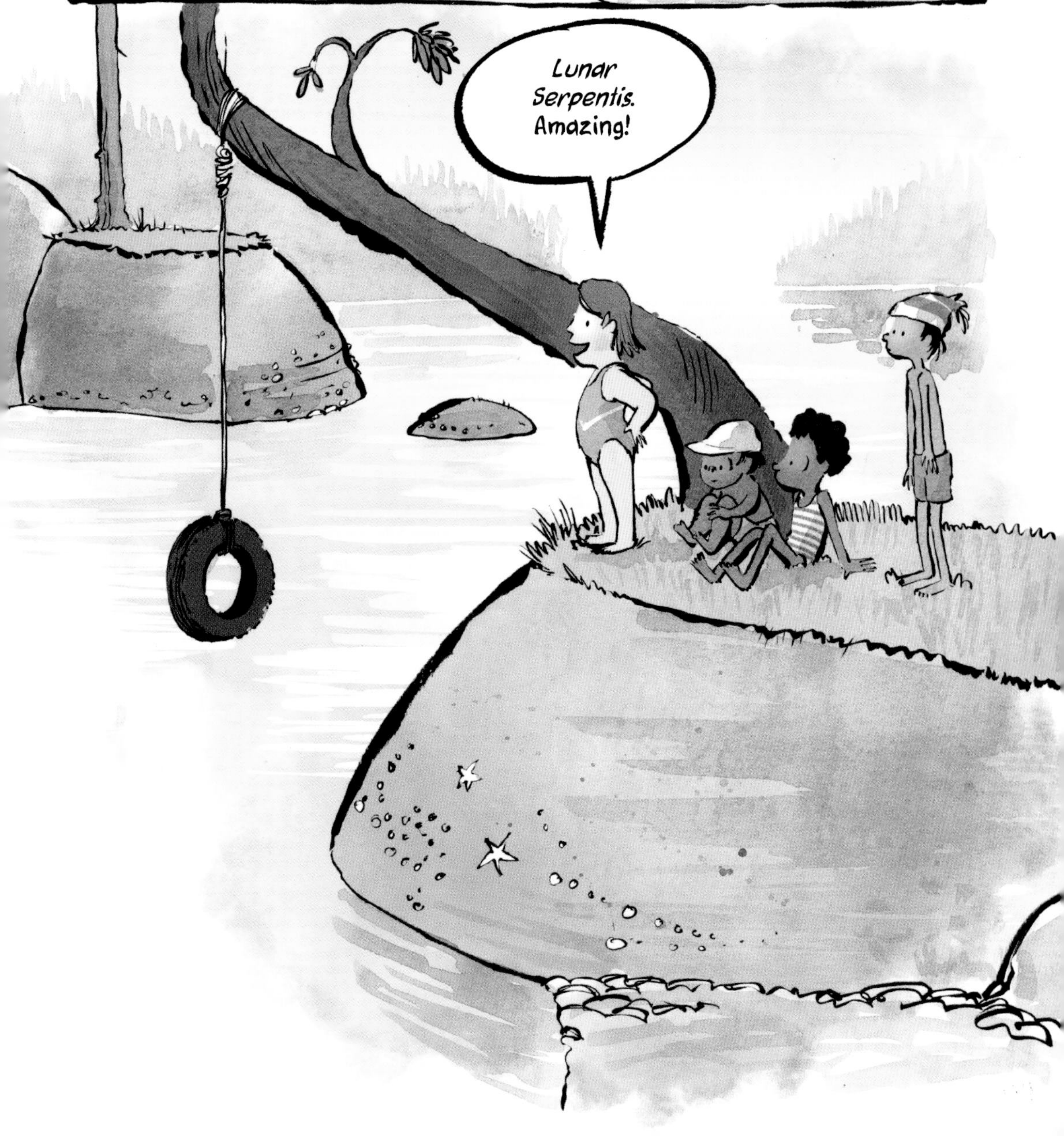
Lunar Serpentis. Amazing!

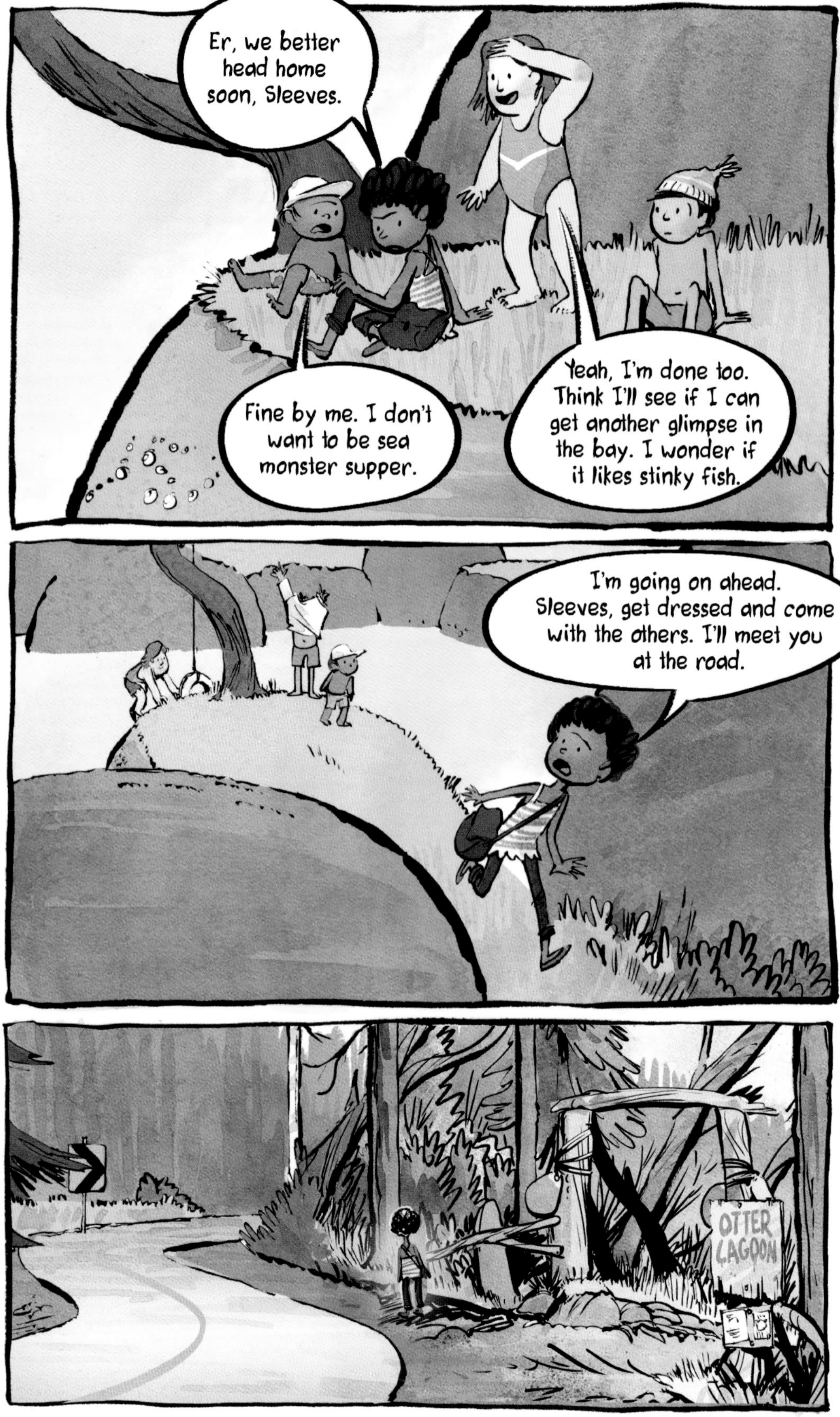
Er, we better head home soon, Sleeves.
Fine by me. I don't want to be sea monster supper.
Yeah, I'm done too. Think I'll see if I can get another glimpse in the bay. I wonder if it likes stinky fish.
I'm going on ahead. Sleeves, get dressed and come with the others. I'll meet you at the road.
OTTER LAGOON

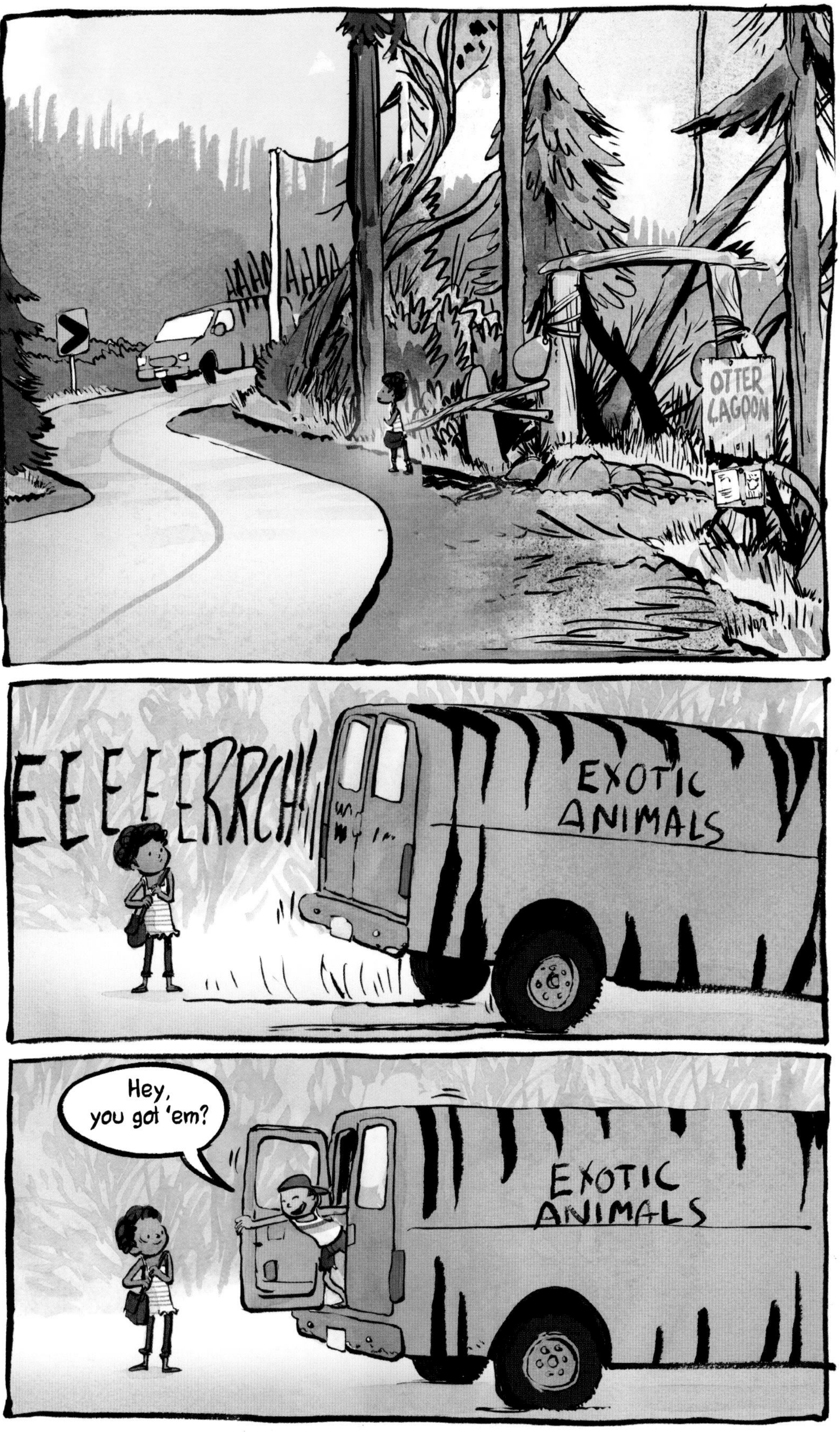
AAAAAAHAAA
OTTER LAGOON
EEEEERRCH!!
EXOTIC ANIMALS
Hey, you got 'em?
EXOTIC ANIMALS

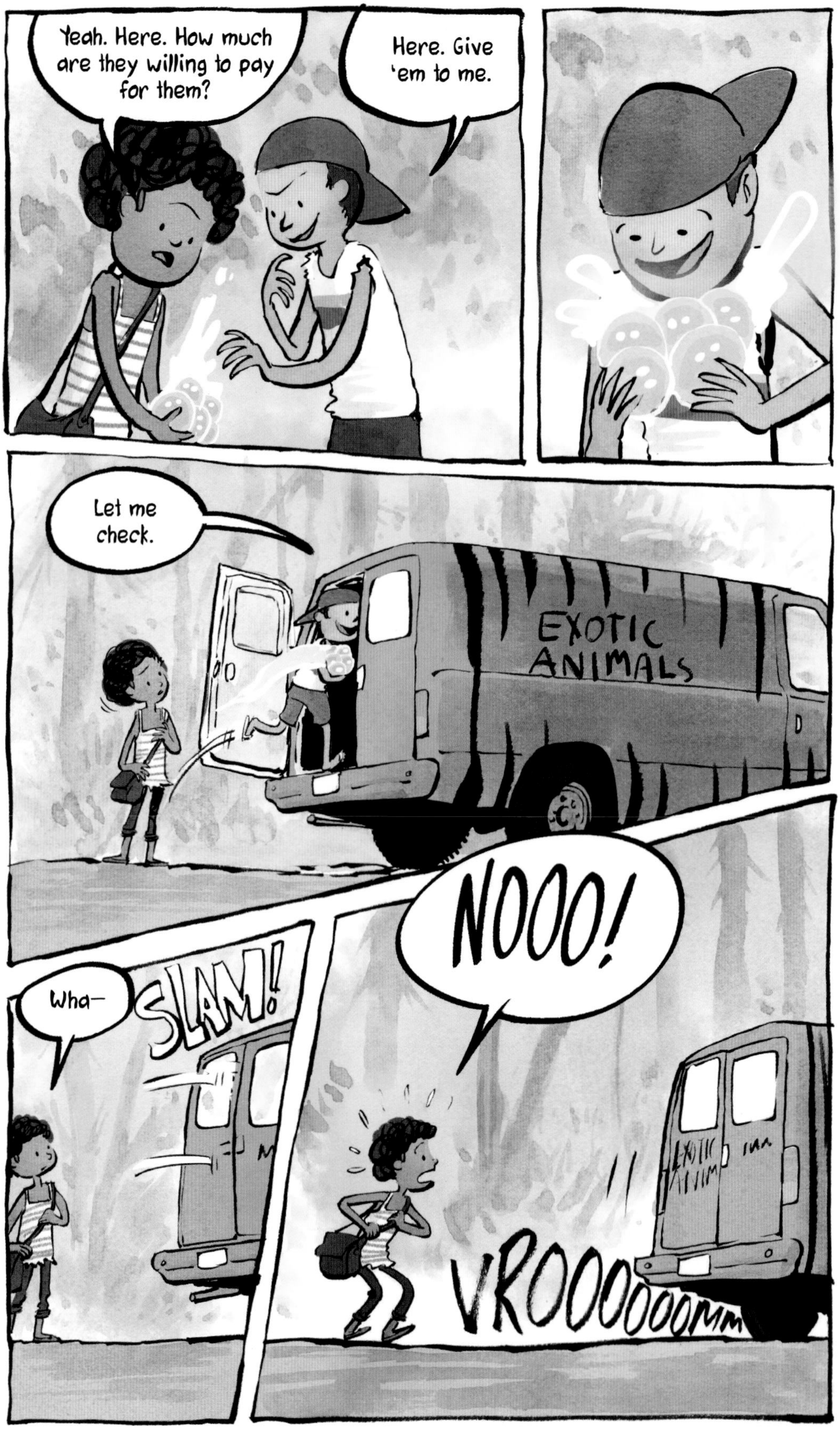
Yeah. Here. How much are they willing to pay for them?
Here. Give 'em to me.
Let me check.
EXOTIC ANIMALS
Wha—
SLAM!
NOOO!
VROOOOOOMM

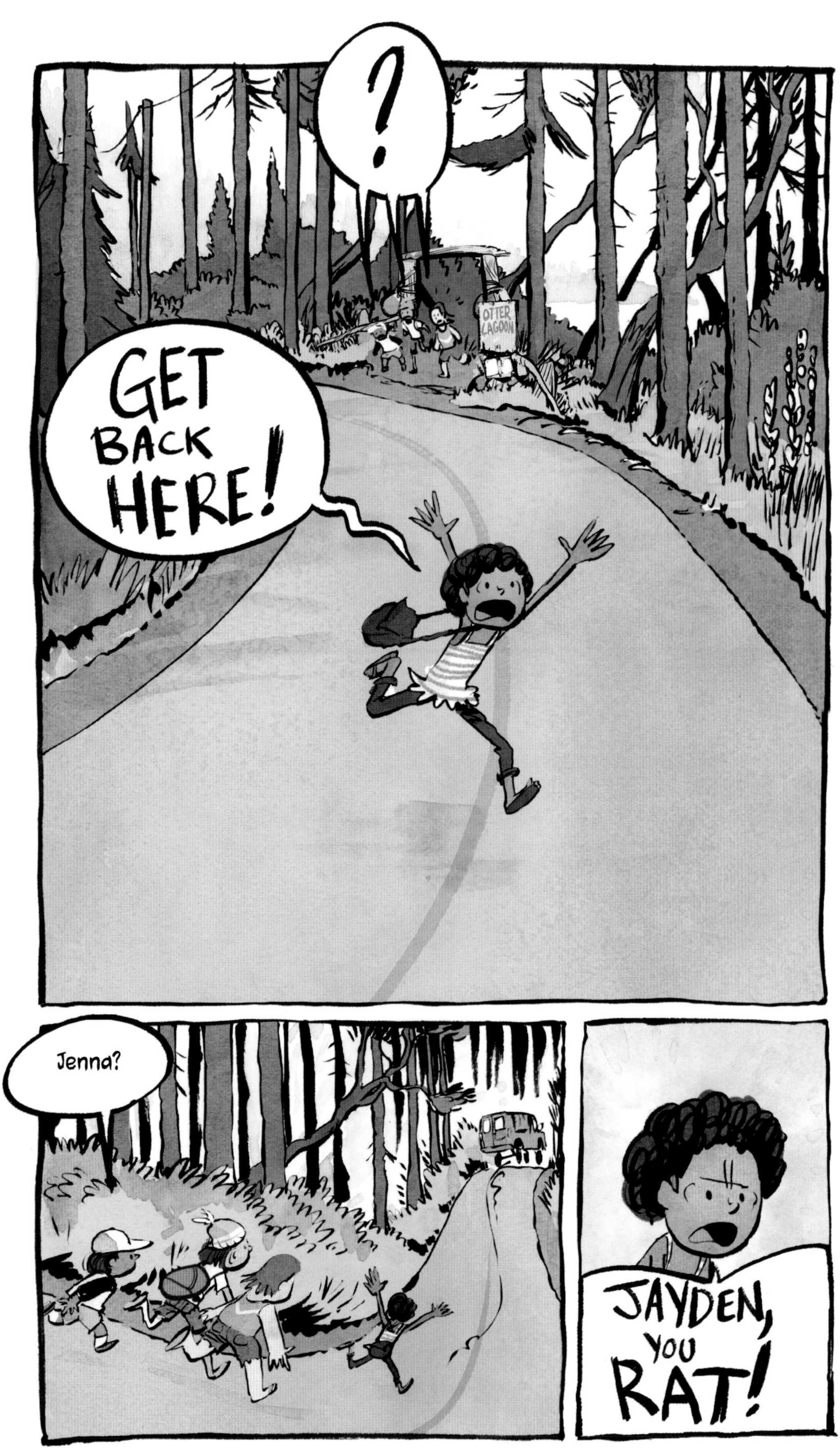
?
OTTER LAGOON
GET BACK HERE!
Jenna?
JAYDEN, YOU RAT!

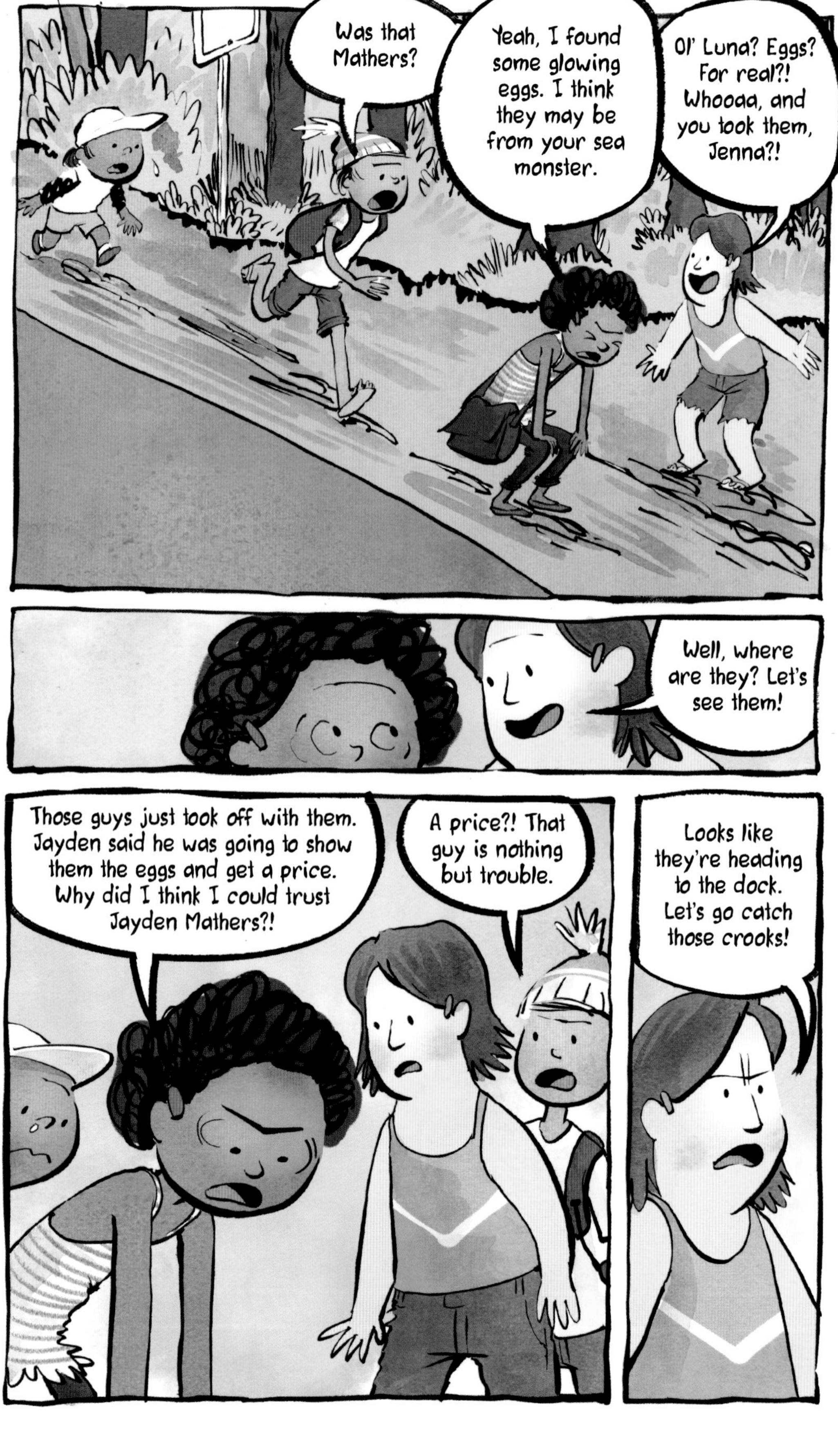
Was that Mathers?
Yeah, I found some glowing eggs. I think they may be from your sea monster.
Ol' Luna? Eggs? For real?! Whooaa, and you took them, Jenna?!
Well, where are they? Let's see them!
Those guys just took off with them. Jayden said he was going to show them the eggs and get a price. Why did I think I could trust Jayden Mathers?!
A price?! That guy is nothing but trouble.
Looks like they're heading to the dock. Let's go catch those crooks!

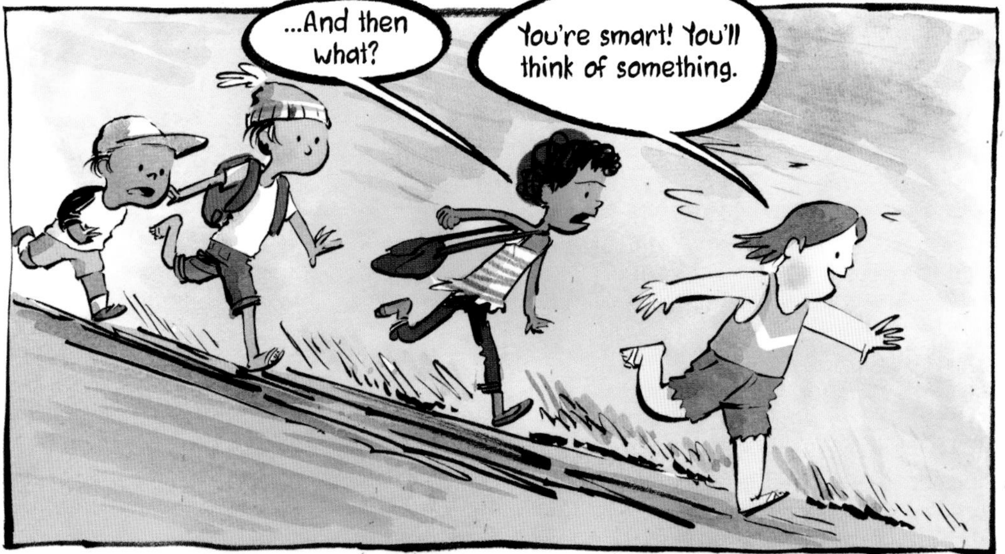
...And then what?
You're smart! You'll think of something.

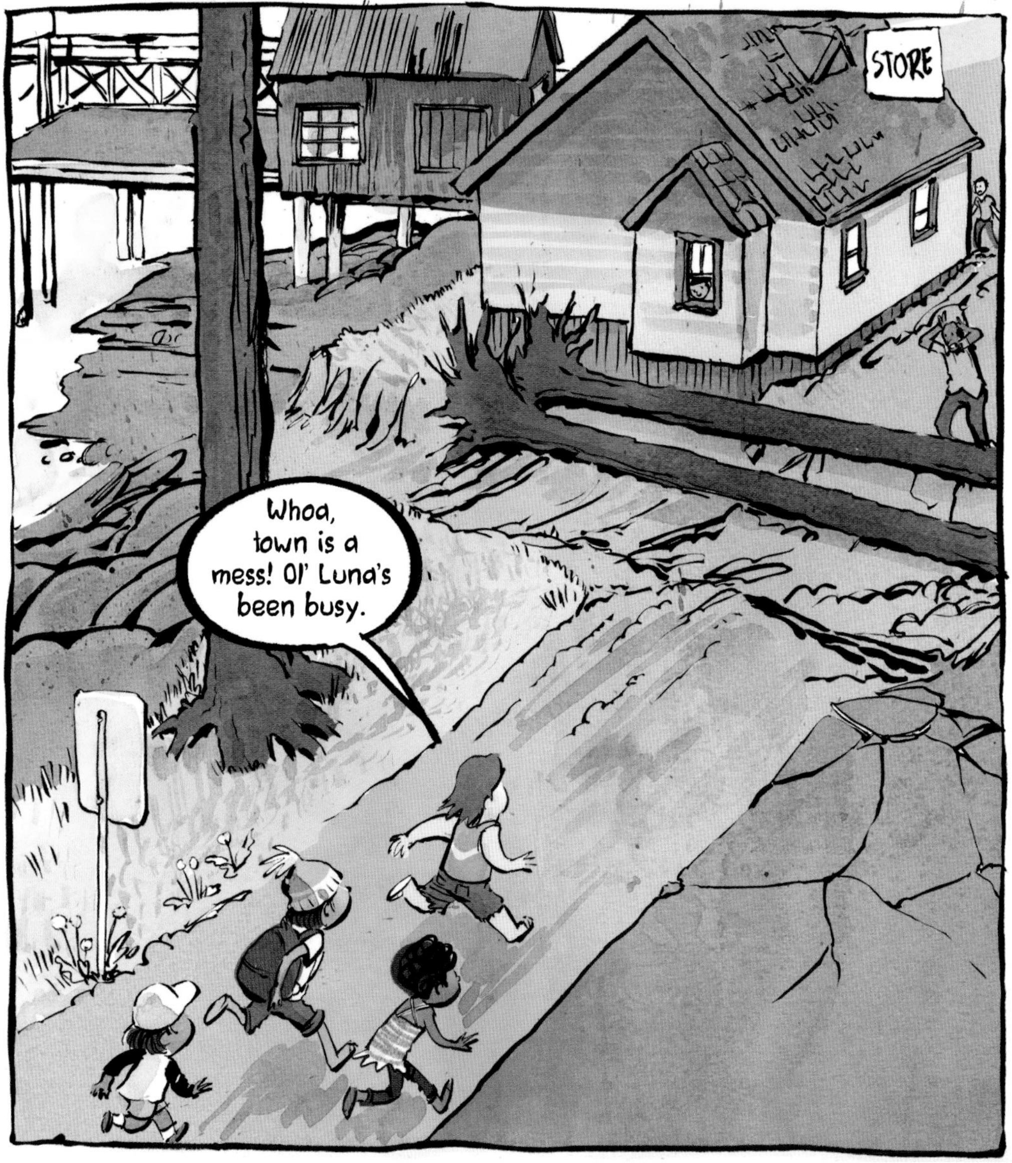
STORE
Whoa, town is a mess! Ol' Luna's been busy.

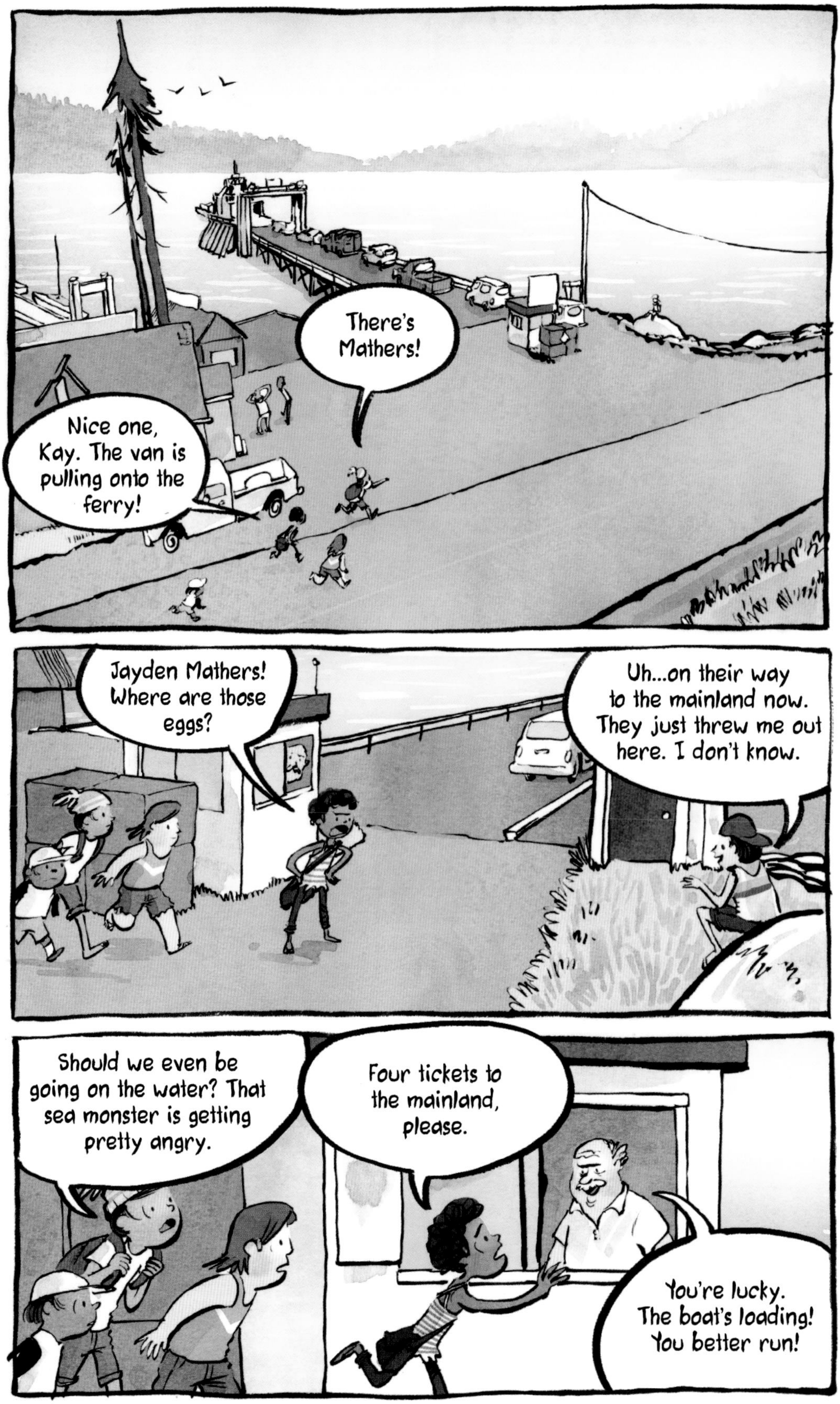
There's Mathers!
Nice one, Kay. The van is pulling onto the ferry!
Jayden Mathers! Where are those eggs?
Uh...on their way to the mainland now. They just threw me out here. I don't know.
Should we even be going on the water? That sea monster is getting pretty angry.
Four tickets to the mainland, please.
You're lucky. The boat's loading! You better run!

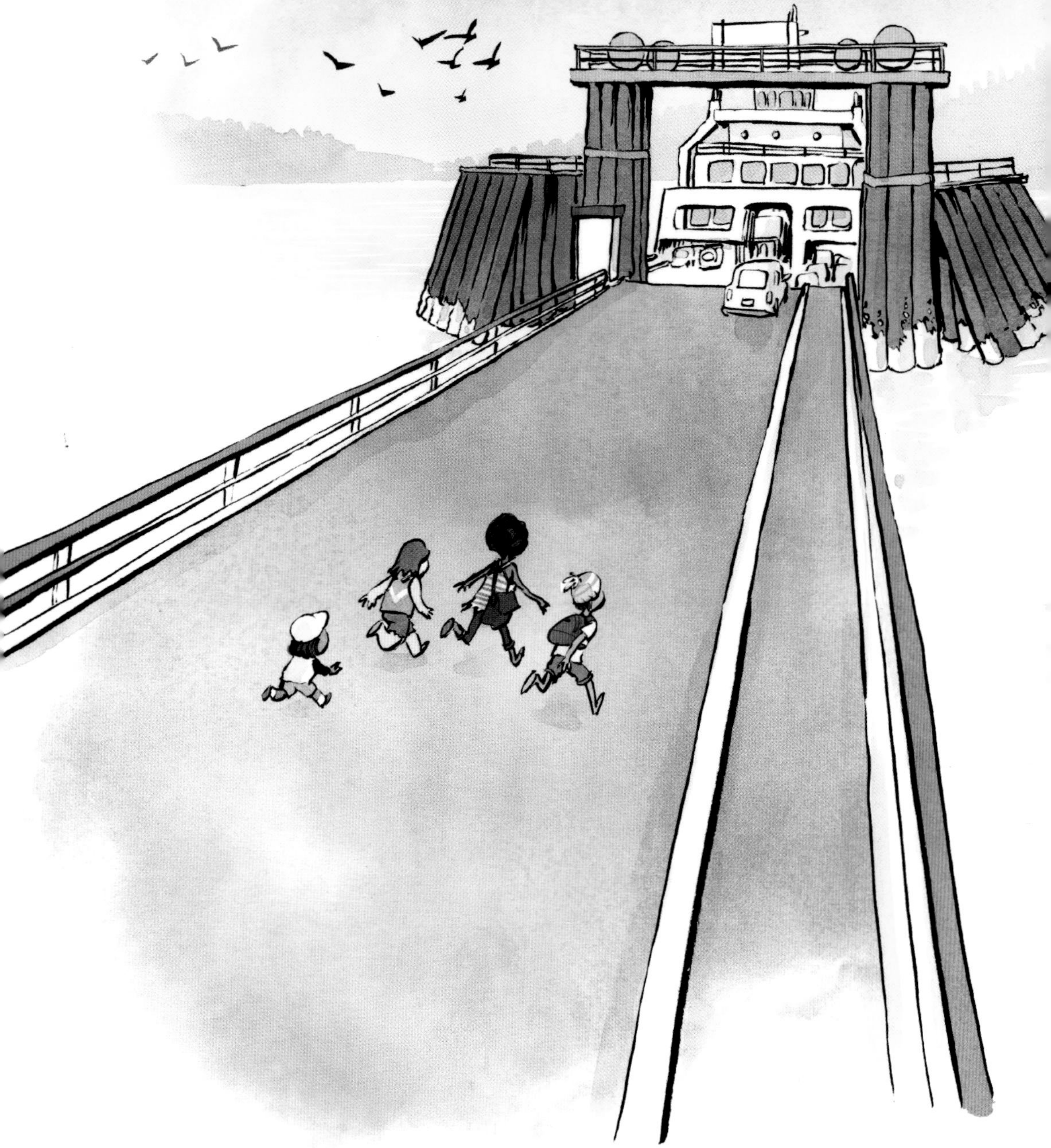

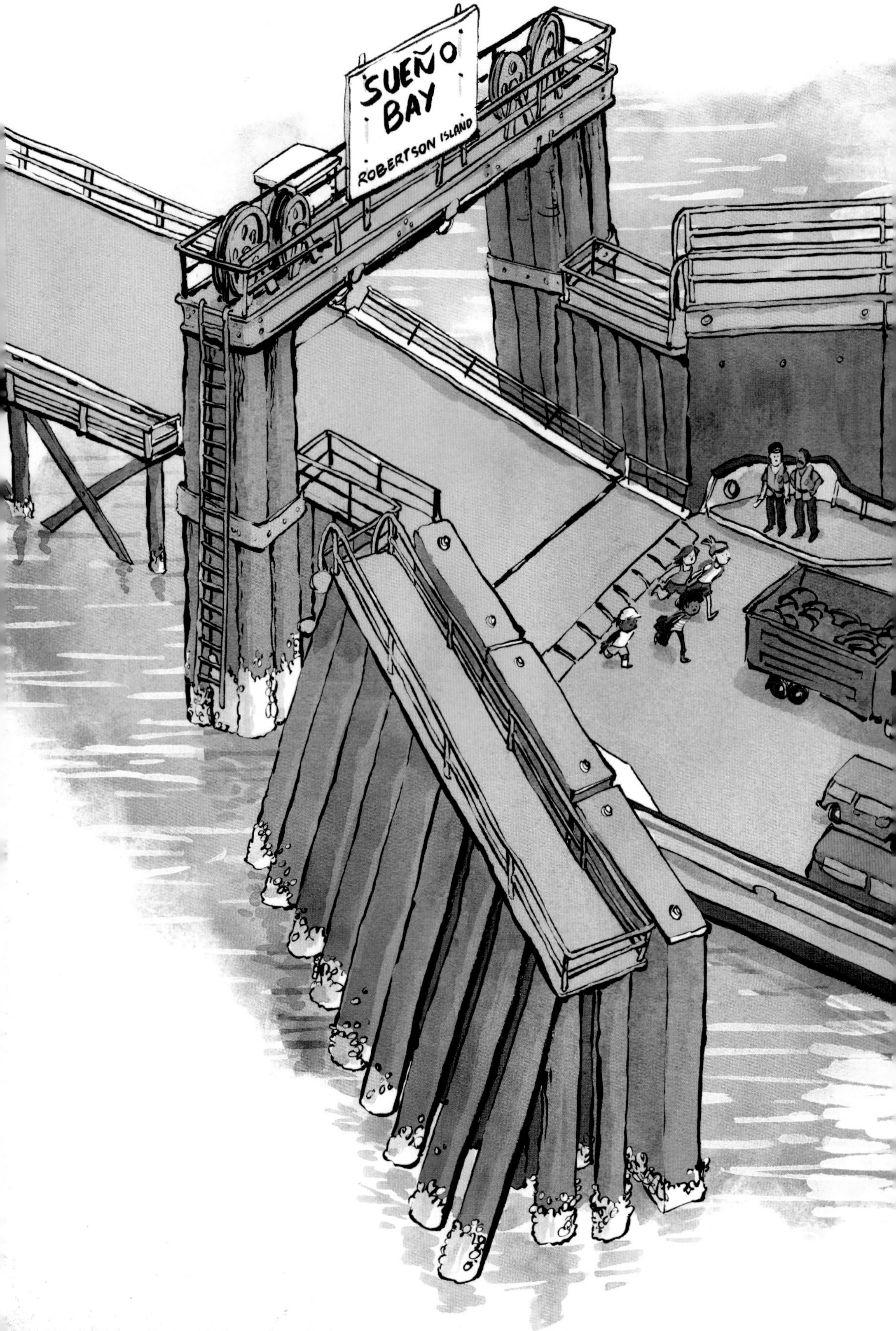
SUEÑO BAY
ROBERTSON ISLAND

CHAPTER FOUR

We're Going to Need a Bigger Boat

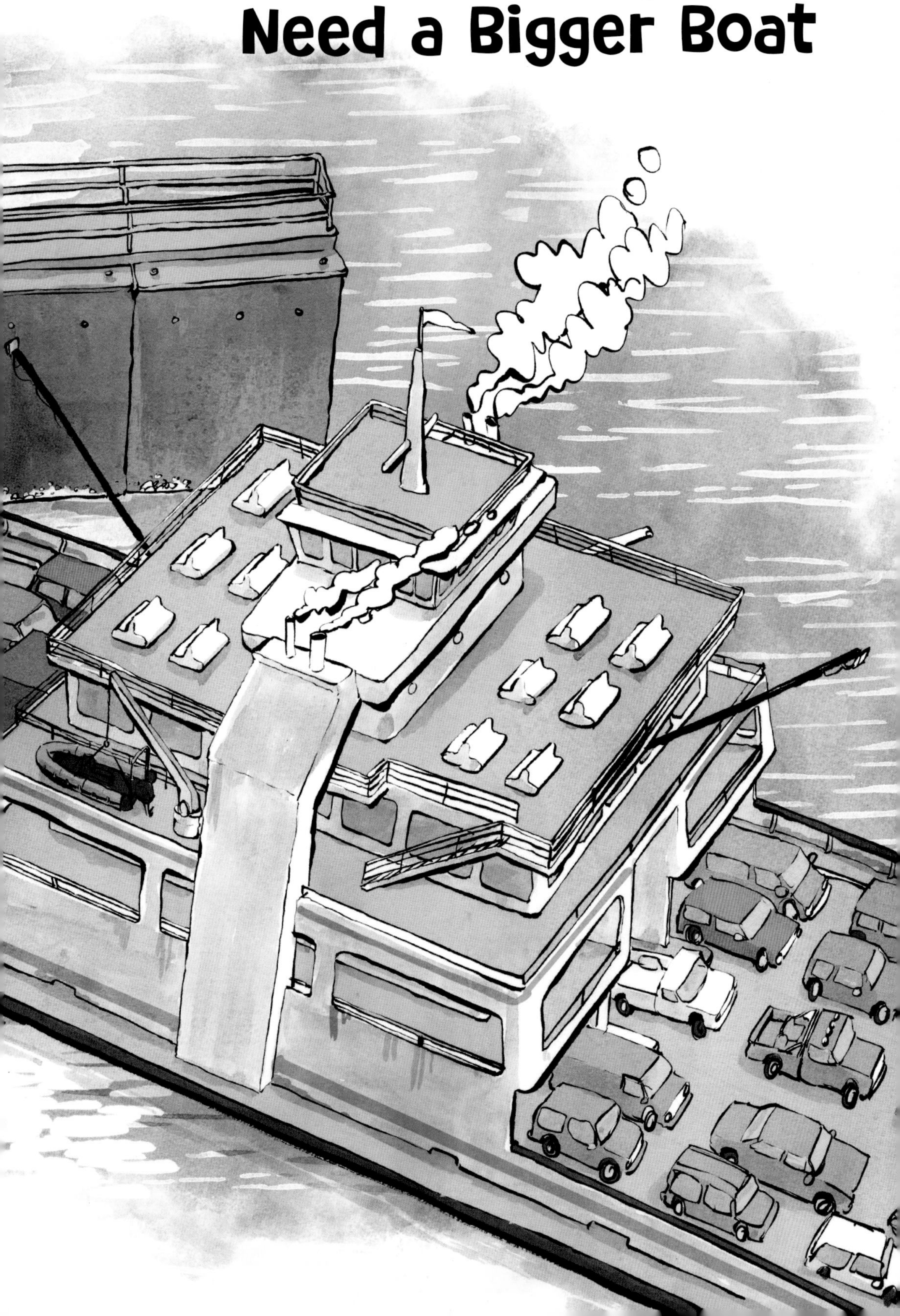

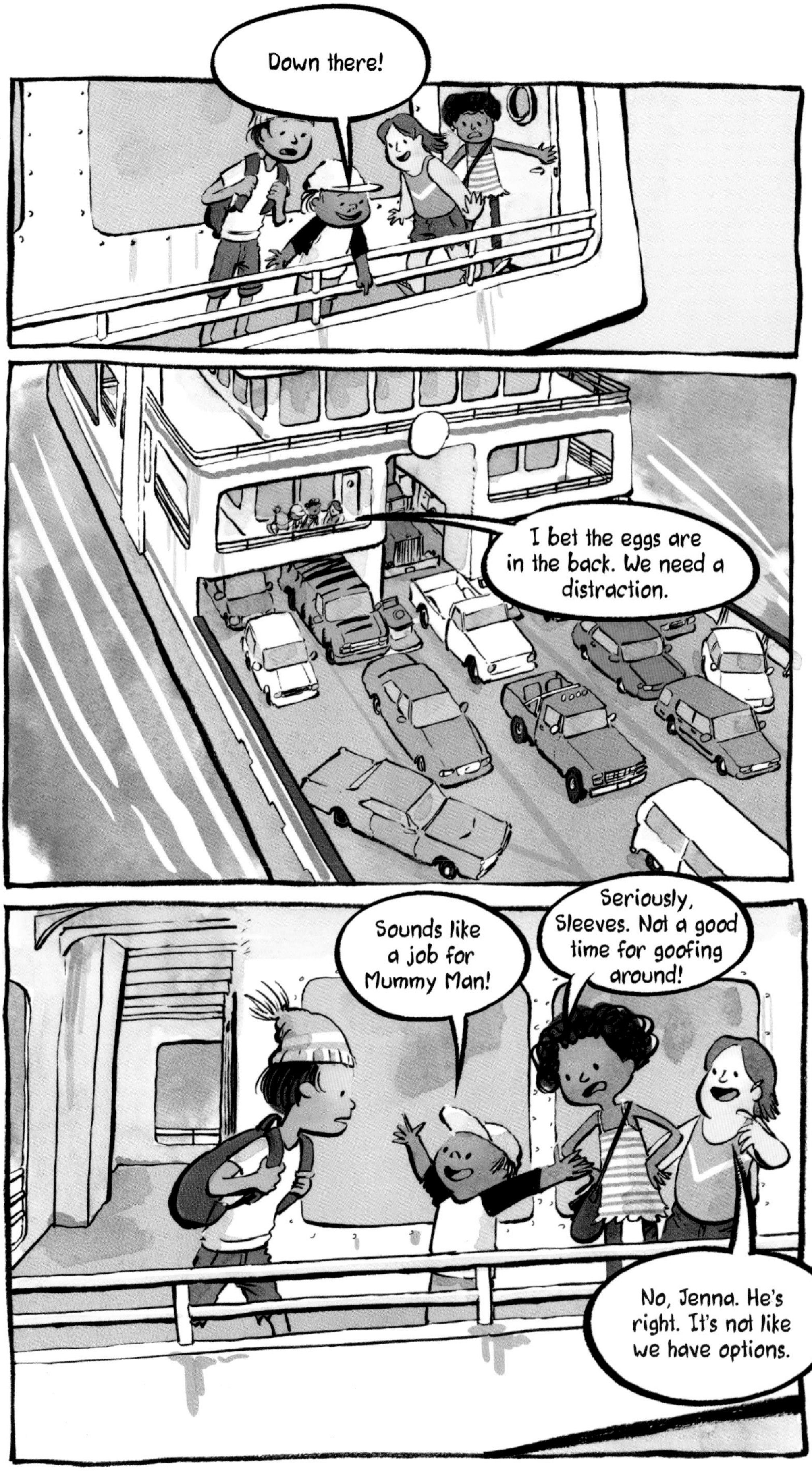
Down there!
I bet the eggs are in the back. We need a distraction.
Sounds like a job for Mummy Man!
Seriously, Sleeves. Not a good time for goofing around!
No, Jenna. He's right. It's not like we have options.

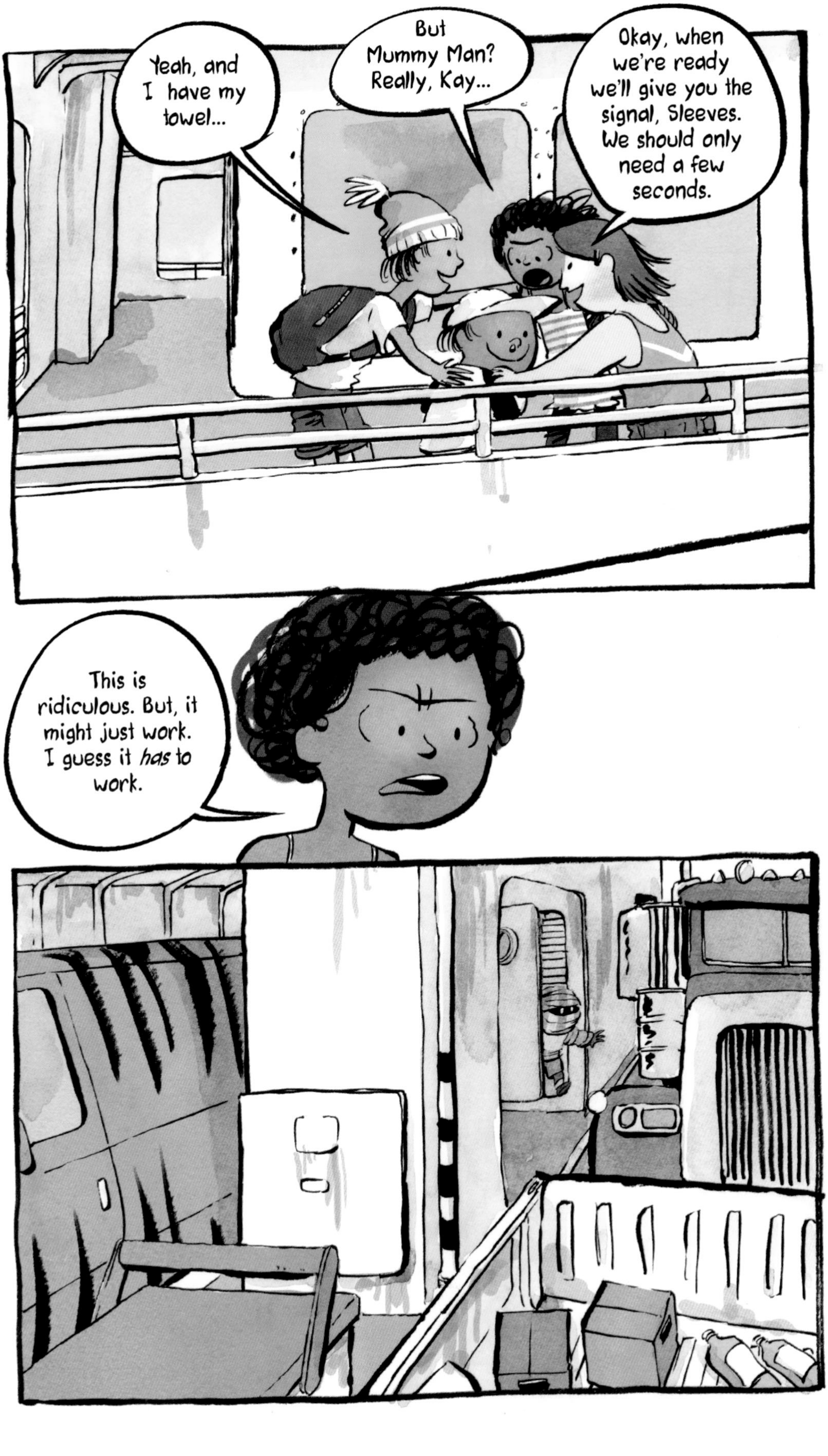
Yeah, and I have my towel...
But Mummy Man? Really, Kay...
Okay, when we're ready we'll give you the signal, Sleeves. We should only need a few seconds.
This is ridiculous. But, it might just work. I guess it *has* to work.

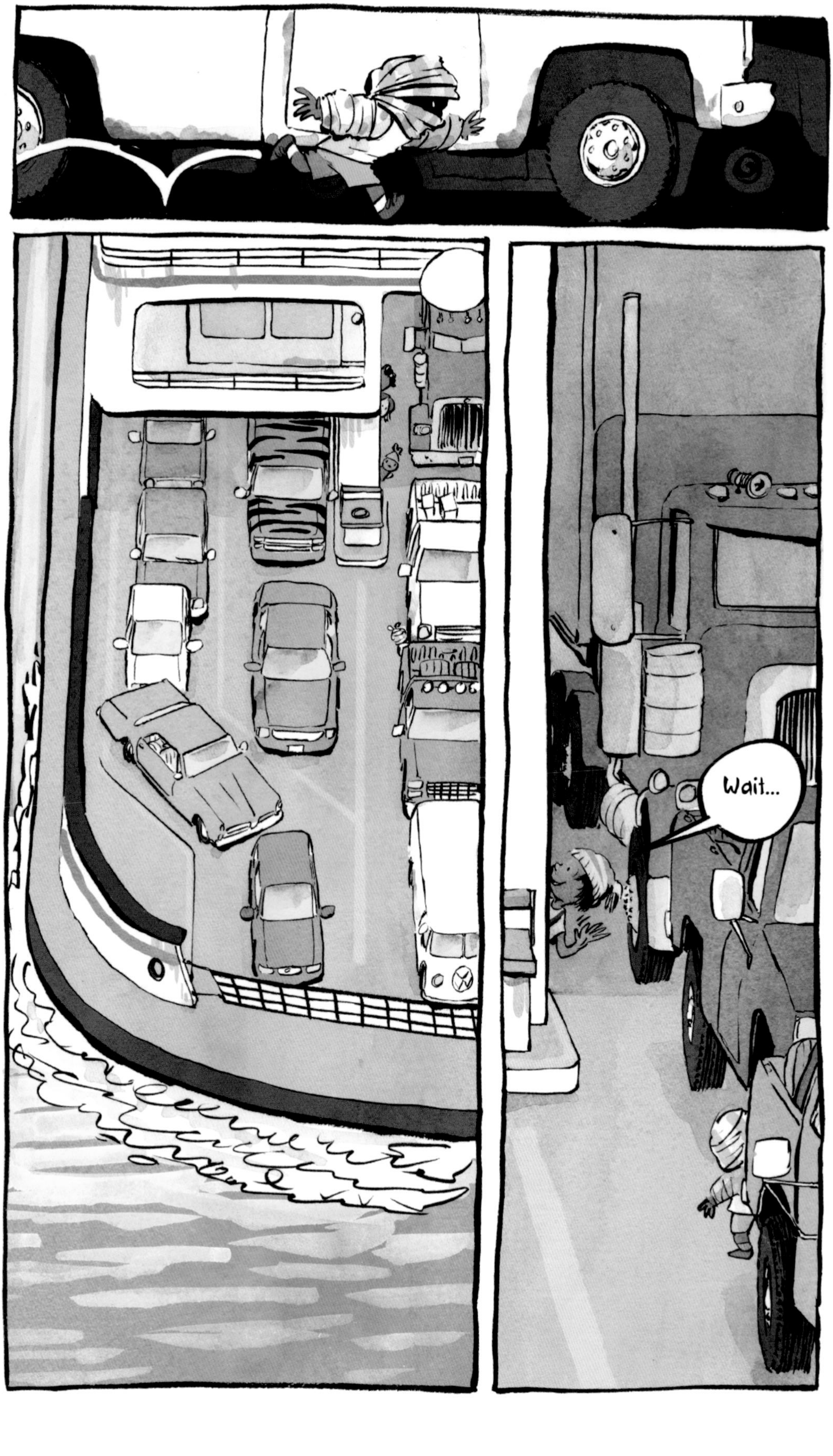

Wait...

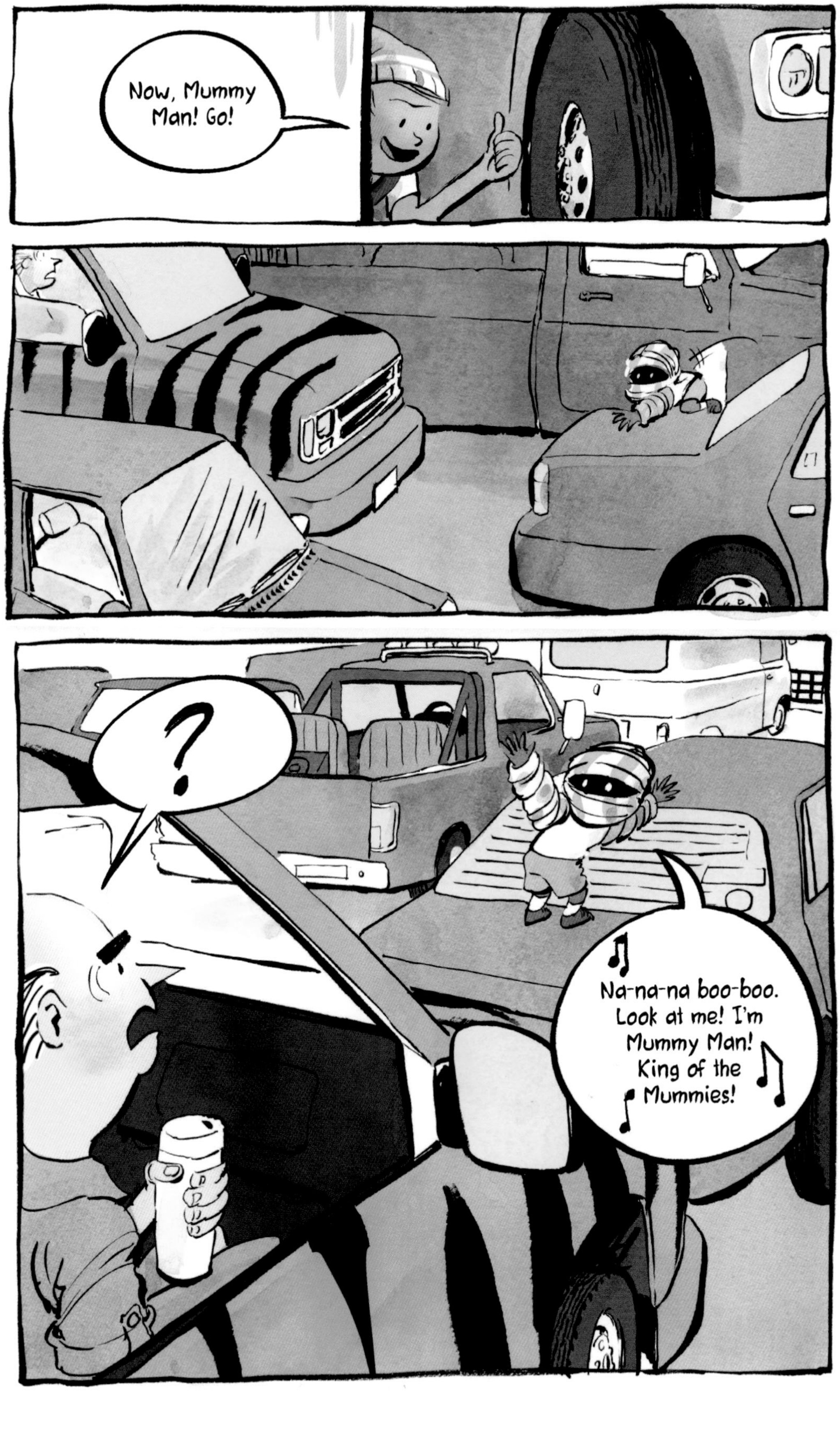
Now, Mummy Man! Go!
?
Na-na-na boo-boo. Look at me! I'm Mummy Man! King of the Mummies!

What is that kid doing?
I told you this island is weird, man.
Coast is clear.
Okay, Jenna, good to go.
EXOTIC ANIMALS

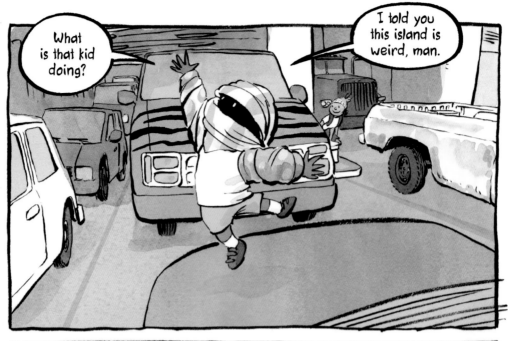

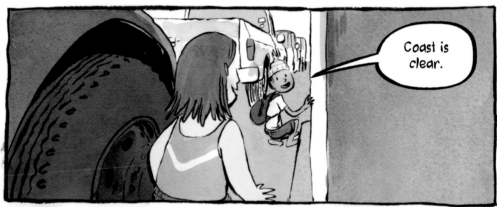

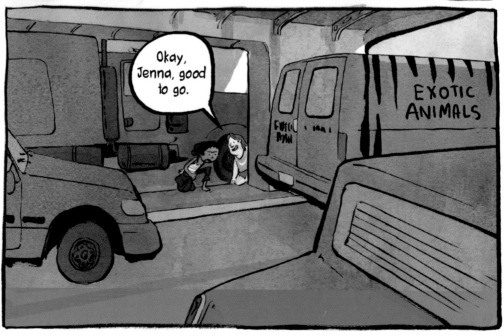

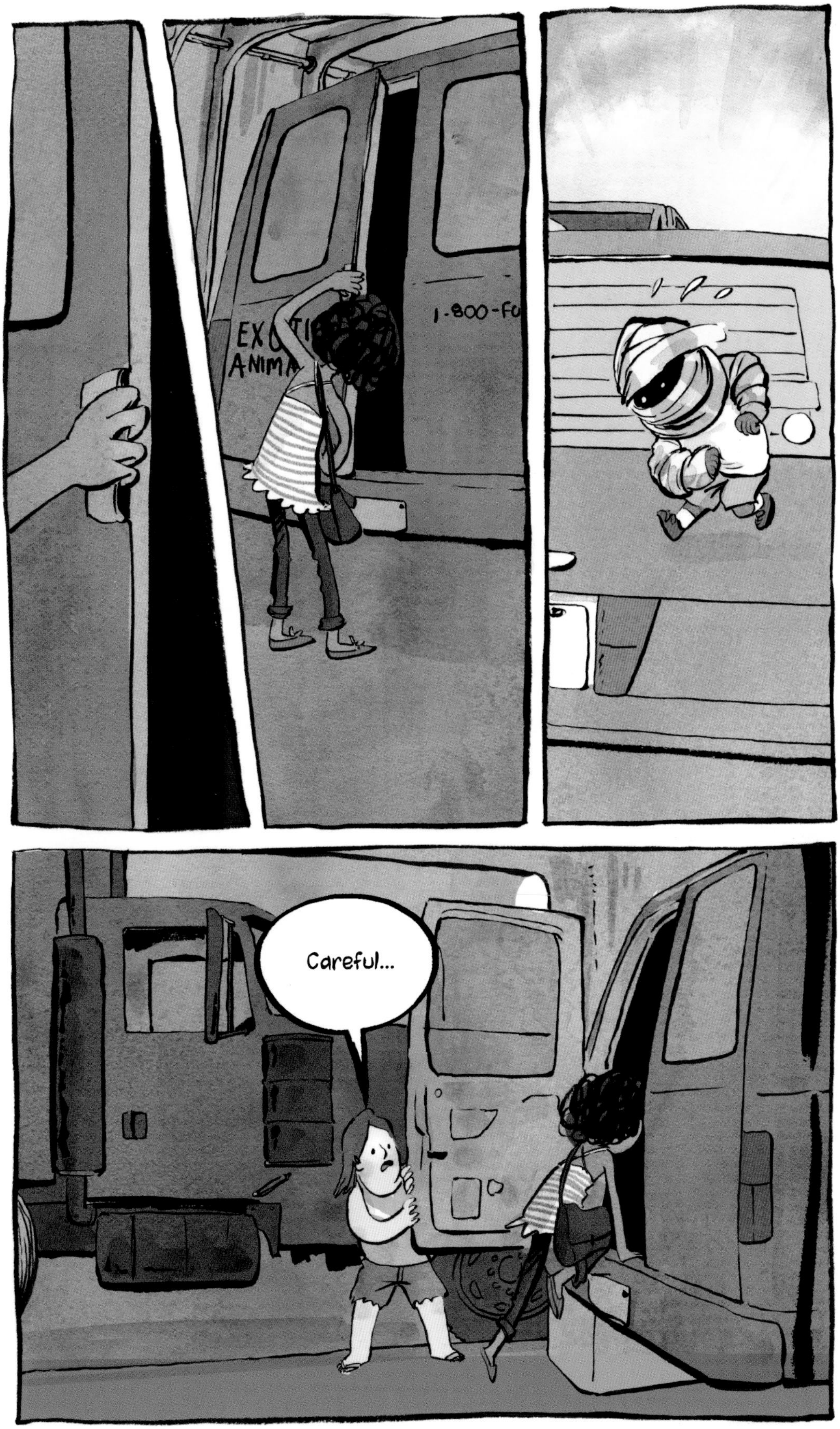
EXOTI
ANIMA
1-800-FU
Careful...

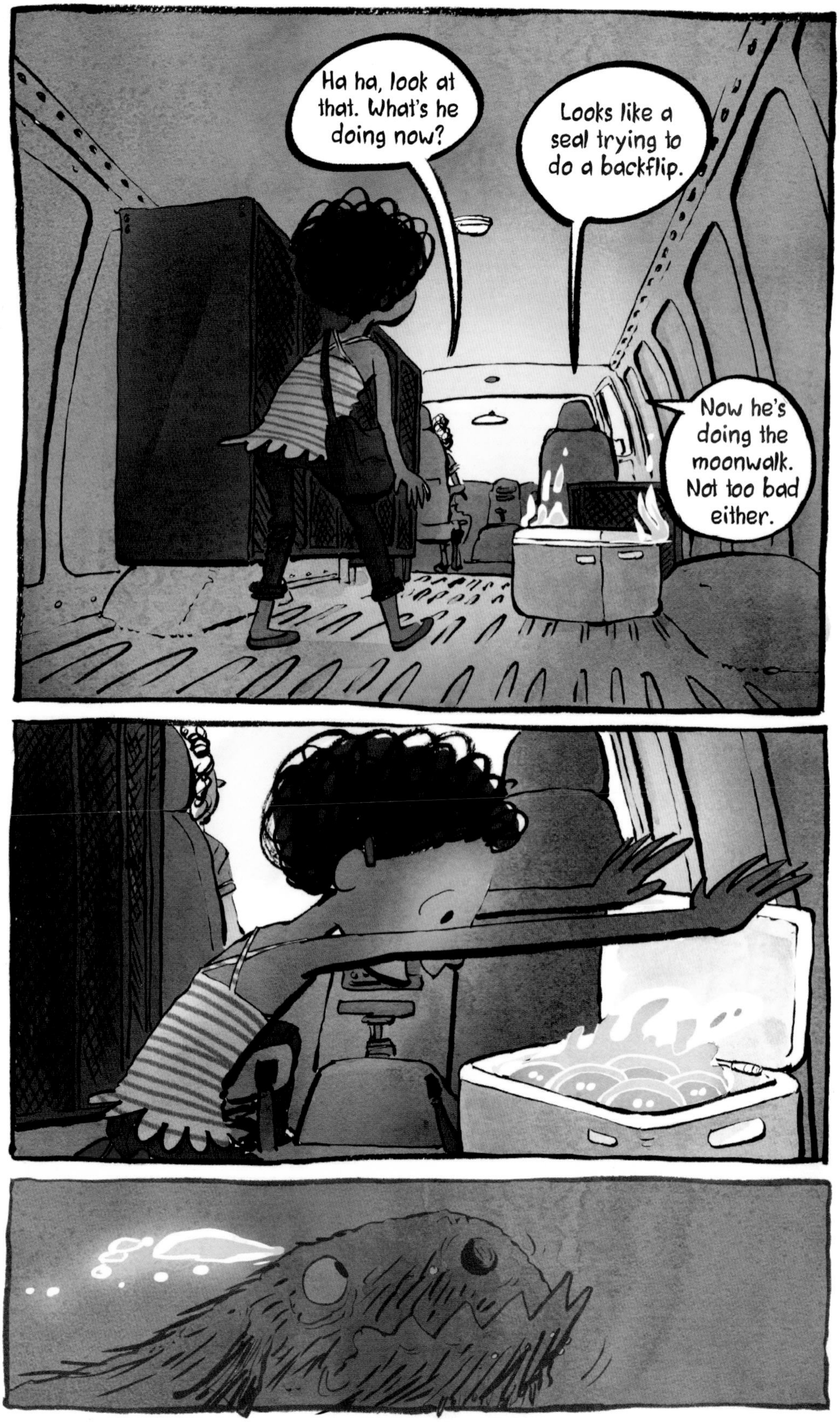
Ha ha, look at that. What's he doing now?
Looks like a seal trying to do a backflip.
Now he's doing the moonwalk. Not too bad either.

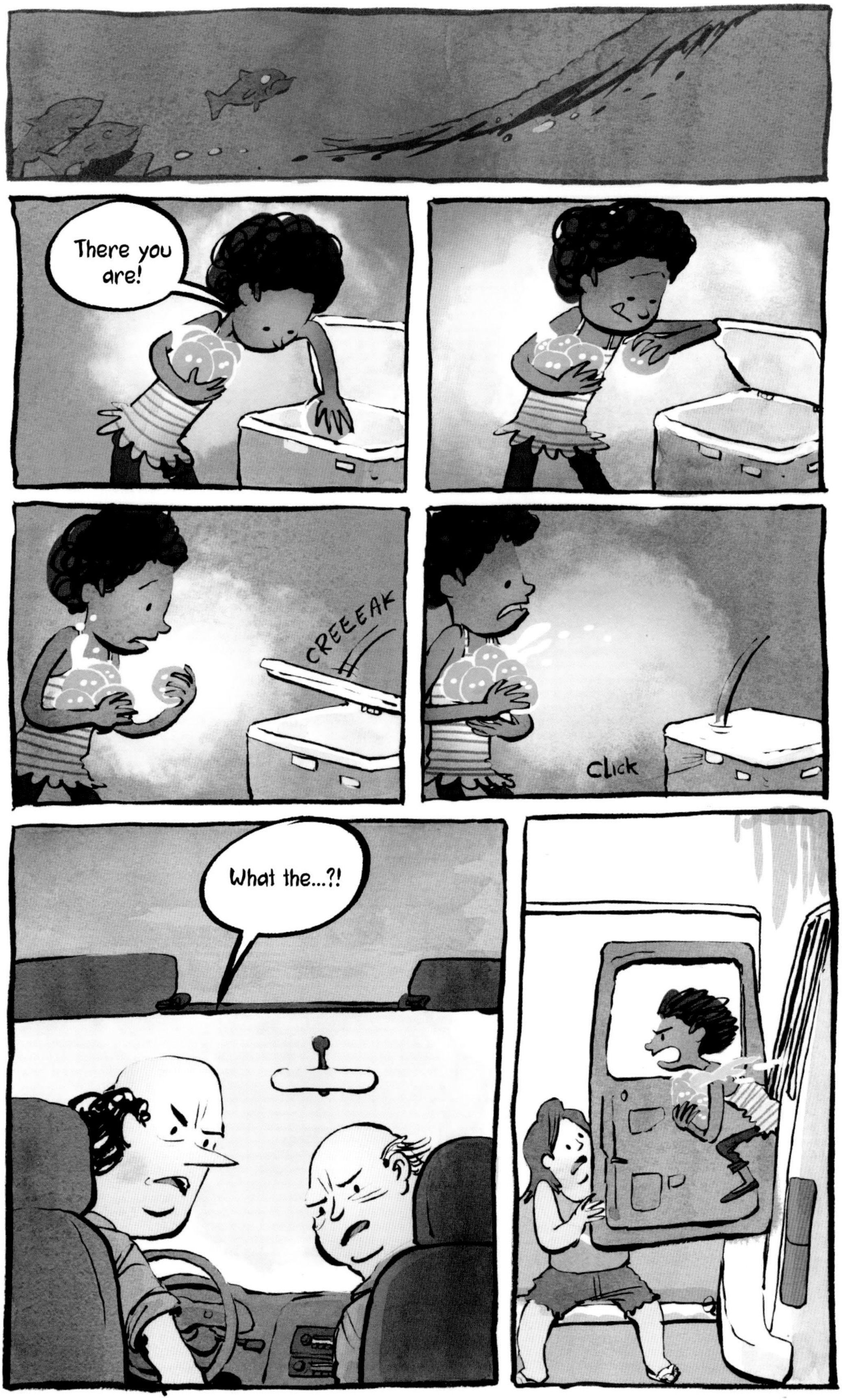
There you are!
CREEEAK
Click
What the...?!

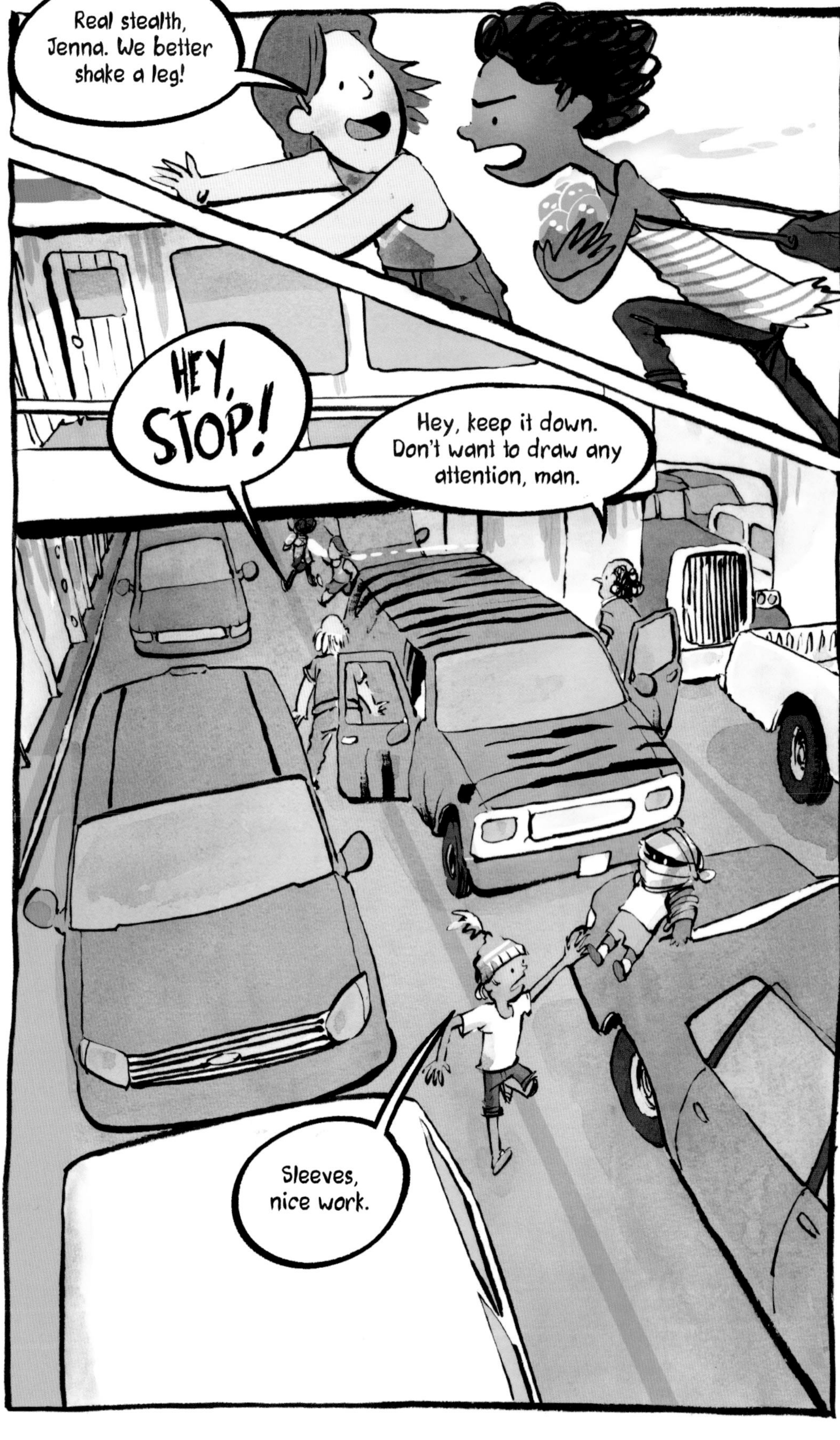
Real stealth, Jenna. We better shake a leg!
HEY, STOP!
Hey, keep it down. Don't want to draw any attention, man.
Sleeves, nice work.

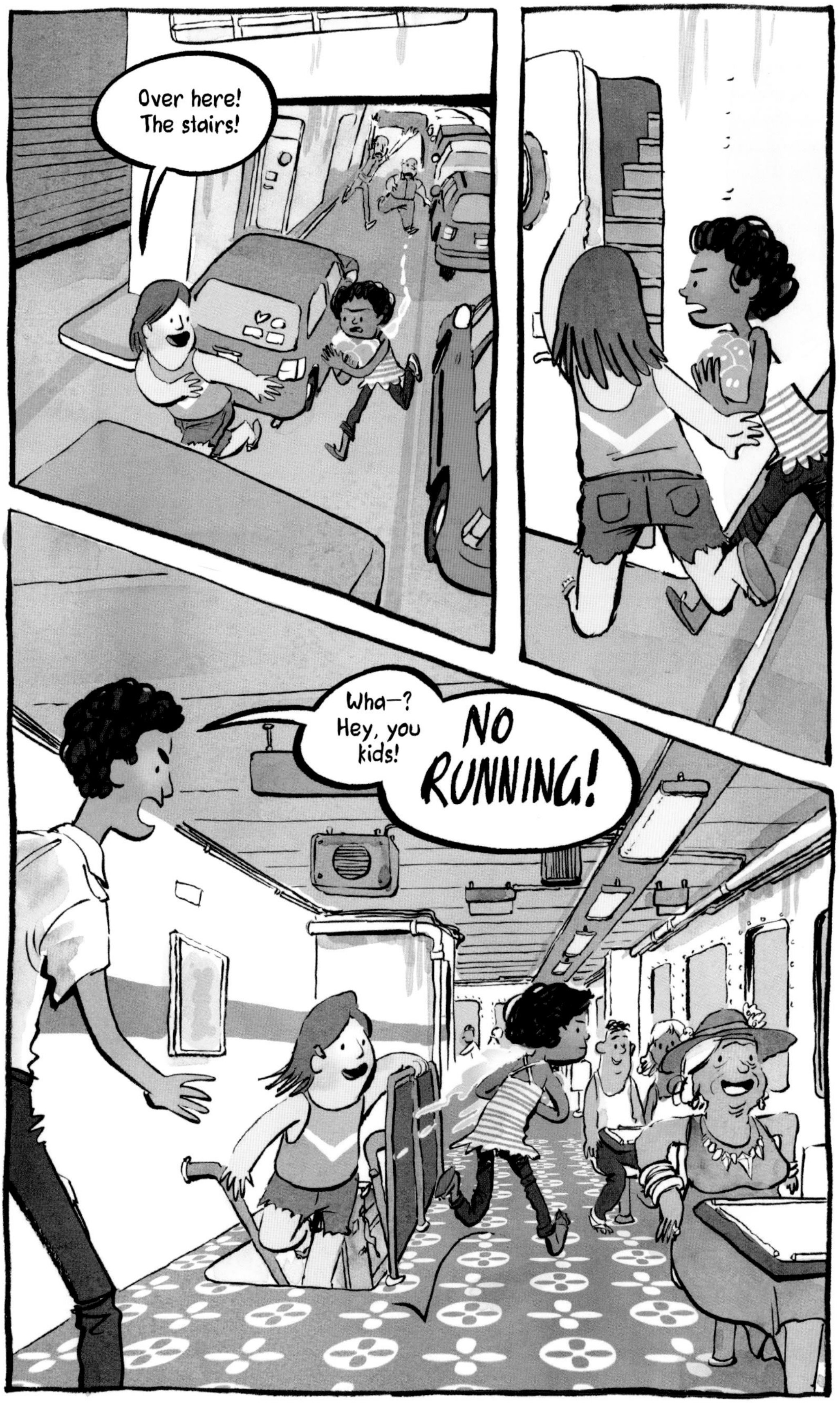
Over here! The stairs!
Wha—? Hey, you kids!
NO RUNNING!

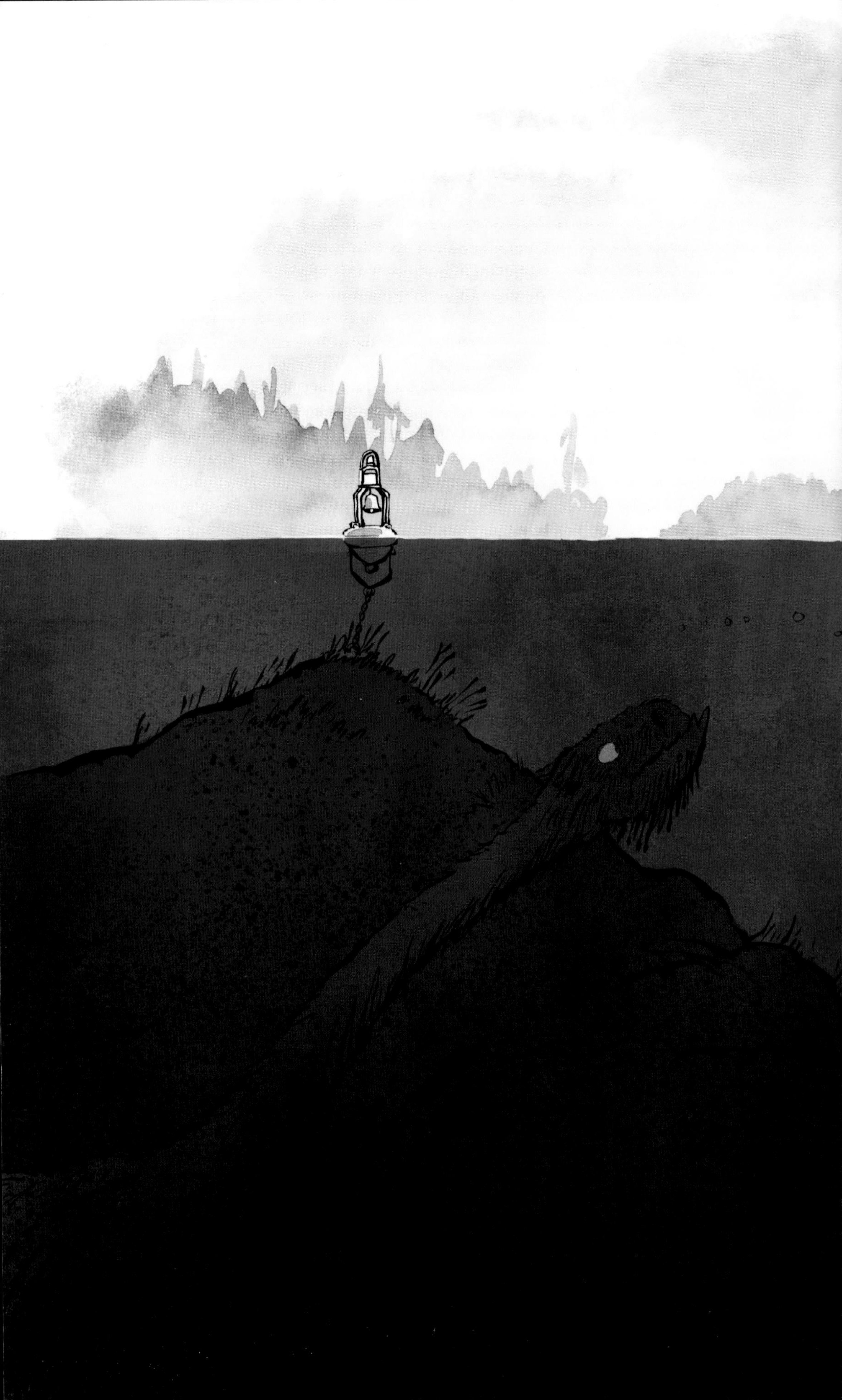

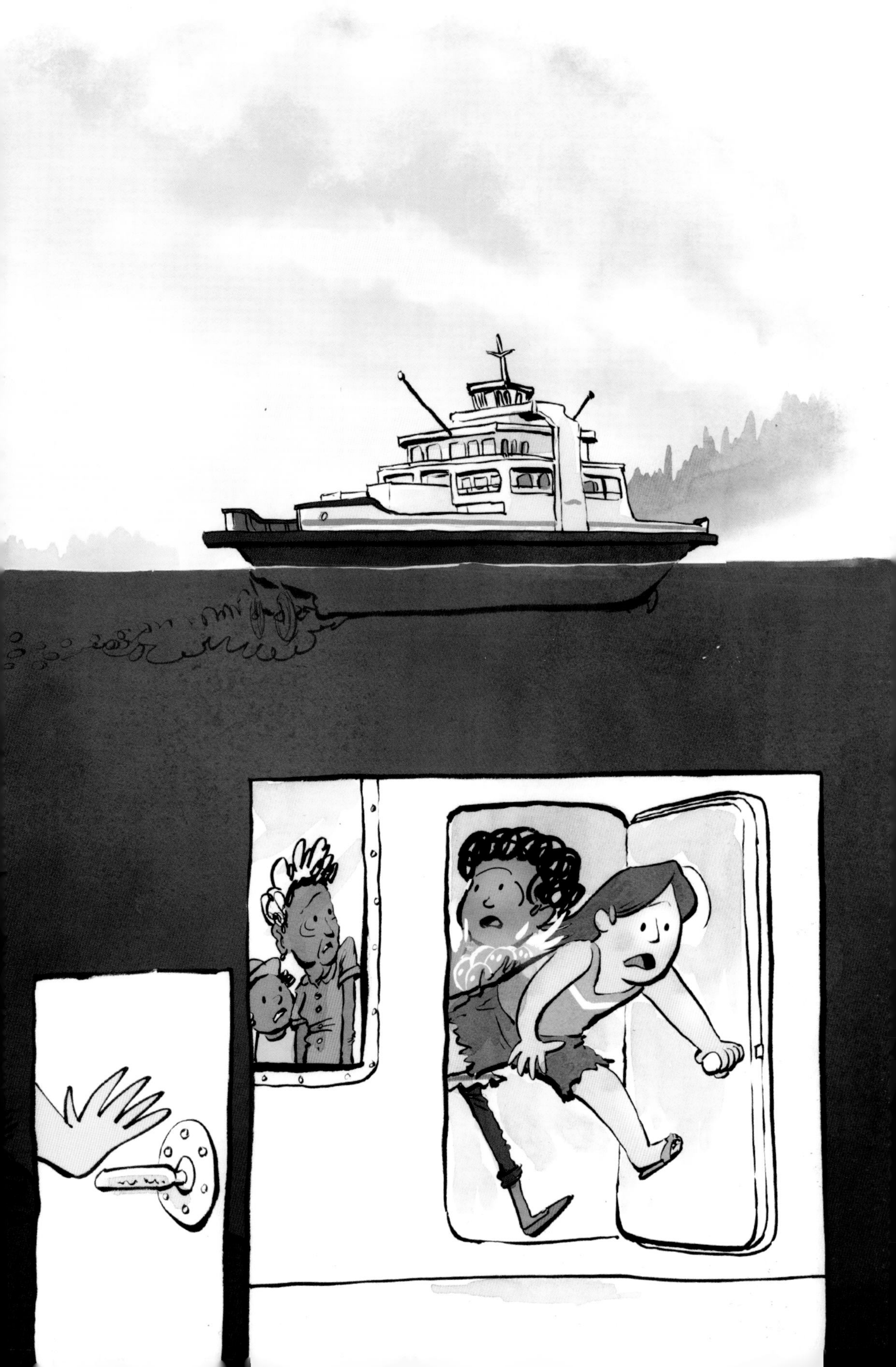

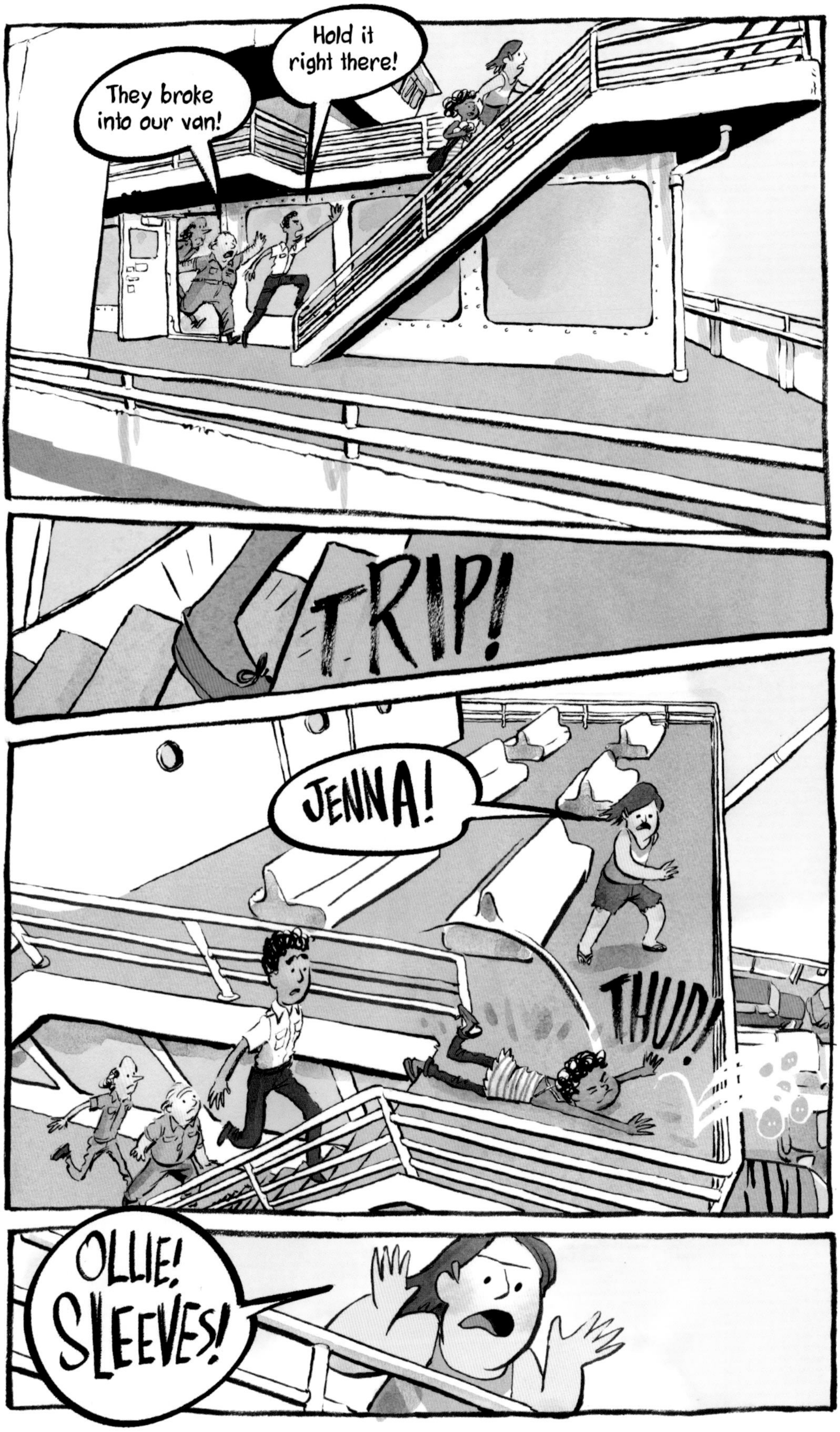
They broke into our van!
Hold it right there!
TRIP!
JENNA!
THUD!
OLLIE! SLEEVES!

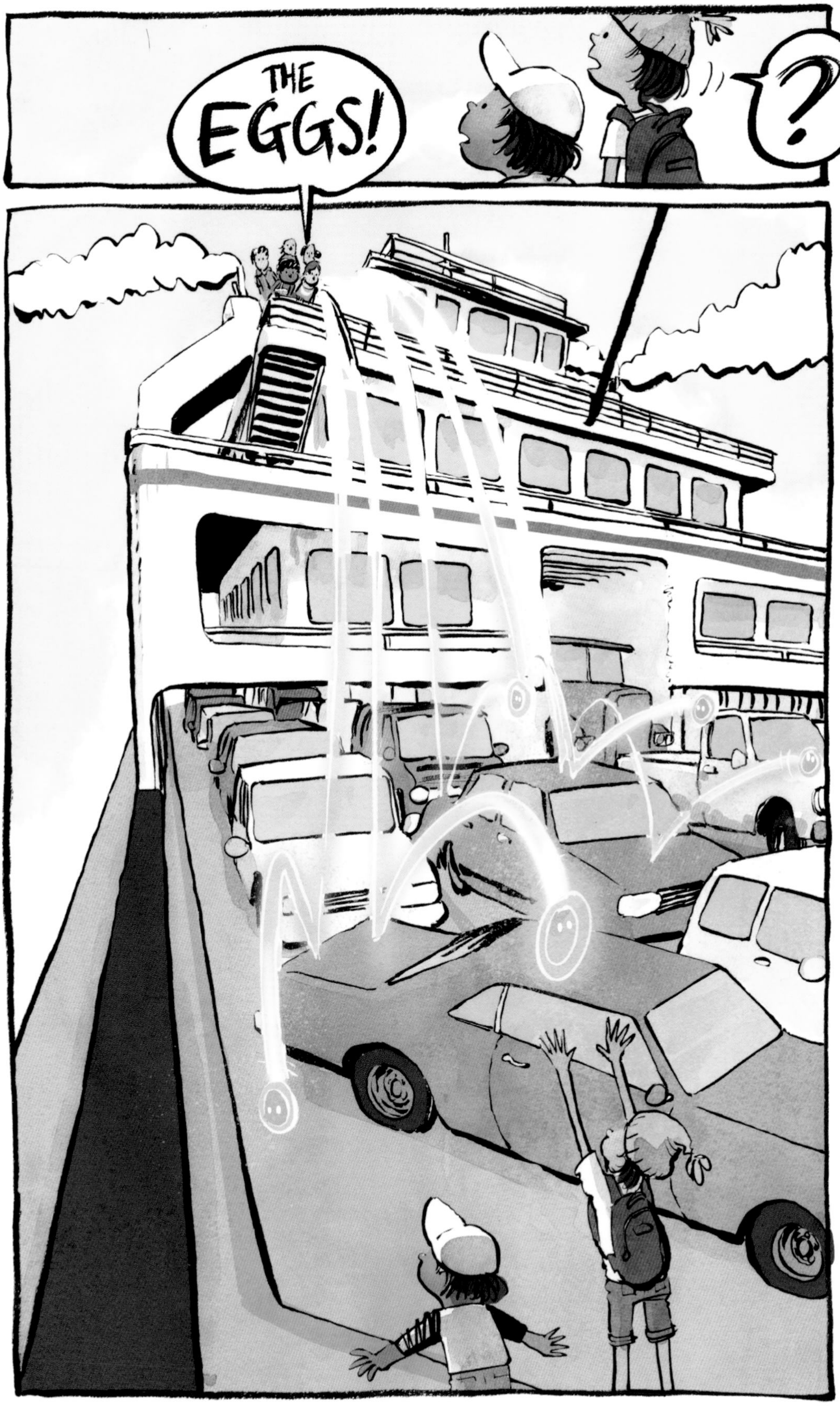
THE EGGS!
?

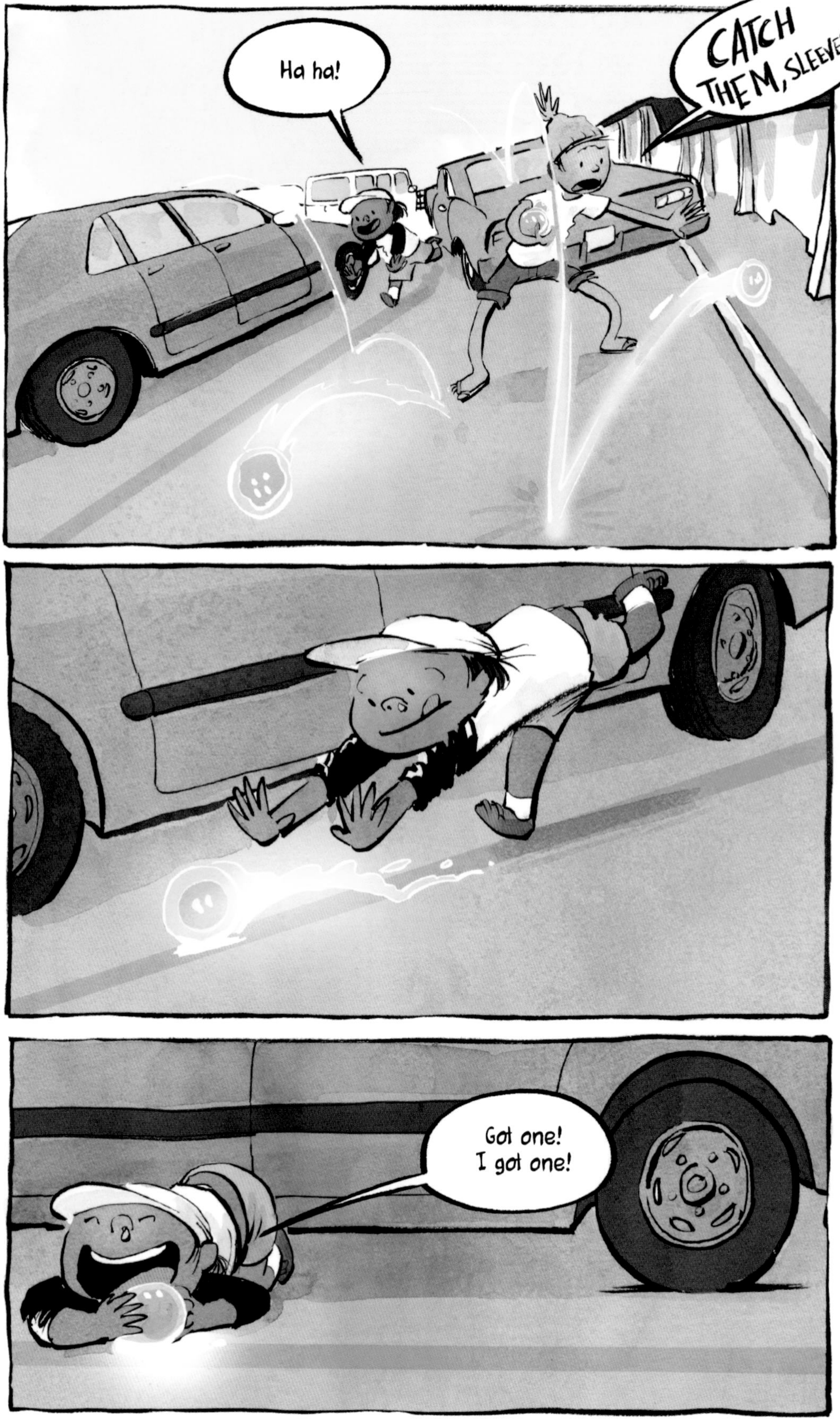
Ha ha!
CATCH THEM, SLEEVES!
Got one! I got one!

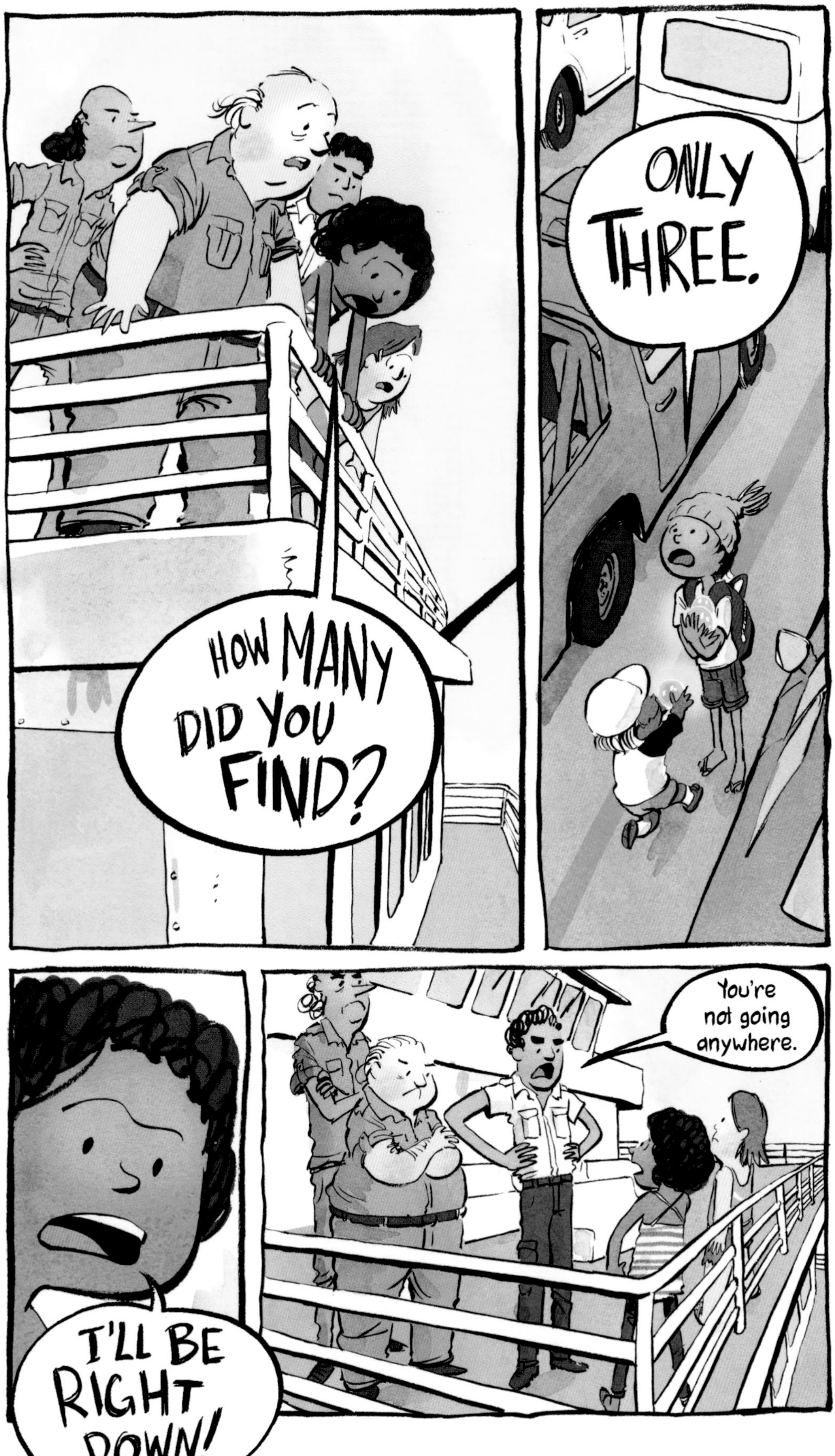
HOW MANY DID YOU FIND?
ONLY THREE.
I'LL BE RIGHT DOWN!
You're not going anywhere.

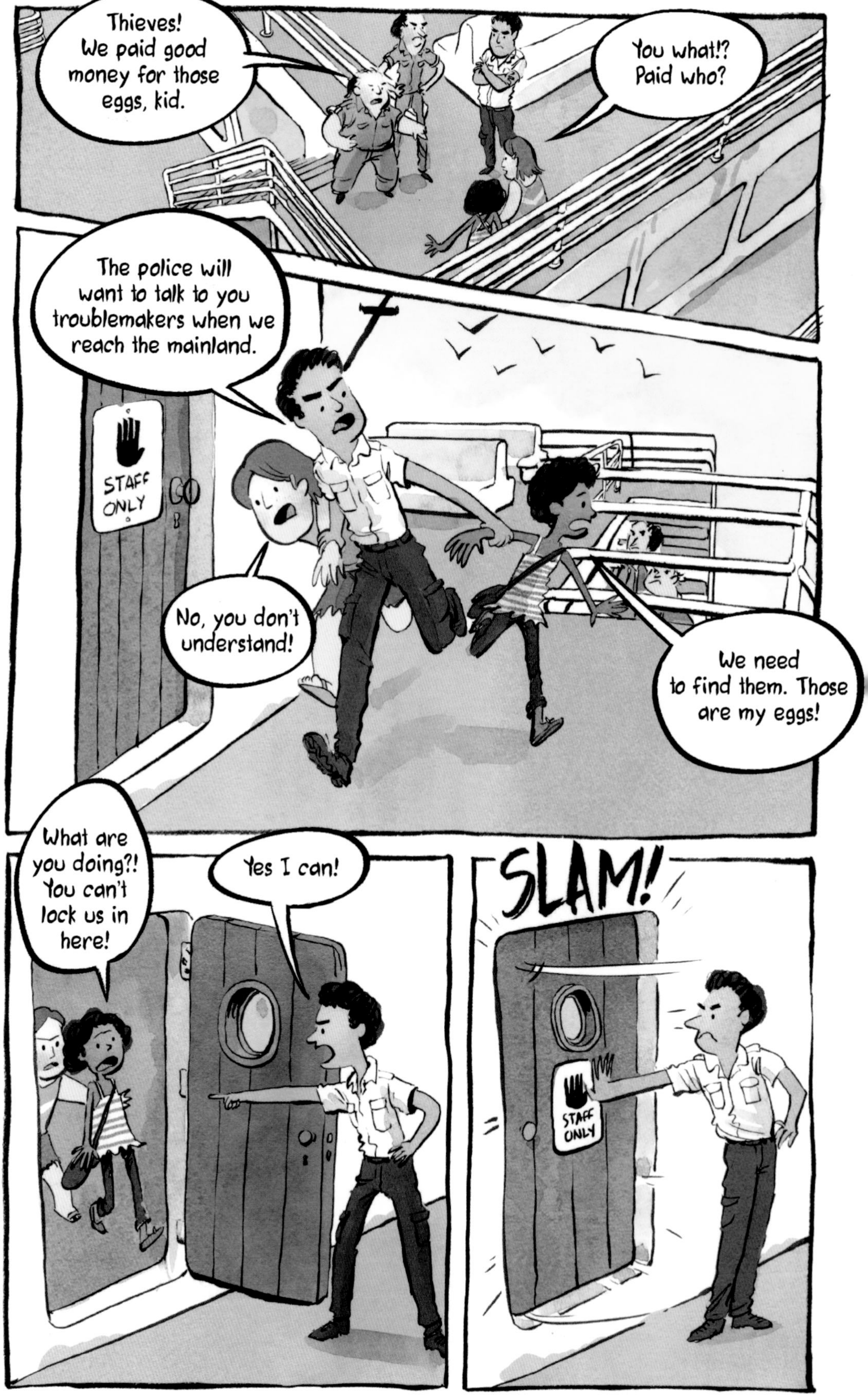
Thieves! We paid good money for those eggs, kid.
You what!? Paid who?
The police will want to talk to you troublemakers when we reach the mainland.
STAFF ONLY
No, you don't understand!
We need to find them. Those are my eggs!
What are you doing?! You can't lock us in here!
Yes I can!
SLAM!
STAFF ONLY

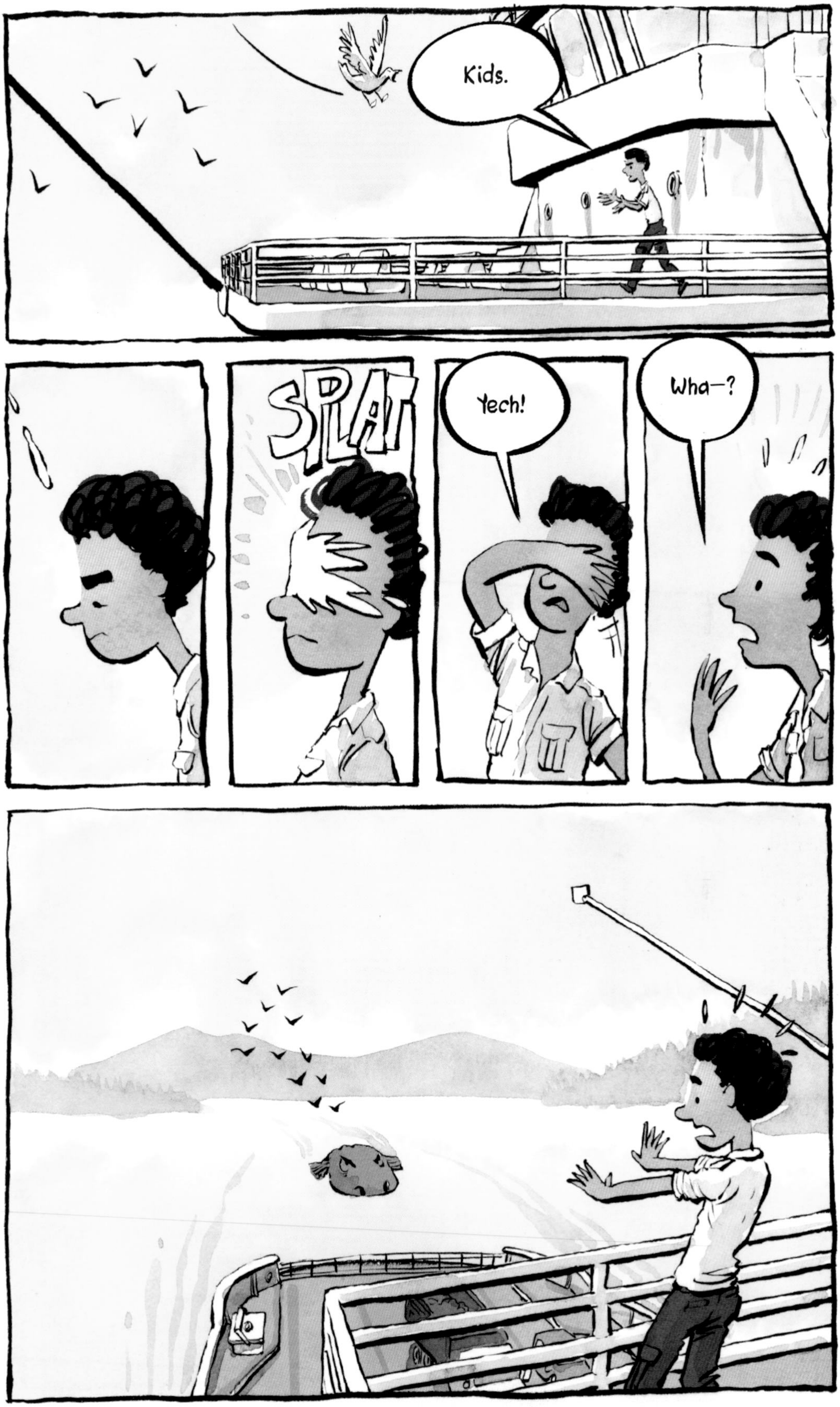
Kids.
SPLAT
Yech!
Wha—?

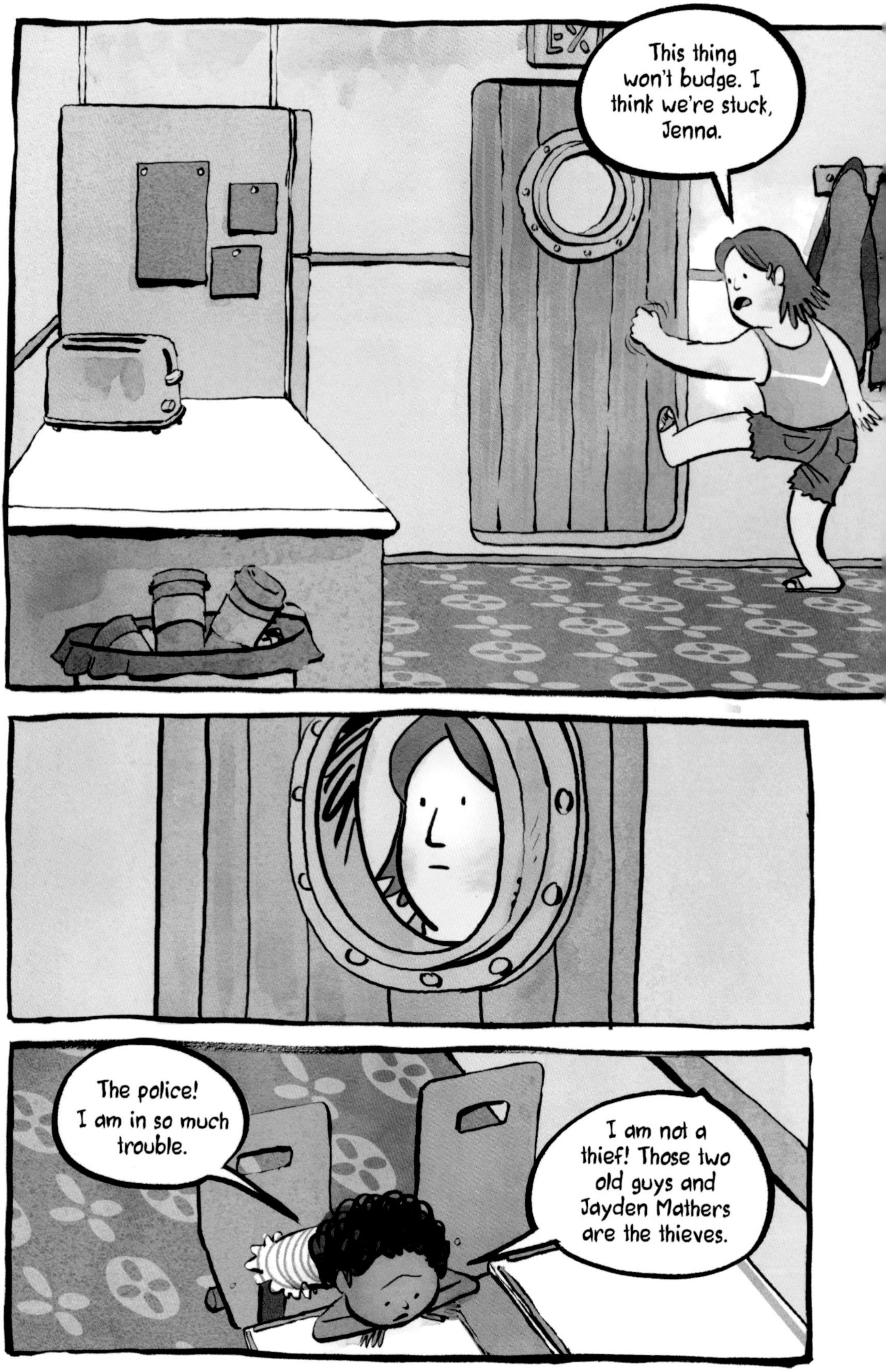
This thing won't budge. I think we're stuck, Jenna.
The police! I am in so much trouble.
I am not a thief! Those two old guys and Jayden Mathers are the thieves.

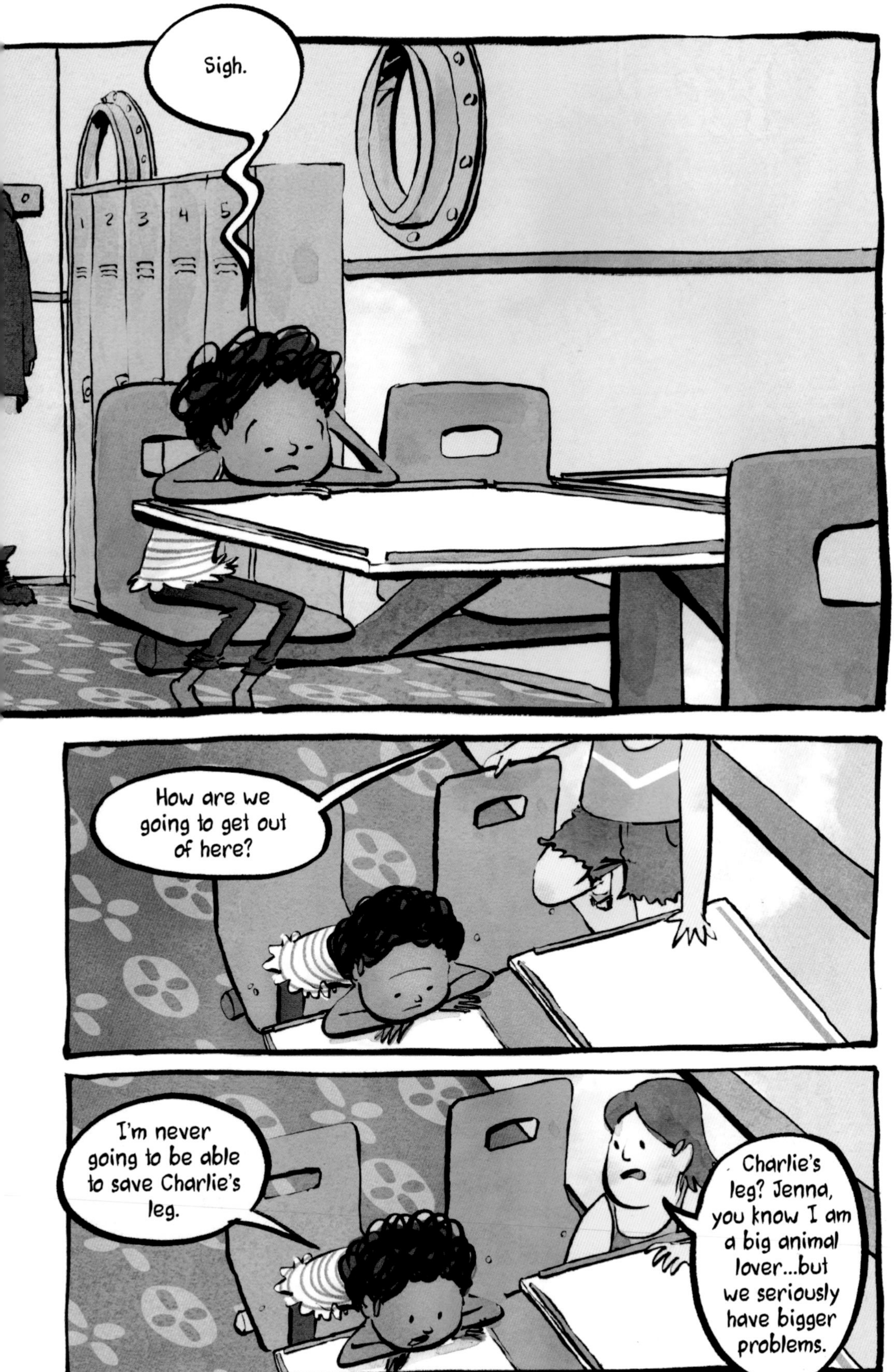
Sigh.
How are we going to get out of here?
I'm never going to be able to save Charlie's leg.
Charlie's leg? Jenna, you know I am a big animal lover...but we seriously have bigger problems.

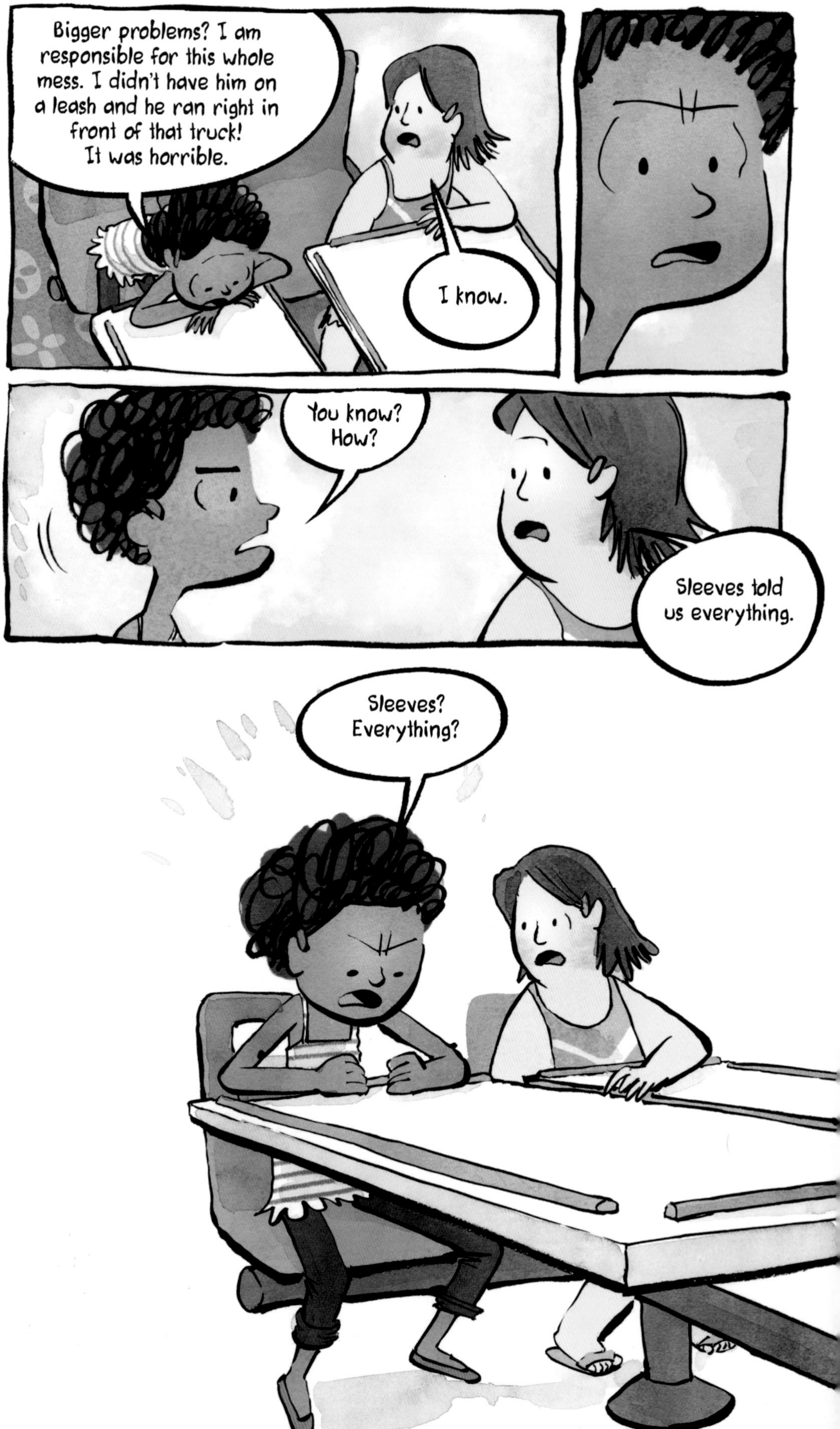
Bigger problems? I am responsible for this whole mess. I didn't have him on a leash and he ran right in front of that truck! It was horrible.
I know.
You know? How?
Sleeves told us everything.
Sleeves? Everything?

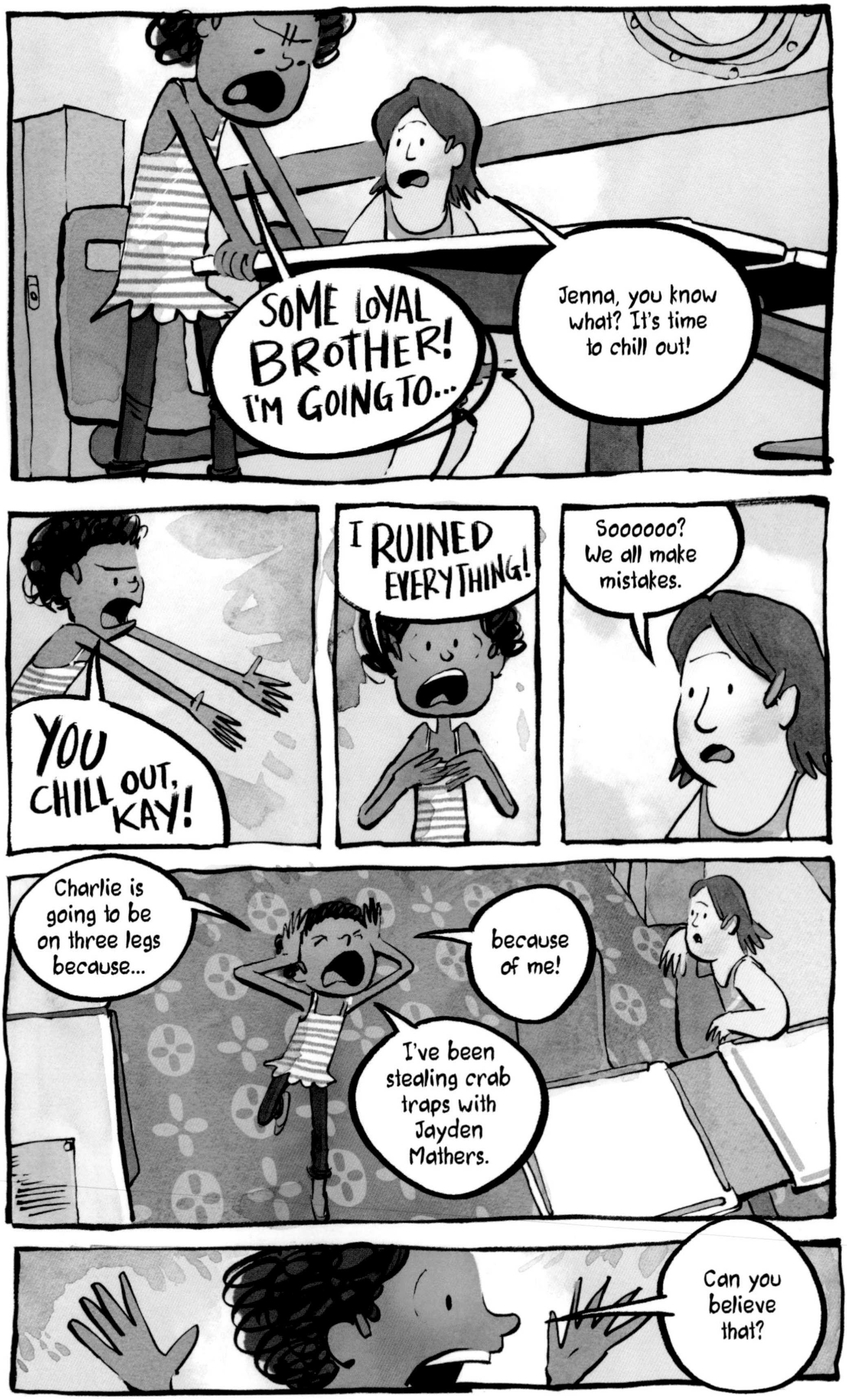
SOME LOYAL BROTHER! I'M GOING TO...
Jenna, you know what? It's time to chill out!
YOU CHILL OUT, KAY!
I RUINED EVERYTHING!
Soooooo? We all make mistakes.
Charlie is going to be on three legs because...
because of me!
I've been stealing crab traps with Jayden Mathers.
Can you believe that?

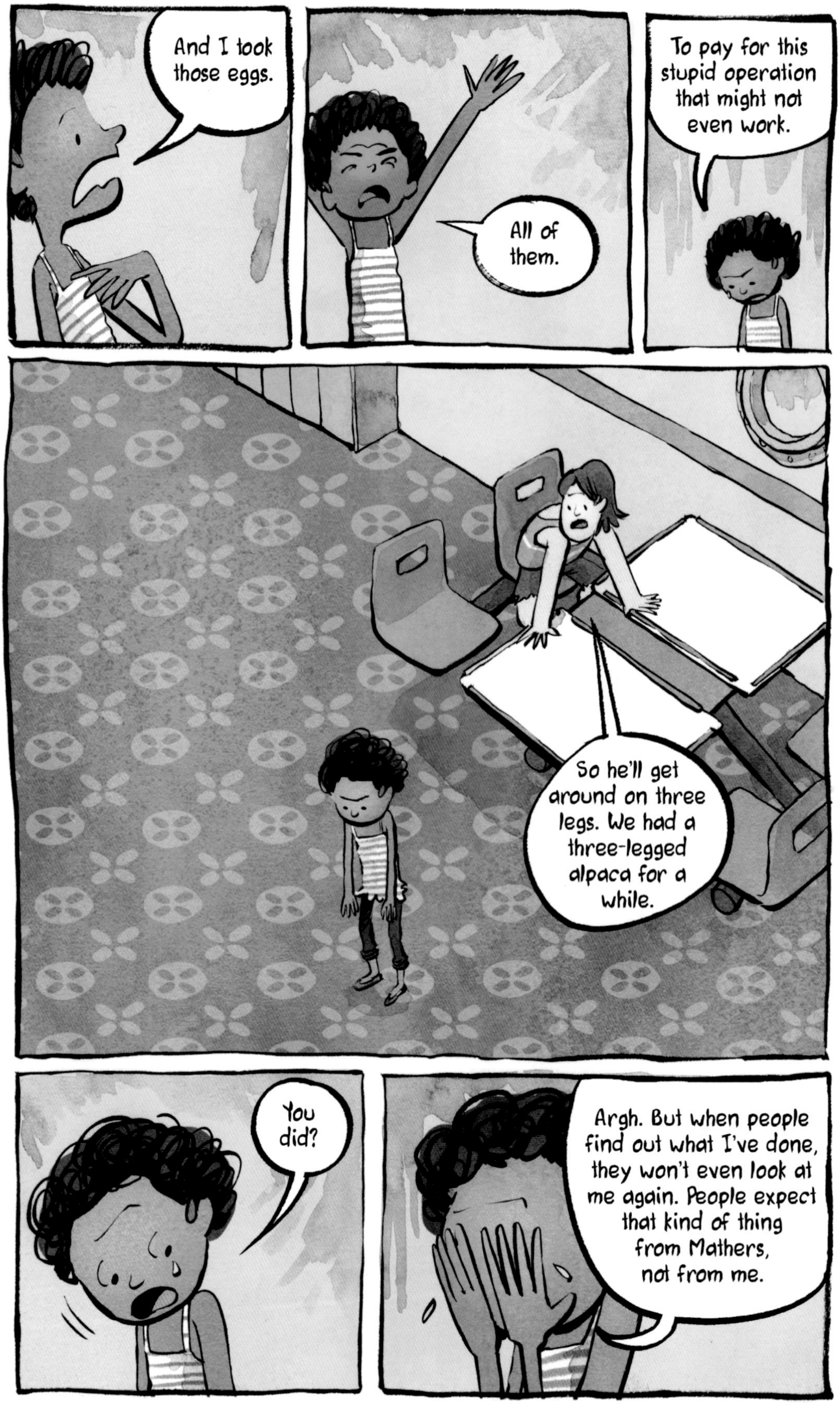
And I took those eggs.
All of them.
To pay for this stupid operation that might not even work.
So he'll get around on three legs. We had a three-legged alpaca for a while.
You did?
Argh. But when people find out what I've done, they won't even look at me again. People expect that kind of thing from Mathers, not from me.

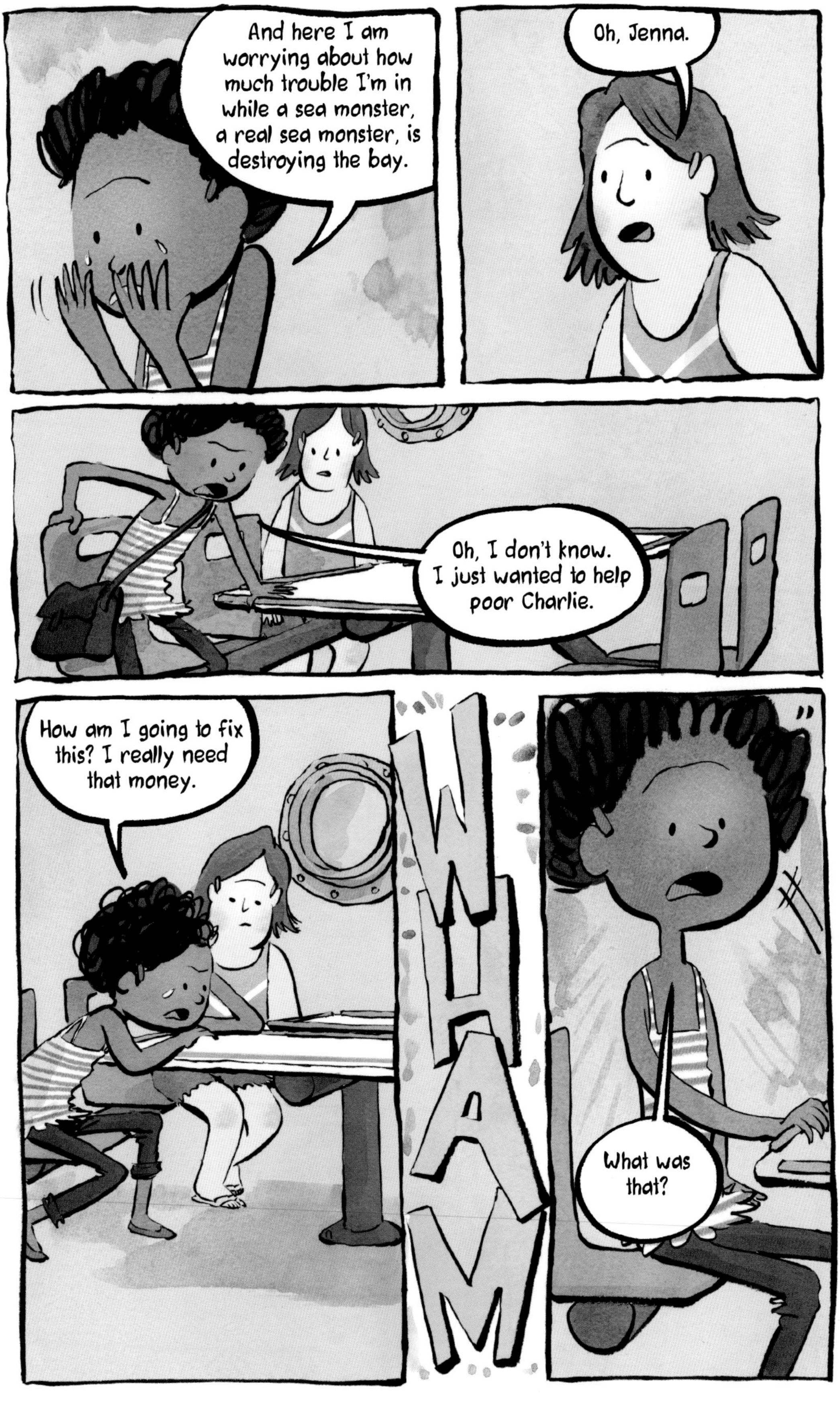
And here I am worrying about how much trouble I'm in while a sea monster, a real sea monster, is destroying the bay.
Oh, Jenna.
Oh, I don't know. I just wanted to help poor Charlie.
How am I going to fix this? I really need that money.
WHAM
What was that?

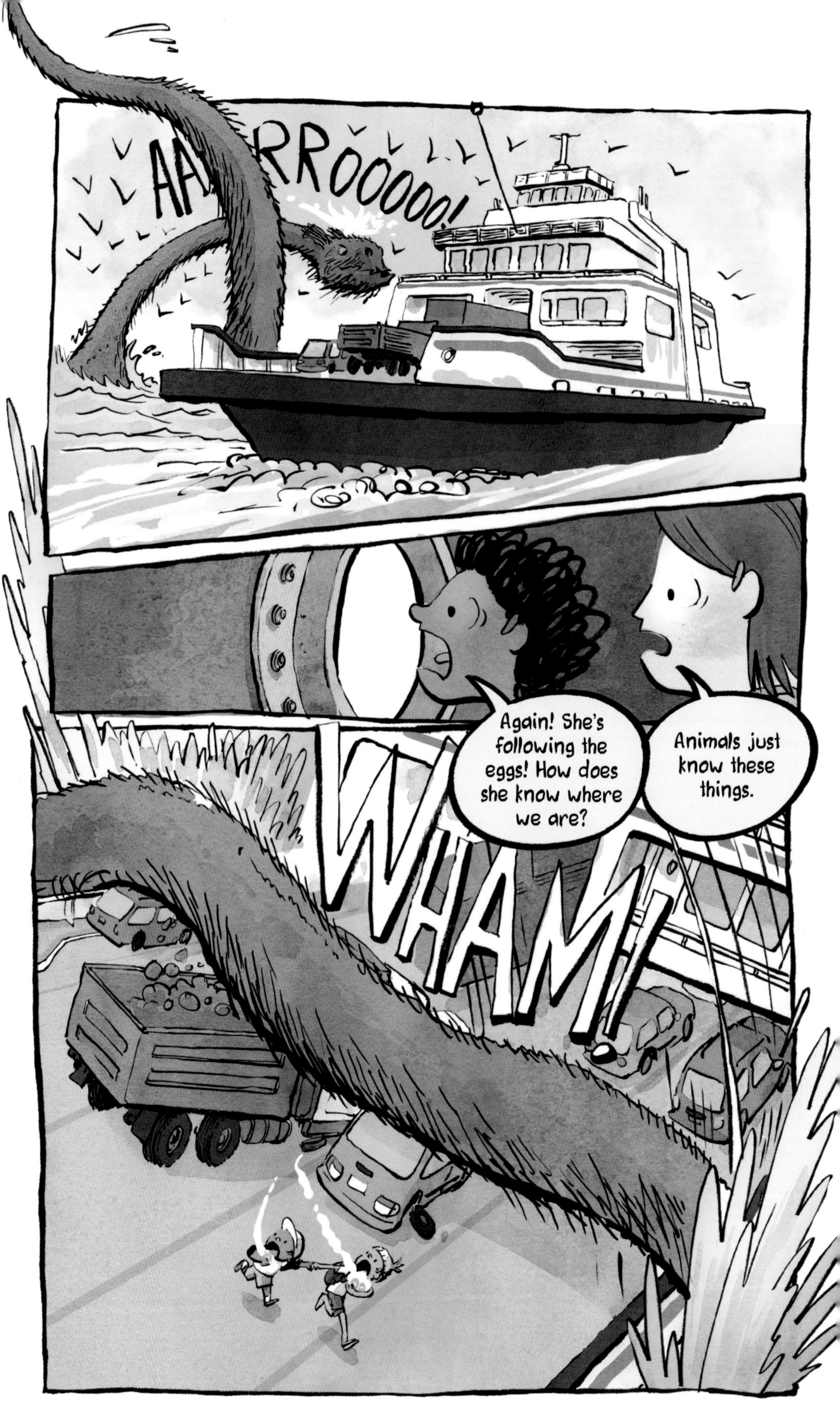
AAARROOOOO!
Again! She's following the eggs! How does she know where we are?
Animals just know these things.
WHAM!

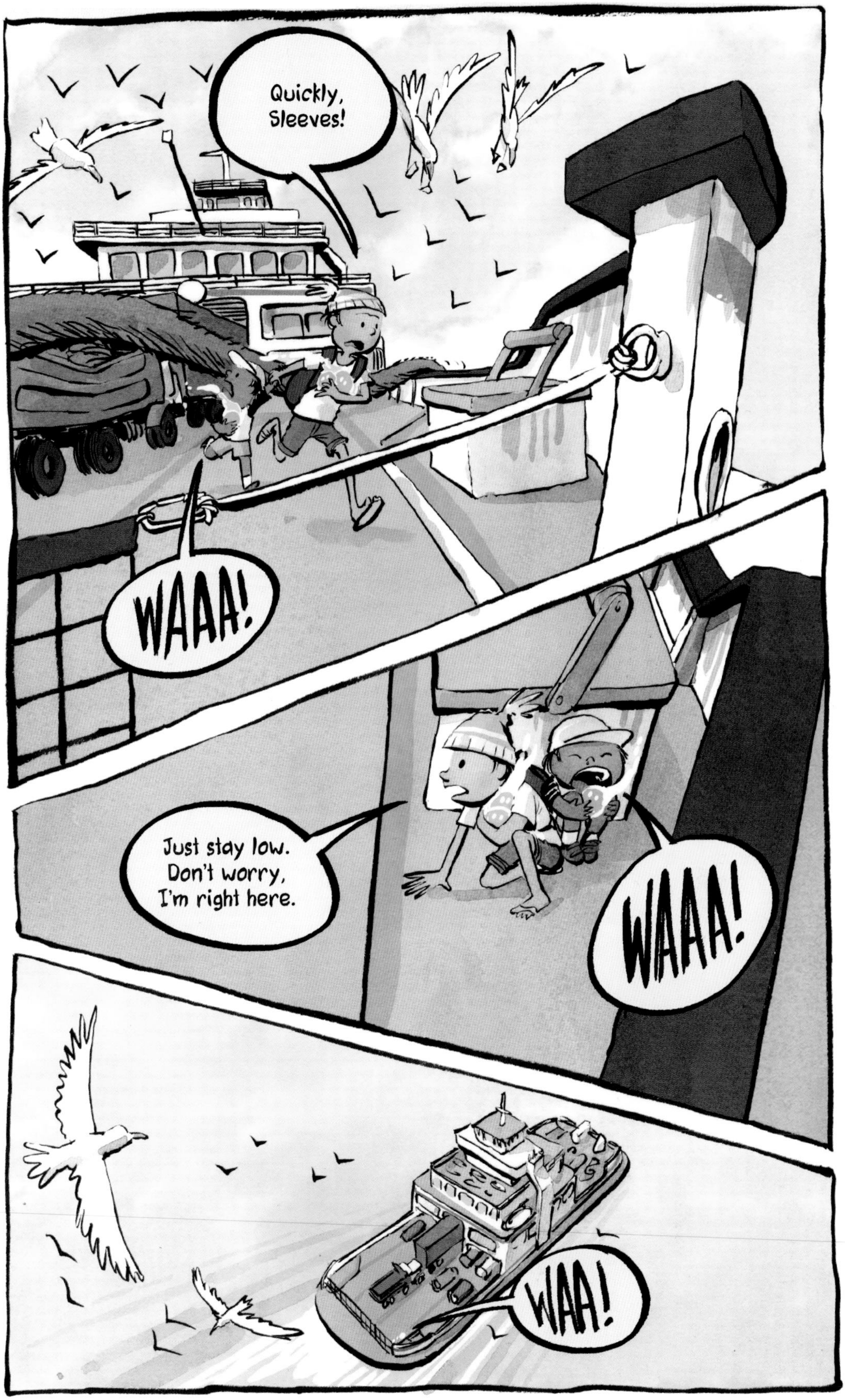

Quickly, Sleeves!
WAAA!
Just stay low. Don't worry, I'm right here.
WAAA!
WAA!

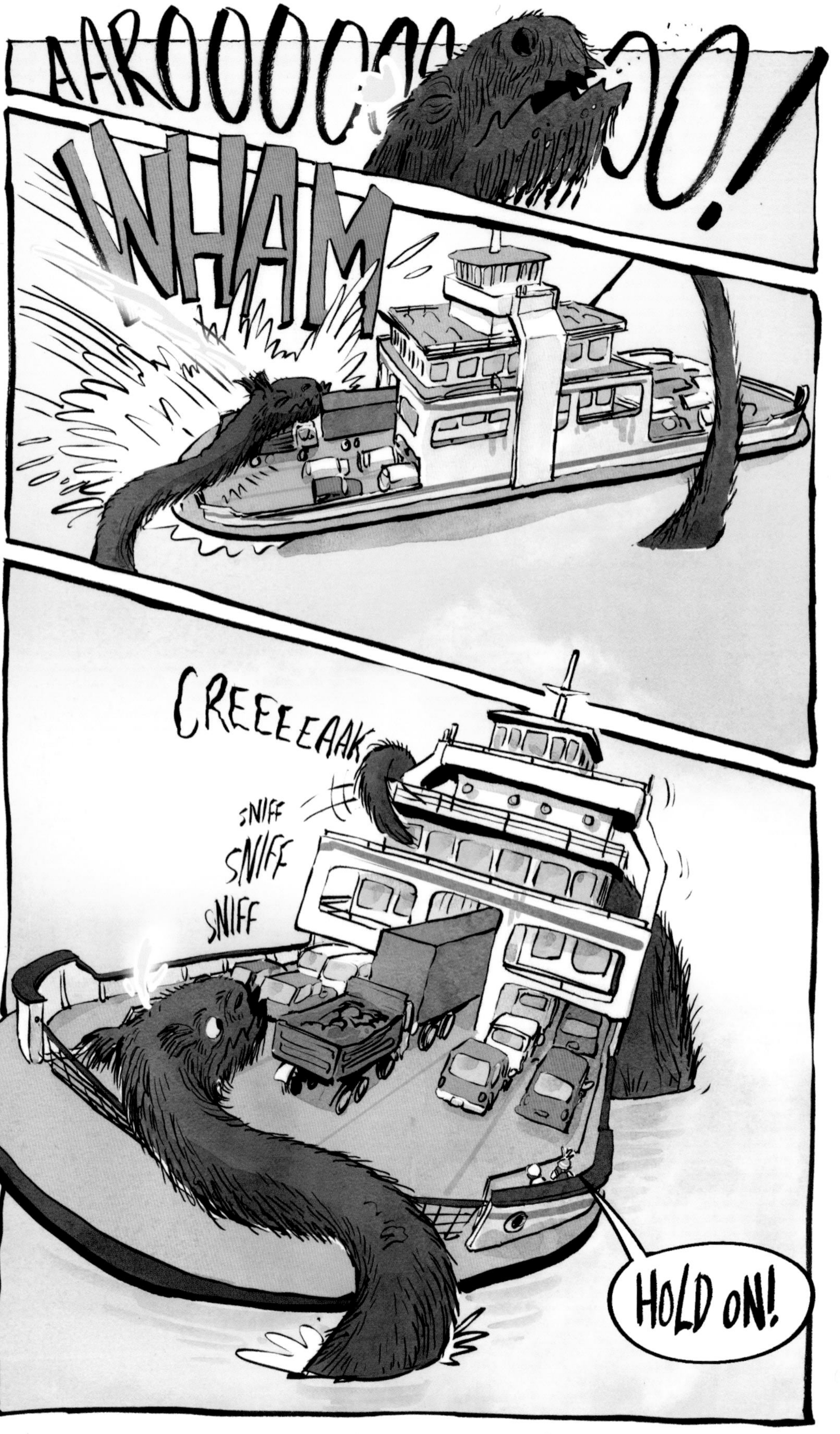

AAROOOOOOOOO!
WHAM
CREEEEAAK
SNIFF
SNIFF
SNIFF
HOLD ON!

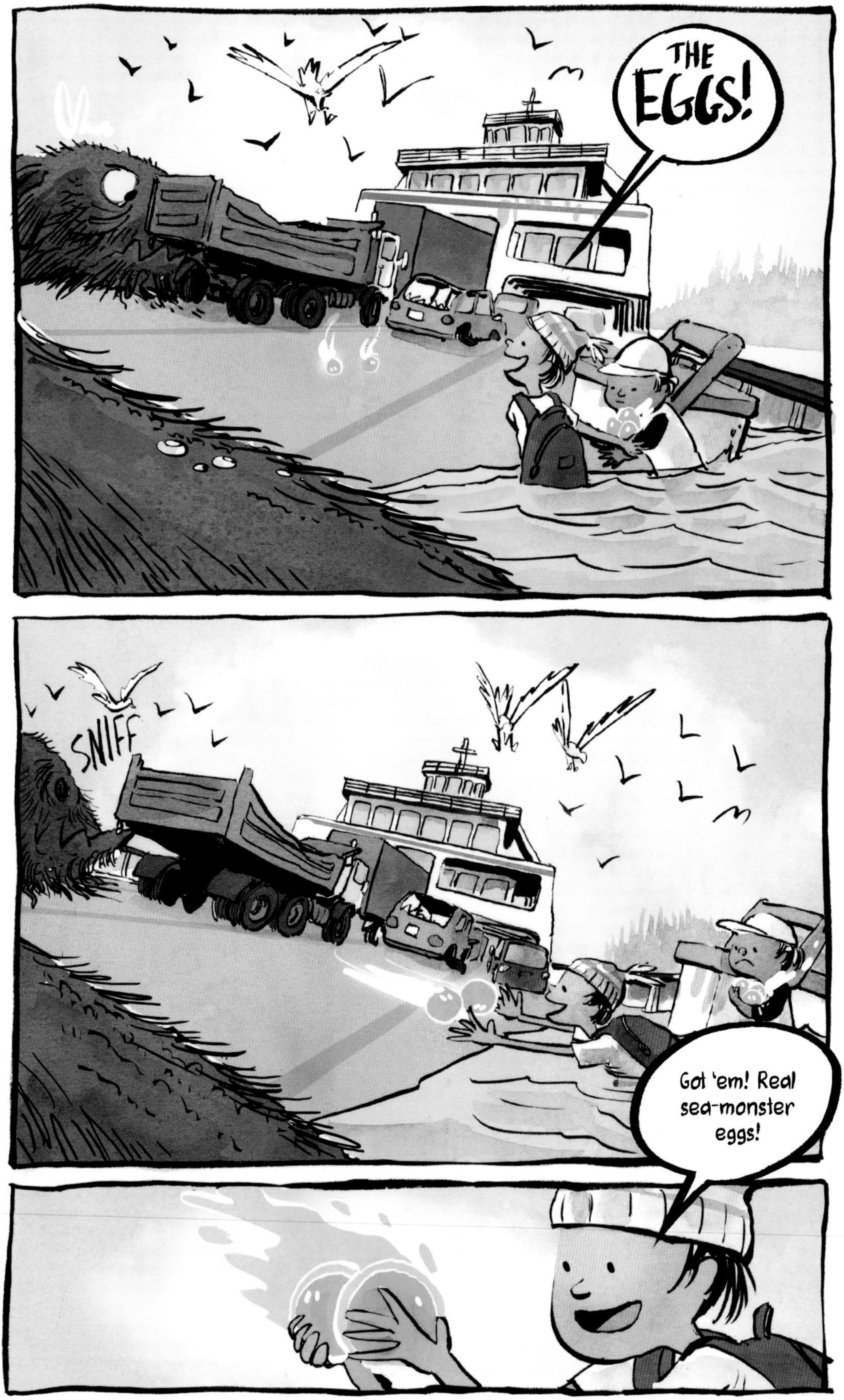
THE EGGS!
SNIFF
Got 'em! Real sea-monster eggs!

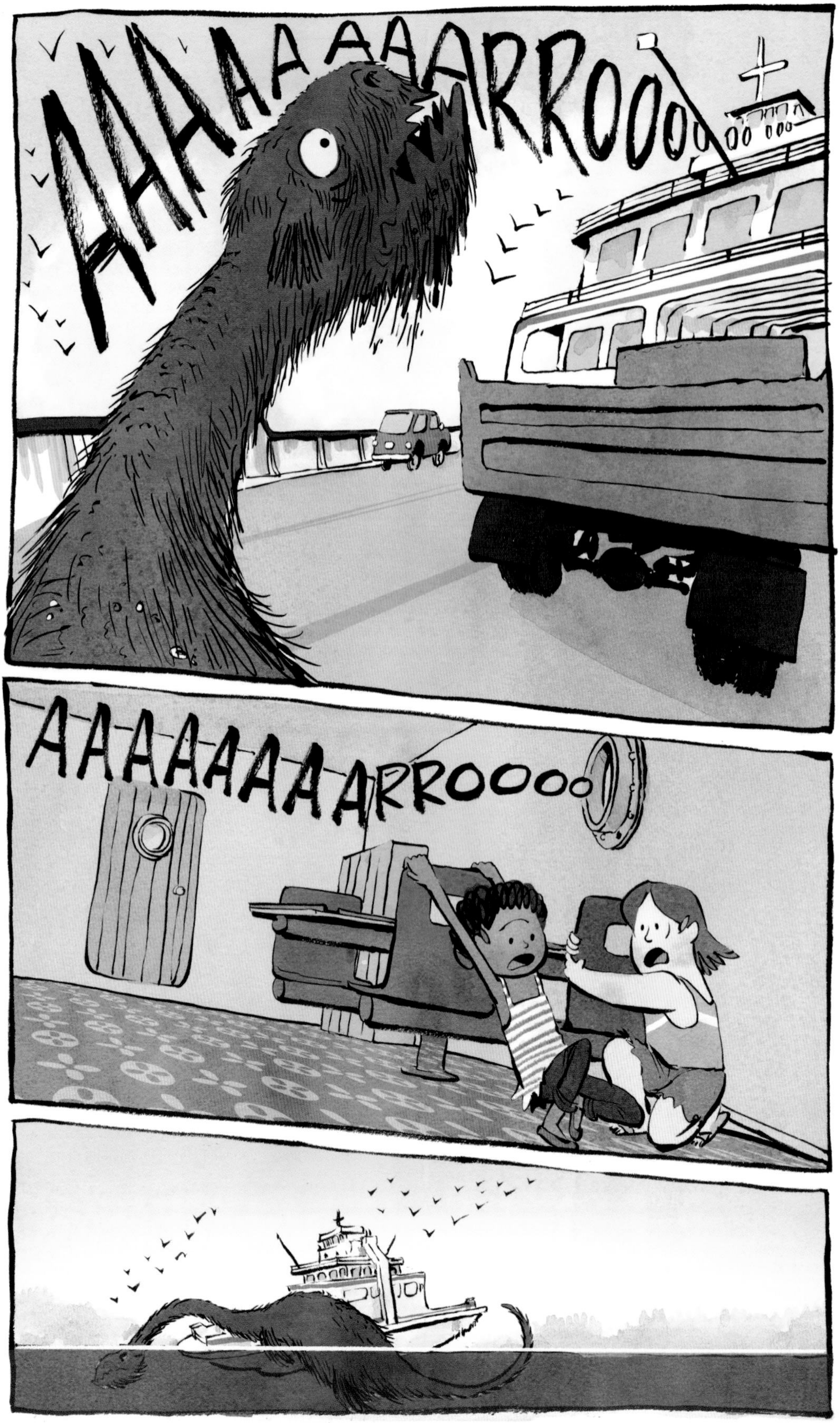
AAAAAAARROOOo
AAAAAAAARROOOo

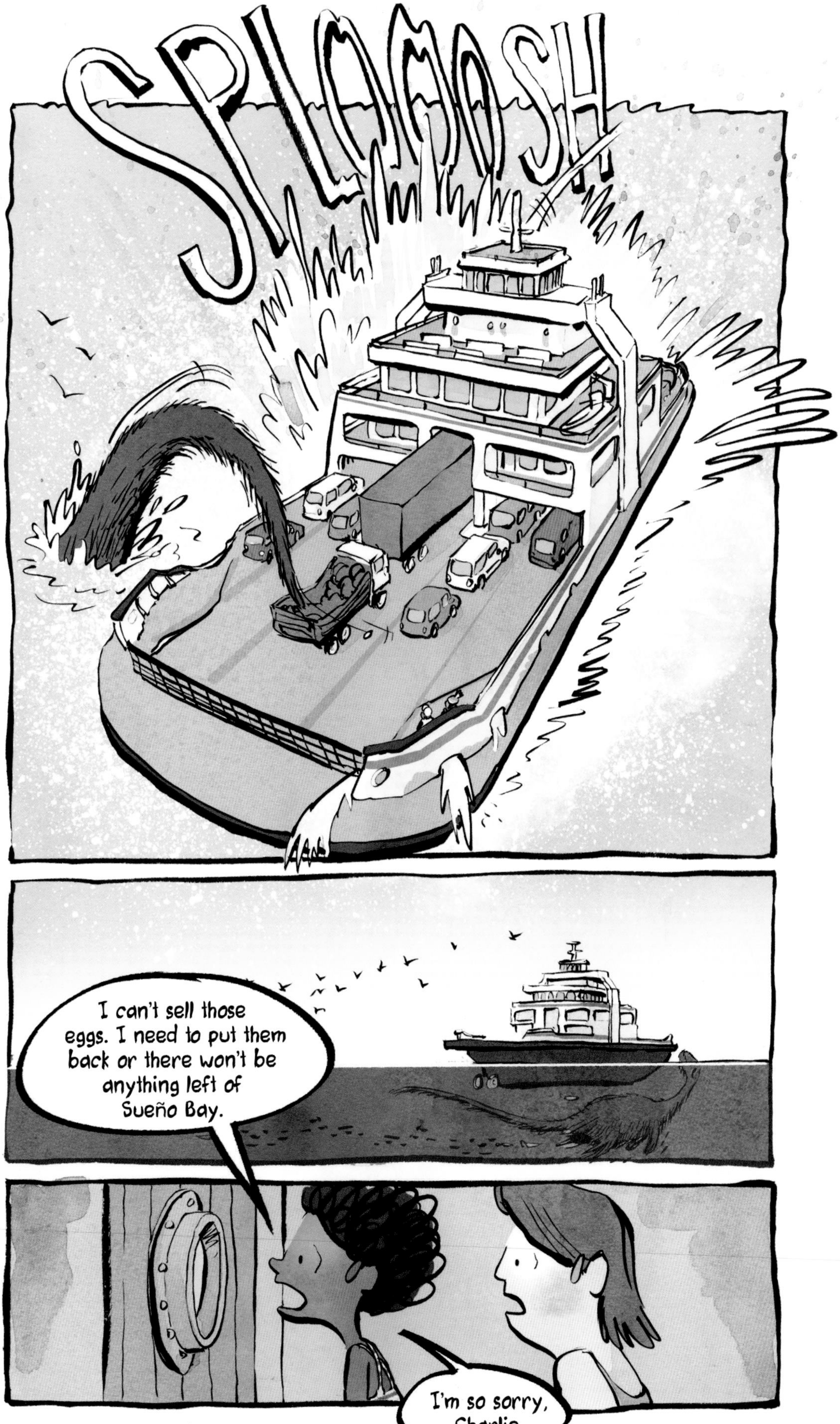
SPLOOOSH
I can't sell those eggs. I need to put them back or there won't be anything left of Sueño Bay.
I'm so sorry, Charlie.

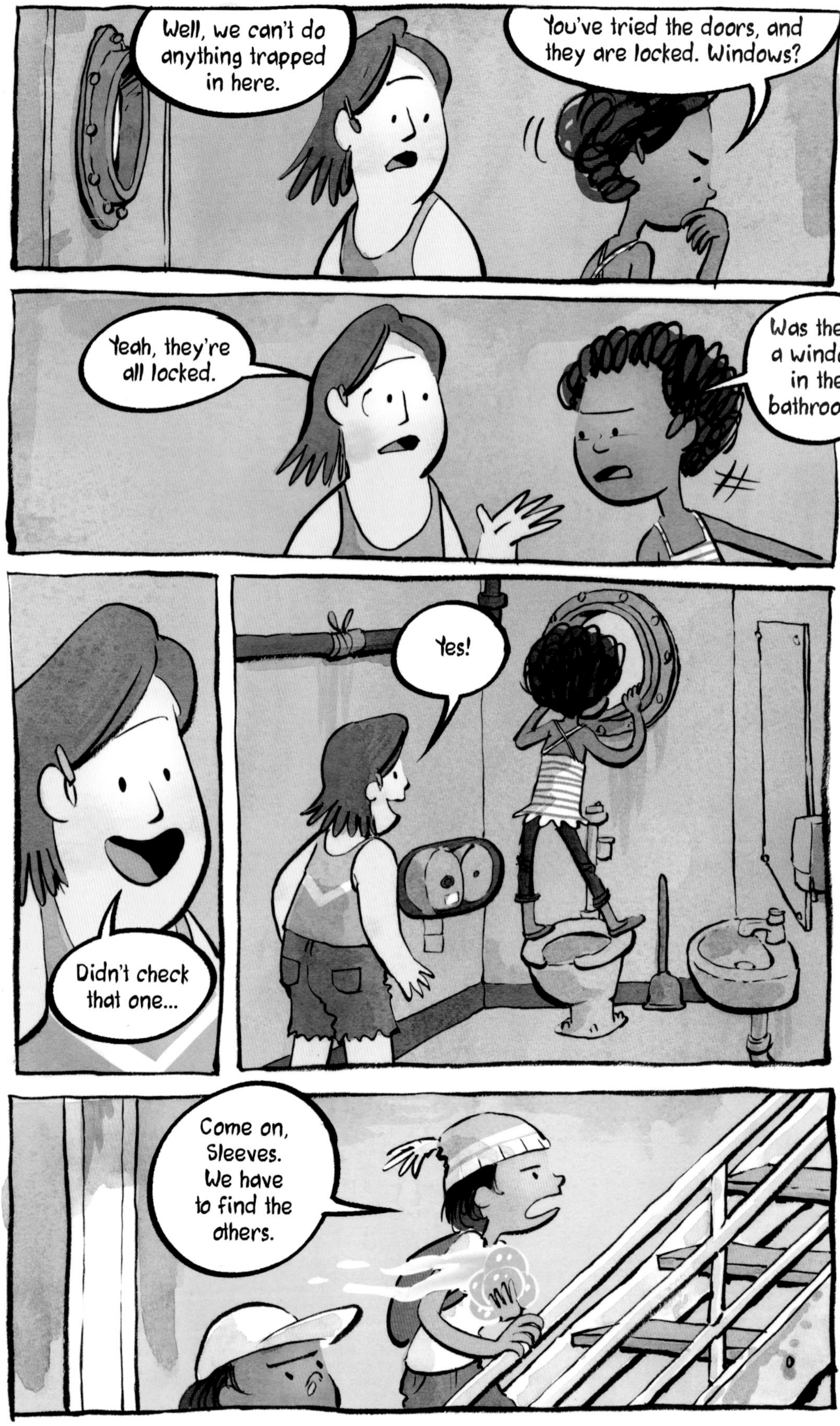
Well, we can't do anything trapped in here.
You've tried the doors, and they are locked. Windows?
Yeah, they're all locked.
Was there a window in the bathroom?
Didn't check that one...
Yes!
Come on, Sleeves. We have to find the others.

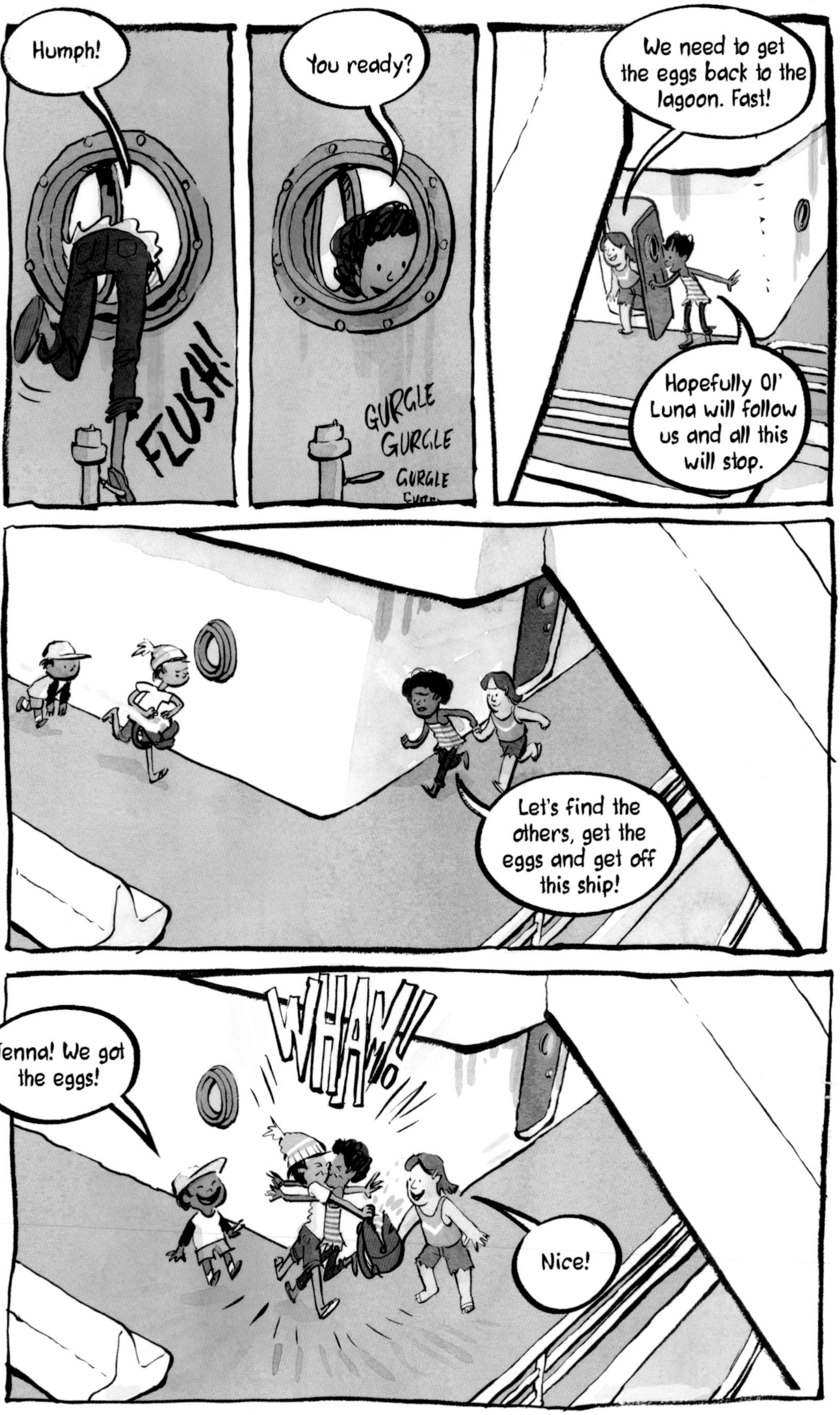

Humph!
FLUSH!
You ready?
GURGLE
GURGLE
GURGLE
We need to get the eggs back to the lagoon. Fast!
Hopefully Ol' Luna will follow us and all this will stop.
Let's find the others, get the eggs and get off this ship!
WHAM!
Jenna! We got the eggs!
Nice!

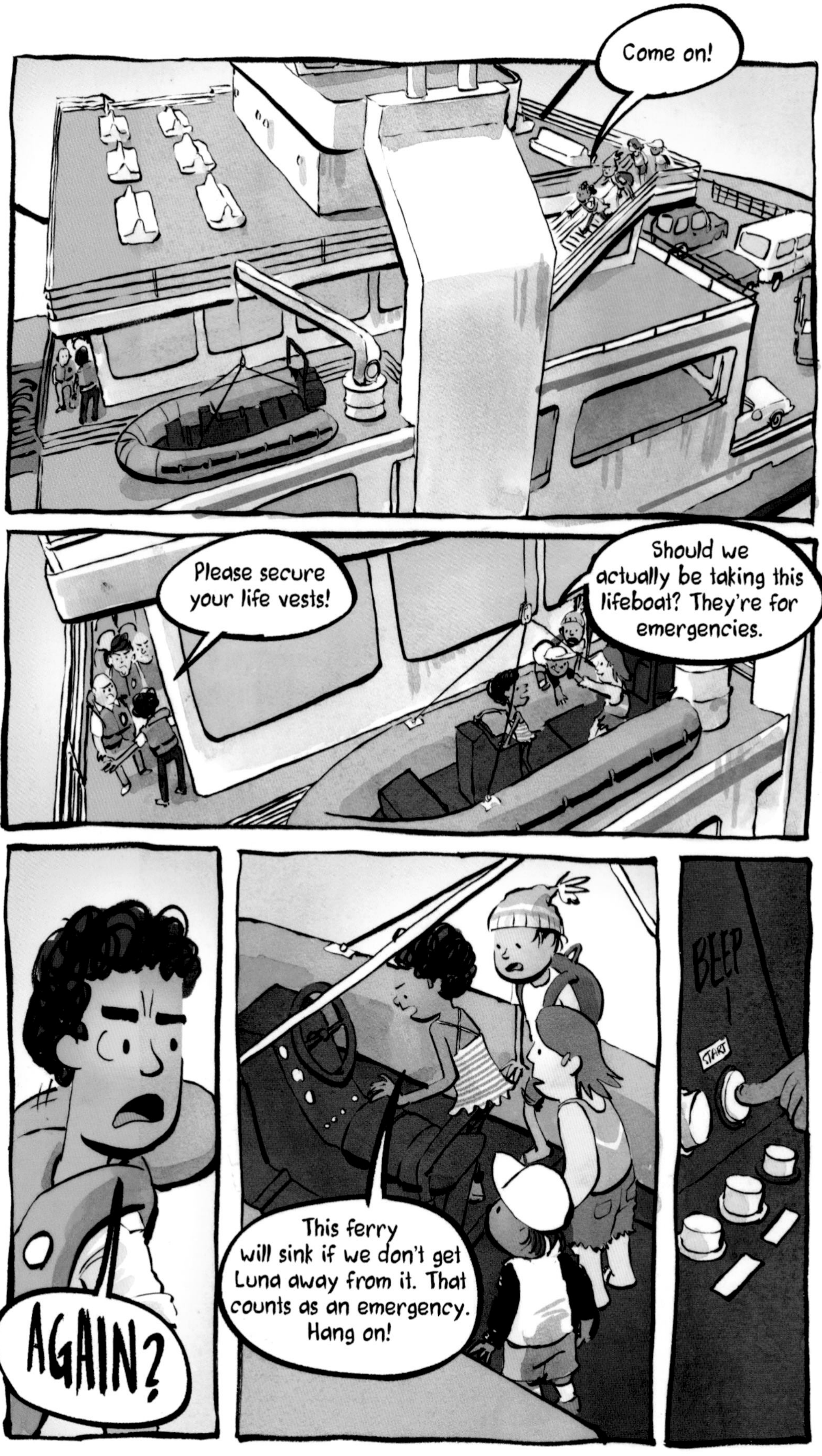
Come on!
Please secure your life vests!
Should we actually be taking this lifeboat? They're for emergencies.
AGAIN?
This ferry will sink if we don't get Luna away from it. That counts as an emergency. Hang on!
BEEP
START

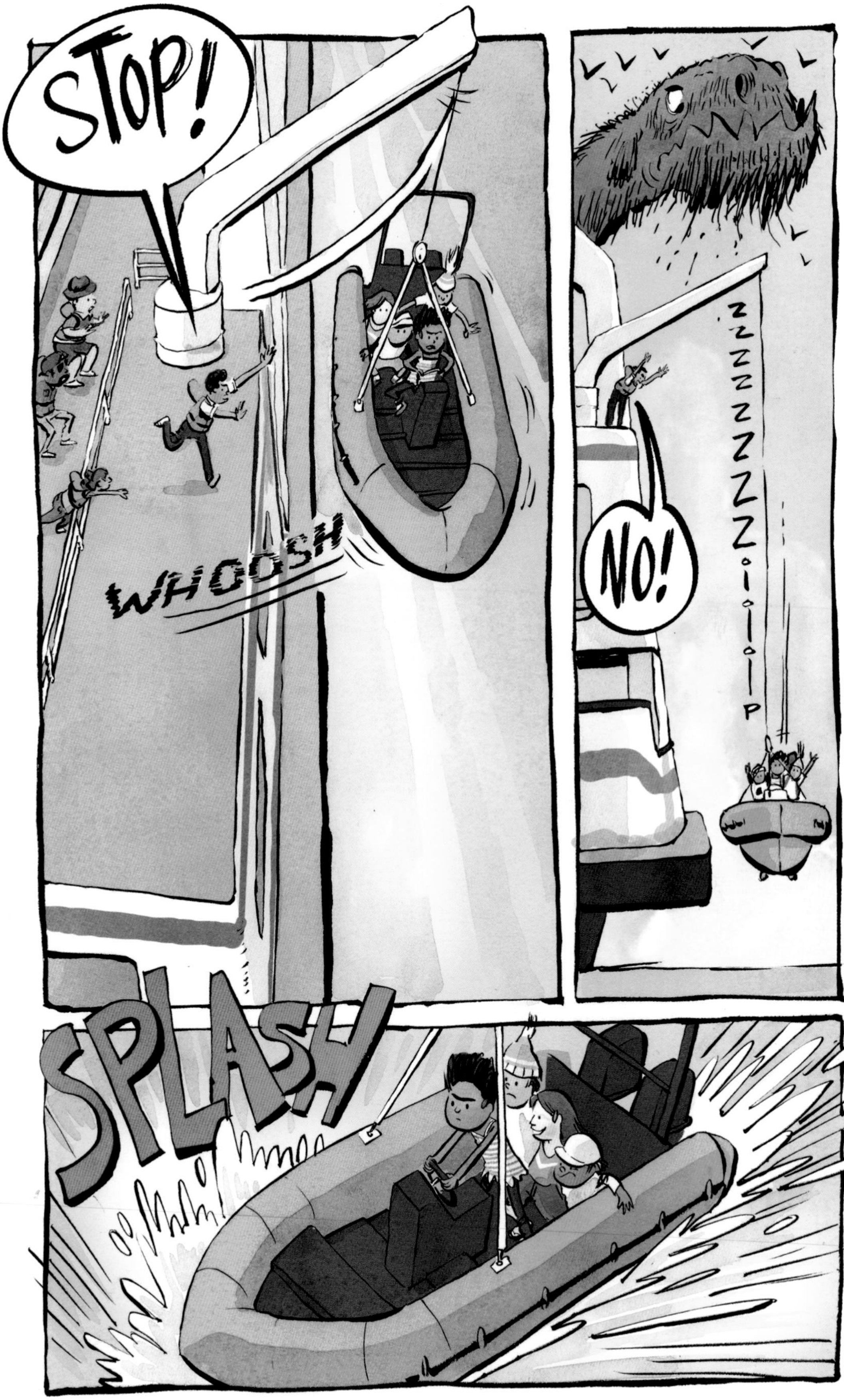
STOP!
WHOOSH
NO!
ZZZZZZZZZ.i.i.l.l.P
SPLASH

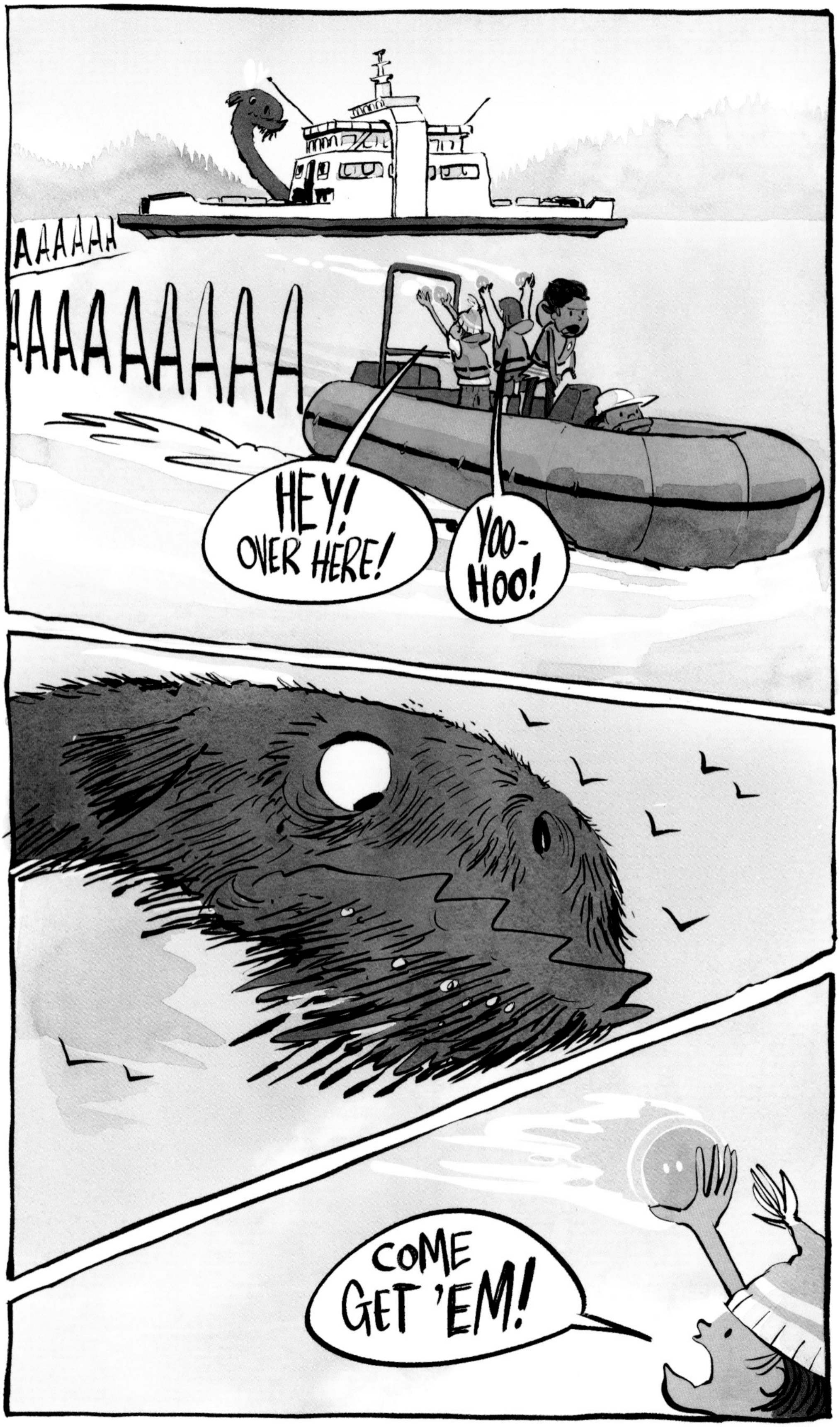

AAAAAH
AAAAAAAAA
HEY! OVER HERE!
YOO-HOO!
COME GET 'EM!

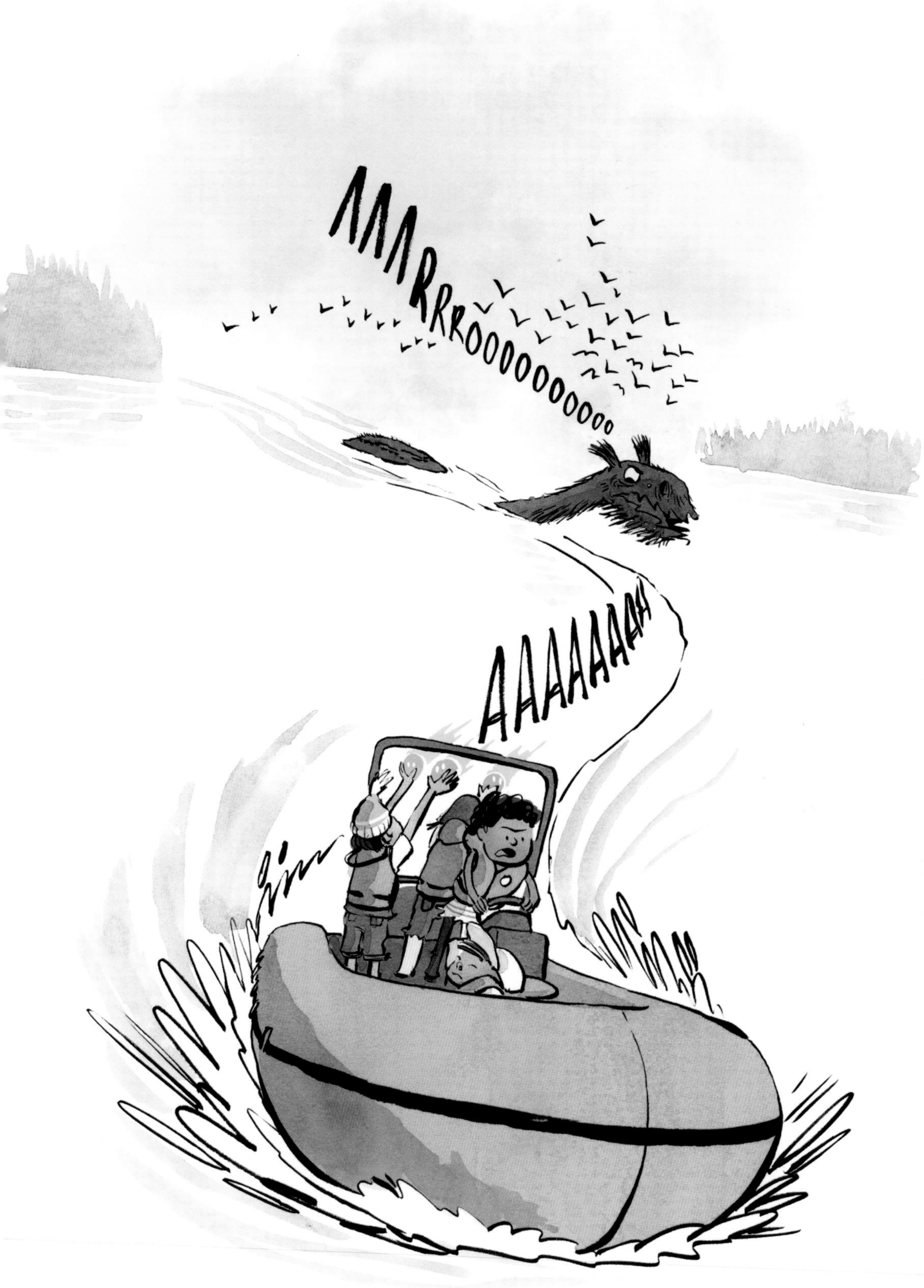
AAARRRROOOOOOOOOOoooo
AAAAAAAH

CHAPTER FIVE

Every One Hundred Years Or So...

AAAAAAAAAAAAAAA

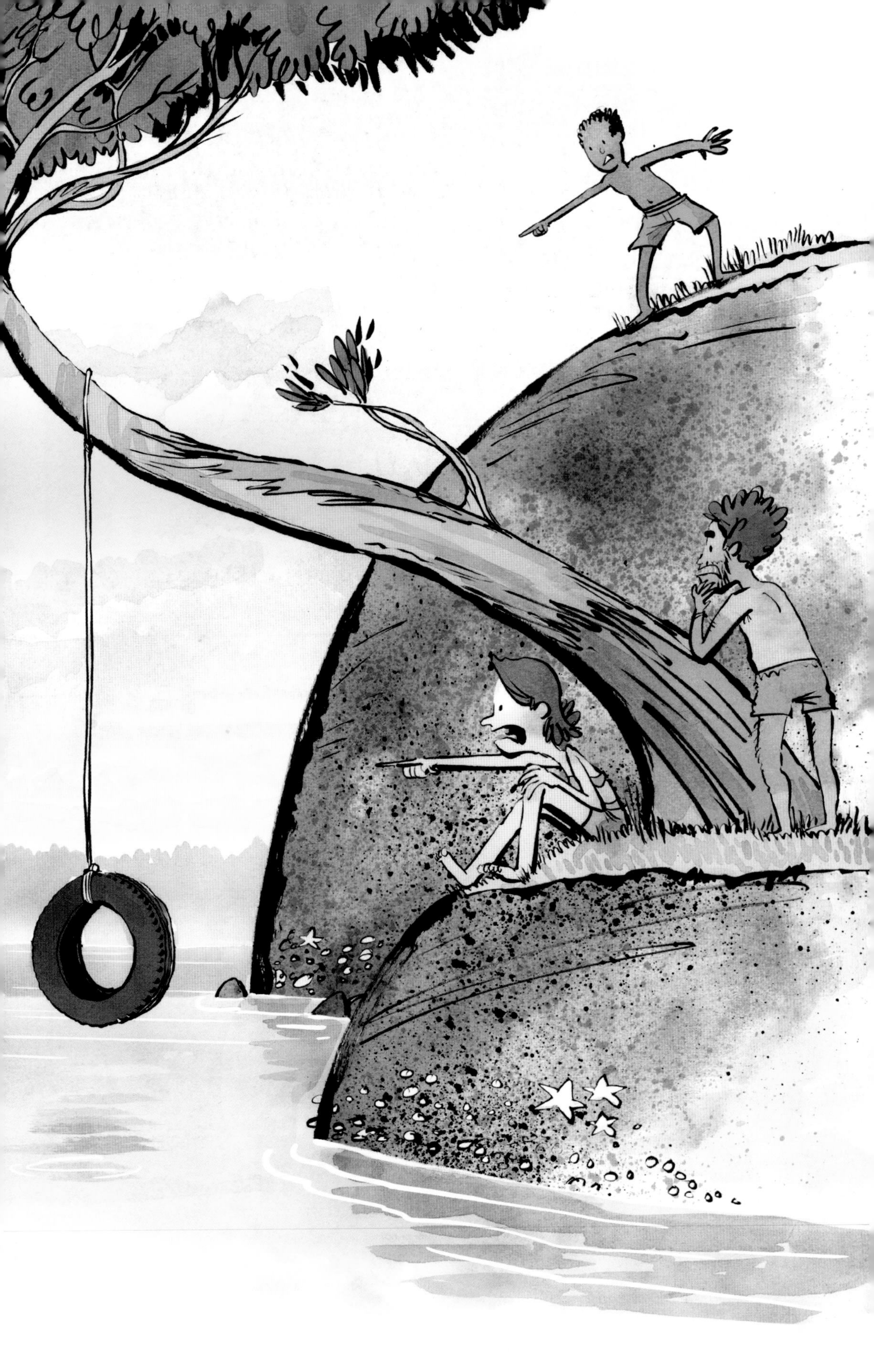

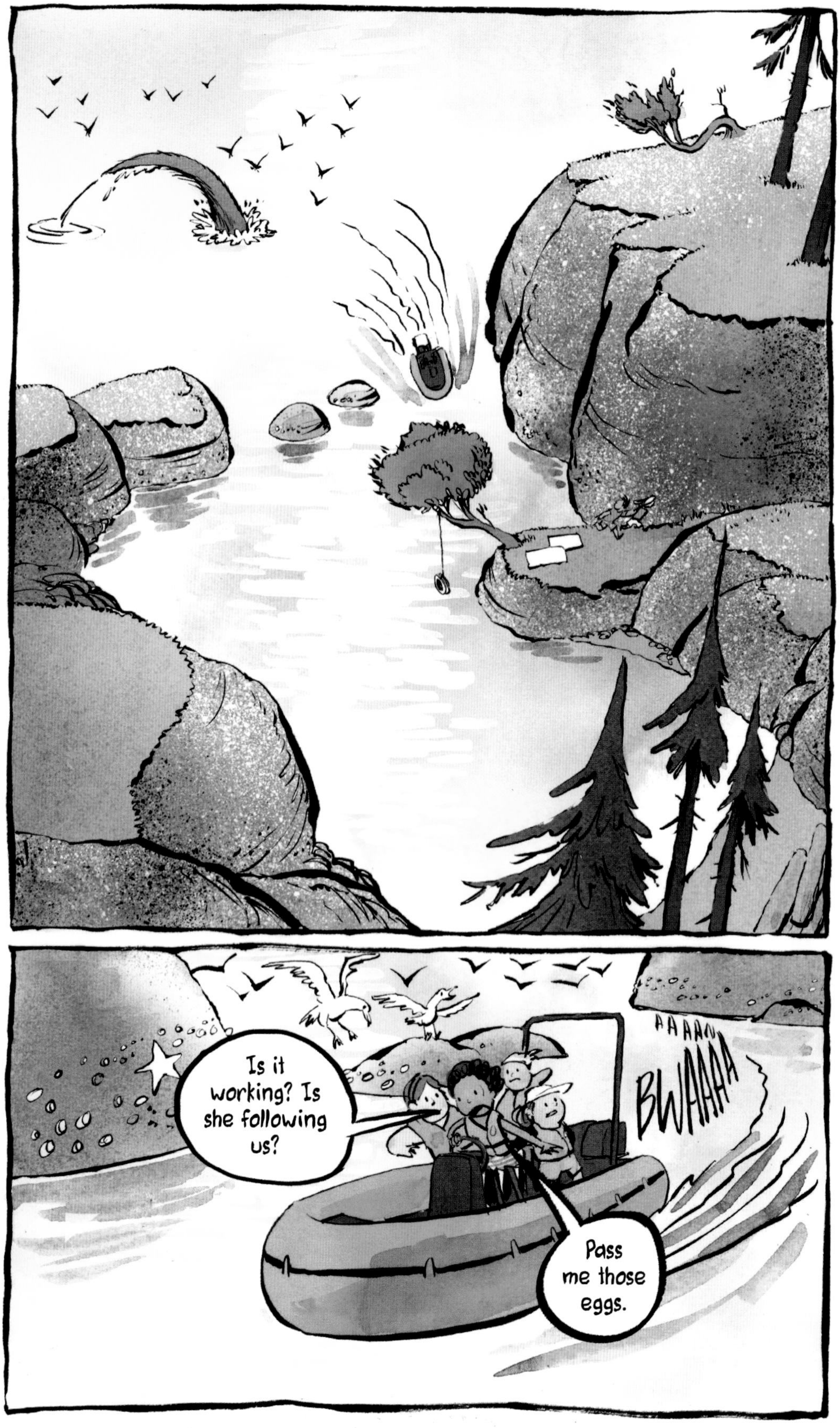

Is it working? Is she following us?
AAAAN BWAAAA
Pass me those eggs.

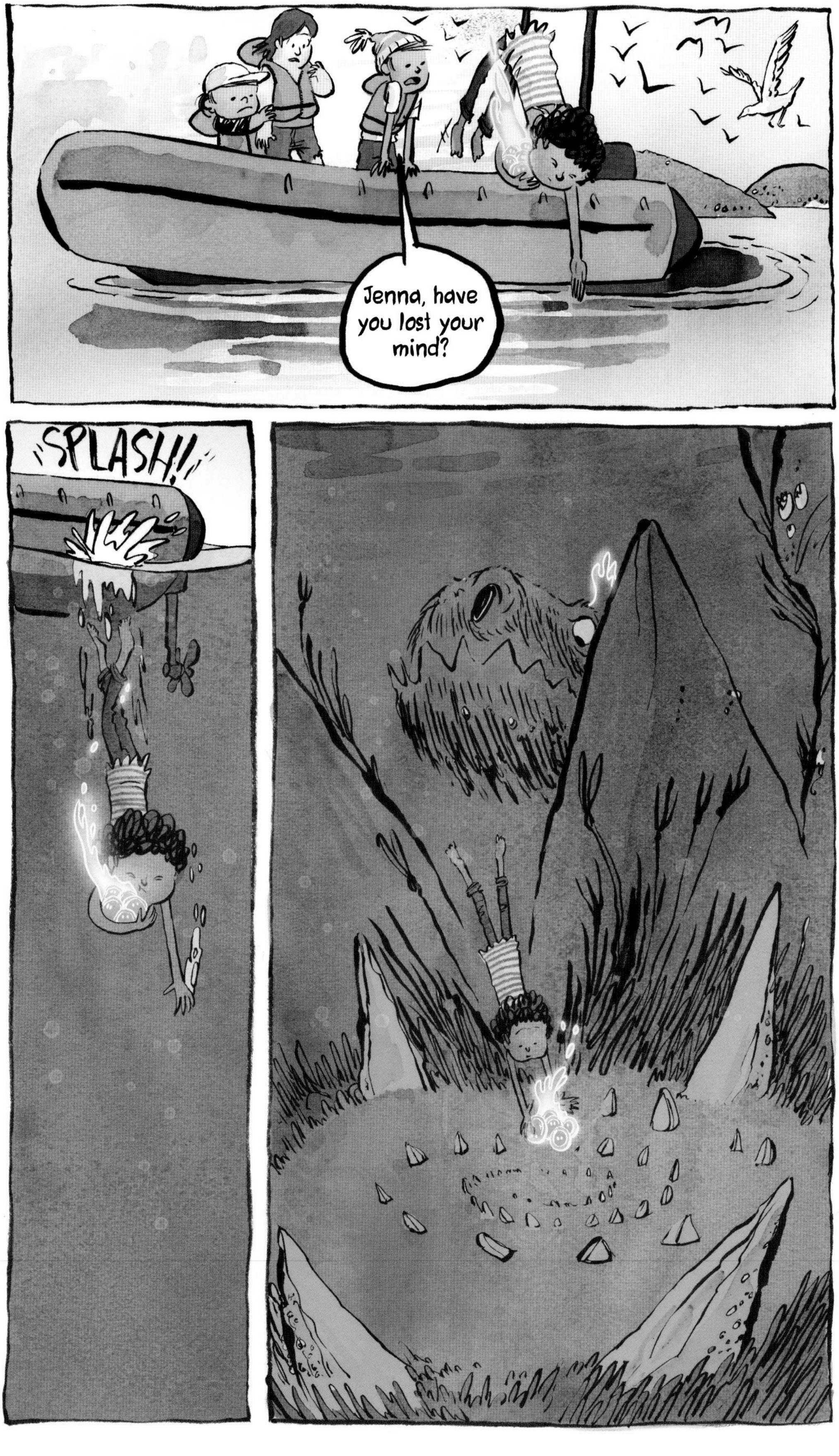
Jenna, have you lost your mind?
SPLASH!!

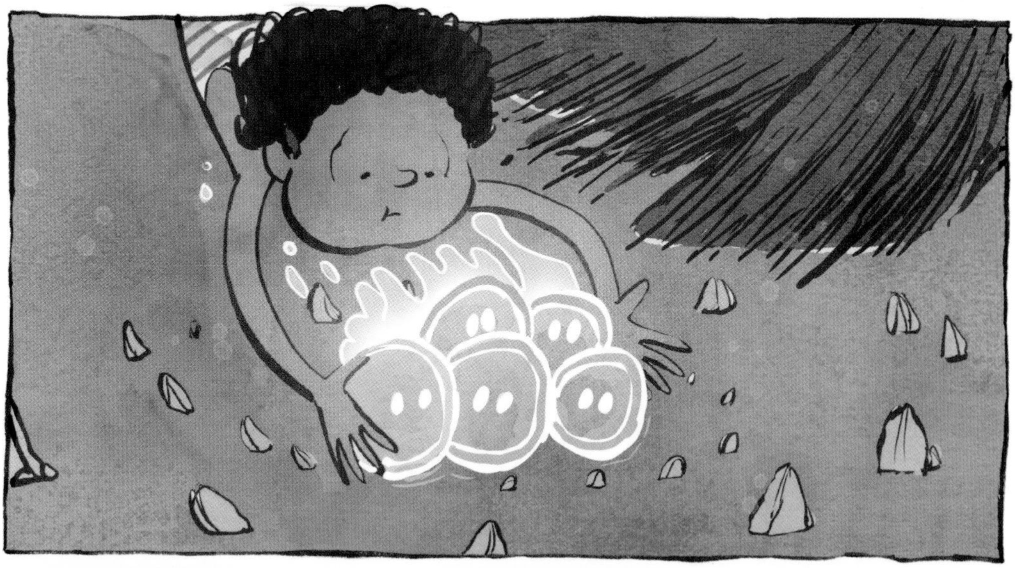

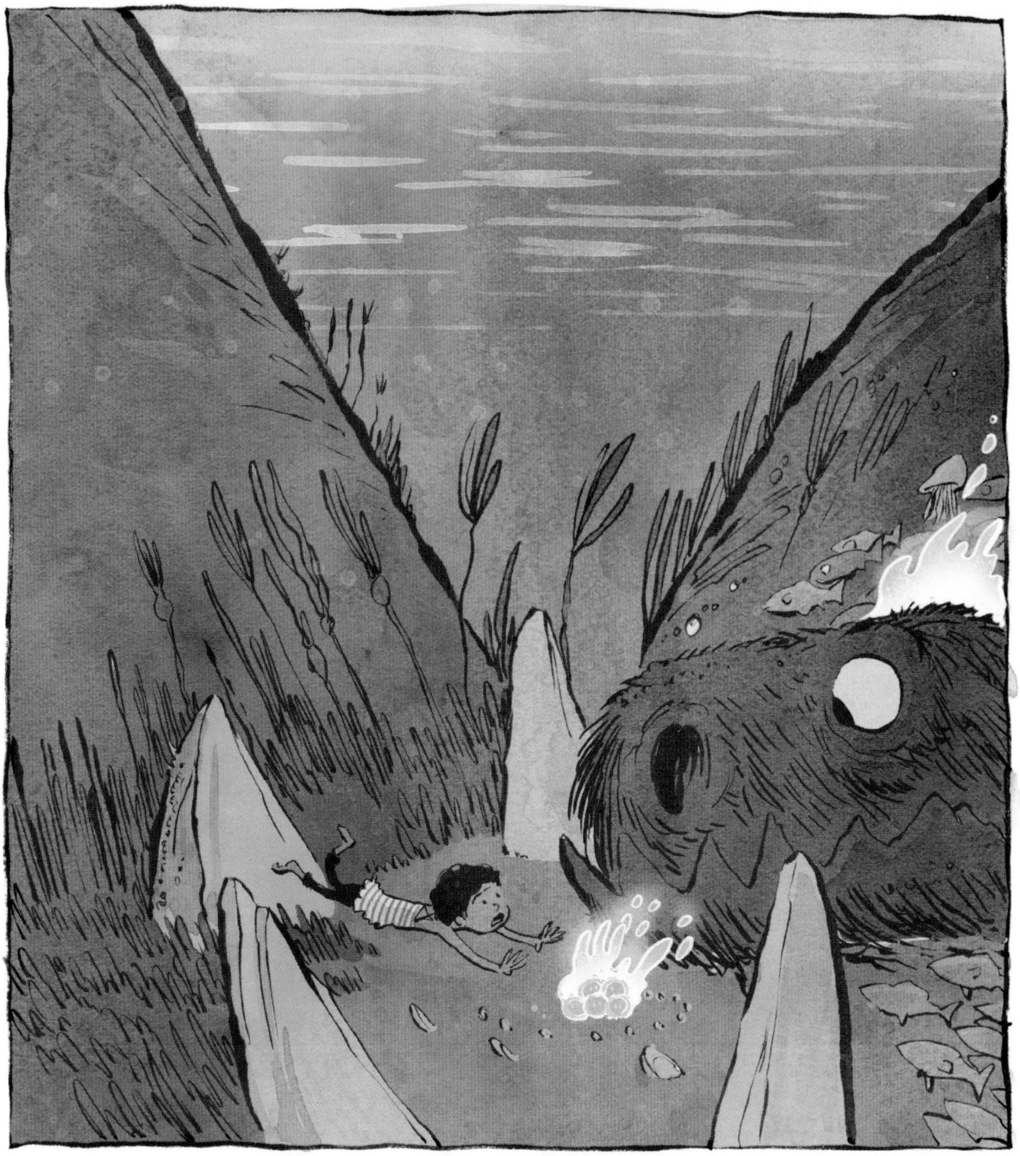

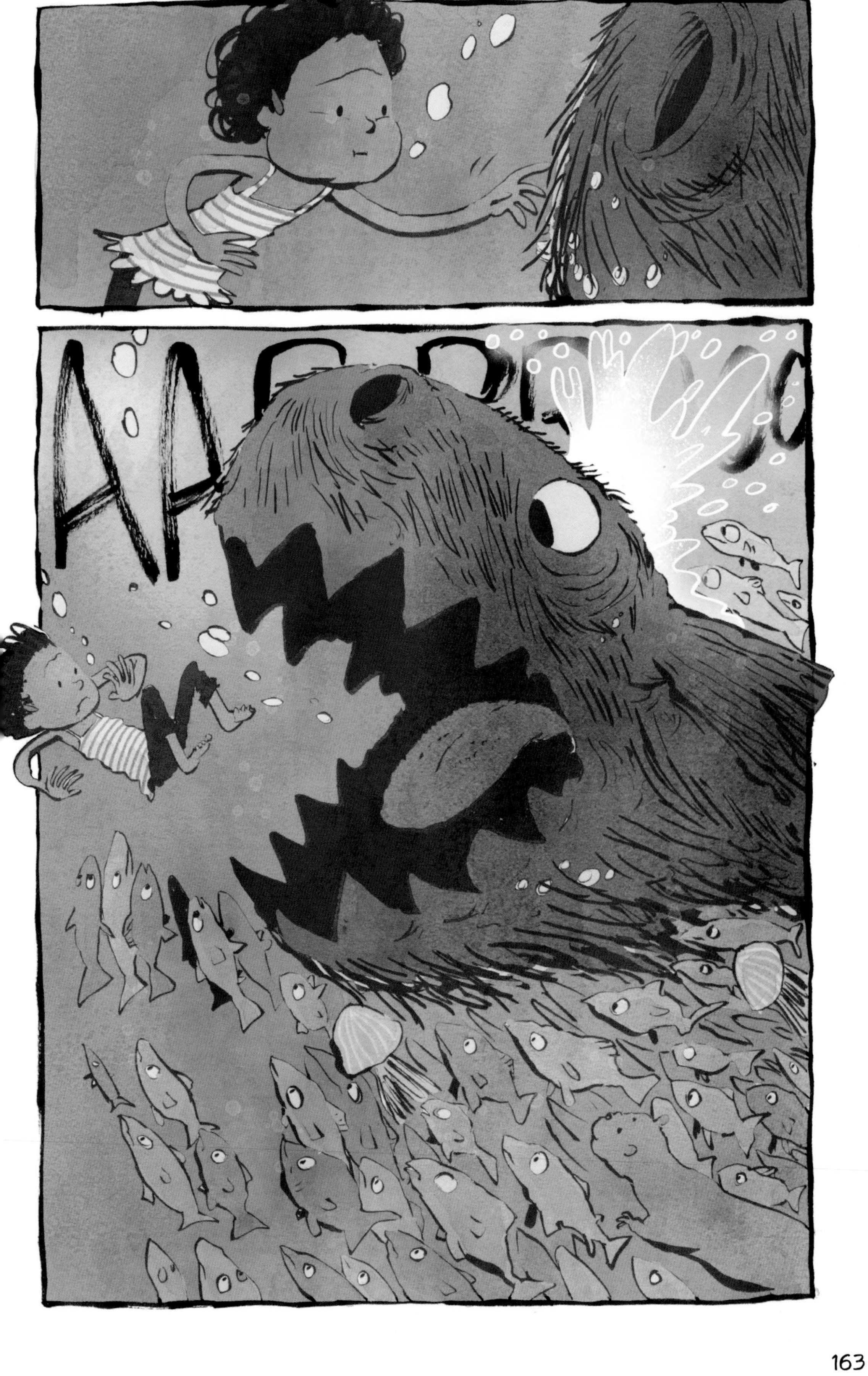

GET ME OUT OF HERE!

AAAAHHHAROOOO

BRUM!

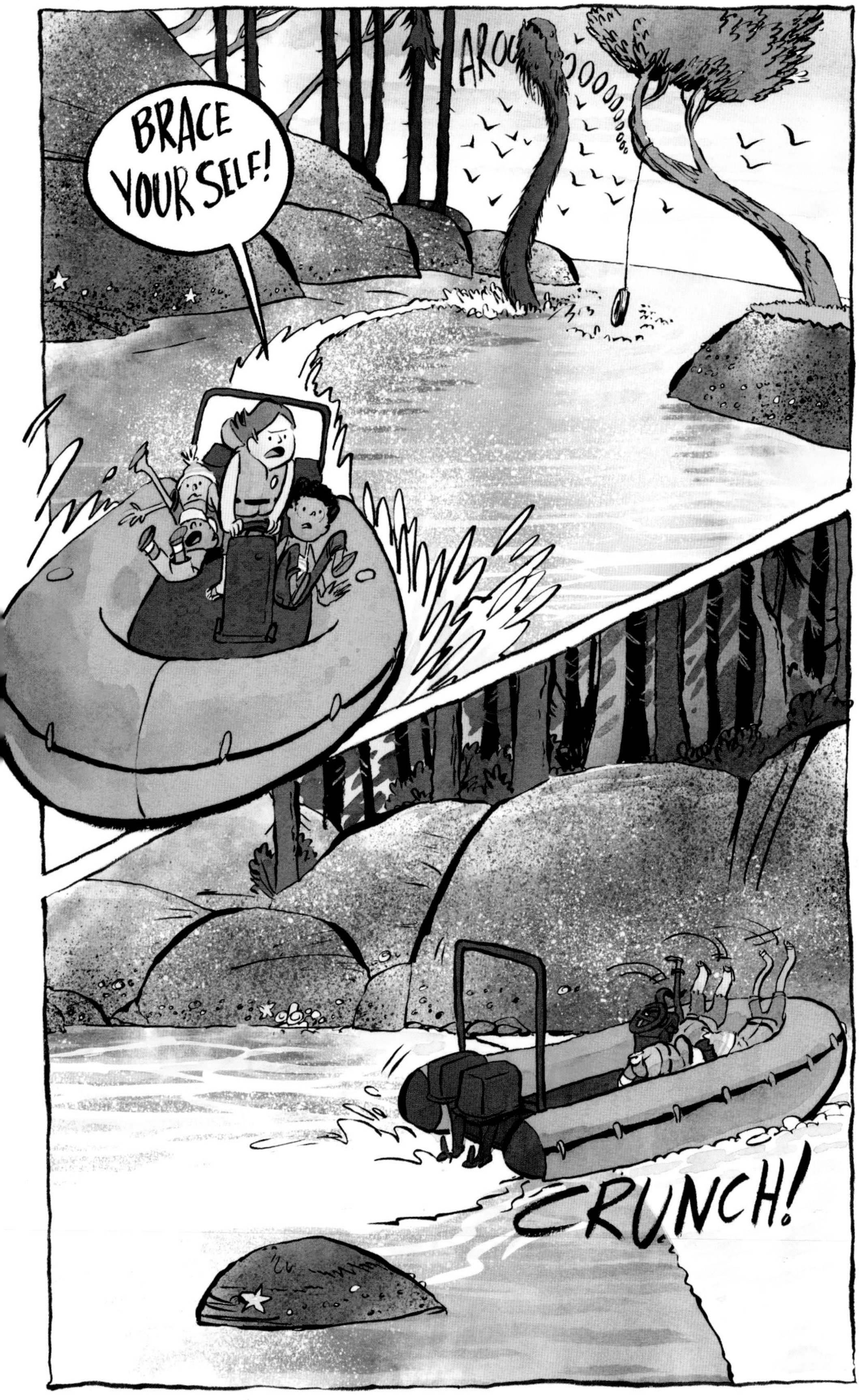
AROOOOOOOOOOOO
BRACE YOUR SELF!
CRUNCH!

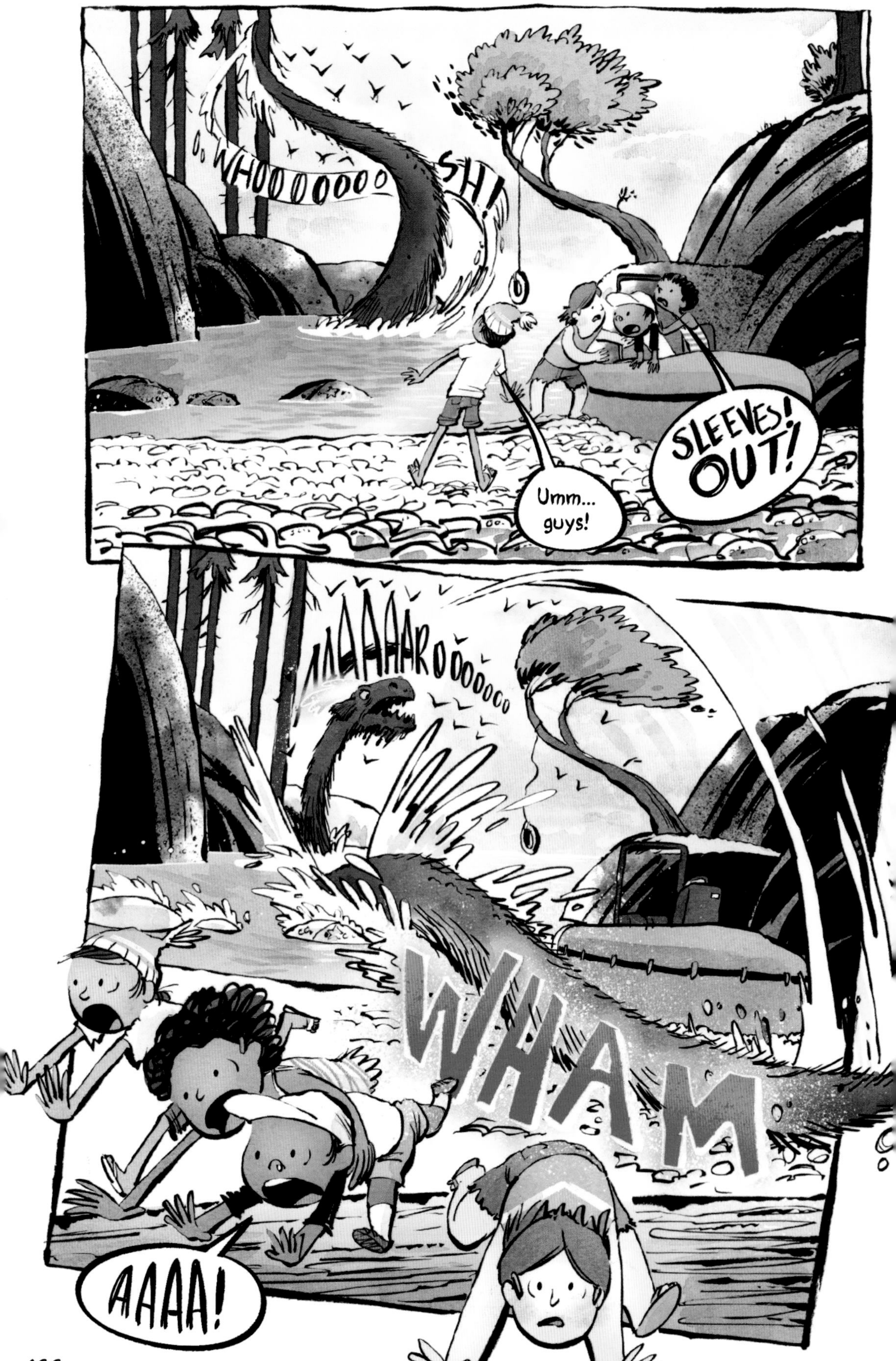
WHOOOOOOOOSH!
Umm... guys!
SLEEVES! OUT!
WAAAAAROOOOOOO
WHAM
AAAA!

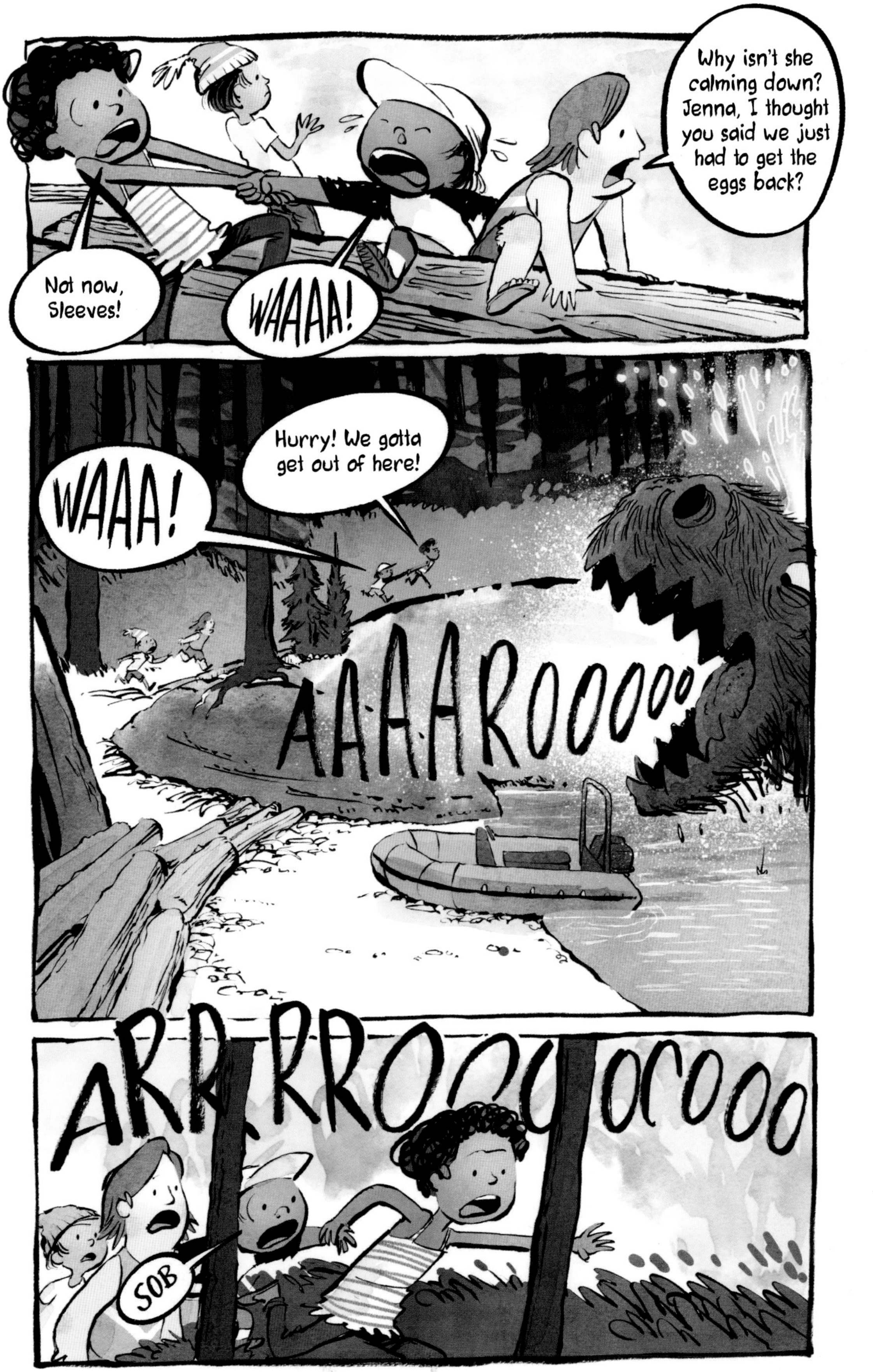
Why isn't she calming down? Jenna, I thought you said we just had to get the eggs back?
Not now, Sleeves!
WAAAA!
Hurry! We gotta get out of here!
WAAA!
AAAAROOOOOO
ARRRRROOOOOOOOO
SOB

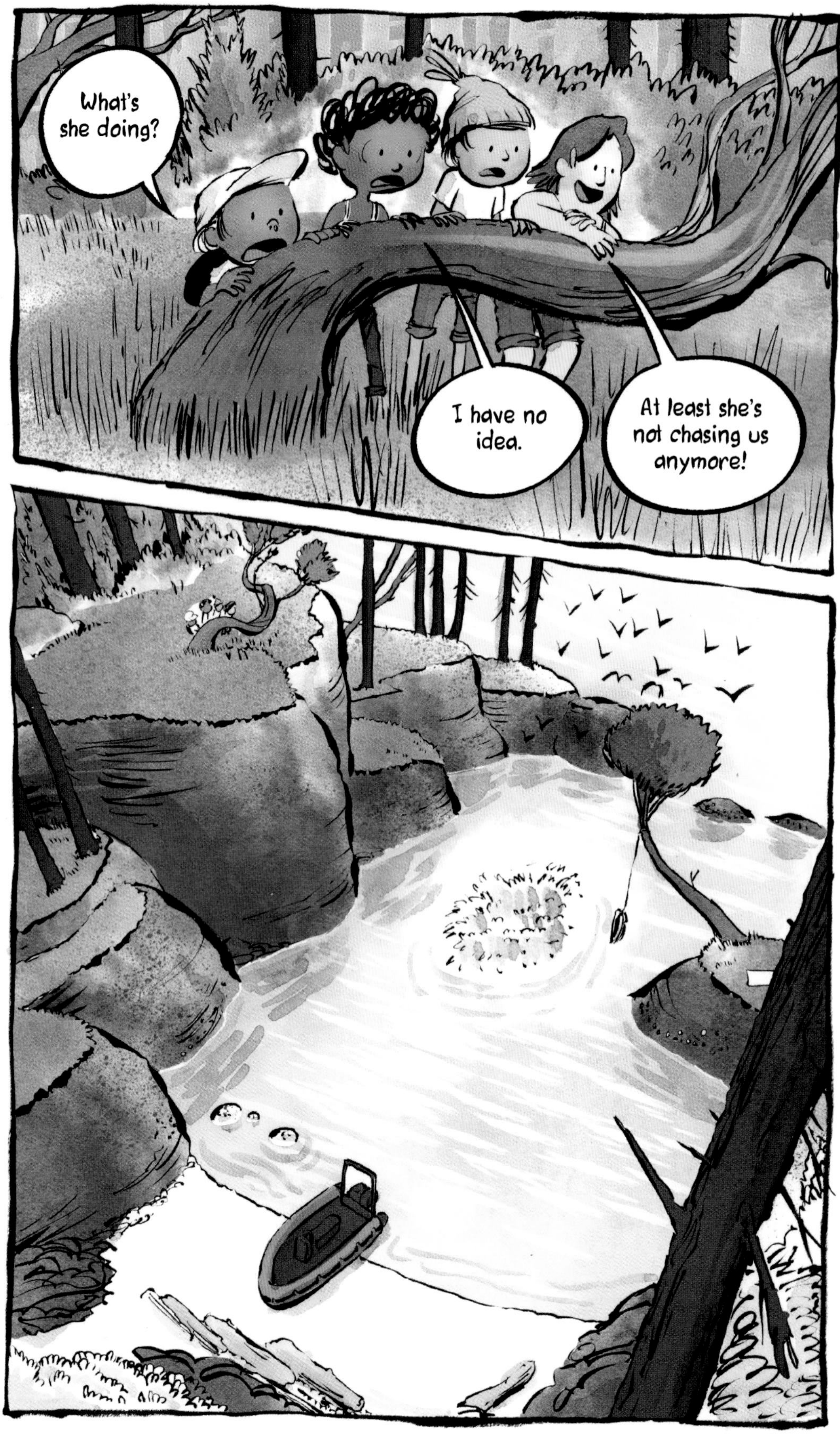
What's she doing?
I have no idea.
At least she's not chasing us anymore!

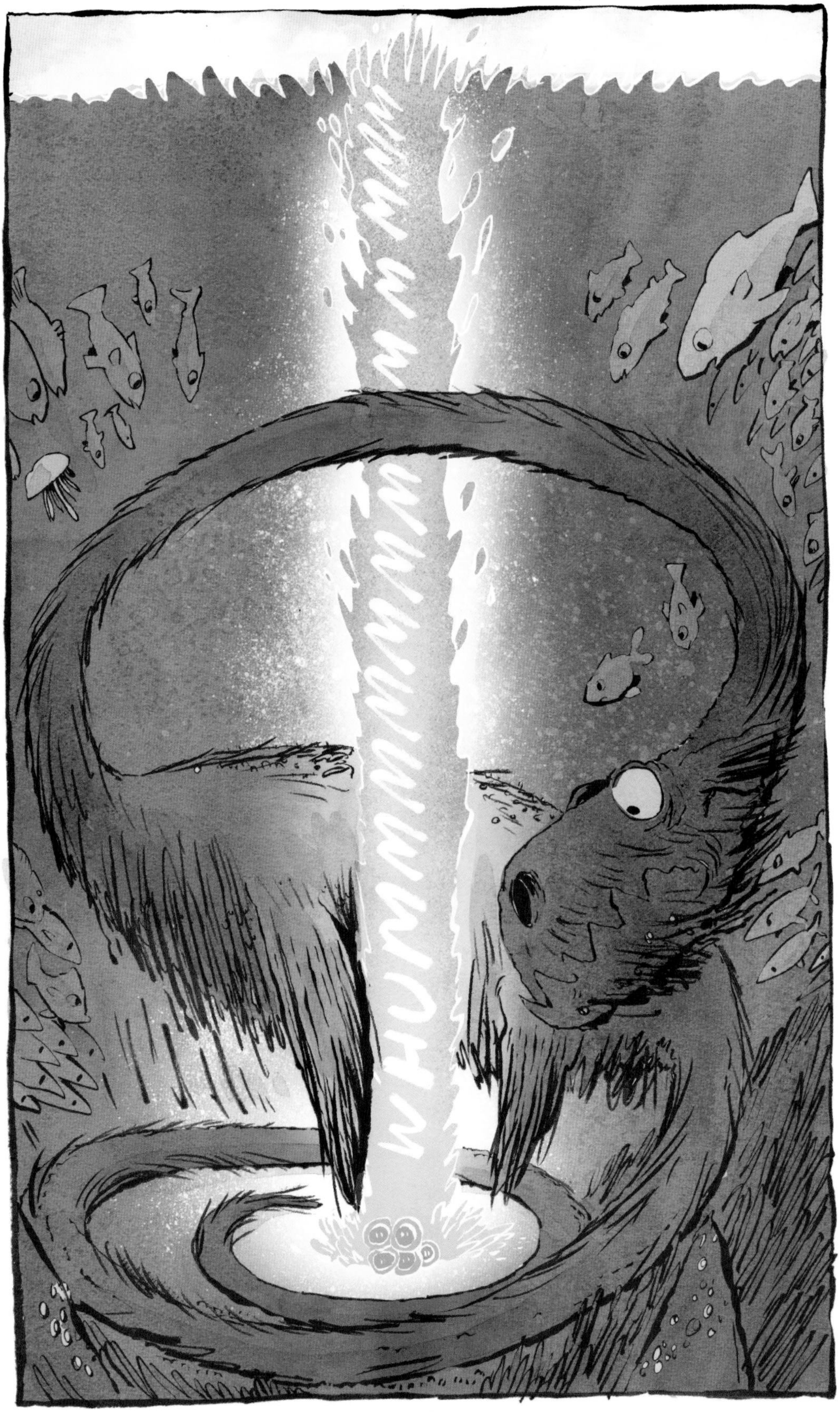

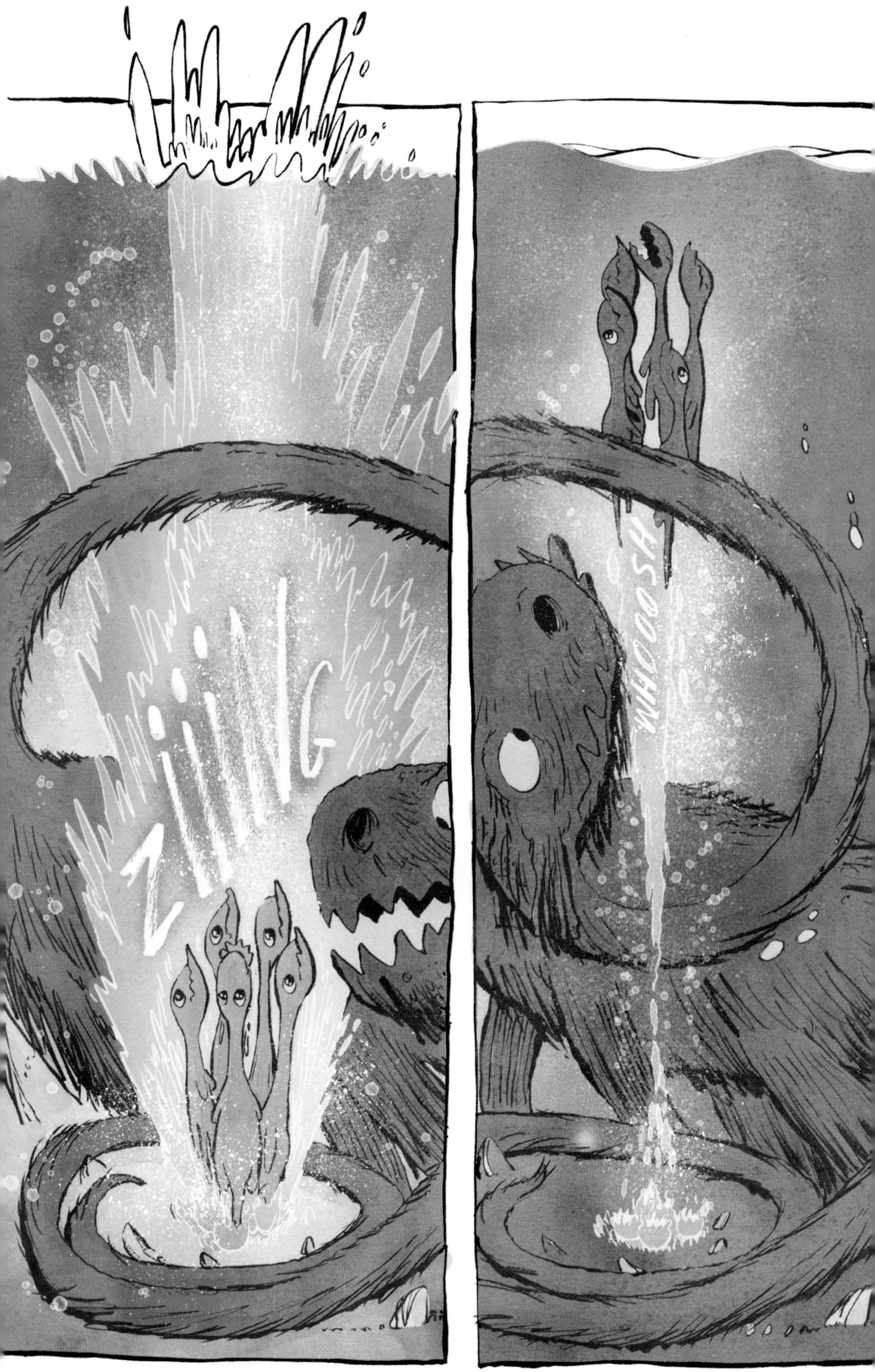
ZIIING
WHOOOSH

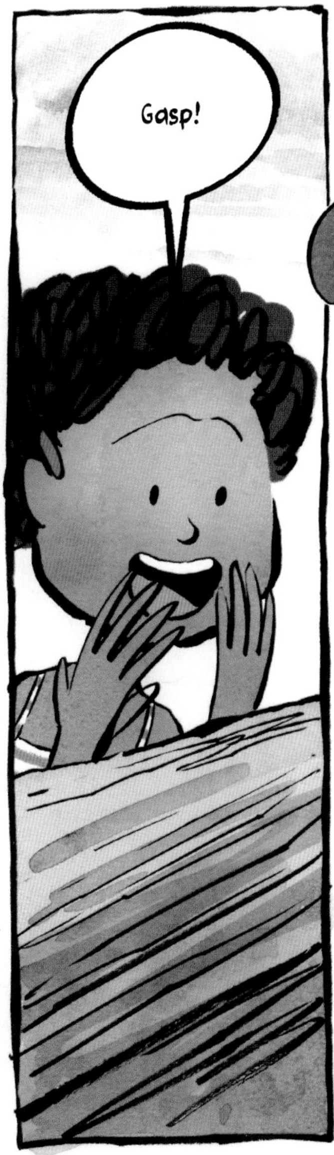
Gasp!

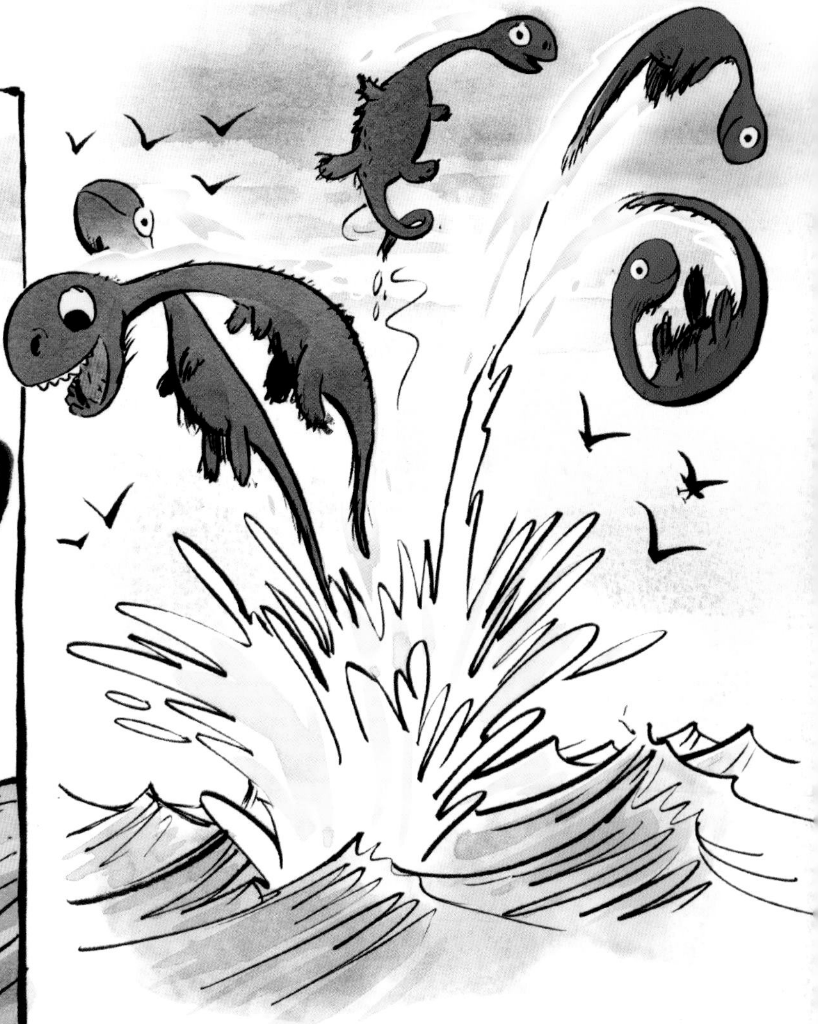

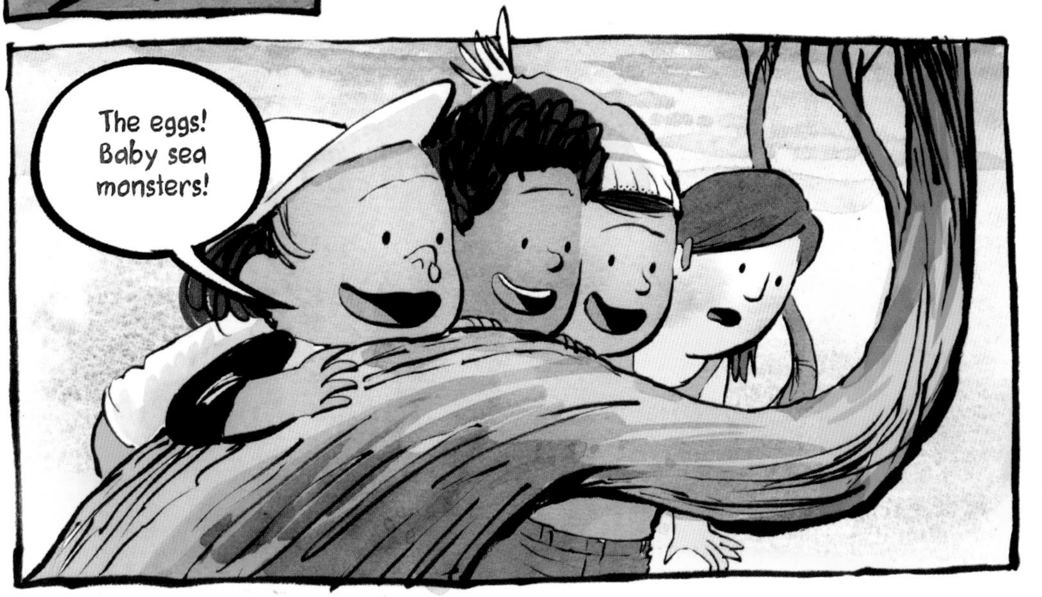
The eggs! Baby sea monsters!

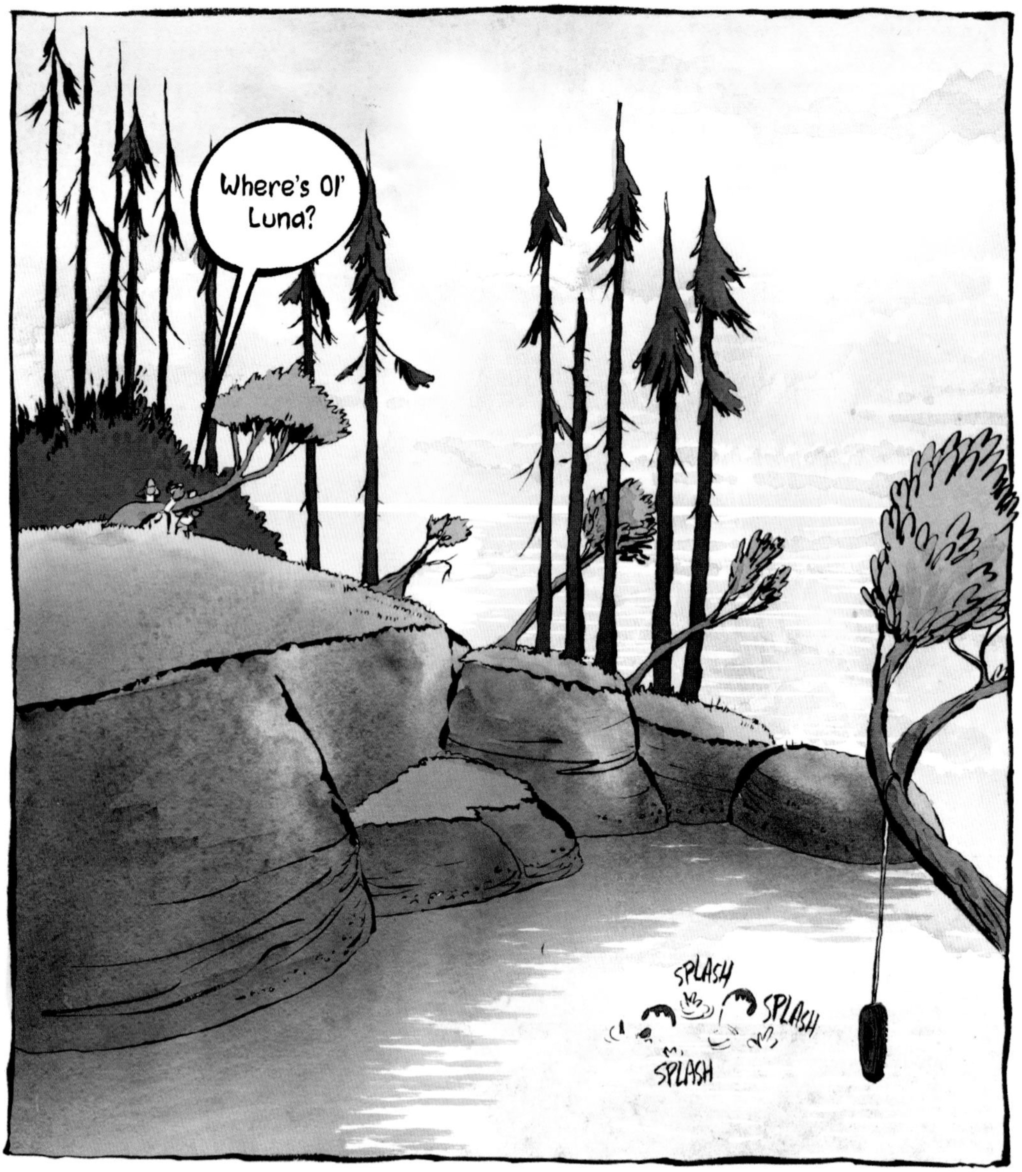
Where's Ol' Luna?
SPLASH
SPLASH
SPLASH

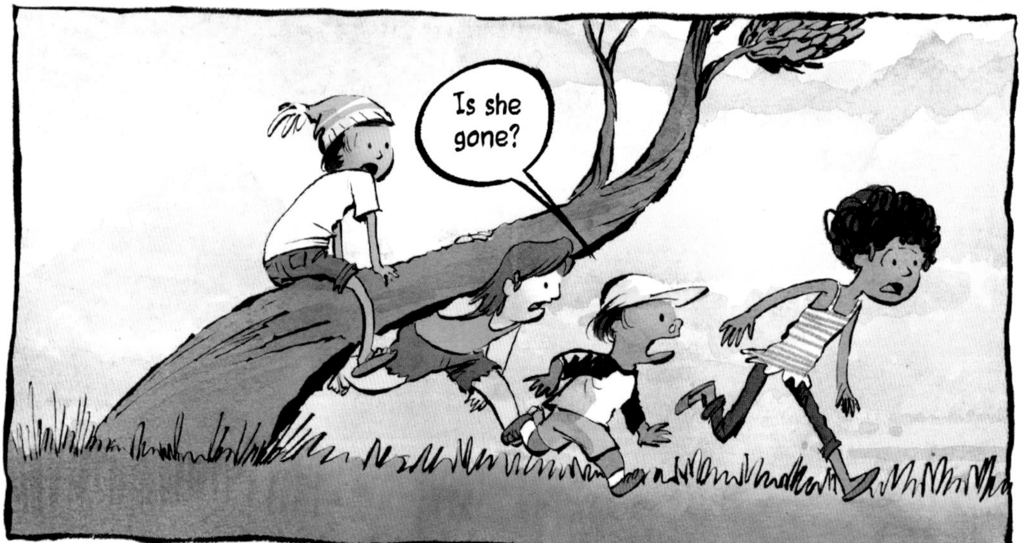
Is she gone?

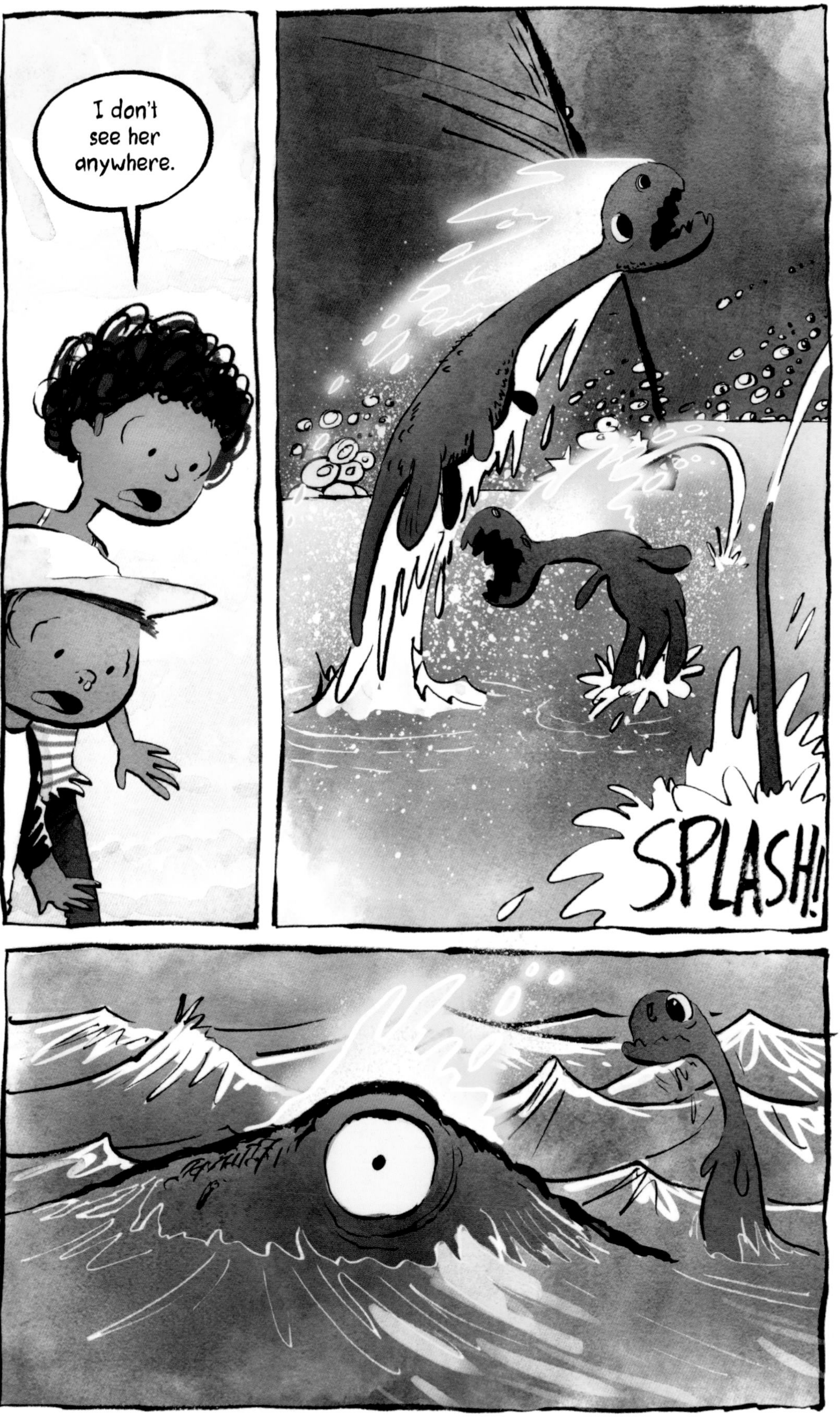
I don't see her anywhere.
SPLASH!

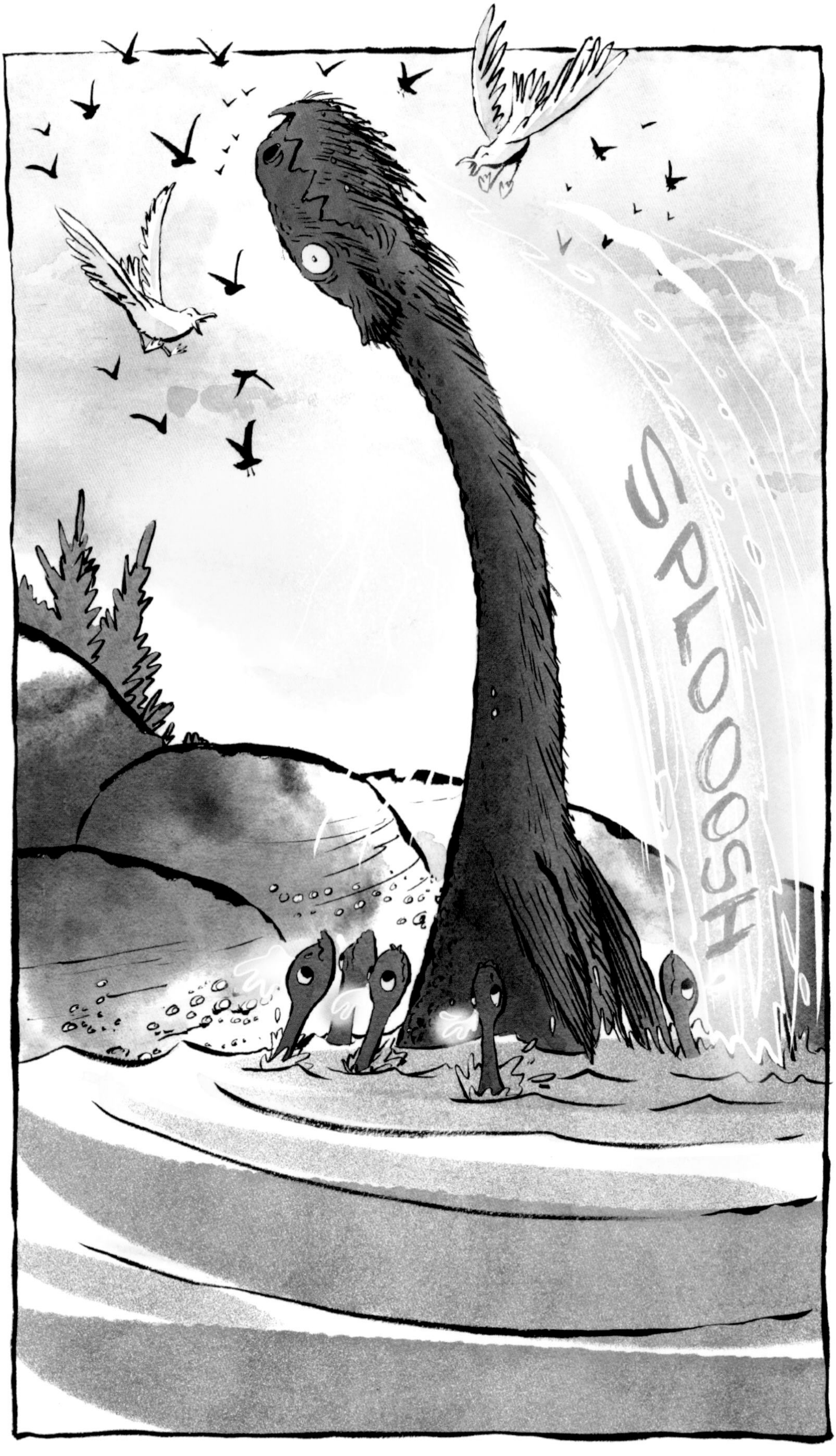
SPLOOOSH

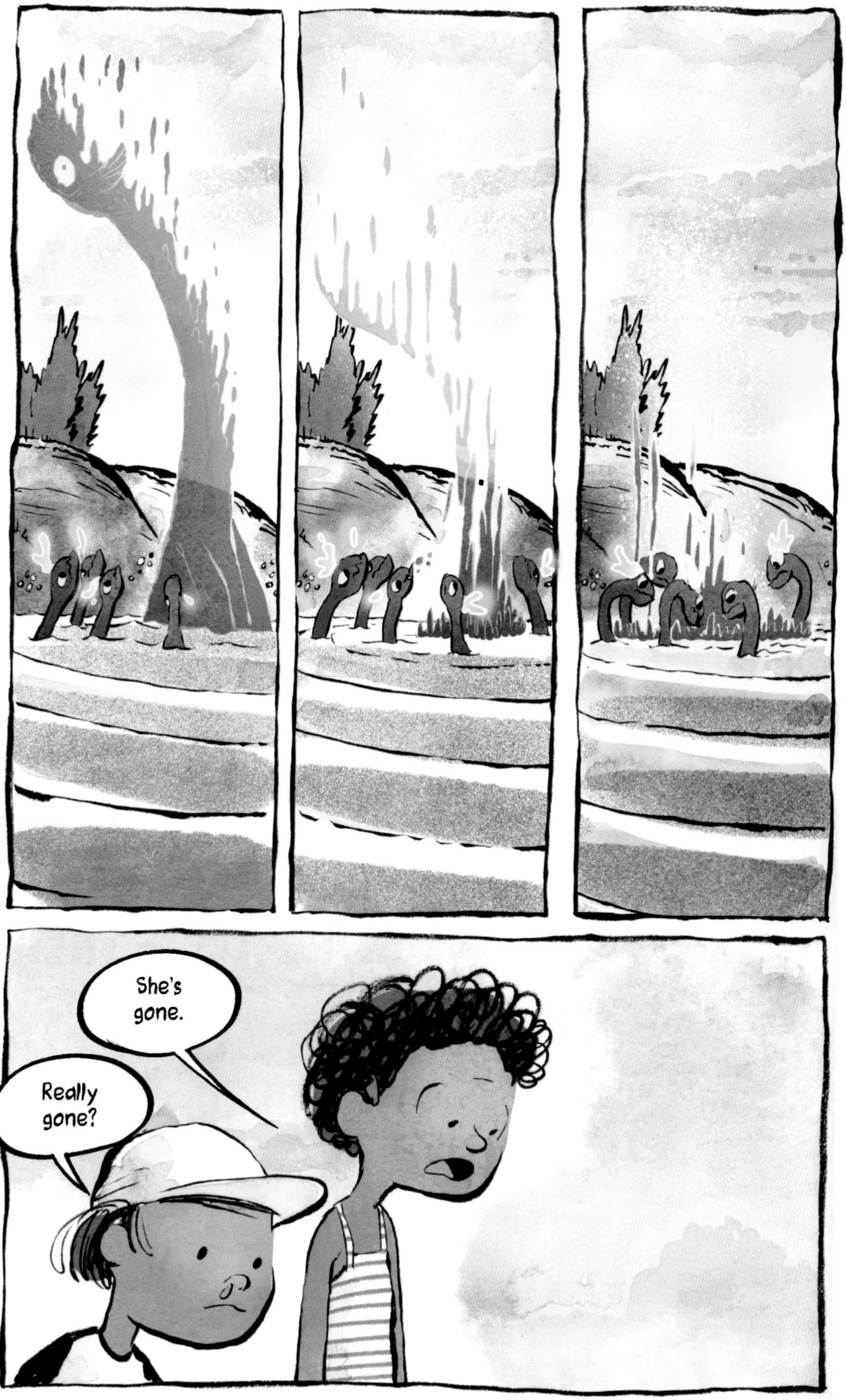
She's gone.
Really gone?

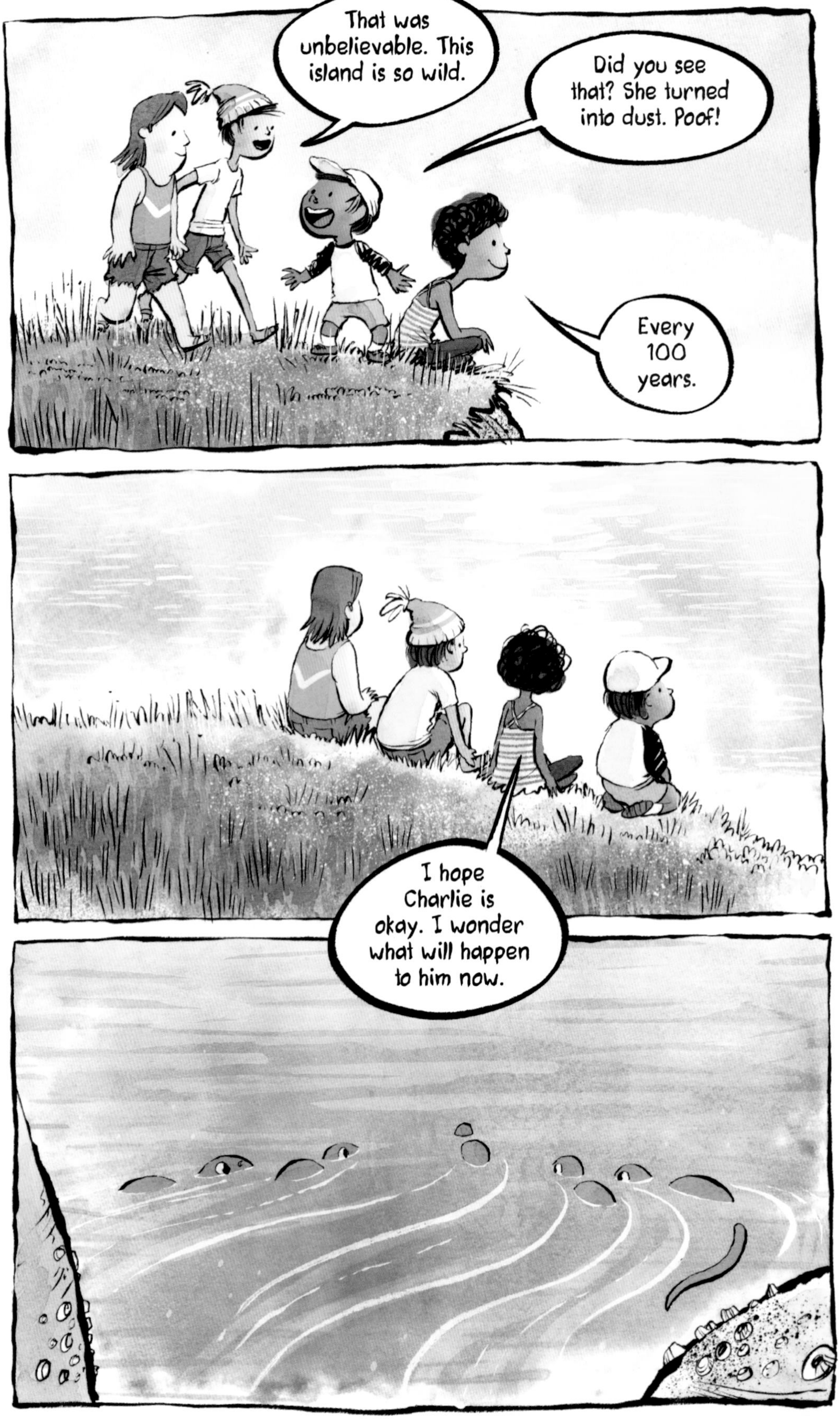
That was unbelievable. This island is so wild.
Did you see that? She turned into dust. Poof!
Every 100 years.
I hope Charlie is okay. I wonder what will happen to him now.

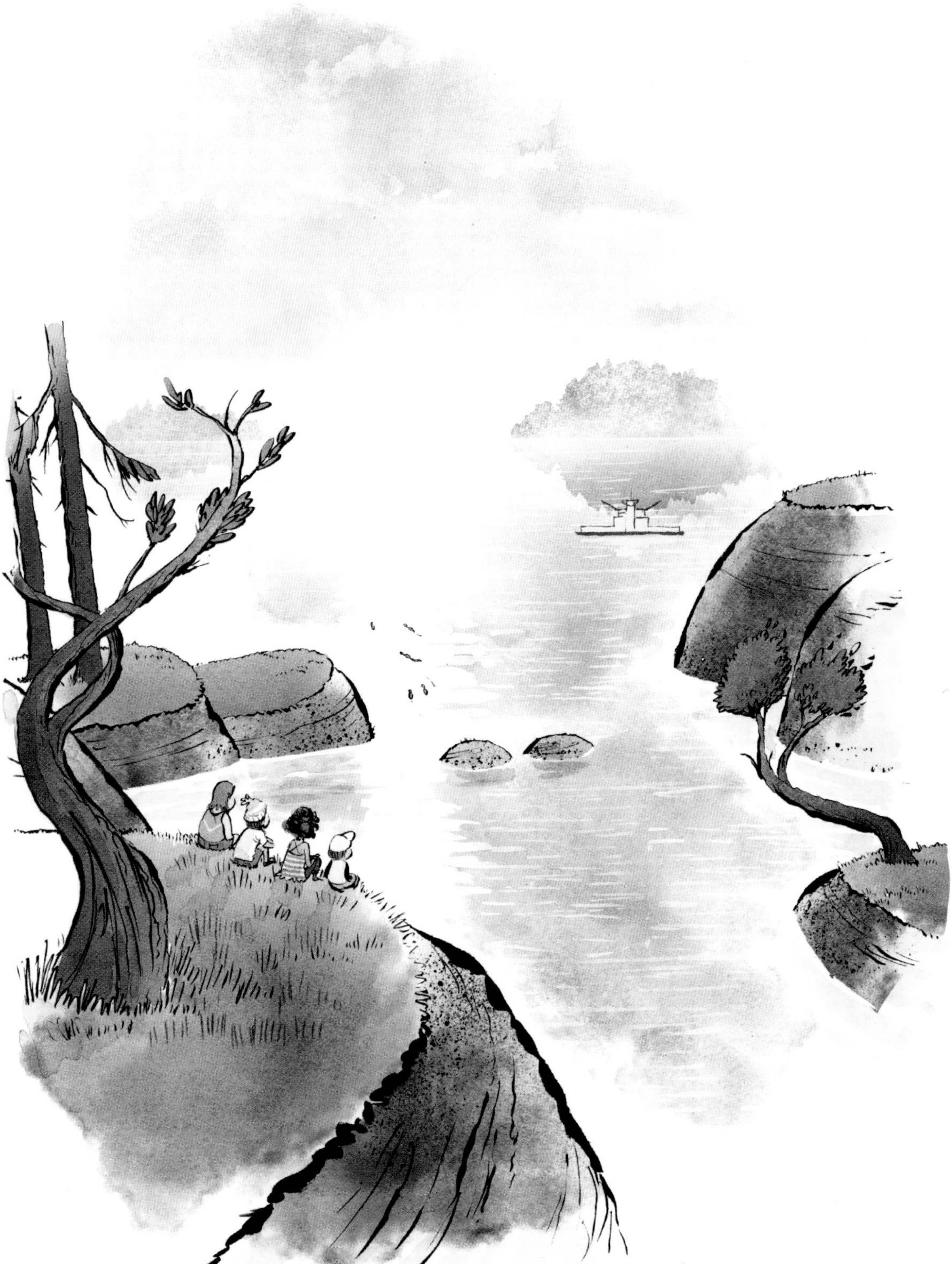

CHAPTER SIX

Cannonball!

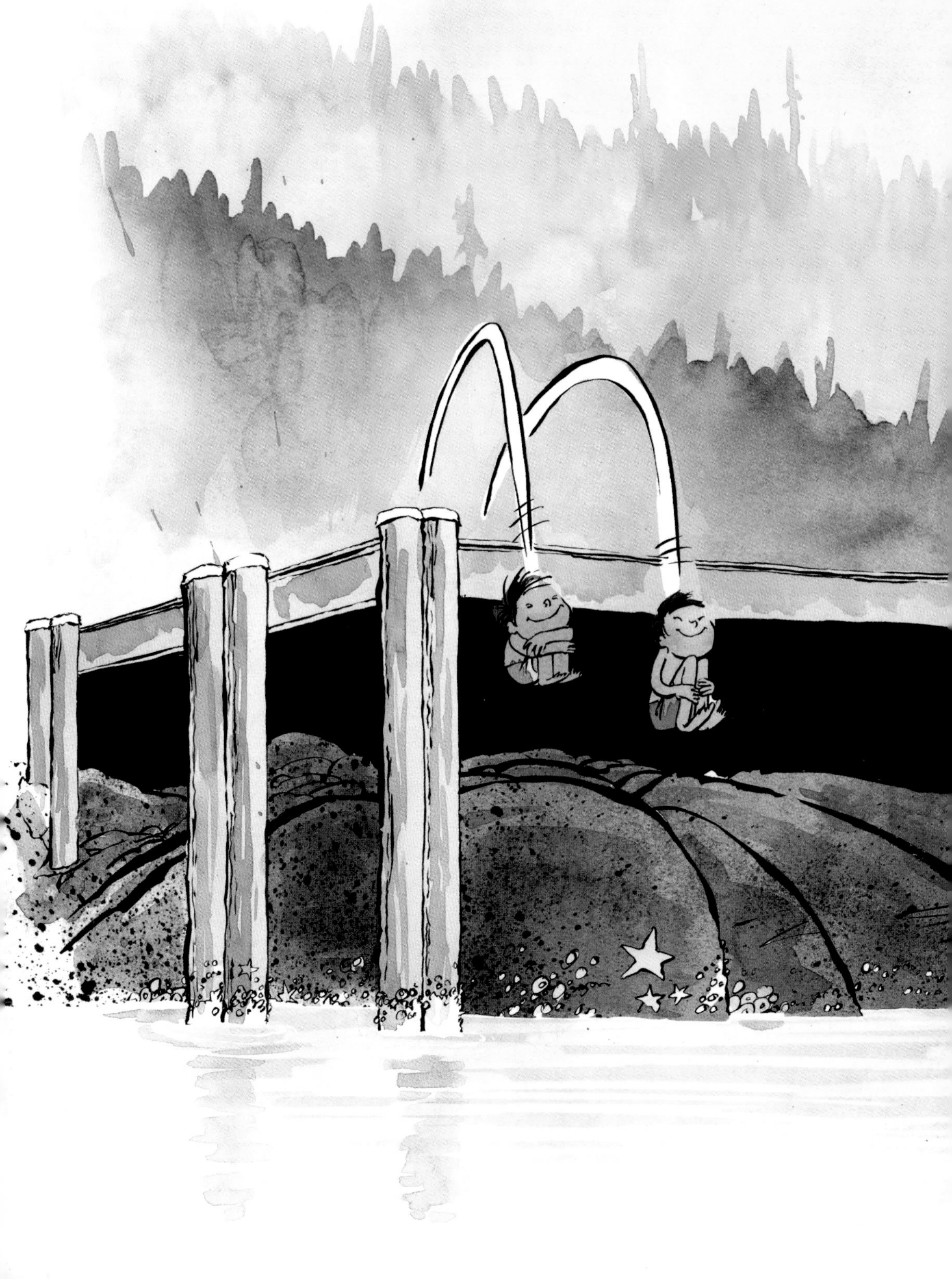

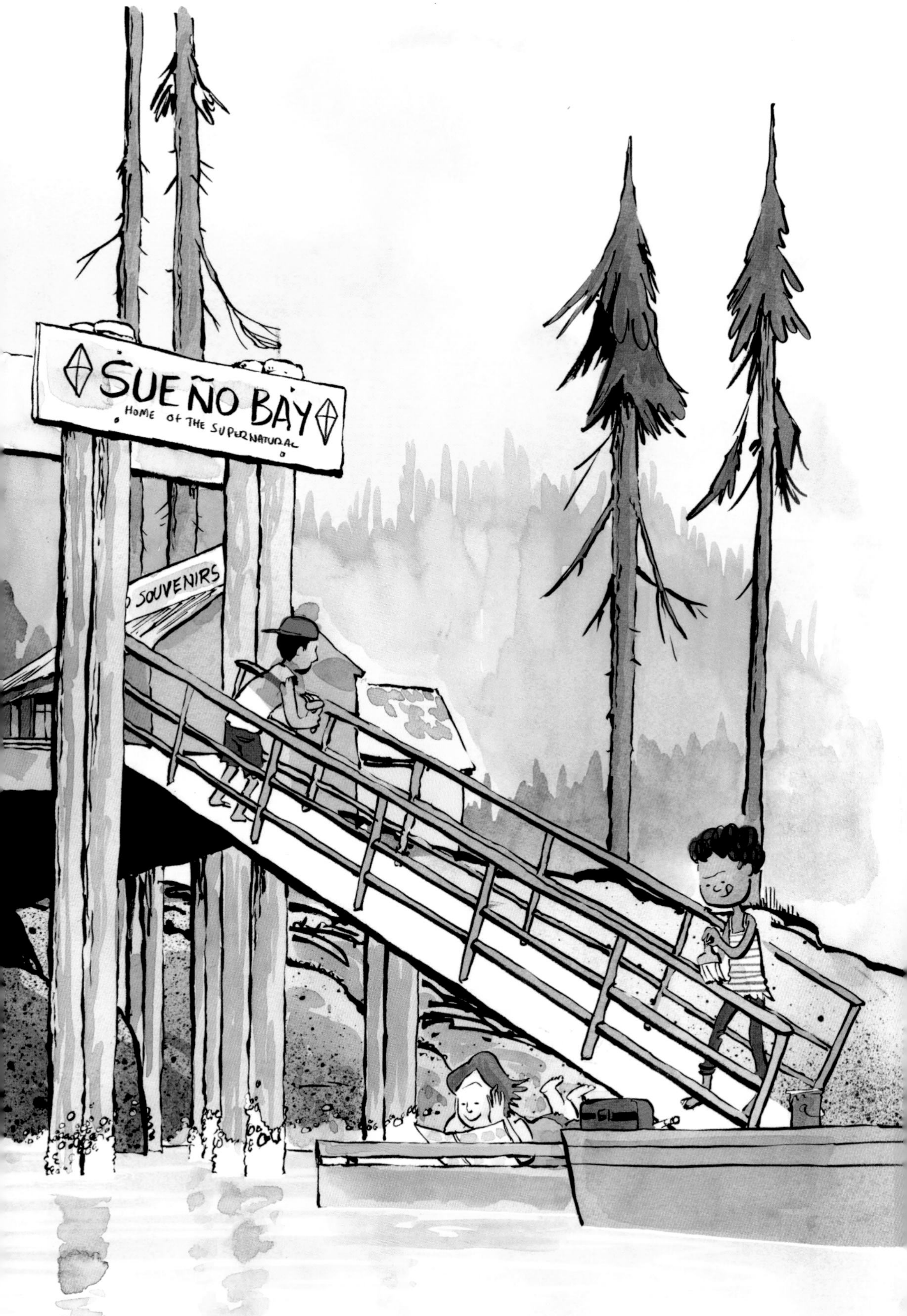
SUE ÑO BAY
HOME OF THE SUPERNATURAL
SOUVENIRS

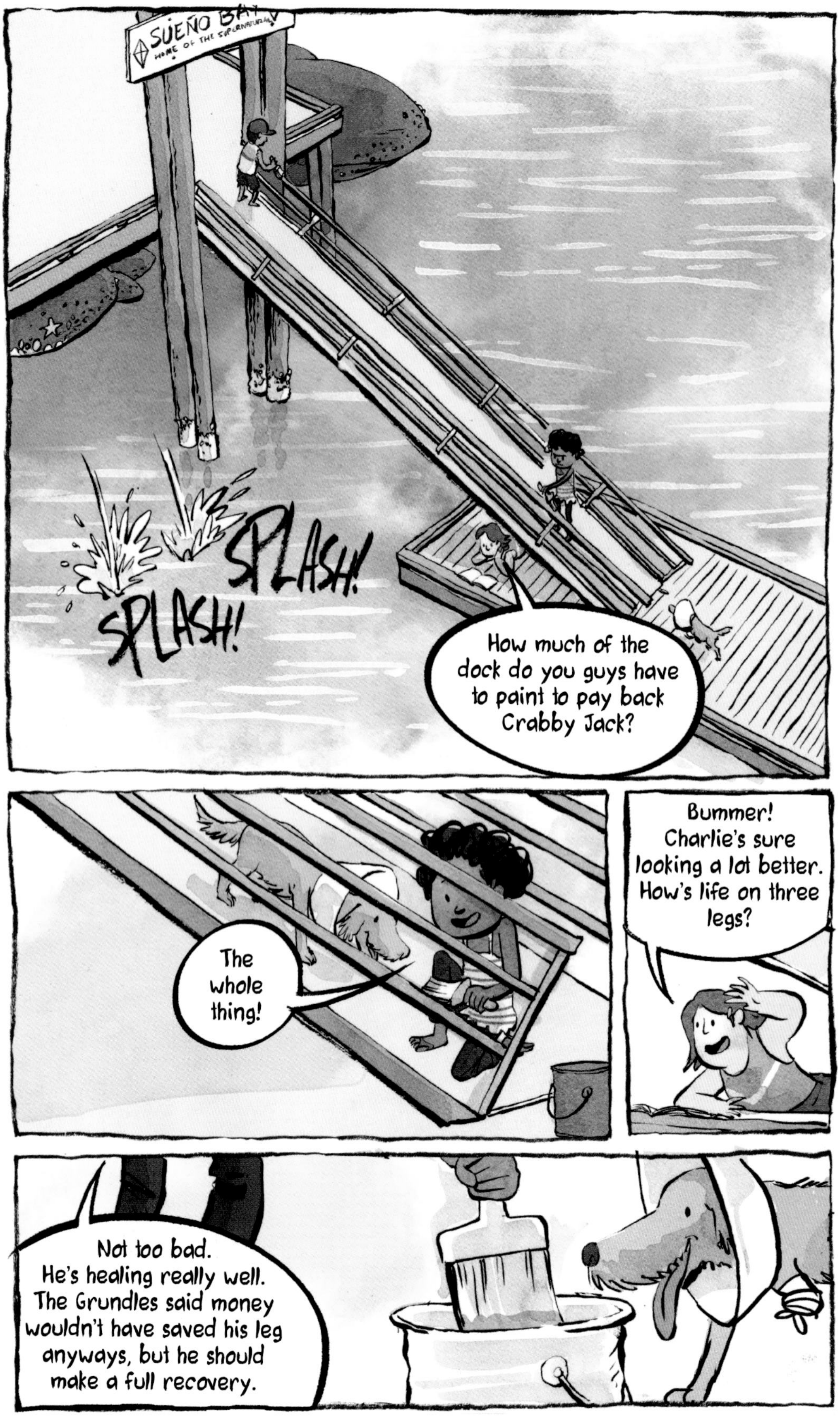
SUEÑO BAY
HOME OF THE SUPERNATURAL
SPLASH!
SPLASH!
How much of the dock do you guys have to paint to pay back Crabby Jack?
The whole thing!
Bummer! Charlie's sure looking a lot better. How's life on three legs?
Not too bad. He's healing really well. The Grundles said money wouldn't have saved his leg anyways, but he should make a full recovery.

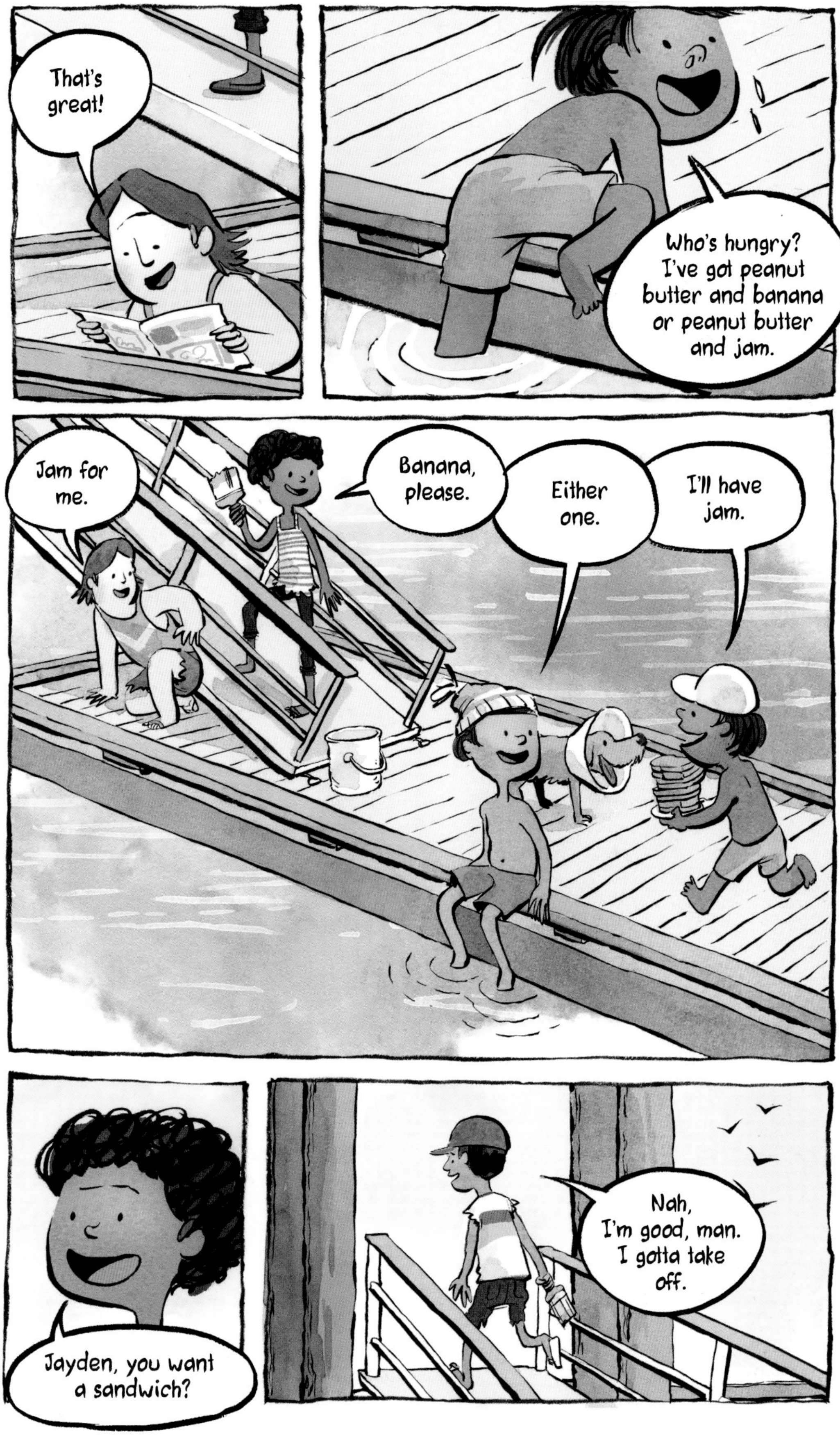
That's great!
Who's hungry? I've got peanut butter and banana or peanut butter and jam.
Jam for me.
Banana, please.
Either one.
I'll have jam.
Jayden, you want a sandwich?
Nah, I'm good, man. I gotta take off.

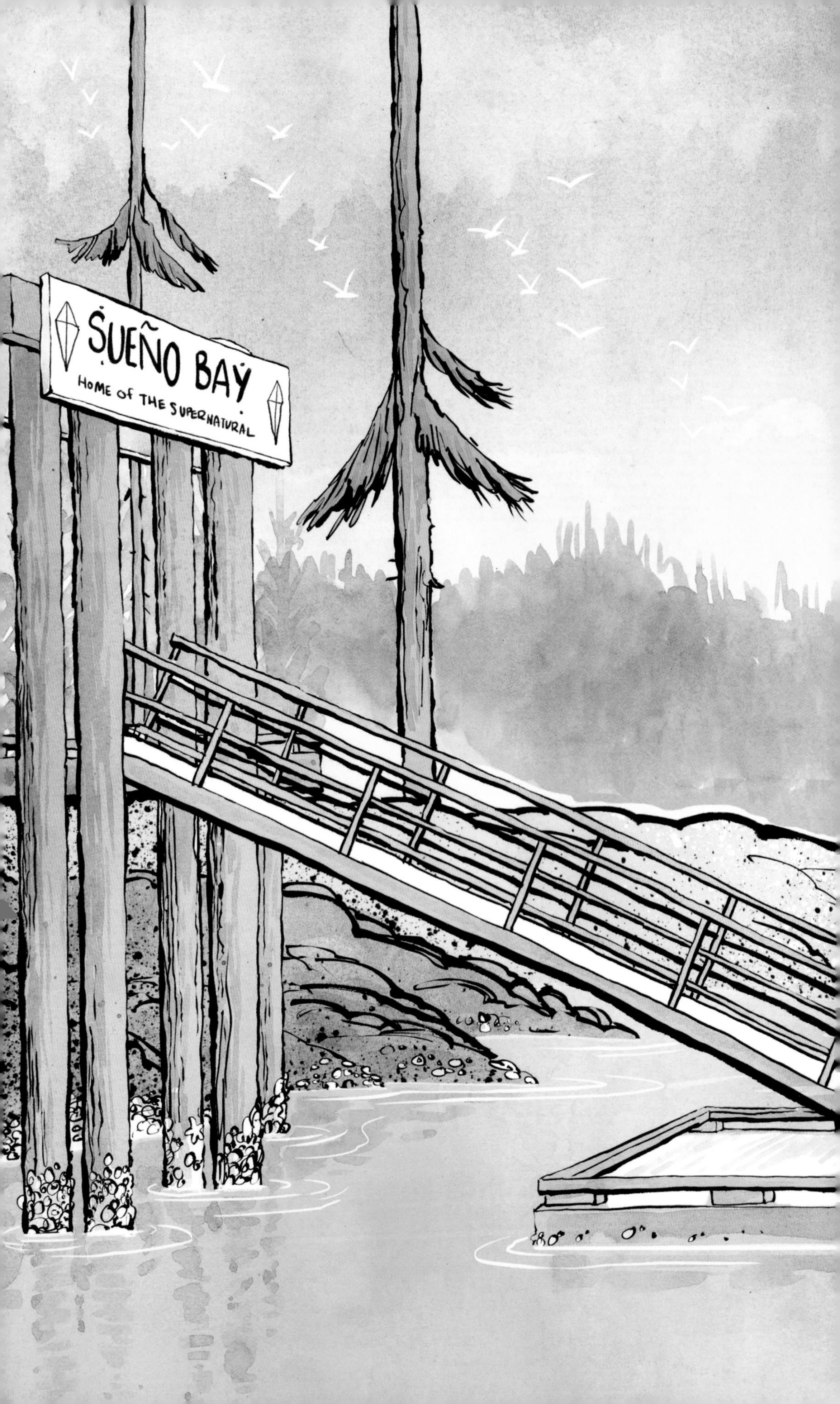
SUEÑO BAY
HOME OF THE SUPERNATURAL

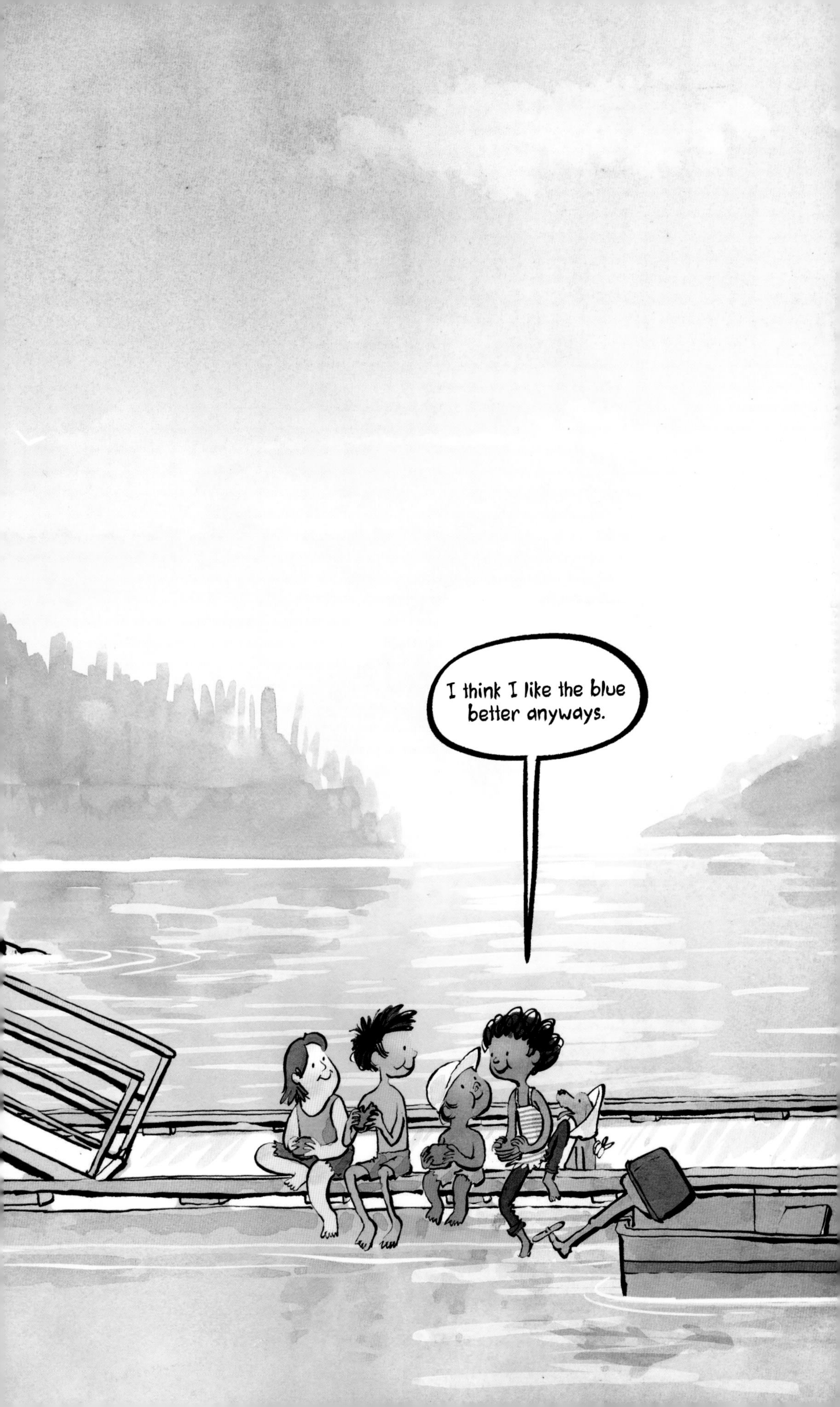
I think I like the blue better anyways.

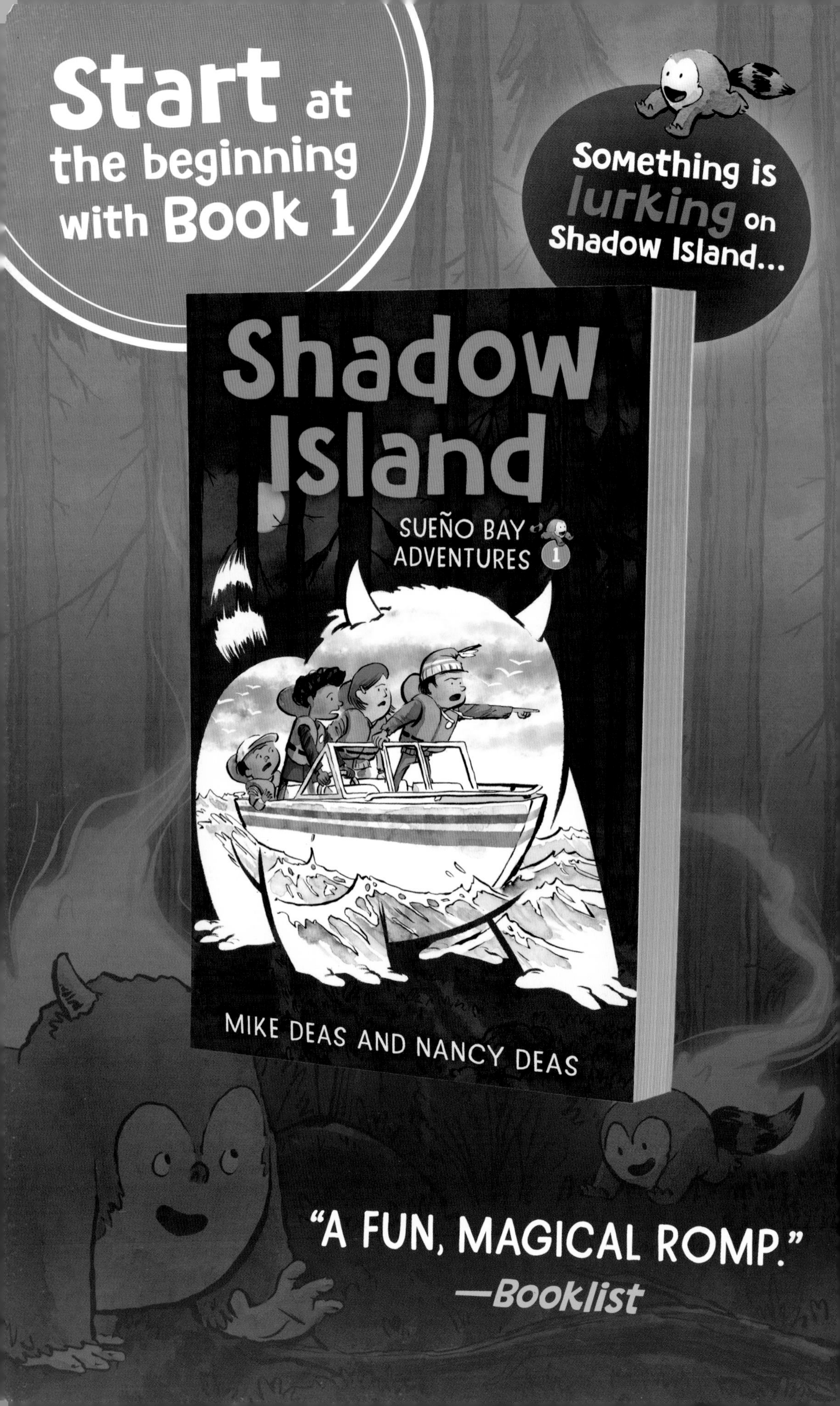
Start at the beginning with Book 1
Something is lurking on Shadow Island...
Shadow Island
SUEÑO BAY ADVENTURES 1
MIKE DEAS AND NANCY DEAS
"A FUN, MAGICAL ROMP."
—Booklist

More action-packed adventure awaits!

"RABBLE-ROUSING, SMART-TALKING KIDS."
—*SCHOOL LIBRARY JOURNAL*

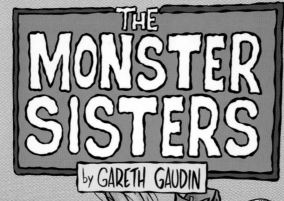

THE MONSTER SISTERS
by GARETH GAUDIN
The Mystery of the Unlocked Cave

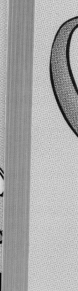

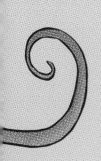

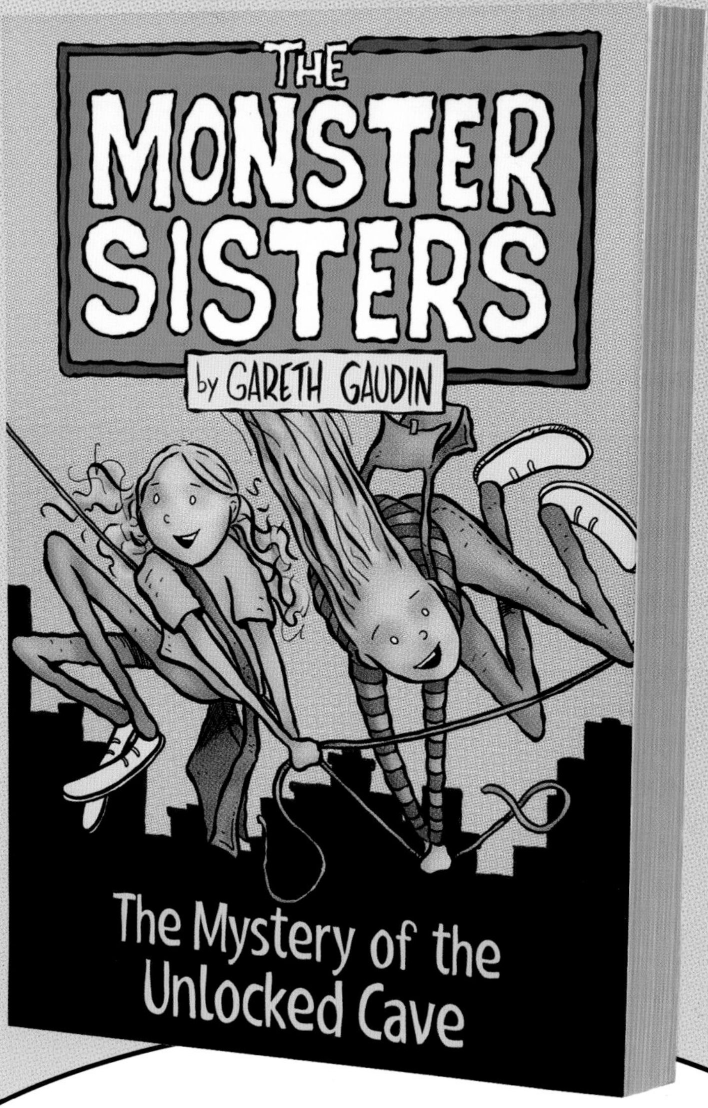

Super sleuths, Enid Jupiter and Lyra Gotham tackle a **MAJOR MONSTER INFESTATION** in their quiet town.

ORCA

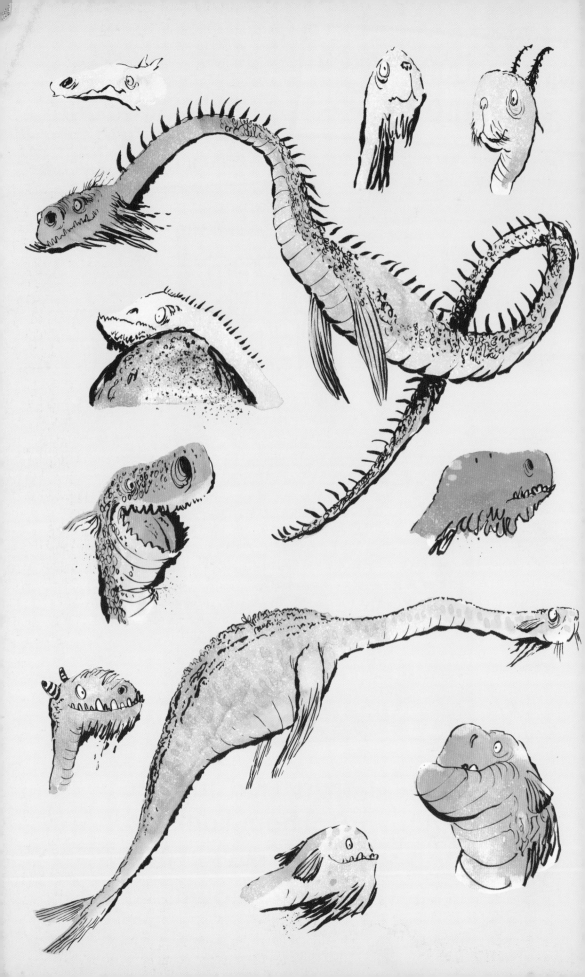

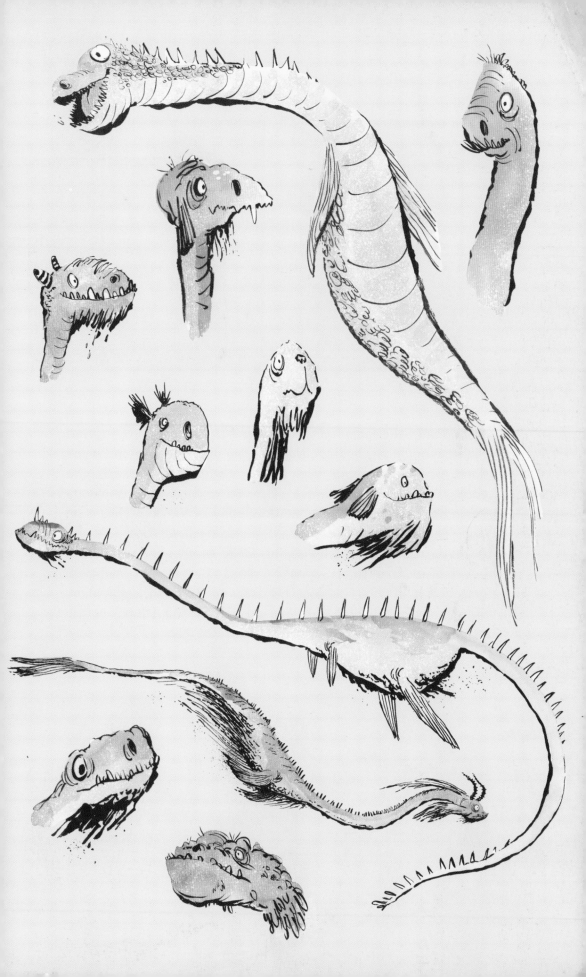

Husband-and-wife team **NANCY** and **MIKE DEAS** enjoyed collaborating on this project. Nancy grew up on a farm on Mayne Island, British Columbia, where she wandered the forests and beaches. She has a great love of travel and adventure. Nancy holds a bachelor of arts from the University of Victoria. Mike is an author/illustrator of graphic novels, including *Dalen and Gole* and the Graphic Guide Adventure series. While he grew up with a love of illustrative storytelling, Capilano College's Commercial Animation program helped Mike fine-tune his drawing skills and imagination. Mike, Nancy and their family live on Salt Spring Island, British Columbia, a magical and mysterious island that inspired Sueño Bay.

SUEÑO BAY ADVENTURES 2

What is waiting in the depths of Otter Lagoon?

Welcome to Sueño Bay, home of the supernatural. When Jenna finds a rare egg in the waters of Otter Lagoon, she unknowingly sets off a sequence of events that could mean the end of the peaceful village of Sueño Bay. In spite of her attempts to keep them out of her business, Jenna can't stop her friends from poking around when the supernatural is involved. And soon enough this crew of young sleuths is in a race against time with...

the greatest Moon Creature they have ever faced!

SUEÑO BAY ADVENTURES 1

Shadow Island

SUEÑO BAY ADVENTURES

MIKE DEAS AND NANCY DEAS

$14.95

ISBN 978-1-4598-1964-1

9 781459 819641

ORCA BOOK PUBLISHERS
orcabook.com